The Mysterious Face

It is often said that one has but one life to live, but that is nonsense. For one who reads, there is no limit to the number of lives that may be lived, for fiction, biography, and history offer an inexhaustible number of lives in many parts of the world, in all periods of time.
—Louis L'Amour

Memory is the diary that we all carry about with us.
—Oscar Wilde

All that mankind has done, thought, gained, or been: it is lying, as in magic preservation, in the pages of books.
—Thomas Carlyle

The Mysterious Face

Peggy Lovelace Ellis

Faraway Publishing
Black Mountain, N.C.

Peggy Lovelace Ellis
76 Wagon Trail
Black Mountain, NC 28711-2565
www.peggyellis.com

First Edition

Cover Design: SelfPubBookCovers.com/VonnaArt

Published by Faraway Publishing
125 Spring View Drive
Black Mountain, NC 28711

Printed in the United States of America

ISBN-13: 979-8-9881761-4-5

Library of Congress Control Number: 2024934844

Romantic Suspense. Cozy Mysteries. Small Town & Rural Cozy Mysteries. Romance. Doppelgängers. Terrorism. Apparitions. Small Town Business. Small Town Life. Contemporary Fiction

For Jim

Fifty-Five Years and Counting

Table of Contents

Acknowledgements

Some people are irreplaceable in my life.

Foremost is my husband, James T. Ellis. He has been my support in too many ways to count throughout our fifty-five years of marriage, and especially during those times when my mind was so busy with characters vying for my attention that I didn't hear him.

No one produces a book without considerable help from others. I'm fortunate to have known and worked with people who willingly listened to me as I droned on about my stories.

Dawn Aldridge Poore (author of Regency mystery and romance series (https://www.amazon.com/Books-Dawn-Aldridge-Poore), Melissa Cook is my ongoing all-round encourager, https://www.melissacook.us, and my sister and my niece, who choose to remain anonymous, always sit in my corner.

Randolph Shaffner shared his publishing expertise in the publication of this book.

My endless appreciation to all.

Chapter 1

New Kid in Town

Overcast skies would depress most people. Not Bianca Rossi. She didn't notice. Her temper was at boiling point. The object waited for her inside. This McDonald's on the edge of Detroit was as crowded with breakfast eaters as she had hoped. Bianca shoved open the door, ignored lines, and jerked out a chair opposite her target.

He spoke before she could open her mouth. "What happened?"

His soft, but menacing, tone irritated her. Nobody uses that tone with Bianca Rossi. The white-haired man filling his face across from her would rue the day he did. "Your pet operative got into his nose candy, that's what."

"Did the cops get him?"

Bianca stared into his steel-gray eyes. Where are this man's brains? "How could they not? He walked right into their arms!"

"What about the stuff?"

"They took everything." Bianca leaned forward, but after glancing around, she relaxed back into the hard plastic chair. "You do realize he won't keep his mouth shut. This idea was ridiculous from the start. You expected destruction of two tunnels and a bridge, all crowded with cars, at the same time, yet you put the stuff in a crackhead's hands. You must have lost your mind."

She leaned forward again. "Tell me. Did the other explosions go off?"

A wicked grin crossed his face. "Are you afraid you missed a big bang? Seeing hundreds of people blown to smithereens?"

Bianca refused him the satisfaction of knowing how much she had wanted to witness the whole shebang. Instead, she sneered. "So, you failed on those bombs too. My first United States adventure, and you blew it. Next time, you should admit the work is beyond you. Let a younger person deal with details."

His bushy eyebrows met when he frowned. "Don't tell me my job. Did the cops see you?"

"I don't know. The crackhead called my name, the one he knew, anyway, so they know someone else was there."

"You'd better leave Detroit. Your face is too well known. Stay away until this fiasco blows over."

"You'll hear from me when I'm ready. Until then, get this into your head. I won't go if you ever partner me with another crackhead."

He eyed her over the cup rim. "You get this into your head. You'll go where I send you."

"You're forgetting something. I'm Miguel Rossi's granddaughter." She shot him a triumphant smile, striding away before he could reply.

Bianca Rossi always has the last word.

ཉ ཉ ཉ ཉ ཉ

"Hey, watch where you're going!"

The harsh masculine voice brought Megan to a standstill. Tilting the umbrella, she met blue eyes boring into hers. Him again. Just what she needed.

Why had she bothered to come into town? She'd debated whether she should while staring out her back window. The heavy rain had blurred the hedge bordering her yard. This was a morning for sleep, not work. Megan had come anyway, because rain might drive people into her shop. Before she could apologize, Fran Riddle's lilting voice called her name.

[2]

"Standing here isn't ideal for introductions, I know. However, Jed, this is Megan Stanfield, who owns Crawfordville's only natural food store. Megan, say hi to Jed Anderson, farmer extraordinaire."

"Hi, Jed. My umbrella didn't watch where it was going," Megan quipped. "Sorry."

"Think nothing of it, Miss Stanfield." He stepped aside, motioning them before him into the diner.

"Have I broken some Southern tradition by being informal?" Megan asked Fran as they slid into a booth. She turned her cup upright for the server who approached, coffee carafes in hand. "Good morning, Mattie. I need high test this morning."

"Same for me," Fran said.

"As my grandmother would say, I think Jed is smitten."

"I don't know how you could reach that conclusion, but, if so, he has chosen a peculiar way of showing it."

"We're cousins, grew up together, so I know him well. He's a nice guy."

"Of all the things I don't need in my life, a smitten man heads the list, so he can snub me all he wants." Megan wouldn't admit this man intrigued her. Still, she asked, "Shouldn't a farmer be feeding chickens, or something, instead of sitting here?"

"Cows, not chickens. He must have finished the milking early." Fran lowered her eyelashes, hiding the twinkle Megan had learned to expect but not trust. "He never came into town this early until you arrived. Now, he's here most mornings, gazing soulfully at you."

Megan almost choked on her coffee. "Not funny. He isn't gazing soulfully at me. He's glaring murderously. Is it me, or does he treat all women this way?"

"Just you. He's ignored all females since he came back from the university."

"Broken relationship probably."

"Not that I ever heard. Still, he might have learned to keep secrets from me."

"Oh, well, no skin off my nose." Megan glanced at her watch. "Time for work."

"For me also."

They parted at the door, Fran to her boutique, Fine Feathers, two blocks away. Megan turned right toward her own shop, Nature's Way, next door. She nodded at several people, none of whom responded.

At times like this, Megan questioned the wisdom of moving to this small town in the North Carolina mountains. She had soon learned there were regulars at the diner eating or having coffee—therefore the logical place to make friends. Didn't happen. Fran was the only person she could call friend, not merely an acquaintance, after several weeks here.

The day was slow—two herbal tea sales only. The shade trees in the square lured her outside where a beautiful orange cat ambled over from the library.

The sun was bright. Fluffy clouds tinged with gray drifted across a sky so blue it looked photoshopped. Megan breathed the fresh mountain air and glanced down the street. She spotted Jed Anderson crossing the square, his fit, muscular body shifting with each step. Sunlight filtering through leaves turned his russet hair to flames. She knew by his sudden stop he'd seen her, so she waved.

A flop-eared beagle slumped at his feet when he stopped beside her. "Hello, Miss Stanfield."

"Hello, again." Megan inhaled deeply. "The flowers smell heavenly after this morning's rain." She patted the dog's head. "Who's your friend?"

"Buddy. I see the town freeloader likes you."

"Isn't Marmalade beautiful?" She ran her fingers through the cat's silky hair. "Won't you join me? My friends call me Megan."

Jed sat on the far edge of the bench, leaving the cat between them. Without turning towards her, he asked, "Why did you come here?"

Megan had needed anonymity, so she had drilled herself in a story to tell inquisitive people. When need be, words flowed from her mouth like water without barriers. This wasn't the first time she'd lived a lie—probably not the last either.

"My grandparents lived here."

"Yeah, I heard. The Abernathies and Malloys, but they're long gone."

"I know. I hoped to find some other relatives."

"Visiting would've settled that."

"I wanted to experience small town life. I'm renting the Malloy homeplace, where my grandmother lived. Maybe that's why I feel I belong here."

The wooden bench creaked under his shifting weight. "Yeah, sure."

"Is a civil conversation beyond your capability?"

"Sorry."

Megan heaved a sigh. Irritating man. "Can you tell me where my grandfather lived?"

"A mile beyond your place. His house is gone now—lightning strike caused a fire. The owner built an A-frame. You've probably seen it."

"The redwood. I'm glad the fire didn't destroy those old trees. I imagine Granddad climbed them, perhaps had a treehouse."

"My dad considered buying your grandmother's place. Only fifty acres or so, but they could be profitable again with work."

"Could you manage two farms?"

"With help. We're dairy farmers although we have an apple orchard too. I want a vegetable garden for the farmers' market. I've wanted to grow pumpkins ever since I made my first jack-o-lantern when I was four."

Swallowing her amusement, Megan wondered what else he hid behind his earlier inflexible face. "Couldn't you find enough space on your farm?"

"Sure, but property is a good investment."

Megan nodded. "I imagine you're right. Have you tried organic gardening?"

"Are you telling me how to run my farm?" Jed demanded. "What do you know about farming? What do you know about beetles eating beans or black spot hitting tomatoes?"

His sudden temper appalled Megan. Don't make waves, she reminded herself. A deep breath steadied her voice. "Nothing! I'm only asking."

"Which shows you don't belong here." Jed strode away, calling the dog over his shoulder.

Buddy gave her a reproachful stare before he ambled after his master.

Megan shook her head in disbelief at Jed's temper. Strangled sounds interrupted her thoughts. A man wearing a faded denim jacket with baggy jeans gazed at her. She'd seen him before, but he didn't appear to be approachable. She didn't want yet another native snubbing her, so she smiled and returned to her store.

ℵ ℵ ℵ ℵ ℵ

Standing in the shadows of a large spruce, he could almost touch the woman when she walked across the square after Jed Anderson rushed away. Why did the sight of her startle him so? He'd been asking himself that question since the first time he saw her weeks ago. He closed his eyes, breathed deeply. She was gone when he opened them again. Her face reminded him of someone—something—unpleasant. He searched his mind without success. He slid his fists into his jacket pockets and shuffled his way homeward.

ന ന ന ന ന

Despite her determination not to think about Jed, he invaded Megan's thoughts when she drove home. His cold blue eyes had warmed while he discussed farming. She didn't know why her question had turned them icy again, but she had dealt with bad-tempered people before. She could do it again.

You don't belong here. Jed's parting words still tumbled in Megan's head when she pushed through the library door for the Fall Festival meeting that evening. She'd let Fran talk her into coming, now she must face unfriendly people. Megan tilted her lips into a slight smile and entered the room.

Conversation dwindled while several pairs of eyes studied her. Megan sighed with relief when she spotted Fran's welcoming expression in a sea of guarded faces.

"Sit here, Megan. Hey, everybody, I'm sure you've seen Megan Stanfield around town. I've recruited her to help with the festival." Turning toward the late arrival, Fran said, "Mrs. Malcolm is our illustrious leader. The fair wouldn't exist without her. You know Catherine Crawford from the library and Sally Jamison, our realtor extraordinaire. You'll sort out the others during our meetings."

"I look forward to becoming better acquainted. I'll help if I can."

Mrs. Malcolm shrugged. "I don't know what an outsider can do, but I reckon your sitting in won't hurt."

Several people averted their eyes, probably embarrassed at their leader's snide remark. Megan bit back a retort.

"Poor woman," Fran whispered. "Her overbearing son-in-law must be giving her problems again. She's normally the sweetest person on the planet."

Megan relaxed when the others turned toward the woman chairing the meeting.

"Sally, I'm counting on you to take charge of crafts again this year. Inez, you'll organize children's games, right?" Receiving their cheerful nods, Mrs. Malcolm studied the other faces. "I need volunteers for food."

"Joyce Pressley has done food for years," a strident voice reminded her. "You can't leave her out just because she isn't here."

"I asked her," Mrs. Malcolm said. "She can't. Her daughter is having her gall bladder taken out, so Joyce has the children indefinitely. There's no way she can take on anything else with four little imps on her hands."

"Maybe Miss Stanfield would like to be in charge," someone said.

Megan ignored the mockery. "This is my first Fall Festival. There must be something simple I can do."

"Sure, there is," Fran said. "We'll need help with making posters, advertising, gathering prizes for the kids' events, for example."

"We'll need help manning the booths, especially crafts tables," Sally said, and the meeting continued.

Later, Megan heard the phone ring when she stepped onto her porch, but the ringing stopped while she fumbled with the key. Probably a wrong number. She didn't expect calls from local people. Outsiders either. No one knows where she is.

The meeting had gone well, Megan reflected while she creamed her face. A few women had talked to her afterwards, so maybe she could hope for better days.

She was in the state of being not asleep yet not fully awake when the phone rang. She glanced at the clock. Who would call her at midnight?

"Hello?" she mumbled into the receiver.

ഇ ഇ ഇ ഇ ഇ

Jed gripped the phone until his knuckles turned white. The newcomer had been on his mind all evening, as she was altogether too often. Her hazel eyes refused to leave his thoughts. At times, they sparkled with green flecks. At other times, she challenged him with gold flecks shooting darts at him. The tawny hair curving around her neck made him forget he didn't care for curly hair.

Since college, no woman had gotten under his skin like this one. Not since Jasmine with her long silky blonde hair, her amused smile, her stated preference for lawyers over farmers. Not since Jasmine had any woman challenged his work. He didn't appreciate interference, especially from a stranger—another city slicker. Still, he shouldn't have lost his temper.

He cleared his throat. "This is Jed Anderson. Did I wake you?"

"I'm awake."

"Umm … It's late, I know. I did call earlier."

"I was out."

This was even harder than he'd thought. "I . . . um, why I called. I apologize for my rudeness this afternoon. I don't know why I talked to you the way I did." Oh, he knew alright. Rudeness was his only defense against her appeal. 'Once bitten, twice shy' became his motto after Jasmine dumped him.

Jed broke into the dragging silence. "I'm sorry I yelled at you."

Megan heaved a sigh. "I guess I was offensive without realizing it. I shouldn't have mentioned organic farming because I don't know anything about the insect problems you face."

"How could you?" Jed apologized again. Must she be so magnanimous? He needed sleep, but he was curious. "I saw you go into the library earlier. Did Fran rope you into helping with the Fall Festival?"

"She's very persuasive. I've read about small town festivals. They sound like fun. Mrs. Malcolm said they've been held here forever."

"She'd know. Carrie Malcolm has chaired that committee all my life at least. Who knows how long before? One of my earliest memories is bobbing for apples. She dragged me out of the tub by my ankles more than once."

"I've never bobbed for apples, but I'm game to try. Making jack-o-lanterns would be fun too, if I could figure out how to do it without cutting off my fingers."

"I'll be your teacher. I'm the best there is, if I do say so myself."

Jed said a hurried goodnight, cutting off her laughter. Why had he spilled his guts? What was it about Megan Stanfield? She'd done the same thing earlier, disarming him. Shaking his head, he slid beneath the covers. Milking came early.

It certainly did. When the alarm rang at five, Jed almost chucked the clock out the window. Eyelids at half-mast, he pulled on jeans and sweatshirt and slipped his bare feet into rubber boots. In the milking barn, he greeted the farmhands with a jaw-breaking yawn. Teat cups proved difficult to attach. Cows complained. As if complaining wasn't enough, one jammed her pointy hoof on his foot. Limping, he finished his chores in tight-lipped silence.

"This is what comes of letting women into your life," Jed muttered. "I even talked to one at midnight, for heaven's sake. From this point on, it's strictly business with Megan Stanfield."

Chapter 2

Who is She?

Early morning chill had not dampened Megan's cheerfulness. She couldn't remember when she'd last faced a new day with positive thoughts. Maybe Jed had changed his mind about her. She would like to think another person had accepted her.

She strolled into the diner. "Hi, Mattie. Bring some decaf to Fran's booth, will you?"

Fran pushed the bowl of creamers toward her. "Aren't we cheerful this morning? Did someone work a magic potion on you?"

"Something better—a five-mile run at daybreak. The crisp air cleared my sinuses like you wouldn't believe." Megan lowered her voice. "You'll never guess who phoned me last night."

"Okay, I won't try. Tell me."

"Jed Anderson."

"After his rudeness yesterday?"

Megan nodded. "At midnight, no less."

"Midnight? What did he want?"

"Much to my surprise, he apologized for his rudeness. After that, he was good-humored, even friendly. Can you believe it?"

"The good-humored part, yes. He's friendly to a fault." Fran picked up her purse. "At midnight, though, when he gets up before roosters crow? Intriguing."

"Guilty conscience, maybe." Megan downed the last of her coffee. "I must check stock this morning before salesmen come."

Minutes later, they stood outside discussing Megan's hair appointment the next afternoon. Megan turned when she heard Jed tell Buddy to stay in the truck. The navy polo shirt topping his faded jeans showed his rippling pecs and biceps. She waited, smiling, but chagrin replaced her anticipation when he hustled by without so much as nodding.

Fran stood openmouthed.

"Men are the most confusing creatures on earth," Megan said. "He was friendly at midnight; now, eight hours later, he snubs me."

"I have no clue. I've known him since we fought over the same Teddy bear. He's never blown hot and cold about any female. You have him floundering like a fish out of water."

The image amused Megan. "So, he can flop back in—sink to the bottom."

Fran joined her quiet laughter and then turned left while Megan turned right.

Megan flicked a feather duster over the merchandise. Not one customer came, but she was getting used to that—used to it, not happy about it. There was one regular, a creepy elderly man, who came for yogurt-covered raisins almost every day. He watched her from the corner of his eye—she watched him the same way—but he never spoke. His only greeting was a nod when he sidled into the store. Tourists avoided this little town a few miles from the interstate. Some days, trekkers wandered in and purchased trail mix or water. There were not enough, though, to keep her business going much longer.

Megan ran her fingers along a rack containing freeze-dried herbs packages. She was proud of this store, the counter arrangements, the merchandise she'd chosen. Her pleasure faded when Jed strode inside bringing all outdoors with him.

She watched him look around the small store over shelves stocked with vegetable noodles, dried fruits, and foods prepared without preservatives. Herbal teas gave off a glorious mixture of scents.

Megan stiffened her spine when Jed focused his smoldering eyes on her. She held his gaze, ready for battle. Megan Elizabeth Stanfield did not cower in the face of angry people.

"This is what you call *health* food?" Jed picked up a tofu package, read the label, and tossed it down again. "Did you actually believe people here would eat this stuff?"

Megan battled an anger, threatening to explode like bombs in Afghanistan. "If you came here to insult me, there's the door."

He ignored her pointing finger.

She gripped her hands behind her back rather than punch his nose, her first inclination. "Why are you so against my having a store here? People might enjoy natural food if they tried it."

"*Natural* food? Natural food is what we grow around here, not what you buy dried out in cellophane bags. You should have learned your mistake by now, so how soon will you leave our town?"

"What makes you think I'm leaving *our* town?" Megan leaned toward him across the counter. "You didn't answer me, Mr. Anderson. Why are you so against my being here?"

He turned to leave but whirled toward her, a range of emotions crossing his face. The fury she could understand, but the uncertainty surprised her.

"My mother, Rosalie Anderson, owns this building. Didn't you read the lease?"

"Of course, I read it. How could I know she's your mother?"

"Anderson . . . Anderson. Not a difficult connection in a small town."

"Common name. What difference does it make anyway?"

"She needs a long term, successful business here, so her income will be stable."

"My business would be successful if people supported a descendant of the town's founders."

"Female logic defeats me."

His answer infuriated her. Megan struggled for words—annihilation in mind—when he continued.

"How can we support your so-called natural food store when you've shown you don't live by your own words?"

"Not live by my words? What can you possibly mean?"

"We've seen you eating. If you believe in natural—really, this borders on artificial—food, why do you eat cheeseburgers, chicken salad, even bacon?"

Megan's jaw dropped. Had he been watching her? Did he stalk her away from the diner too? The idea disturbed her. However, his question was logical and deserved a logical answer. Gathering her wits, Megan explained. "Moderation is the key to good health, Jed. Yes, you've seen me eating meat. What you haven't seen is the food I eat at home, which balances what I eat anywhere else."

"I don't want to see it if you cook using this stuff."

With supreme effort, she ignored his mutters. "I'm neither a vegan nor an animal rights activist, but surely you can understand lessening animal products with an increase in vegetables untainted with chemicals . . . ."

"There you go again, on your high horse about chemicals. I wish you'd take your fancy ideas out of my mother's building."

"Does she want to break my lease?" His hesitancy answered her, so Megan pressed her advantage. "Perhaps she should tell me so herself."

"My mother is a saint." The fierce words barely escaped his clenched jaws. "She'd give away her last cent if she thought someone needed it, so I manage her business. If she caters to business failures, she'll soon be bankrupt." Turning on his heel, Jed stormed out of the room and slammed out the door.

Bristling at his unjust rebuke, Megan watched him cross the street. His long legs reached his truck faster than she'd thought possible. She turned away when the engine roared to life. The loudmouthed nuisance would kill himself. Good riddance.

Nevertheless, Jed Anderson had made her think.

Megan crossed the street into the square where she settled on the wooden bench facing her shop. Leaning back, she gazed at the quiet scene. An elderly woman gripped the stair railing of an old clapboard building with a door marked Nathanial Sykes, Attorney at Law. Farther along the street, three men sat on the porch of Dillon's hardware store. Trees stood in stark contrast against the baby blue sky. Flowerbeds surrounding trees added color. Far above, a plane droned its way to somewhere. Closer, birds sang in the trees. The peacefulness calmed her nerves. Her money worries faded.

ഇ ഇ ഇ ഇ ഇ

He stayed in the shadows until Jed drove away. His head throbbed and his breath came in spurts while he studied the unknown woman. Her profile had attracted his attention, the smile tugged at his memory. He watched her walk across the street. Her movement was familiar too, long strides yet not masculine, so why didn't the way she moved bother him? He gritted his teeth and hurried away.

ഇ ഇ ഇ ഇ ഇ

Mike Williams glanced up from the flyer on his desk when a rat-a-tat-tat on the door admitted Sheriff Frank Anderson, his chief supporter when he moved here from Atlanta two years ago. Some people hadn't wanted an outsider. Their attitude added difficulty, adapting from big city homicide detective to small town police chief. Frank, a native, had quietly helped him during those first few months, asking no questions Mike didn't want to answer. He admired the older man, a demanding cop with no hidden agenda, his voice enough to make sinners confess. From what he'd seen, the sheriff was straight as a yardstick.

Frank settled into a chair beside the desk. "You wanted to see me?"

"Read this."

He handed Frank the flyer, the reason he had asked the sheriff to stop by police headquarters today. If this had landed on Mike's Atlanta desk, he wouldn't have given it much more than a quick read before passing it on. Not here, though—not this flyer, because he knows the face. He sees it most mornings having breakfast across from Fran Riddle.

Frank glanced at the flyer but then slowly read it through. "Son of a gun, a terrorist right here in our midst. She looks so innocent too. You'd never know there was anything hidden behind her beautiful face."

"I saw her with Jed Anderson. He's your cousin, right?"

"Yeah, so is Fran Riddle, who latched onto Megan the moment the newcomer hit town not long ago. They've been close friends ever since."

"Think they'd be willing to help?"

"They will, or I'll know the reason why." Frank smashed his cigarette butt in the stoneware saucer Mike shoved toward him.

"We don't want to go off half-cocked calling Feds without something concrete," Mike said. "We'll talk to them, starting with Jed."

"There might be questions, if he comes here. How about I take this to his farm on my own time? I'm there often enough no one will question my presence."

"Sounds good. Just be sure no one suspects." He grinned at Frank's raised eyebrows. "Sorry. I don't mean to teach you your business."

"Oh, I daresay you could teach me plenty, big city cop that you are." Frank tucked the folded flyer into his pocket and, with a half salute, headed out the door.

ᴎᴎᴎᴎᴎ

Later, wearing worn jeans and denim shirt, Frank knocked a rat-tat-tat before walking into the farmhouse where his Aunt Rosalie lived. This had been his second home since his wife died eight years earlier. "I invited myself to supper."

"Why am I not surprised?" Rosalie asked with a laugh. "Somehow, you manage to be here right when Pearl has meatloaf and potatoes ready."

"Meatloaf and potatoes, ah, yes, food for a hungry man." Frank helped her to her feet keeping her in the circle of his arm while they crossed the hall toward the kitchen. She was frail, but she didn't let multiple sclerosis slow her much.

"How's your apple crop this year?" Frank asked Jed, around a mouthful of mashed potatoes.

"Good. We could use some rain though."

They touched on the problem of finding enough part-time help during picking season. Jed didn't make any bones about hiring only local people. There was no question about their legality either. Farming had enough issues without adding illegal immigrants into the mix.

Frank shoved his cup toward Pearl Gasperson when she served coffee. When his aunt became ill, Pearl had moved in to help her, much to the family's eternal gratitude but over Rosalie's protests. Pearl had stated she needed work, Rosalie needed help, so they were a match. Rosalie, the softhearted woman she is, stopped arguing.

"Thanks, Old Lady," Frank said. Pearl was only a few years older than he was, but her hair was already white when she was in high school. He—the smart-mouthed adolescent he was—had insisted she was really an old woman pretending to be young.

"You're welcome, you old buzzard. Are you still persecuting innocent people?"

"Every chance I get."

Pearl left the room on a wave of laughter.

Frank sipped his coffee. He needed to get Jed away so they could talk. Inspiration came when he glanced around the room at paintings which Rosalie had done years before. She'd considered a career in painting, but that ended when she married. One was of Jed astride Brownie, his first pony.

"I heard you bought another horse."

"You bet. Hero's Pride. Come, give me your opinion."

Frank snorted. "As if I know anything about horses."

Of even height, they matched steps toward the stable. There, they passed some occupied stalls before reaching the last one where a dark stallion bumped the half door.

Jed ran his hand down the long mane. "Sorry, boy, no ride tonight. Frank wants to natter at me."

"How do you know?" Frank demanded.

Jed laughed. "You've been eyeing me since you walked in the door. I learned what that meant when you took me to task over childish pranks."

"Did I rake you over the coals often?"

"Too often for my comfort anyway."

"Ah, the trials of being older. This time I'm not here regarding your misdemeanors but about another person's felonies."

"I'm not aware I know anybody committing felonies. The idea of a felon living in a town of 10,000-or-so people intrigues me." Jed led the way back to the house.

"Is anybody else around?"

"No, all the hands left earlier." Jed closed the office door. "Have a seat, and let's hear it."

Frank pulled the folded flyer from his jacket pocket, showing only the picture. "Look familiar?"

"Megan Stanfield." Jed unfolded the flyer and read the information. "Bianca? Terrorist? No way."

"You didn't read everything. She started in Milan during the second world war with a resistance group working for the Allies."

Jed's mouth gaped like a trout after bait. "World War Two? *Megan*?"

"I'm telling you what Interpol thinks. This woman dropped from sight after the war but reemerged on the sixties war protest scene."

"Twenty years later?" Jed asked. "Possible, I guess. She would be in her late thirties, trying to recapture her youth."

"Could be. Still searching for the fountain of youth when she was in the Middle East during the seventies raising a fuss with the Israelis."

"Late forties and still protesting? Sounds like retarded development. She'd be in her nineties, now, and on the rampage again. No way. I know plastic surgeons can do wonders, but they can't stop natural aging. If this is the same woman, she found the fountain of youth somewhere along the way."

"The Feds don't say this is the same woman. They say the description has followed terrorist activities throughout the years. There are two photographs, same face, different places, different decades. They believe plastic surgery is the answer."

"How?"

"Women changing their appearance to match a known resistance worker, making people think she's the same woman."

Jed shook his head. "Bizarre thinking. Now she's in our small town where she sticks out like a sore thumb. I'm not buying it."

"Look at the date, Jed. See it the way the Feds will when we report the woman's—what's the word I want? —looks just like her."

"Doppelgänger?"

"Right. This woman's doppelgänger is here. The woman on the wanted poster tried to blow up Detroit tunnels this past July. If I remember correctly, Megan Stanfield came here from Detroit about the same time."

"Unusual, Frank, I grant you. I don't recall two strangers have ever moved here during the same month."

"Two? Oh, I'd forgotten an old codger who rents one of Sally's cabins at Mirror Lake. I see him around town nearly every day. If Megan Stanfield is involved with terrorists, is he? Or is he keeping an eye on her in case she talks? Or protecting her if someone starts asking questions?"

"I can't see their being terrorists. A doppelgänger must be the answer. If Megan were guilty, she wouldn't admit being from Detroit but, instead, choose anywhere else in the world for her ancestral hometown."

"You might be right." Frank pushed for something definite to confirm his belief the FBI, Interpol, and everyone else was on a wild goose chase. "So, you don't have any suspicions she isn't who she says she is or came here for any reason other than the one she gave?"

"I doubted her for my own reasons," Jed admitted.

"Are you going to tell me what they were, or are?"

Jed shrugged. "She attracts me, which I don't want, so I scoffed when she told me why she came south. Her reason is credible, though: her grandparents' homeplace. Both sets were natives."

"Yeah, the Abernathies and Malloys. I know the names, but don't remember any of the people. They died out years ago, so she chose a good cover."

"I don't believe it."

"Okay, humor me here. The flyer doesn't give much detail, yet it does indicate that face has been involved in terrorist activities for several decades."

"Don't you see? Megan can't be the person pictured there. She's too young. The whole idea is beyond preposterous."

"Plastic surgery, Jed, remember? During your intimate moments . . . ."

Jed snorted. "We don't have intimate moments. We're barely civil to each other."

Frank cocked one eyebrow. "The most attractive female to hit this town in who knows how long, yet you haven't made a play? You're slipping, Cuz, but do this for me. Check behind her ears . . . ."

"Her *ears*?"

"Yes, her ears." Frank contained his impatience. The request sounded ridiculous to him too. "I understand surgeons take nips and tucks behind ears in face lifts. Anyhow, look behind her ears without raising suspicions. Understand this. I'll have your hide if she disappears before we have enough information for the Feds. You hear me?"

"I hear you. I heard her tell Fran she has an appointment with Deborah Hayes tomorrow, getting her hair cut. I'll talk to Deb beforehand, let her do the spying."

"Will your old flame do it without running her mouth?"

"I'll think of some story, not sure Megan isn't lying about her age, her face is too perfect, or something. You know what this town is like, Frank. Half the people will know something is in the air by lunchtime tomorrow; the other half, by dinnertime."

"Yes, but make sure you aren't the pipeline. Get it done soonest."

"Okay, I'm on it, even if I do think the whole thing is out of left field."

"Just do it." Frank heaved himself from the chair. "Tell Aunt Rosalie I'll be back when I get hungry again."

Chapter 3

Decision Time

Megan's anger at Jed simmered during a brisk walk from town. This is home, she murmured, even if not permanent. Finding the fully-furnished, two-story, white clapboard house, the Malloy homeplace with long front and back porches, had been fortuitous. Her family homeplace was comfortable—looked like what it was: lived in over time. Only a mile from her shop too. Being at home didn't ease her anger toward Jed Anderson. She paced the floor until her feet hurt. Picking up cushions, she beat them to a fare-thee-well and threw them on the sofa, but that didn't help. Her brain was still ready to explode.

He thought her business was a failure, did he? What was he doing to help? Not one thing. If his mother's investment concerned him, why wasn't he helping? Why wasn't he buying something—snacks at least? He could enjoy several items if he would try them. Why didn't he encourage people to patronize her business? And he thinks she isn't logical!

Megan thought longingly of throwing the last sofa pillow at the vexatious man. Yes, a good word: vexatious. Pestiferous is even better. She marched out to the back porch and plopped into her favorite Boston rocker, where the motion kept time with her furious digging for words describing Jed Anderson. Irksome. Troublesome. Tiresome. Aggravating. Upsetting. Infuriating.

Her brain slowed over words. The rocker motion became a gentle sway. Soon after her arrival, Megan learned night falls softly in the mountains. At this hour, she enjoyed the quiet sounds of the waning day. Small animals crossing the yard crunching the leaves, a car motor in the distance, the mild ripple of breezes through the trees always soothed her.

Crawfordville was a peaceful place—except for Jed Anderson—unlike any place Megan had ever been, although she missed the excitement of city life. Circumstances being what they were, she must ignore the past for now, must live her story. She roused herself from memories. Bedtime.

Megan had been asleep only moments when the ringing phone woke her. She opened one eye enough to check the clock. Midnight.

"Hello?" She cleared her throat. "Hello? Who's there?"

"Jed. Jed Anderson." His voice faded into silence.

Great. Does he make phone calls at any time except midnight? "Did you think of something more for your rant?"

"Uh, I called to apologize."

"Again?"

"I was out of line this afternoon. I shouldn't have criticized you or your store."

"No, you shouldn't have." Her anger came back, icy this time. "Your rudeness was uncalled for. I didn't appreciate it one bit."

"My mother's investment is important."

He couldn't appease her with anything short of full apology. "Do you always show your concern for her by insulting her tenants?"

"No, no I don't. I do apologize. I'm sorry I was rude. I'll try not to let it happen again."

Don't make waves. Deep breath. Megan accepted his apology.

"Maybe we can sit down one day to discuss the situation in a rational way."

Rational? When had he ever been rational with her? Her granddad's voice popped into her mind. He had often quieted her temper with one phrase when someone had insulted her. Humor cools animosity. Another deep breath. "Good idea. Midnight apologies might become habitual."

"True."

"The cows might kick you if you milk them without a proper night's rest."

"They haven't yet, and I haven't had a decent night's rest since the first time I saw you."

A click followed by the dial tone sounded loud in her ear. Megan stared at the phone with disbelief. She couldn't remember the last time someone—anyone—had left her speechless.

ꙩ ꙩ ꙩ ꙩ ꙩ

"Confound it," Jed muttered after he broke the connection. Megan had done it again—disarmed him with friendly words in her delightful accent. Not Yankee. Something else. Did people in the upper Midwest have accents? At the beginning of his call, she had shown only contempt with good reason. However, he'd been right about his mother's business. He only went about it the wrong way.

He still wanted Megan Stanfield away from here, not only because she got under his skin but for the town's sake. The fuss following a terrorist accusation would be bad for Crawfordville. However, yelling at her wasn't getting the job done. The echo of his father's words surrounded him. "You'll catch more flies with honey than with vinegar." He would smother her with honey, Jed decided.

The image of amber dripping from her face stayed with him as he drifted into sleep.

ꙩ ꙩ ꙩ ꙩ ꙩ

Sleep was impossible after Jed's call, so Megan went to the kitchen for chamomile tea. His call had not only disturbed her sleep but had reminded her of a major concern. Money. Before going into hiding, she limited money access to avoid scrutiny. She'd misjudged her financial needs. How much longer could she manage? She leaned against a window facing the backyard while her mind sifted through various solutions.

Her thoughts stopped when something white rose from the ground through the scant branches of the hedge and hovered for what seemed an eternity before fading downward. Megan waited for the . . . the thing to rise again. It didn't.

Megan considered what she'd seen. A white blob with no definite shape but uneven edges rose straight up and came down the same way. She didn't hear a sound through the closed window. Could she have imagined it? Megan admitted her thought processes were off kilter since the Detroit fiasco, still she was far from irrational. No, the image was just moonlight filtering through the trees—couldn't be anything else. Could it?

What a day. Only one sale, the confrontation with Jed, and his midnight call. A trick of light upset her. She snuggled on the sofa beneath a down comforter. Tomorrow would be better. Couldn't be worse.

Megan should have remembered not to test fate.

Fran's raised eyebrows greeted Megan at Fine Feathers the next morning.

"Your face would dry up milk cows," Fran said. "Help me fold the dust covers while you tell me what's wrong."

Megan shrugged. She'd opened a business to keep her mind occupied until better days came. They surely would, she'd told herself. They must. This small town didn't have a health food store, so she had leased space in a prime location.

This morning, she had done some hard thinking while she walked toward town. All she could see ahead was trouble. She was almost ready to admit her business was a failure. Looking into her future in Crawfordville was like peering through a heavy mist. She folded another cover before replying. "Decision time—do I stay, or do I leave?"

"Oh, no, Megan," Fran pleaded. "You can't mean that. Think about why you came. You'll realize you must stay."

Megan smoothed the muslin edges while she eased into the role she'd rehearsed. "I came to get away from the triple-locked doors, the traffic, the panhandlers, the . . . well, you get the picture even if you've never had the experience."

Megan handed Fran the last dust cover. "Why do people think I came for any reason other than what I've told them? I wanted a simpler, quieter life. I suppose I'm a sixties throwback."

"Crawfordville isn't a commune, by any means, but I guess closer to nature than big cities. You must realize small town people are suspicious of outsiders with new ideas."

"I suppose a health food store is innovative here. My business could be a success, though, if people would try natural food. After all, they don't have to eat only health food. I don't."

"Are things really so bad?"

Megan answered the hesitant question with a jerky nod. "Do you think my lack of business is because people believe I don't live by my words about healthy eating?"

"Where did you get such an idea?" Fran asked. "I've never heard anything so absurd."

"Jed." Megan clapped a hand across her mouth. "Oh, no! I wasn't going to burden you with this." Nevertheless, words tumbled over each other while she recounted their stupid argument.

"I know Aunt Rosalie owns your building—her parents had a grocery store there long years ago—but I can't see her throwing you out on your ear. She's almost the saint Jed thinks she is. You're keeping up with the rent, aren't you?"

"So far, I am. I know my lease protects me from ejection while I do, but maybe I should leave. I can't risk Mrs. Anderson's livelihood."

"Megan, don't say anything about leaving." Fran leaned against a counter, urgency coloring her voice. "Aunt Rosalie doesn't depend on rental income from your store. Her parents and Jed's father left her a wealthy woman. I doubt she has ever touched her capital. Don't let Jed's attitude send you away. You're already part of this town. Other people feel the same way. Sally, for one, Catherine is another. This town needs young businesswomen. The mayor said so at the last Chamber of Commerce meeting, remember? Robin emphasized establishing a business is a way we can keep our young women here. Otherwise, we will lose them to Asheville or Atlanta."

"I'll soon be part of Crawfordsville's homeless, not its businesswomen. My business is a dismal failure. I've heard people come for fall leaf color and hoped they would give my store a needed money infusion to keep me going until spring. According to the weather report, leaf color won't change for a few weeks. I'm not sure I can wait. I'll soon be completely broke. I even studied the newspaper's help-wanted ads. There isn't anything else for me here."

Fran nodded as she swished a feather duster across the counter.

A thought popped out of nowhere and lodged in Megan's brain. She pondered the idea, oblivious to her surroundings. She'd come here to hide until she could deal with her future. That time had not yet come. Grasping Fran's arm, she asked, "What do you think about a different business—one which sells a variety, so I won't depend on one kind of product?"

"A sort of modified general store?"

Megan leaned forward to answer Fran's doubting question. "Crawfordville doesn't have a card shop, or a gift shop, or a crafts shop, and goodness knows what else. So, why not have everything under one roof? I already lease the perfect location. I must give the idea more thought, however."

Fran opened but closed her mouth without speaking.

"Do you think my idea would work here?" Megan heard the timidity in her question, as second thoughts battered her brain. She didn't know whether she wanted encouragement or a swift denial.

"I thought you said you were down to your last dime."

Almost, still the idea wouldn't go away. Her idea nibbled at the edges of Megan's mind like a finicky eater while she walked toward her shop. Did she have enough money? She couldn't ask family for money because her lifestyle would horrify them. A bank loan? Megan dug in her mental heels. Her grandfather's disapproval of debt buzzed through her brain. No debt. There must be another way.

The natural foods supplier might take back the stock, perhaps with a refund, which buoyed her for a moment. A second thought made her shoulders slump. She didn't remember the contract containing a clause about refunds. New stock costs would take her last dime if she had to start over again.

Megan studied the store fittings from a new perspective. Would her present counters and shelves work? She pictured their holding yarn instead of noodles, greeting cards instead of tofu. No, cards needed shelves with slots. Where would she get the money for them? Unless the supplier gave her the refund. One slim chance. That's all she had. One minute Megan was excited—surely, the distributor would understand—the next she was in the dumps. There was no reason he should.

Success is the bottom line. She had to succeed if she stayed here for any length of time, which she must do.

Megan's decision left her quivering.

Chapter 4

Suspicion

The morning after Frank's orders regarding Megan, Jed hesitated at the hair salon door with a glance around before he stepped outside. Maybe no one would see him leave the pink-painted storefront. No such luck. He should have used the back door after talking with Deborah. With a self-conscious grin, Jed slid into step with Jack Kincaid, ignoring his amusement.

Most times, small town life was good. This was not one of them. Not only had his old flame teased him, he had to contend with his banker's humor.

"Morning, Jed. Deborah should have used more sticky stuff on your hair."

"She ran out, I reckon." Jed pushed open the diner door hoping Jack would drop the subject. He didn't. Jed left half an hour later with considerable relief. Seeing Megan having breakfast with Fran directly in his line of view didn't help. Wanting her gone because she messed with his libido was one thing. Sneaking around asking questions was another. He'd seen her in a temper, also cool as a cucumber in the face of his disdain. He'd seen her relaxed with Fran as she was this morning. Her eyes reflected her every emotion. No way could Megan Stanfield be a terrorist. Ridiculous to think otherwise.

Jed left his fieldhands herding cattle to the adjoining field and returned to town in late afternoon feeling only disgust with himself. True, he must pry into Megan's life or Frank would nail his hide to the barn door, which didn't ease his guilt.

"So, you didn't find any scars." Jed had browsed through the hardware store until Deborah closed her shop. From the window, he had watched Megan leave the salon, her long legs carrying her down the street and out of sight, before he waylaid Deborah hurrying to her car.

"Jed, what's going on? I've noticed your attitude toward Megan—all your friends have—so why do you need information about a woman you pretend means nothing to you?"

"Pretend?" He widened his eyes. "Not pretense, Debi darling. How can I possibly care for any woman after you broke my heart in high school? You wouldn't even go to the senior prom with me. Wounded me for life."

Deborah leaned against her SUV, a grin on her face. "Now I understand why you flit from woman to woman like bees after honey, never lighting anywhere long enough to get snagged."

"Exactly. Now aren't you ashamed of yourself for dumping me for my best friend?"

"Oh, no, Jed. Your memory is faulty. You did the dumping when a blonde Jezebel from Brevard caught your eye."

"Don't remind me of her. You're to blame that she got her claws into me. I would never have noticed her if you hadn't broken my heart."

"Face it, Redhead. You couldn't resist when she batted her false eyelashes at you."

"No way!" This banter was amusing—remembering his teen years was always fun—but Jed needed answers for Frank. "Any scars?"

Deborah sobered. "No scars behind her ears or anywhere else on her head or neck. No facial wrinkles or scarred eyelids either. I've never seen such perfect skin. I thought it was cosmetics until I looked close. Megan appears to be in her mid-twenties, although I understand she's several years older."

Jed kept his relief under wraps. "Thanks."

"I don't know what's happening, Jed, and I can see you won't tell me. However, you should know I've heard whispers that Megan came here because she's in trouble. Hiding in this small town, although she could lose herself in a big city easier."

"I know you don't gossip, Deborah, so I won't ask you to keep my questions under your hat. I can tell you this much. Your information is a help, not a hindrance for Megan."

Jed strode away. The sooner he called Frank, the sooner he could put the whole mess behind him.

ꝶ ꝶ ꝶ ꝶ ꝶ

"Is Mike in?" Frank stopped at the front desk. He agreed with Jed. Megan Stanfield was not the face on the flyer. She might identify her, though, so it was time for questions.

"Come in, Frank." Mike waved him toward a chair. "Coffee?"

"I've drunk enough this morning to float a battleship, so I'll pass. Megan Stanfield's hairdresser said there are no scars of any kind on Megan's head, neck, or face, so no surgery hides advanced years or different appearance. This appears to rule her out as the terrorist, if copycat plastic surgery is in the equation."

Mike nodded. "The next question is do we question her before we call the Feds?"

"You've never dealt with the local FBI agent. I have. John Patterson is protective of his position. We will do well to let him handle the interrogation if we want future cooperation from him."

Mike reached for the phone and cradled it after a few words. "Patterson will be here in an hour. Megan should be here then."

Frank glanced at his watch. Almost lunch time. "Megan normally closes her shop for an hour, so she's probably in the diner. Shall I ask her to come here, or will you?"

"I would rather do almost anything else. She lives in my jurisdiction, though, so I'll do it. I gather Patterson can get rough?"

"Verbally, yes," Frank said. "He has a quick temper too. Okay if I'm here? He learned the hard way some time back that I won't tolerate any kind of abuse from him."

"I'll be glad to have you."

"By the way, Mike, I've never known Patterson to be punctual. I understand Sally Jamison subs for Megan when the need arises. You might suggest Sally keep the shop all afternoon. I won't be surprised if Patterson, when he eventually gets here, takes the rest of the day at least."

ﬗ ﬗ ﬗ ﬗ ﬗ

"Hi, Mike, join us for lunch?" Megan scooted toward the wall moving her plate along with her. "I can vouch for the Reuben sandwich."

"Sounds good. Hey, Fran. What's that stuff you're eating?"

"Beef goulash. Okay but not out of the ordinary." Fran offered him a bite.

Mike chewed and swallowed. "No thanks, I'll stick with the sandwich even though Megan didn't offer me a bite."

"Guess I'm a pig. I want all of it!" The diner had grown quiet when the cop joined Megan's booth. "Okay, Mike, this is too early for your usual lunch, so does your presence now have anything to do with the whispers I've encountered since yesterday?"

"I haven't heard any whispers, Megan, but we do want you at the station after you finish lunch. You might be there all afternoon, so arrange for someone to cover you at the store. Can I depend on you?"

Megan only nodded, but Fran pushed for answers.

"Why, Mike? People have accepted Megan, some genuinely like her even though she's an outsider. Suddenly, they're avoiding her, shunning her almost. There's even talk of criminal activity. You sitting with us adds to rumors, so for heaven's sake tell us what's going on."

"I can't." He hurried away leaving Megan and Fran staring at each other.

Mike's going to arrest me. Megan shivered at the thought, something new for her.

Fran pushed away her plate. "Megan, is there something you want to tell me?"

Great. Even her one close friend suspects her of doing who knows what, but she had her answer ready. "I don't have a clue what's going on, Fran. I've never even had a speeding ticket."

"I believe you, but there must be a reason for the gossip. In my shop this morning, two women kept staring at me. I confronted them. You know me. I believe in being direct. One said, since I'm your best friend, I should know all about it. The other pulled her out the door before she could say anything else."

"Is my shop the reason?"

"Why would what you sell interest the police? At any rate, you'll find out this afternoon, so call me when the police finish. I must get back to work, and you have a date with a handsome cop."

"Some date. I'd better call Sally." Megan shoved her plate away. The sandwich lost its appeal.

Ꙅ Ꙅ Ꙅ Ꙅ Ꙅ

He wrapped his arms across his scrawny chest and watched the woman leave the diner after the cop left in an almighty hurry. She must have done something bad, committed a crime. But if so, why hadn't Mike Williams arrested her? Instead, she had gone into her shop. If she's a criminal, is he one too? If he'd spent time behind bars, he'd have tattoos, wouldn't he? He didn't. Not even one from his Army years. His temples started throbbing. He needed to remember, he told himself again. He *must* remember else these headaches would be the death of him for sure.

ריריריריר

"Have you talked to her? The woman on the flyer?" The eager voice preceded a man of slight build, hair more salt than pepper. Ignoring the deputy who tugged at his arm, he shoved open the police chief's door, taking up a bulldog stance. A younger man stood at his shoulder.

Mike turned from the window and studied the man who had barged into his office unannounced. Presumably the expected FBI agent. Frank had been right. The federal agents were more than an hour late. Mike Williams, small town police chief though he now was, had dealt with self-important officials in Atlanta too many times to let this one intimidate him. He studied the man a moment longer and then turned toward Frank.

"Do you know these men?"

Frank picked up Mike's reaction and stared at the men for a long moment. "Ummm. Yes, I've met them before. The older one is John Patterson, Senior FBI agent in the Asheville office. The younger one is agent Nicholas Burke." Frank turned toward the Feds. "This is Michael Williams, Crawfordville's police chief."

Patterson glared at Frank. "Why are you here? This has nothing to do with you. Espionage is a federal matter."

Mike watched with amusement when Frank drew himself to his full height, several inches taller, many pounds heavier than the Fed. After so many years of law enforcement, the sheriff was tough as an old boot. No minor federal official would bully him.

"This is my county." Frank tapped his badge. "Everything happening here is my business. Naturally, I'm here."

"Okay, introductions are out of the way, please be seated." Mike met the agent's glare with one of his own. "You've wasted our time as well as Megan Stanfield's long enough."

"Her name is Megan Stanfield? She's the woman on this flyer?"

"That's the name of the local woman who resembles the face on the flyer, yes. However, we don't believe she's the same woman. She might identify her, though. The resemblance is outstanding, but Ms. Stanfield is too young . . . ."

"I'm not stupid! One woman hasn't been behind multiple decades of terrorism. However, there's no question the same face has created havoc over several decades. I want the woman who has it now."

Frank intervened. "The photo is twenty years old. Ms. Stanfield is too young."

"Plastic surgery works wonders . . . ."

". . . but leaves scars. Ms. Stanfield has none."

Patterson ignored his comment. "Tell me what you know about her."

Mike recounted what he knew. "Her reason for moving here is reasonable. She wanted to find some family after her grandmother's death last winter. The timing is coincidental."

“I don’t believe in coincidence. Somebody with that face tried to blow up Detroit tunnels in July. Somebody with that face shows up here in July, admitting she came from Detroit. Must be the same person. Get her in here now.”

Mike pushed a buzzer and asked for Megan.

Chapter 5

Questions, Questions, Questions

When Megan entered the small room, three men stood. One man lounged in a plastic molded chair, glancing from the flyer to her face. Before she could reach the chair that Mike indicated, the man jumped to his feet and took two strides toward her. When she stepped backward, he followed, holding the flyer next to her face.

"Get out of her face, Patterson!" Frank could move fast for such a big man, but Mike was faster. He yanked Patterson around before the sheriff could knock the agent on his keister.

"You don't intimidate a witness in my office." Mike jerked a thumb sideways. "You keep your distance. Furthermore, you will ask questions in a reasonable manner, or I'll call your boss."

Patterson stepped toward the chair but didn't stop the tirade.

"The picture is her, a known terrorist wanted all over the world. You're obstructing justice, Williams." Patterson slapped Mike's desk. "I'll call Atlanta myself."

Megan collapsed into the chair Frank held for her. "Terrorist? Me? Why would he think I'm a terrorist? Who is he anyway?"

"Patterson, sit down." As soon as the agent collapsed into a chair, Mike spoke.

"Megan, these two men are John Patterson and Nicholas Burke, FBI agents."

"*FBI*? Why are they interested in me?"

"Because you're a known terrorist," Patterson shouted.

Mike pushed the intercom. "Brittany, get me FBI headquarters in Atlanta."

"Not necessary." Patterson shrugged off his junior's arm. He took a deep breath "We've searched for that face for decades. I became overly excited finding the current owner."

"Will someone please tell me what's happening here?" Megan glared around the room, at last focusing on Mike, seated behind a battered metal desk. The blinds behind him were open wide, allowing full sunlight to flood the room and into her face. "I've had enough of whispers, finger pointing, and now this man's tirade. Why Am I Here?"

Mike took over. "You're due an explanation, Megan. First, though, you need to answer some questions." He punched the recorder button and said a few words of introduction. "Now, Mr. Patterson, start your questions."

Patterson thrust the flyer toward Megan. "That's you."

Megan glanced at it, frowned, and then looked closer, reading the information beneath the picture. "No, this isn't me. Who is she, this Bianca person? I've never heard of her."

"You're Bianca. Denial won't get you anywhere, so admit it."

Mike met her eyes. "The photo does look like you. Can you identify her?"

Megan shook her head. "I can only repeat, it isn't me. I don't know her, but she looks older than I am. What did he mean, searching for me for many years? I haven't been hard to find. Any number of people could have directed him to me. I'm still waiting for an explanation."

"She's right. Patterson," Mike said. "You're not asking questions; you're telling her she's a terrorist."

Patterson gritted his teeth. "Are you a United States citizen?"

"Yes."

"Were you born in the United States?"

"Yes."

"Are you sure you were not born in Milan, Italy?"

"Yes."

"An outright lie." Patterson controlled himself again. "During the mid-forties, a woman with your face was part of the Italian Underground working in Milan."

"The mid-forties! Are you out of your mind? I was born in 1990, which you would know if you had bothered to see my birth certificate before making your wild accusations."

"I said someone with your face. Your face dropped from sight during the fifties, re-emerged in sixties war protests, created more chaos throughout the seventies and eighties. Since then, a woman with your face has left destruction over a large part of the world, including failed efforts in Detroit this past July. I contend you are this latest woman."

Megan stared at him. "You cannot possibly be serious. The same face? Somebody is feeding you a line of unbelievable absurdity. Are you sure you have an actual photograph, not a computer-generated picture?"

"This is a real photograph," Patterson insisted. "People captured that face on film during both the sixties and the nineties. This past July, an eyewitness described her. He picked your picture from a line-up. Now, Bianca, tell us your real surname."

"I repeat, I am not whoever she is. My name is not Bianca. I am Megan Elizabeth Stanfield, born March tenth, 1990, Detroit, Michigan, United States of America. My parents are Reid and Susan Stanfield, residents of Detroit, although they are traveling now. I can direct you to their home where you can talk to the servants. They've all known me since my birth."

Mike intervened again. "Megan, will you give us information about your schooling, church, and anything else helpful for Patterson to trace your background?"

"I'll do whatever necessary to clear up this absurd situation."

"You heard her, Patterson, so verifying what she has told you should be the next order of business."

"What's to keep her from disappearing again?"

"I'm not going anywhere." Megan pointed out the obvious. "Staying here is to my benefit because I know I'm innocent."

"No! The face, man, look at the face!" Patterson waved the flyer. "She is at least the third generation with a face involved in terrorism. For over seventy years, law enforcement agencies all over the world have sought that face. Can you wonder I want to hold the current owner, now that I have her in my grasp? Be reasonable!"

Mike exchanged a long look with Frank. They knew Patterson was right. They would have to confine her.

"We'll hold Ms. Stanfield for you."

"You're going to put me in jail?"

Mike met her horrified gaze. "We must, Megan, until he is certain you aren't the woman who he thinks you are. You're not under arrest. You're a material witness only."

"Not under arrest? You're putting me in jail, so what's the difference? Besides, you can't keep me without a warrant." She'd read that somewhere and hoped it was true.

"Megan, we can hold you for forty-eight hours as a material witness. You won't have an arrest record."

"That doesn't make any difference. This will finish me here all because I look like someone else, which isn't fair. I'm not her. I'm not!"

"Your friends . . . ."

"What friends, Mike? Few people speak to me now. No one will after this gets out, all because of my face. I can't do anything about it. I was born with this face!"

"You have a famous, or infamous, face, Megan." Mike believed her, yet agreed with the FBI he could not risk her disappearing.

Megan bit her inner lip to stop the trembling. "How long must I stay here?"

"We'll keep you only until Patterson verifies your history."

"He has no intention of verifying anything, Surely, you noticed that neither agent made even one note."

Frank agreed. "She's right, Mike. Patterson has no intention of looking into her life."

"There's no need. She's guilty. I don't trust rubes to keep her, so I'm taking her into custody."

"No, you're not. You have no authority in my office unless I give it to you." Mike refrained from knocking the smug look off Patterson's face. Instead, he punched the intercom button. "Get me Fred Higgins with the FBI in Atlanta. No one else."

Patterson rose half way out of the chair but settled back.

"Nabbing a person wanted all over the world would be a notch in your gun, wouldn't it, Patterson?" Frank shook his head. "You're getting ahead of the evidence again. What about possible fingerprints? Surely Interpol has some for comparison."

"I have all I need."

"Fred? Mike Williams, here. We're on speaker phone. How are you doing? Faye and the kids?" After a bit more chitchat, he said, "I have a situation involving an agent."

He explained. "Megan Stanfield's appearance matches the flyer photo. I'm willing to keep her in my jail while the FBI investigates her Detroit history."

"What's the problem?"

"John Patterson from the Asheville office has taken no notes. Furthermore, he stated he does not intend to investigate anything. He has declared her guilt based on her face."

"I've never had reason to doubt your word, Mike, still I must see this woman for myself before I can make a decision of such importance. So, keep her on ice until I get there."

"Any idea when?"

"Before the day is over is the best I can say."

"Right." Mike cradled the phone. "Patterson, you and Burke are to be here too."

"I wouldn't miss it. Fred will agree with me, you'll see." He left the room with Burke at his heels.

"I want to know one thing." Megan broke the silence. "Can any reasonable person truly believe my face has been floating around since the forties?"

Frank answered. "I've never found John Patterson to be reasonable."

Megan gripped her hands together. "Mike, are you keeping me now?"

"I must."

"Look at it this way," Frank said. "If we don't keep you in jail here, the Feds will take custody as soon as you walk out the door. When they would release you is anybody's guess. You're better off here."

"Better off? A relative term."

ᚢ ᚢ ᚢ ᚢ ᚢ

The cell door slammed shut leaving Megan on the inside in a room smaller than her closet. *So, this is what a cell looks like. None of the comforts of home.* She took a deep breath. What had gone so terribly wrong that this could happen to her? The terrorism issue had blown up in her face, the face too well known to officials for her comfort.

The only sounds were inside her head as she debated her next move. No one had listened when she voiced her innocence earlier. She couldn't kid herself. They probably never would. Her face condemned her. Sure, she could obtain formidable help with just one phone call, but she'd learned one lesson early in life. If she got into a mess, she should expect to get herself out. Megan Elizabeth Stanfield would find a way. She must.

When the cell door opened two hours later, Megan settled her face into a blank. There was no way on earth she would let anyone know she was not in complete control of her life.

"I've never heard anything so idiotic!" Fran's disgusted voice preceded her through the door. "*Megan Stanfield* a terrorist? She won't even step on a bug, for heaven's sake! She steps over them."

Megan almost smiled. If Fran were in charge, the entire FBI would be on bended knee, begging forgiveness before the day was over.

The door slammed shut, leaving Fran inside. "You're not a terrorist! You can bet I told them so."

"I did too. They didn't listen." Megan shot her a rueful grin. "Can you believe this? If it isn't one thing, it's another. Failing business isn't enough; now this terrorist accusation. What next? How did you hear about this ridiculous charge? Don't tell me the news is all over town already."

They sat shoulder to shoulder on the cot. "Gossip is all over town that Mike arrested you. Naturally, there's speculation, but no one knows why. I learned the reason when I overheard cops talking in the lobby."

"I don't understand how people knew something was wrong before I did. They started staring early this morning and haven't stopped." Megan's laughter was self-mockery. "Seeing so many people coming into the store thrilled me. I thought they had accepted me at least enough to sample my stock. However, my merchandise didn't interest them—only *moi*."

"God would strike me dead if I expressed my opinion of these people whom I've known all my life."

Megan smiled at the vehemence. "I doubt you even know such language, but I'm not proud of my own thoughts. I hate to think what my family will do when they hear."

"Have you called anyone?"

"No. The only family I have is in Europe where I hope they stay until this is over." She'd never wished anything more.

The cell door opened admitting Alice Morrison, one of Megan's few regular customers. Considering her job, she probably needed regular infusions of the soothing herbal teas. "The FBI agent has arrived from Atlanta, Megan. They're ready for you."

Mr. Higgins must have come in the helicopter that Megan had heard a few minutes earlier. Calmness was the key.

"I'm going with her," Fran stated.

"You can't, Fran. You can wait in the lobby while they talk." Alice's voice was polite but allowed for no contradiction.

"I'll see you afterwards, no matter what they say," Megan assured her.

After Fran left, Alice touched Megan's upper arm, not quite grasping it yet prepared to do so.

Megan gave her a slight smile, repeating her earlier assurance. "Running is the farthest thing from my mind. Staying here is to my benefit because I know I'm innocent."

"Routine."

She kept step with the policewoman. Senseless violence was the best description of terrorist activities she'd ever read. Bottom line, someone must pay. Her argument would be she was that person because of her face. Megan Elizabeth Stanfield would not show fear. Only absolute confidence would get her through this ordeal.

"Fred, I know this is a federal matter, but is it okay if we local cops sit in on your interrogation?"

"Certainly, Mike. If there's anything I miss or if either you or the sheriff has questions, ask them. I haven't had time to look into the situation, so both of you are closer to the situation than I."

So, Megan thought, she was subject to questions from all these law officers. Daunting, but she kept her voice steady when she greeted them.

Footsteps outside the door faded while Megan concentrated on Fred Higgins. She stood up to his scrutiny until he motioned her toward a chair. She sat still, her ankles crossed, her hands limp in her lap. She couldn't recall exercising this much self-control since her grandmother had condemned her fidgeting when she was seven.

"Ms. Stanfield, except for age, this photo is your image. Have you had surgery on your head? Facelift? Eye lift? Laser?"

"No, sir."

"May I search for scars on your head?"

"Yes, sir."

By sheer willpower, she held her head still while he inspected behind her ears and ran his fingers over her skull. Not quite a massage but close. She would have enjoyed it under other circumstances.

Satisfied, he returned to his chair. "No scars, not even hairline size."

John Patterson spoke. "Some cosmetics cover even the worst scars."

Without looking at him, Megan lifted her purse from the floor. She was surprised they'd allowed her to keep it. Common sense told her someone had searched it thoroughly.

"Look out! She's going for a gun!"

"Don't be stupid, Patterson." Frank glared at him. "I searched her purse myself."

"I don't trust you." Patterson pointed a finger at the sheriff. "You'll do anything to protect the people around here."

"Yes, I protect my people from authorities who overstep their legal boundaries, something you should have learned before now." He pointed his own finger at Patterson.

"Both of you hush, or leave the room." Higgins waited for silence before he asked, "What do you need from your purse, Ms. Stanfield?"

"Wipes to clean the cosmetics off my face, which might satisfy Mr. Patterson." When Higgins nodded, Megan pulled out a package, showing it around the room. Pulling out a tissue, she methodically wiped her face and tossed the stained wipe. She didn't know why she'd put on her face today, completely contrary to her usual morning routine. Yes, she did. Nightmares about money had prevented rest. She'd covered the ravages, never dreaming she would show her baggy eyes to anyone today.

When she had scrubbed her face clean, using multiple tissues, Higgins inspected it again. "No scars. Not even from acne."

Never had Megan been more pleased with her flawless skin.

Patterson's whining voice rose. "People hid scars in other ways. Or, she might have had her face restructured."

Higgins stared him into silence. Turning toward Mike, he said, "Keep Ms. Stanfield while I investigate her story."

"No investigation is necessary, I tell you, Fred!" Patterson protested. "Look at her face! Scars or no scars, restructured or not, that face is the one law men all over the world want. Interpol will agree with me, you'll see."

Fred again stared him into silence. "I suggest you go back to Asheville if you want to remain in your current position. You have enough other cases to keep you busy."

Megan watched the silent struggle until Patterson relented to the younger agent's arm-tugging. With one last glare at her, he stalked from the room, muttering they would soon admit he was right.

"How long will I be here?"

"A few days at most," Higgins said. "Give me some names. I'll call my counterpart in Detroit first thing tomorrow." She gave him the information he wanted and watched him shove his notes into a battered leather briefcase. Then, shaking hands all around, he left.

Megan shook her head. "He won't call anybody. Regardless of the way he frowned Mr. Patterson into silence, I'll bet he agrees with him. They have me. A bird in hand, you know."

"We won't let that happen," Frank assured her.

Mike reiterated Frank's vow. "However, I don't believe our intervention will be necessary. I worked with Fred several times connected with my Atlanta cases. He has never gone back on his word."

Fran stormed into Mike's office, demanding answers. Turning on Frank, she threatened him with mayhem for keeping Megan.

"Calm down, Cuz. She's better off with us than in the Feds' custody. Now, Alice will take her back to her cell. You find out what she needs for a few days." He nodded toward Mike and left.

Minutes later, Fran left Megan's cell with list in hand. "I'll get you out of here, if it means I go to Detroit myself. I can ask questions as well as any FBI agent. Probably better."

Sitting on the bunk, Megan heard the door shut and the key turn. She was alone. Time for thought without pretense. Prison loomed large.

Chapter 6

Doppelgänger?

"Earth to Jed!"

He jerked his attention toward his mother.

"I've spoken twice, Son. What's bothering you?"

"Sorry, Mom. I didn't mean to upset you." He should have gone outside to walk off his apprehension about Megan Stanfield. He wanted her gone, far from Crawfordville, far from his presence. This terrorist business might be the best way to get rid of her. Terrorist activities meant death in some countries. Here, terrorism means lifetime imprisonment, at the least. He didn't want her at Leavenworth, just away from here.

"I'm more curious than upset. Pacing and muttering are not like you."

Before Jed found a soothing answer, the doorbell rang, followed by the opening door.

"Anybody home?"

"Come in, Frank." Relieved, Jed met him at the door of his mother's room, converted from the seldom-used formal living room when MS prevented her climbing stairs.

"Hey, Frank. Tell me what's going on. Jed's as jumpy as a cat near a rocking chair, but he isn't talking."

Frank eased his bulk into the glider chair beside her recliner and leaned over to kiss her cheek. "Aunt Rosalie, you're a sight for sore eyes after a long day."

"Cut the flattery, Frankie. I'm never inquisitive about official business unless it pertains to us. This does, otherwise Jed wouldn't be on edge, so out with it."

"Mom owns that building on the square. How will this situation affect her investment, if the allegations are true?" Jed questioned.

"I don't see why it should have any effect. I thought you might be worried, Jed, so I came."

"I'm waiting."

Frank turned toward her. "I apologize, Aunt Rosalie. Briefly, Megan Stanfield, who has the natural food store in your building, bears a striking—we could say almost identical—facial resemblance to a well-known international terrorist. The Feds have questioned her. Mike Williams and I have also. I don't believe she's involved, nor does Mike. The FBI requested we keep her while they verify her story."

"How terrible for her. When will you get the FBI's decision?"

"We hope not more than a few days."

"She has no family here, if I remember correctly. Does she have everything she needs? Maybe I should visit her, let her know she isn't alone."

Jed shook his head. "Mom, this is the reason I didn't tell you. I knew you would exert yourself too much if I did."

"Aunt Rosalie, your soft heart always goes out to anyone in trouble. However, Fran has befriended Megan from the moment she arrived and has already taken necessities to her."

"If you're sure she doesn't need me . . . ."

"I'm sure." Frank patted her hand. "As I said, this has been a long day. I'm ready for home. We have the matter under control, so you put it out of your head."

Jed followed him to the door. "Thanks, Frank."

ꑌ ꑌ ꑌ ꑌ

The key turned in the lock, breaking the dead silence. Megan had been in jail only two days, yet it seemed like an eternity. She was sure the sun had risen each morning and set each evening, even though she hadn't seen either. She'd spent the endless hours thinking, unable to concentrate on the books Fran supplied.

What would she do if no one ever believed her? The FBI might not question the people she had listed. Someone might lie about Megan Stanfield. She *must* get out of this cell. Her chest constricted. She slowed her breathing and changed the directions of her thoughts toward a new, different store.

Megan had enumerated what she would do when she left jail. If . . . . No, she refused to go there. She would call for help, readily available because of who she is. Her immediate agenda was a long, hot, bubble bath, accompanied by properly brewed Darjeeling. Next on her list was calling the natural food rep. Then, she would start pricing the different counters she would need, followed by calls to distributors for new merchandise.

"They're ready for you, Megan."

She studied Alice's face, which revealed nothing. Gripping her purse, Megan straightened her shoulders as she walked beside the policewoman. Through the glass door, she saw Fran waiting.

"I came right over when Frank called me. He won't let me go into Mike's office though."

"Having you close by is enough."

Alice opened the office door, urging Megan inside before she released her hold on Megan's arm.

Megan's trembling knees threatened to give way, and her heart beat a tattoo against her ribs as she stepped inside to meet her fate.

She looked at each face—the sheriff, the police chief, three FBI agents—too many people in this small office. Only one face was not blank. John Patterson scowled at her. Her heart leaped. Surely, he would gloat if he'd learned she was guilty. She sat in the chair

Fred Higgins indicated, never taking her gaze from his face. Was he satisfied with what his Detroit agent had learned? Reflecting on the past, she had selected bits of the Megan Stanfield history, which she drilled into her brain for inquisitive people. Now she would learn whether she'd been successful.

"Ms. Stanfield, our agent supplied a detailed report. He talked with your parents' servants, your former employer, and your pastor." He glanced at a paper in his hand. "He also interviewed your grandparents' attorney."

Megan focused on Fred Higgins. So far, so good.

"Our agent spoke by phone to the now-retired head mistress of your boarding school. Also, both the dean and the department chairman at the University of Michigan business school."

She'd had several run-ins with the department chairman over her coursework. Megan had insisted international finance did not interest her. Could he still hold a grudge after all these years?

"My agent's report is quite clear." He paused, while he shuffled papers.

Would he never finish?

"His report shows without any doubt you are not the person pictured on the flyer."

The room tilted. Pulling herself from the blackness surrounding her, Megan gulped water pouring into her mouth. She was not that person. What else was he saying? She pushed away the hand holding the cup and forced herself to attention.

"Also clear is the fact you are not, nor have you ever been, involved with terrorism anywhere. However, the resemblance is so obvious we must ask who she is."

Megan met his gaze. She would suggest a doppelgänger. Her heart fluttered with excitement one moment but then slowed to snail's pace. No one would believe something so farfetched, something from a David Baldacci thriller. Nevertheless . . . , "I have no clue who she is. I've spent these two days thinking. The way I see it, there is only one possibility. Doppelgänger."

"She's lying, Fred!"

"Sit down, Patterson. When I want your opinion, I'll ask for it." Higgins turned back to Megan. "I've heard of doppelgängers, but I've never seen evidence such exists. However, your resemblance to the flyer is unbelievable, so perhaps they do. Okay, we know you're an only child. Do you have cousins, no matter how far removed?"

"None. Neither of my parents has siblings. All my grandparents are dead. If I have more distant relatives, I've never heard of them."

"Based on our limited knowledge, the terrorist activity began seventy some odd years ago in Italy. Do you have any connections there?"

She kept her answers brief. "No, sir."

"Do you know anyone who does?"

"No, sir."

"Have you traveled in Italy?"

"The only time I've traveled outside the States was when I was ten years old. I don't remember whether we went to Italy."

"What places do you remember?"

"London, because we saw the changing of the guard. Paris was one boring museum after another. Those are the places I remember, but I know we went to Switzerland. My parents wanted to check possible boarding schools."

"Yet you attended a private school in Detroit."

"Yes, because I rebelled at being so far from my grandfather." Megan anticipated the next question and schooled her features into blandness.

"Your parents travel a great deal."

"Yes, sir. They've been in Europe several weeks."

"Italy?"

"I don't know their schedule, but I've never heard either mention Italy. They prefer Paris and Zurich."

He studied her face, which she kept calm by sheer determination. She needed to hurry him along. "Mr. Higgins, terrorism is unconscionable. If I could help you, I would. Truly. I just don't see how I can."

"I don't either, Ms. Stanfield, but if anything comes to mind, anything you might have heard about distant relatives, for instance, you report to Mike immediately. Understood?"

"Yes, sir."

Frank spoke for the first time. "There's something I don't understand. If this face is so well known around the world, how come I've never heard of it?"

"I wondered about that too, so I did a little research. This appears to be the first time anyone with this face has made an appearance in the United States. She has exercised her destructive behavior mostly throughout the Middle East and the European eastern bloc with a few excursions into Africa and South America."

He stood. "Okay, we've finished here, Mike. If you hear anything else, call me ASAP."

"I will."

Megan's breathing eased. "Mr. Higgins, will you tell me if you learn that person's identity? I don't want to go through life haunted by her."

He assured her he would and left, ushering the other agents out the door, despite Patterson's resistance.

When the door clicked shut, Megan released the shudders she had locked inside throughout the ordeal. The door slammed open. She straightened her shoulders, smoothing her face into a mask. She fought the need to escape hands that gripped her shoulders but relaxed when Fran pulled her up and drew her into a strong hug.

"You're not guilty, you're not! I won't let them keep you here any longer. You hear me, Frank Anderson? I'll give you so much trouble you won't know what hit you."

"Everybody in the building probably hears you, Cuz."

"They're not keeping me, Fran. I can't leave this place fast enough. Will you bring my stuff from the cell? I don't ever want to go back there."

"Wait in the lobby," Mike said. "Alice will bring Megan's possessions while she signs some papers. Another ten minutes, and you can leave."

ꙥ ꙥ ꙥ ꙥ ꙥ

Megan was aware of every floor squeak when she headed toward outside and freedom. Stepping through the doorway, she closed the door with a solid pull.

Megan lost herself in this first moment of freedom. A train whistled somewhere. Closer, children's shrill chatter assaulted her ears. Sun glinted off parked cars. Aromas drifted from the bakery down the street. She breathed deeply, and lifted her face to the sun.

Fran touched her arm. "Are you going to your shop?"

"No. Tell Sally I'll open tomorrow. Right now, home is what I need."

"I can drive you."

Megan shook her head. She needed fresh air. She needed to stretch her legs. Most of all, she needed to be alone. Taking the bag of her possessions from Fran, she gave her a one-armed hug. "I don't know how to thank you."

"Not necessary."

Megan strode toward home and the long, hot, rose-scented bubble bath she had promised herself.

An hour later, she pulled herself from the now tepid bath. Keeping her mind blank, she brewed a pot of Darjeeling, which she carried to the back porch. Late afternoon sun struck the porch at an angle, increasing the heat, but it was cold in the shadows of her mind.

Gripping the teacup, she could fight something off no longer. Megan Elizabeth Stanfield was free, but she admitted what she had blocked from her mind for fear that knowledge would show in her face.

I know the face on the flyer.

Chapter 7

Impossible!

Mother.

Megan had struggled not to tell the cops the face on the flyer was not an unknown doppelgänger. For once, her unruly tongue didn't outrun her brain. *Could Susan Elaine Abernathy Stanfield be a terrorist?* Every ounce of sense Megan had refuted the possibility. There was no way her mother's inane conversation was an act. Her dumb blonde stupidity was not an act either. Megan thought back over life with her mother, who had always been the same—incompetent, bumbling, helpless, mind like a sieve. No way could she be involved with terrorism. Yet who else was there? No one.

Should Megan *confess*? She could withstand prison better than her mother could. The enormity of the situation overwhelmed her. Didn't her life have enough issues without this? She was not a terrorist, although they hadn't believed her until her references had checked out. John Patterson still didn't. That face was not her, so it must be her mother. There was no one else.

Megan visualized the flyer picture, the face shape was so familiar, the sculpted eyebrows never needed plucking, the high cheek bones, the lush lashes, the eyes. Megan's heart skipped a beat. The eyes were wrong! They were hard, not sparkling. She'd never seen photographs, or even snapshots, where her mother's eyes didn't sparkle. Her mother said the sparkles came from thinking happy thoughts. Split personality? No. Megan would cling to her stated doppelgänger theory until the Feds found the real terrorist. If they did. They must.

For her own satisfaction—if not anyone else's—maybe she could learn her mother's schedule over the past few years. She could check the internet for terrorist activities at the same time in the same place her parents traveled. Megan had never understood her parents' whim to wander around the world, but now she wished she had been her mother's tag-along-Tulu.

She wouldn't have the last two years, though. She wouldn't have left David.

David.

Sometimes his memory sneaked up on her, but this wasn't one of those times. Instead, it hit her like a barrage of gunfire on a well-trodden path to her brain.

Megan had spent the years after college at home, instead of joining her friends in New York's banking world. Even though Detroit was her home, she knew so few people that she'd sat alone in more restaurants than she could count or wanted to remember.

Then, she'd met handsome, debonair, successful David Andrew Blackwell. Megan's life changed at that moment—no more being alone, no more avoiding social events because everyone else had someone. Now she had someone, someone who escorted her to trendy places, someone who focused on her, no matter who else was around. She reveled in David's attention with his prematurely silver hair, eyes that matched his hair until his temper erupted. They turned to metallic pewter, then. She'd seen others flinch before that blazing fire, but he had only directed his ire at her once, the last time she saw him.

Everything ended.

David told her six months ago he'd met someone else. Megan had seen his waning interest, although she had denied it during those early days when he didn't call. However, on the last evening she saw him, he stood outside their favorite restaurant, a petite blonde clinging to his arm. Megan had to accept she'd lost him. He was her first love. The emptiness in her chest indicated he might also be her last.

Slow to unwind after the stress of the past few weeks, Megan curled up on the porch swing, as her thoughts wandered to her last months at home. She could easily have lost herself there. In weak moments, she longed for the hustle and bustle of the life she had known. She refrained from asking herself how long she could be happy away from city life.

The sunset turned the sky indigo and then black. Megan still sat motionless. The only light came from the moon peeking over the trees and fireflies dancing around the back yard. The quiet now was so deep as to be almost tangible. The night stillness brought back all the old loneliness. Good times slid into bad times, separated, mingled again. If she were not careful, she had told herself, she would become a recluse.

Maybe she should have bought a kitten after all. Megan had considered it during the days and nights following David's rejection. A cat would be loyal for life, not like a man. But she'd known, somewhere in the recesses of her mind, a cat's company was not the answer. She would become an eccentric old woman living in a house filled with felines, never speaking to another human.

The mere possibility had brought about a spate of activity eventually taking her out of Detroit. Her break-up with David had given Megan legitimate reason to find some place where no one knew her. She chose this little North Carolina town, her ancestral hometown. She ordered herself to put the past behind. Megan Elizabeth Stanfield refused to be trapped by memories. Insanity lay there.

No one here knew about David. Wouldn't Jed Anderson crow, if he knew her lover had dumped her?

Megan didn't intend for anyone to know anything about her Detroit life.

ꑭ ꑭ ꑭ ꑭ ꑭ

Jed messed around the barn, keeping an eye out for Frank. Surely, he would report on the FBI meeting with Megan. When the Honda turned into the drive, Jed hurried toward it. "Well?"

"Can I at least get out of the car? Let's go inside. Aunt Rosalie will want to hear this too."

She raised anxious eyes when they stepped into her room. "Well?"

Frank shook his head. "Like mother, like son. In a nutshell, the FBI cleared Megan. They're satisfied she isn't a terrorist but again asked her about the face on the flyer. She couldn't help them. She's safely at home again."

"Patterson? Is he satisfied?"

"He'll never admit he might be wrong, demanded we contact Interpol, but Higgins is satisfied. Now, Jed, do you think I might have some sweet tea to lubricate my parched throat?"

Three glasses of tea later, Frank left, and Jed headed back to the barn. The others might be satisfied Megan isn't a terrorist, but he wasn't sure.

"Calm down, King. I need to talk with Dad."

Saddled, he let his mount gallop away its fidgets across the flat pasture but slowed when they reached the foot of the mountain: his biggest challenge, therefore irresistible, when he rode his first pony. He'd been sure he could touch the sun from the top, but never got there.

Jed sat quietly while King's breathing returned to normal. Together, they ducked branches as the horse picked his way through a thick stand of oak trees.

Probably should thin them next year and replant some areas. How fortunate he was that his great-grandfather had seen the ongoing need for timber on the farm. They had never left home to obtain lumber for outbuildings until Jed's father had stopped using their own lumber mill, instead supplying work to a down-and-out sawmill several years ago.

Halfway up the mountain, Jed stopped at an overlook where he dismounted and dropped King's reins so he could munch among the wildflowers, while Jed traveled down memory lane, something he didn't often do.

"This is where you found me, Dad, remember? I was lost and Brownie hadn't learned the way home. You didn't blister my backside for riding without telling anyone, but you were probably tempted. Instead, you dried my tears and held my four-year-old body close, with Brownie following behind us. You didn't even fuss at me for riding bareback."

Thereafter, his dad had brought him here for "discussions," as Dad had called them when youthful peccadillos had warranted more than raised eyebrows.

Jed stared into the distance, lost in thought this time.

"I'm confused, Dad. You're probably thinking, 'not again.' You helped me put Jasmine out of my life. I didn't have much choice then, because she married someone else. My problem is another woman though. Megan could be worse. Is she a terrorist? The FBI have absolved her, but her face is so much like the wanted poster I'm not sure she hasn't fooled them.

"You know she's gotten under my skin. I can't even look at any other woman without Megan's image intervening. I'm trying to make her leave town, go back to Detroit, or even the moon—anywhere away from here. I admit, though, I doubt her leaving would get Megan Stanfield out of my mind."

Jed listened for an answer in the breeze. He didn't hear his dad's voice but was calmer, although still not convinced of Megan's innocence.

"Her face, Dad. Her face!"

Chapter 8

New Business

"Fran, you're back!" Megan called across the square. Fran had flown to New York the day after Megan left the jail and settled back into the life that she was carving out for herself. She'd answered all questions with a smile but doubted anyone believed her "mistaken identity" explanation. She ignored the stares that still came her way. "How was your trip?"

"Successful—you'll love the new fashions I found— but tiring. We'll talk about me later. What's new with you?"

"Let's find a place to talk. The diner is like Grand Central Station this morning."

"You're certainly full of vim, vigor, and vitality," Fran told her. "The library should be quiet at this hour. I'll even forego my third cup of coffee."

"Poor baby," Megan teased.

Marmalade meowed a greeting, as he slipped between their feet, when Fran opened the door.

"Morning, Catherine," Fran greeted the librarian. "We're looking for a place we can hear ourselves think."

"You've found it." She waved them toward the reading section. "Has Megan given you her news?"

Fran glanced toward Megan, the question in her eyes easing when Megan's lips tilted upward at the corners. "I saw her store windows are almost bare."

"There's more, but she'll tell you," Catherine said. "Take your time. I'd better warn you, though. Mrs. Harwood's third graders will invade at ten."

Megan and Fran settled into Queen Anne chairs. "I've done it!"

"I'm in favor of your doing anything that brings a sparkle to your eyes, so tell."

Megan started with the thoughts that battled in her brain after leaving Fran's boutique—before Mike jailed her. She'd decided maybe, just maybe, she could stay here. She would set aside enough moving money if she must leave and risk the rest of her funds here. Past thirty—now or never for success.

"So, I've had a busy week."

"Good thinking. Now, details, woman, details!"

"I'm changing my business like we discussed. The natural food salesman agreed to take back most of the merchandise on my shelves. I'll keep the herbal teas, dried fruit, trail mixes, and the bottled water. Hikers buy them. There's one man who buys yogurt raisins almost daily, never anything else. He makes me nervous because he only comes in when I'm alone. He doesn't walk. He creeps."

"Sounds like the man renting at Mirror Lake. I heard he visited the area in his younger years. Has arthritis, I understand."

"Okay his physical condition could explain the way he walks." Megan's tension eased a little. "Anyway, I'm keeping those things in the front window until I reopen so I'll have a few sales. Sally will give me some guidance on which crafts to stock."

"She's good with all sorts of needlework, so you made a good choice there. Okay, your new business will have herbal teas, dried fruits, trail mixes, bottled water, and crafts. What else?"

"I'm stocking cards, wrapping paper, collectibles, the whole bit. The Hallmark distributor will make a delivery when I tell him which day. I can hardly wait to get everything in place."

"I'm excited for you, Megan. This new business will be successful. I'm betting on it."

Pangs of uncertainty shot through Megan. Even though she'd made her decision, the wee hours of the morning still brought doubts after a recurring nightmare woke her. Would she ever stop hearing a cell door slam shut with her inside? She'd always believed anyone in jail was guilty. Not anymore. Megan squared her shoulders. "I'll make this store work. I won't—I *will not*—go back to the rat race I left behind. That's my past life, not my future."

"That's the spirit."

"Would you believe John Patterson came here?"

"No! Didn't you tell me the Atlanta guy said he must stay away from you?"

Megan nodded. "I caught him peeping through the store window yesterday. He stared all the time I was dialing Mike Williams. He didn't even budge when Mike walked up behind him."

"What did Mike do?"

"Sent him on his way after talking to him. Mike told me Patterson was still suspicious, and my empty store added fire to his belief."

"You told him why your store is empty."

"I did and politely too, despite Mike's barely suppressed suspicions. Didn't he just make my day."

"Oh, well, when you open your new business, Mike's suspicion, at least, will disappear. I doubt Patterson's ever will. Mike hasn't been here long, but Frank says he knows his business. I've never known my cousin to be wrong about anything, much to my chagrin as a teenager."

"I'm afraid you're right about Patterson. I have visions of him dogging my footsteps right on through eternity." Megan hesitated. "I must confess. I don't want people hurt, but I almost wish the woman with my face would do something outrageous, in Europe or somewhere else far away. Not kill anybody, you understand, but verify my innocence, even to John Patterson."

"Something like that might prove necessary with him."

"Afraid so." Megan headed for the doorway but then pivoted on her heel. "By the way, the Fall Festival committee meets tonight."

"Thanks. I didn't check my calendar this morning."

"See you there." Megan turned toward her store. There were still several things she must do before going to Asheville.

Soon after seven, Megan hurried up the library steps, tired from an afternoon of talking with several of Asheville's small business owners, primarily women but a couple of men. The owners had been helpful, probably because her business would be far enough away not to cut too much into theirs, which worked both ways.

Megan's head buzzed with what she'd learned during her whirlwind tour through downtown shops, which she should have done before she opened Nature's Way. She should have remembered what one university professor had said: Failure to plan equals plan to fail. Call it impatience, or more likely, temporary brain failure.

"Here she is now." Fran beckoned her toward a chair in the suddenly silent room. "I told the ladies about your new shop."

"I believe you'll find my new store both interesting and helpful, besides saving some travel time between here and Asheville." Megan hoped she sounded more confident than she felt. "I'm looking forward to opening for business."

"Sally said you will stock craft supplies," Mrs. Malcolm said. "Will you include materials for flower arrangements? Both live and dried?"

"Absolutely. I've never been a crafts person, so I have a lot to learn, but Sally offered her help while I get this new business underway. I would appreciate any suggestions all of you might have."

Cathie Adams said, "This isn't precisely a craft, but a local place for art supplies would be great. My choice has been driving to Asheville or ordering through the internet. Neither is satisfactory."

"I'll look into art supplies." Megan made notes of suggestions until Mrs. Malcolm called them to order.

"Megan, I'm glad you're making the change. We need this kind of store. Now, let's discuss plans for the festival."

Arriving home later, Megan made her way down the hallway toward the bathroom. The day had been so exciting she didn't think she'd be able to sleep, but a long, hot, rose-scented bath might help. She knew the jail smell, as she thought of it, was long gone from her body, but she hadn't been able to wash it from her mind.

Megan stepped out of the tub when the water was tepid, her eyelids heavy with sleep. She toweled herself dry and snuggled between the sheets.

The ringing phone pulled her from the depths of sleep. She groped for it without opening her eyes.

Jed again.

"Must be midnight," she mumbled. "Do you need to apologize for something?"

His laughter was soft, almost seductive. "Not this time. I just wanted to talk. This is the only time I can find you at home. You've become a regular gadabout. However, I don't believe you're fully awake, so I'll call you tomorrow."

"Okay, good night. Remember, don't turn your back on the cows." She fumbled the receiver back into its cradle with his chuckles ringing in her ear. His voice, not loud and abusive, but quiet and gentle, surprised her. It would be nice if he always spoke this way, but she knew better than to expect change. One word from her could set him off.

Late the following afternoon, Megan was busy re-arranging movable shelves when Jed strolled inside. He'd said he would *call*, hadn't he?

"What happened to your merchandise?"

Megan adjusted a rolling counter to an angle and stood back for a broader view. Satisfied, she turned toward the back of the store. "Break time. Care for some coffee?"

"No thanks." Jed propped his shoulder against the wall. "Are you going out of business? Leaving town?"

She stirred some hazelnut creamer into the steaming brew. Even when he stood still, his energy hummed around her. Enervating—something she must avoid at all costs. "I can't decide if you sound hopeful or disappointed."

"Curious."

"No, I'm not going out of business nor leaving town. I'm opening a different kind of store."

"How different?" Jed straightened away from the door frame. "No more so-called health food?"

She'd had more than enough censure from him. Her tone was crisp. "Do you want to hear my plans, or would you rather be disagreeable?"

"Alright, let's hear them."

His grudging tone irritated her, but Megan kept her voice neutral. "I'm opening a general merchandise store."

"Good grief! Next thing I know you'll be selling oceanfront property in Arizona."

"There's no such thing!"

"Somebody wrote that line in a song. I gather you don't care for country music."

"Certainly not. I like big bands and pop singers like Frank Sinatra."

"What? No Motown? You're from Detroit too. For shame!" He grinned at her until she returned it.

"My grandfather guided my choice of music. He had stacks of old 78s you wouldn't believe. We spent hours listening to them. Later, he gave me LPs when the 78s got too scratchy."

Remembering her early happiness eased Megan's irritation. "There are all sorts of shops Crawfordville doesn't have—greeting cards, collectibles, craft supplies, for instance. I decided to have them under one roof. I'll stop carrying anything that doesn't sell and soon have what the town needs. The ladies were enthusiastic at the festival meeting last night, so my new store should be successful. What do you think?"

Jed studied her face, searching for who knows what. "Sounds good, but do you know anything about managing a business?"

"I managed a health food store back home for several years. My mistake here was beginning without determining what the town needed. I knew better—just didn't think it through."

"I didn't know what you did there." His mouth turned up at one corner. "Perhaps you're not the scatterbrain I thought you were."

"Scatterbrain?" Megan sputtered, her earlier irritation turning to anger. "How dare you say such a thing?"

"You haven't given me any reason to believe otherwise." His gaze turned frosty at her tone.

"I am *not* scatterbrained," Megan informed him through clenched teeth. "I couldn't have managed a master's degree in business administration if I were, but what would farmers know about university degrees?"

"For your information, I have degrees in agriculture and in business. I also studied enough veterinary medicine to take care of my cattle except in extreme cases. Need I say I'm succeeding better with my education than you are with yours?"

Before Megan could answer, Jed stormed from the store, leaving the door wide open.

She followed him. She'd forgotten Fran had mentioned Jed's university days. Maybe she'd been a tiny bit hasty. Megan stepped outside the door, watching Jed stride toward his truck. She didn't notice the scruffy man until he collided with her.

Megan steadied herself by grasping the denim-clad arms of the man who stared at her in the square. He pulled himself free before she could apologize. He glanced over his shoulder before scuttling away, baggy jeans flapping around his legs. This time his face was different. Rather than the puzzled expression he'd worn then, something else bothered him. Panic? Fear? Surely not. Megan had experienced several reactions since she'd come here, but fear wasn't one of them. Why would this man fear her? Maybe he'd seen the terrorist in action and mistaken her for the other woman. Megan shivered. Would she ever be free of fear?

ༀ ༀ ༀ ༀ ༀ

The man scurried around the corner where he dropped onto a wooden bench outside the open florist shop door. Gulping breaths of mingled flower scent, he concentrated on calming himself. He could identify only one. Roses. His heart hammered against his ribs. He forced himself to think. Smile. Long stride. Hair. Now roses. In near desperation, he beat his fists against his knees.

He'd watched that woman leave the jail, walking away free after only a couple of days, so she wasn't a criminal. He must not be either, but that didn't help him remember why she made his heart race or his head ache.

He focused on his surroundings. People edged around him on the sidewalk. Standing with an effort, he walked across the square, hoping his knees would support him to the car. His breath came in jerky exhalations. He must not collapse. He might have to answer questions. He didn't have answers.

ɯ ɯ ɯ ɯ ɯ

By evening, Megan had worked herself into a temper tantrum the way she did when she was three years old and begged to visit her grandfather, when her mother refused to take her. Now the grown-up Megan paced the floor, muttering deprecations against men in general but one man, in particular. Women who earn master's degrees are not scatterbrained. David never called her scatterbrained. Prudish, yes. Dull, yes, but not scatterbrained. He'd thought her intelligent.

Still, Jed hadn't called her scatterbrained either. That admission came hard. He only said he'd thought it. Megan collapsed into a rocking chair on the screened back porch, still fretting over the insult. Movement beyond the screen caught her attention. Squinting, she watched something white glide along the hedge top and disappear. A definite shape this time. Human shape, face turned toward her, one arm lifted in greeting. Megan told herself—again—only a trick of the moonlight. Must be. There's no such thing as ghosts.

Twilight had brought out chirping crickets contrasting with the nearby deep voiced bullfrog. Around the area, birds nestled into the trees, tweeting their goodnights. When the insects grew quiet, so did

Megan's nerves. Her scrambled thoughts made her uncomfortable. The trick of moonlight didn't bother her. She would not think about the terrorist, but there was Jed. She'd been rude to him. There was no getting around it. The moon climbed higher; the usual night sounds stopped. Still, Megan sat, reliving the scene in her store—not her finest hour. Returning indoors, she looked at the clock. Almost midnight.

Would Jed call tonight and apologize?

Why should he be the one to apologize, a niggling little voice demanded, the same voice Granddad had called her conscience. Always listen, he'd cautioned. Her conscience would never lead her astray. Maybe not, but its nagging was a nuisance, like now. The irritating voice continued. Your temper flared first. He was only teasing when he said scatterbrain. You should've noticed his smile.

"Oh, alright. I'll apologize to him. I guess if he calls in the middle of the night, I can too." The door stuck when she tried to yank it open. "Calm down, you nitwit," Megan muttered and tried the door again. She thumbed the smallest phone directory she'd ever seen. Several Andersons, but only one J. Anderson. She punched numbers.

Not worth it. Not worth it. Not worth it! She grumbled until he answered.

"Jed?" Her voice cracked like an adolescent boy. She cleared her throat. "Jed, Megan here. Megan Stanfield. I called to apologize for losing my temper this afternoon."

When he didn't answer, Megan tried again. "I overreacted. My conscience told me you were teasing me. I shouldn't have gone off the deep end. Can you forgive me for being so hasty?"

After another long moment, she asked, "Jed, are you there?"

"Yeah, I'm here. I've never had an apology from any woman for anything, Megan. You left me speechless. I shouldn't have been so hasty with my temper either. I apologize too. Let's forget the whole thing—put it behind us—okay?"

Jed was being magnanimous, which she didn't deserve. "Yes, let's do. Uh, will I see you tomorrow? Oh, I forgot tomorrow is Saturday. I hadn't planned to have breakfast at the diner."

He paused again. "The diner isn't the only place we can meet."

Megan reminded herself friendliness overcomes animosity. "Perhaps you can have dinner with me here."

"You're on. What time?"

"Six-thirty? Okay, I'll see you then." Megan cradled the phone and admonished herself. What had possessed her? The invitation had popped out of her mouth, unplanned and unwanted. Now she was committed to having this unpredictable man at her dinner table. What could she cook for him? She'd think of something, might even surprise him with some tofu. Wouldn't that be a laugh?

ぬ ぬ ぬ ぬ ぬ

Grinning, Jed held the phone a moment, listening to the dial tone. Imagine, a woman apologized to him. Would wonders never cease? And just think how much honey he could pour over her unsuspecting head. He'd goofed big time on that this afternoon, but he would make up for his mistake tomorrow night. When he saw her empty store shelves, he'd thought his campaign was over before it started good and hadn't known whether to be happy or sad. Pouring honey was fun, and he wanted to pour more. Lots more.

Phone calls wouldn't do the whole trick though. He would begin his personal campaign in earnest tomorrow. She wouldn't know what had hit her until too late. Was that a twinge of guilt? If so, he pushed it away. She should have gone back to Detroit voluntarily, just admitted her business was a failure and left, he told himself with a self-righteous air. It was her own fault if, no, when she got hurt.

Chapter 9

Perverse Creature

Megan fluffed her hair, still damp from the shower. Another restless night, waking again to questions. How had she gotten herself into this mess? What was she going to cook for Jed Anderson? They would never agree on food. She'd bet her last pair of pantyhose on that. When a robin began his incessant chatter at early dawn, Megan had given up getting more sleep. Now she leaned against her kitchen counter, holding the phone in a death grip.

"Fran, how do you cook green beans for a farmer?"

"How do I do what?" Fran's voice came sleepily over the distance.

"Cook green beans for a farmer. Wake up, Fran, it's a new day. Answer me."

"Megan, do you realize it's six o'clock in the *morning*? Human beings aren't supposed to be awake at this hour."

"Really? I've already run five miles."

"Heaven deliver me from energetic people."

"How's this for an idea, lazybones? I'll cook breakfast while you tell me about the beans."

"I don't want tofu or anything healthy but tasteless."

"How does a cheese omelet sound? I even have some homemade bread."

"You bake bread? From *scratch*? Unbelievable."

"Doubting Thomas! I will be truthful, though. Carrie Malcolm gave me a loaf of her famous sour dough. She's mellowing toward me."

"I told you it would only take time," Fran reminded her. "Are you going to fix me some grits too?"

"Grits are a Southern thing, right? I've seen them on the diner's menu, but I never bothered to find out what they are. I eat hash browns instead. I do at least know they're potatoes."

"I've read cheese grits are popular up north."

"Not in any restaurant I know."

"You need an education. Give me half an hour."

Megan had grated the Provolone and was cracking eggs into a bowl when Fran breezed through the doorway carrying a box.

"What are these things you called grits?" Megan eyed the box.

Fran laughed. "The box won't bite you. I promise."

Breakfast over, Megan said, "I can't say I care much for grits, although stirring strawberry preserves into them made them edible. I wonder if my grandparents ever added preserves."

"I doubt anyone did before this morning."

"I feel my grandmother's presence here, especially outside," Megan confided. "She's urging me to plant flowers, which I don't understand, because I know nothing about gardening. At least that's how I interpret my feeling. She knew I'm hopeless with plants. I heard her tell someone that I'm the only person on earth who ever killed a . . . oh what's the word . . . something that begins with 'fill'."

"A plant beginning with 'fill'?" A frown married Fran's face. "Surely you don't mean a philodendron? I've heard they survive anything."

"Philodendron, that's the word. Mine died, and Grandmother never trusted me with anything else that was green. I remember the Christmas after that she took all the green candy out of the dish before she offered it to me. The candy was spearmint, which I loved, but she said I would kill it."

When Fran stopped laughing, she said, "If you're serious about planting flowers, you can find some books at the library."

"Maybe I will. I guess I can find instructions on YouTube too."

"Probably so. Everything else is available there. Come to think of it, the last woman who lived here, Ruth Caddell was her name, had flower beds which the entire neighborhood envied. The house stood empty for several years after she died, so weeds undoubtedly choked the beds. Have you found any?"

Megan admitted she hadn't paid attention to the yard. "My business has been on my mind."

"Makes sense. I imagine we can find the flower beds though." Fran checked her watch. "I still have some time, so let's look now."

They found one when Megan stumbled. She fell flat on the ground, sliding forward. "Ouch! The leaves have rocks under them."

They cleared enough to realize the stones had once outlined the flowerbed borders.

"This is a start, even if I did nearly break my neck finding it." Megan wrinkled her nose when she brushed rotting leaves from her hands.

"Looks like growing flowers is in your immediate future." Fran said as she started the car.

"You think?"

In late morning, Megan crossed the square and climbed the library steps. She sighed with relief when Catherine didn't blink an eye at having a jailbird in her library. Jailbird. Megan heard someone mutter that word outside the diner yesterday. She'd pretended not to hear. "I want a book which tells me everything about gardens. I warn you, I've never done any gardening."

The librarian grinned. "Okay, tell me what you want to plant—flowers, vegetables, or shrubs."

"Flowers. Fran and I found a place where someone else had some, but I don't know what kind. The area is sunny in the morning, if that tells you anything."

"Considerable." Catherine handed her three books. "These should get you started. I recommend you start preparing the beds now. You'll want to plant bulbs soon, but you have work before that."

"Bulbs? Like tulips? They grow this far south?"

"Sure, also daffodils. Hyacinths too. I understand it's almost impossible to fail with them."

"Don't even mention failure," Megan pleaded. "You'll jinx me for sure. Okay, I'll follow your advice. How do I prepare the soil?"

"The largest book will tell you. Speaking of books, are you familiar with John Sherwood's British mysteries? His protagonist is a horticulturist named Celia Grant, who goes around sticking her nose where it doesn't belong. She solves murders before the police can. Sherwood's books might inspire you."

"Growing flowers or solving murders? I need all the inspiration for flowers I can get, so lead me to him. Just don't wish any murders on me." Murders. Bombs. Terrorism. That face. *Her* face. Magen shuddered.

Tucking the books into the car trunk, she headed for the supermarket on the edge of town.

ন ন ন ন ন

He darted away from the produce section when the woman came into sight. After moving some cans aside, he watched his nemesis place snap beans on the scale. His nemesis. Yes, that's what she was, causing these horrible headaches which start above his eyebrows, sweep across the top of his head, and settle at the base of his skull. He'd never had them until he saw her. When she turned toward him, he hurried down the aisle. He paid for a large bottle of aspirin, turning his head when she carried her loaded basket into the next checkout line. He needed to face her. Didn't want to face her. Couldn't face her. His head hurt too much to deal with her now.

ℕ ℕ ℕ ℕ ℕ

At six o'clock, Megan stared into her closet. She had no idea what a local woman wore when she invited a man for dinner. Short skirt with a long tunic? Long skirt with a frilly blouse? Burgundy palazzo pants with a pink silk blouse? David had told her this shade put roses in her cheeks. No. Megan refused to go there, refused to remember the last time she wore this blouse. A white jersey worked as well. She stepped into silver-colored flats and hurried down the stairs to make last-minute preparations.

Jed rang the doorbell at six-thirty on the dot. Megan opened the door and tried not to stare at the gorgeous creature standing there. What the blue jacket did to his eyes was dangerous to any woman's equilibrium.

"Hey, Jed." Megan led the way to the living room where she'd set a tray of wine and glasses on a side table. At the last minute, she'd realized she didn't know what beverage he would prefer but decided he could drink what she had, or nothing. "Dinner will be a few more minutes. Would you care for an aperitif?"

"What? Oh, whatever you're having will be fine. Excuse my staring. For a moment, I thought I was looking at a movie star."

"You flatter me." What had gotten into Jed? Flattery did not sit well on his lips. "You do your jacket proud."

He lifted his glass in a toast. "We'll consider ourselves fully complimented as the beautiful people we are."

"Hear, hear!" Megan tapped her glass against his. "Now, you can sit here like a guest, or you can help me serve dinner in the kitchen."

"The kitchen for me." He trailed after her. "Wow! The kitchen didn't look like this when I delivered groceries. Mrs. Caddell must have taken out walls to give this spaciousness."

"I'm pleased with the scheme too," Megan said, glancing around the long room. Someone had perfect taste. She was fortunate the blonde oak cabinets and creamy appliances were part of the house. Sunshine yellow walls around the appliances blended into pastel yellow in the dining area, which blended into the creamy walls of the sitting area. Curtains, on the other hand, blended from creamy in the kitchen to pastel yellow and to sunshine yellow in the sitting area. A happy room.

"I've never lived any place with a kitchen large enough to turn around in, much less space for chairs. If this is a typical Southern kitchen, I'm all for it."

"Not typical. Now, how can I help?"

"Take the salads from the fridge while I dish up the trout almandine and veggies." With a quick look at the table, Megan motioned for him to take his seat next to her at one end. She held her breath while he tasted the buttered green beans, which she'd seasoned with fresh basil and toasted sesame seeds sprinkled on top. She'd completely forgotten to get Fran's advice, so she'd cooked the beans until she figured they were ready.

An incident from earlier at the grocery store flashed into Megan's mind. That man spied on her when she was getting the beans. Was he stalking her? The thought sent chills down her spine until she pushed it away as ridiculous. Why would anyone stalk Megan Elizabeth Stanfield? No reason whatever. Just a coincidence that she saw him so often. The square. The diner. The supermarket. Crawfordville is a small town, she reminded herself.

Jed met her gaze. "If you always cook beans this way, I'll eat crow the rest of my life and far beyond. They're different but good."

Megan released her breath. "They did turn out well, considering I'd never cooked green beans before. Back home, we mostly dunk them in boiling, salted water and toss them with a bit of seasoned olive oil. Crunchy. I vowed I would never eat another green bean after I left home."

"Why cook them now?"

"To prove I could."

Jed broke the silence following her admission. "You've mentioned your grandparents but not your parents."

"They're socialites, always traveling. They have a home outside Detroit but have never spent much time there. Nor in their Manhattan apartment, although they're there more than in Detroit."

"Even when you were small?"

"They've always spent more time traveling than at home. They're somewhere in Europe now."

Megan remembered how their rejection had hurt during her childhood. Still did. She hadn't felt wanted by anyone after her beloved grandfather died when she was fifteen. Her grandmother had always traveled a lot too, leaving them alone. Those were the only fun times with her family she could remember.

"You lived with your grandparents?"

"I visited them a lot but spent most of my time either at boarding school, in summer camp, or with our servants."

He was silent for a long moment. "I don't have an answer."

"There's nothing to answer, Jed. My life was the same as many girls I knew, so I didn't expect anything different."

"I suppose I should keep my opinions to myself." Jed pushed aside his dessert dish, perhaps harder than necessary. "I've never eaten better cheese cake."

"Thank you." Megan chuckled. "I could say I used an old family recipe, but lightning might strike me dead. I bought it at the bakery."

They chatted about town activities, while he loaded the dishwasher after she scraped the dishes. They took their coffee to the comfortable chairs at the other end of the room.

Setting his cup on the coffee table, Jed glanced at the John Sherwood book lying there. "You read mysteries. I bought this one for my mother."

"You haven't told me about your parents."

"Dad died five years ago—drunk driver hit him head-on. Multiple Sclerosis keeps Mother mostly at home, although she does walk inside the house with help."

"I'm sorry she's unwell," Megan sympathized.

"She doesn't let MS bother her over much," he responded and picked up his coffee cup.

Megan changed the subject. "Guess what I've decided."

"Do you mean other than the store?"

She nodded. "I'm going to plant flowers."

"Uh huh. Dig holes, stick in plants, leave them."

"I found some books at the library," she answered his skepticism.

"I've never seen books pull weeds." He shot her a challenging look. "Can you tell flowers from weeds?"

"Catherine and Fran think I can." Perverse creature. He could at least encourage her. Megan curbed her mounting irritation. "Grandmother is apparently urging me, so I'll try."

"Your grandmother is urging you to plant flowers? The one who died recently, or another one?"

"She died last January. I never knew my paternal grandmother." Megan ignored his mocking grin. "My feeling is puzzling, I admit. I've never considered gardening, yet during the past few days, the feeling that I should has become almost urgent. The urge seems to come from my grandmother, which is weird, because she knew I don't have the knack."

"Voices in the wind, I suppose, or maybe tapping in the walls?"

Jed's deadpan delivery told her what he thought of ghosts. They don't exist. Didn't she feel the same way? Nevertheless, ... "You don't believe spirits live on after death?"

His raised eyebrows answered her. "Have you seen one?"

"No, I haven't seen anything," Megan fudged, telling herself again the white blob was a trick of light both times. "I have this intense feeling someone is in the backyard. I would have expected an impression inside the house, though, wouldn't you?"

"I believe inside is the usual place people, uh, visualize them." He stood. "I must head home. Milking time comes early."

"Yes, do get plenty of rest. We don't want the cows kicking you."

"Never. Thanks for dinner. I enjoyed the evening."

After he stepped onto the porch, he gazed into her eyes, almost like an afterthought, while a slow, deliberate smile crossed his face before leaving. Standing inside the door, she listened as the Bronco's sounds faded. Megan congratulated herself on a successful evening and gave herself full credit. They hadn't come to blows, although she'd come close to throwing her coffee cup at him at one point.

က္က က္က က္က က္က က္က

Jed stood on the porch until he heard the deadbolt lock click into place before striding to his Bronco.

Megan had surprised him, not only her appearance. She always wore her clothes well, but her sheer beauty stunned him. Still, the biggest surprise was the food. He had not known what to expect, even debated eating a sandwich before coming because Megan might think a wedge of lettuce was a complete meal.

Jed chuckled but sobered when he remembered her childhood. He didn't understand people who neglected their children after bringing them into the world. His parents had showered attention on him, never missing his 4H competitions or ball games. His grandparents had turned out on every occasion. Uncles, aunts too. Even his shy great-uncle Dan watched from a distance.

Why had Megan really moved here? Jed had not swallowed the ancestor nonsense. Oh, well, that didn't matter. He just wanted her to leave town. Anywhere out of his sight and hearing. After he'd poured more honey. He didn't know when he'd enjoyed anything so much.

Jed whistled as he let himself into the back door at the farm, the only home he'd ever known. The housekeeper had left a light burning for him. He didn't need the waiting food after all.

After refrigerating the food, he gazed around the room with new insight. He considered possible changes while he crossed the hall toward his mother's bedroom. A sitting area might save his mother from the boredom of staying in one room except at mealtimes. She could keep Pearl company. A light showed under the door, so he tapped and went inside.

"Still awake?" Jed studied her face for pain but saw only her usual sweet smile. He would like to think he could deal with a serious disease with her grace but doubted he could.

"I got so interested in the new Heather Graham mystery I couldn't bear to put down the book. Did you have a pleasant time?"

"Very." Jed sat beside her bed as he recounted the details. "You'll like Megan. She reads mysteries too."

She laughed with him. "High recommendation, indeed! I look forward to meeting her. I'm glad Frank settled her legal mess. Megan must have been terrified."

"With good reason. Punishment for terrorism is brutal. She seemed okay this evening, although she didn't mention her ordeal."

Jed planted a kiss on his mother's lined cheek and went away, whistling. Yes, it had been a very pleasant evening. He hadn't crossed swords with Megan even once, poured lots of honey too. Their rapport wouldn't last, though. Jed would almost bet the farm on that.

ꞮꞮ ꞮꞮ ꞮꞮ ꞮꞮ ꞮꞮ

"Turn on the TV, CNN, now!"
"Fran, what are you doing up at midnight?"
"Just turn on the TV, Megan!"

This just in from New Scotland Yard. Authorities released some information about the woman who daringly robbed one of London's top private banks earlier today. The mysterious face, which has plagued the world since the mid-1940s, has struck again! However, contrary to her usual actions, no one died. Interpol is on the search. Stay tuned. We'll give more information as it reaches us.

"She got away again. Megan, you do understand no one, not even John Patterson, can still believe you're guilty! Not after this woman's brazen behavior. Daylight robbery, for heaven's sake!"

Something else crowded Megan's thoughts. "Fran, did I cause this? Did I somehow send her a silent message that made her do this? ESP, or something?"

"Oh, for Pete's sake, Megan! Stop looking on the dark side. There is no way you could have caused this or anything else that woman does, so put her behavior out of your mind and get some sleep. Tomorrow, tell Mike to make sure those FBI people know about this."

"Okay. Good night."

Sleep was still elusive, but she dropped off again after an hour of trying to convince herself she wasn't responsible for that woman's actions.

Chapter 10

Meeting Her Landlady

"My mother told me crowing roosters and whistling women always come to bad ends."

Megan turned toward Jed's amused voice. "Then, I'm doomed for sure, because whistling is one of my besetting sins."

The weekend had been pleasant. Monday morning found Megan working with renewed energy when Jed strolled inside her store.

"I missed you in the diner this morning."

"Would you believe I haven't had my first cup of coffee today? The Hallmark distributor showed up at seven. I've been hard at it ever since. What do you think of my displays?"

"They're more interesting than dried seaweed anyway." His lips twitched when she shook a playful finger at him.

"Jed, some subjects are off limits," Fran warned when she swept through the doorway, her challis skirt swirling around her ankles. "Megan, the store looks great. Jed, where do you think you're going?"

"I can see you don't have a proper appreciation of masculine attention. I'll get back to the farm where I'm appreciated."

"Ha! Who appreciates you at the farm? Just tell me that," Fran retorted.

"Cows!"

"Never mind the cows. Make yourself useful around here."

"No," Megan protested. He would probably order her around. She could make this new business a success by herself. She didn't need help from an overbearing male. Hearing the silence left in the wake of her protest, she backtracked. "I mean, I'm sure Jed shouldn't take time from his own business for mine. He's much too busy on the farm, what with cows and apples. I can manage."

Jed answered after a noticeable pause. "Nonsense. I'll deal with shelving in the back, while you and Fran arrange the cards."

Megan gave in despite her inclination otherwise.

"Okay." She directed him with a few words and then turned toward Fran. "I want the crafts all the way across the store. I believe they'll need almost half the space from front to back."

"I agree crafts will be your main draw. Crafts are a tremendous business around here, especially during tourist season."

"A brilliant idea—well," Megan corrected herself, "an idea anyway popped into my head last night."

"Do tell."

Megan handed her a box of birthday cards, gesturing toward the slotted shelves. "One minute I think this idea is great, the next I decide the whole thing is an imposition—too much for an absolute stranger to ask."

"Except you're not an absolute stranger, Megan. You have friends here."

"Acquaintances are more like it. However, what if I ask some local women to do craft demonstrations during the first couple of weeks after I open the store? I'm thinking about a grand opening or get-acquainted-with-the-store promotion. I could pay them with gift certificates for items of their choice." Megan ended on a doubtful note.

"I think they'd jump at the idea," Fran assured her. "Don't you agree, Jed?"

"Sounds good. Megan, you might be surprised at how many rural people throughout these mountains depend on selling crafts for their primary income." He stood back, looking at his work. "Now what else can I do?"

Megan assured him she could handle the rest, not adding she expected to change what he'd done when she was alone.

"Okay, I'll get back to the farm."

With a word of thanks, Megan turned back toward Fran.

"See you later, Jed," Fran said, closing the door behind him.

Megan frowned when she saw Fran's puzzled face. "What's wrong?"

The other opened her mouth but shook her head without answering. She continued slotting cards.

Heat filled Megan's face when she realized the problem. "Go ahead, say it. I was rude to Jed."

"I don't understand why, Megan. You two started out on the wrong foot, I know—although I still don't understand the cause—but he's being helpful now. We would have needed hours putting up the shelves and bins. He did the job in only twenty minutes."

Megan's recent dinner with Jed flashed through her mind. One-time thing. Never again, she assured herself. After a noticeable pause, she answered. "I don't want to have anything to do with him."

"Jed, or any man?"

"Okay, any man." Megan turned her face away when she muttered the words. She didn't know whether she hoped Fran would pursue the matter or ignore it.

"You must have your reasons. I won't be nosy, still maybe you should give the matter more thought. A man can be handy to have around and not just for handyman stuff. Women alone are conspicuous at any social event around here."

"I hadn't thought of that." Megan knew the feeling. "Now, back to what I was saying about my idea. Perhaps one or two women would give lessons for a small fee, using my store for the meeting place. I could put a few chairs in my stockroom, which is clean. Also heated. No charge."

"You should bring it up at the festival meeting tonight. I'll buy your coffee every morning for a week if you have at least five people who are eager to head the list."

"Deal," Megan agreed.

 enenenenen

There were seven.

After explaining her ideas, Megan's heart sank to her toes in the moment of silence that filled the library meeting room before voices vied with each other with suggestions.

"You can count on me for dried flower arranging," Carrie Malcolm said. "This is the perfect time, because the autumn blooming season is winding down. People like to enjoy their flowers outside until late fall. I'll supply the flowers"

"I'll demonstrate preparing and painting designs on ordinary flowerpots and small river rocks. That sort of thing." Mrs. Willoughby, the elementary school art teacher, chimed in.

"I can teach almost any kind of needlework," Sally Jamison told her. "Put me down for whatever you want me to do."

Fliss Ryan offered knitting lessons. Others offered quilting and embroidery, crochet, and macramé.

Megan sighed with relief at their reactions. "I plan to open the store this Saturday. We can begin the demonstrations on Monday. I'll make some posters and depend on all of you to spread the word too."

"Sounds great," Catherine Crawford assured her. "I have absolutely no craft ability, but I volunteer to read stories to children at the library while their mothers are at your place."

"Marvelous idea," exclaimed Fran. "I'll help. The only time I tried crafts, the teacher said she'd heard of people with ten thumbs, but I was the first she'd ever seen."

Amid the general merriment, Megan exchanged a triumphant smile with Fran. *This* business would be successful. She would happily pay for her own coffee too.

ꙡ ꙡ ꙡ ꙡ ꙡ

On Wednesday afternoon, Megan stood inside her store appraising the results of her diligence over the past few days. The food and card selections occupied the left side culminating at the door into the stockroom, where she set up her office. Crafts occupied the back wall, with the gift items on the right. With the cash register also on the right between the ceramics and the windows, she could monitor the entire store with the help of a large, ceiling-mounted mirror. She nodded in satisfaction.

"Are you ready to call it a day?"

Megan whirled toward the door when a masculine voice interrupted her absorption.

"I believe so, Jed. I can't think of anything else I need to do until tomorrow morning when the craft supplies come."

"Could I show you the backwoods?"

Megan hesitated. He looked too appealing standing there with his hands thrust in the back pockets of his well-worn jeans. However, as Fran had said, a male escort was always handy to have around. "Sounds great. I haven't seen much except the drive between here and Asheville."

"Okay, lock up."

They drove the back roads, pausing in small towns long enough for Megan to browse the roadside markets of fresh vegetables. Mostly they enjoyed the tranquility of the mountains, the fluffy, white clouds drifting across the baby blue sky.

"This whole area has changed since I was a kid." Jed's pensive voice faded for a long moment. "Dad had a World War Two jeep he'd found in a junkyard somewhere. After we rebuilt it, we drove around for hours on end without seeing any houses. Now they dot the mountain sides."

"There's little industry, so how can you account for the growth?"

"Tourism. People visit through the years and love the area. This is a great area for retirement. Some people think there are too many retirees. They do bring their retirement accounts with them, though, so we shouldn't complain."

"Look!"

Megan's exclamation made Jed pull the truck onto the wide shoulder. She jumped out of the truck and dug her phone from her pocket to snap pictures of a long, narrow waterfall surrounded by a panorama of gold, crimson, and orange leaves against an evergreen backdrop.

"Michigan has woods—I haven't spent all my time pounding pavement—yet I've never seen such color in my life. So vivid, so alive. And that waterfall *ripples*. Pictures don't show that."

"I thought I was prejudiced when I told people the Smokies are the greatest," Jed admitted. "Of course, I must admit the nearby Blue Ridge Mountains have their own claim to beauty."

Megan turned her attention to the waterfall. "I've read that sometimes there's a cave behind the water. Do you think there might be one here?"

"I've never explored this one. Shall we find out? I warn you the ravine might be deeper, rougher than it appears from here. Mountainsides can be treacherous to maneuver."

Megan glanced at her jeans and runners. "I should be okay."

They picked their way over gnarled tree roots and through lush growth. Rough going was right. Megan's feet slipped, landing her on her derrière. Jed might need to pull her back up the mountainside. The idea amused her. Real he-man stuff.

On the road, the waterfall had been a murmur on the breeze, but deeper into the gorge, the murmur became a roar. At the bottom, they stood on a mossy cushion and peered behind the curtain of water. Edging closer, Megan reveled in the fine mist that caressed her face.

"Sorry, no cave," Jed shouted above the roar and turned to go.

Back in the truck, Megan panted for breath, even though Jed had helped her. She'd never had such an afternoon of simple pleasure. David wouldn't have stood for it. He preferred planes to cars, nightclubs to the splendor of nature. Paved streets to mountain treks. Neon lights to sunlight.

"When are you coming back from wherever you are?"

Jed's voice brought Megan's attention back to her surroundings. "I was thinking."

"Care to share?"

"Oh, just the sheer beauty around here," she fudged. "The mixture of leaf colors, the mist on my face, the wonder of waterfalls. So different from anything I've ever known."

Megan felt his gaze on her face for a moment, but he didn't speak before he eased the truck back onto the road. The light played across the truck hood as they passed under overhanging branches of the towering trees, which crowded the roadsides. They returned to Crawfordville in October's early twilight, stopping at a farmhouse restaurant called Gert's Place for a supper of broiled trout, green beans cooked with ham, and creamed corn.

"Ummm!" Megan put down her fork. "I must learn how to cook corn that way."

Jed laughed and led the way to the door.

"Would you like to stop by the farm for a few minutes? Mom will still be awake. You can compare notes on the latest mysteries."

Dread skittered along Megan's spine at the thought of meeting her landlady. She was in wrinkled jeans, for goodness sakes, not dressed right for meeting anyone of importance. What if she doesn't like me? Should I mention my business? No. She might order me from her building, even her house if she thinks I'm chasing her precious son.

Megan didn't see how she could avoid an introduction, so she fibbed. "I would enjoy meeting her. Seeing your farm too."

"I'm afraid it's too dark to see much of the farm tonight, but perhaps you can come on another day." He swung the truck into a graveled driveway and, moments later, braked at the steps of an old rock house, bleak in the weak moonlight. The stones breathed endurance, as if the house had roots planted deep underground.

Inside, Jed called, "Mom? I've brought you a visitor."

He led Megan toward a room on the right. Mrs. Anderson was sitting in bed, pillows plumped around her, several books on the headboard shelf, one in her hands.

When Jed introduced them, Megan smiled into the blue eyes so much like Jed's. "I'm happy to meet you, Mrs. Anderson. Jed told me you enjoy reading mysteries too."

"I sure do, Miss Stanfield. I read every cozy I can get, but I've started reading some suspense too." She held up her book. a silver bookmark tucked inside about halfway through. "A friend recently gifted me with this David Baldacci book which I'm enjoying. He writes legal thrillers."

"Please call me Megan, Mrs. Anderson. I've read some books by Baldacci. He's an excellent writer. You might enjoy Michael Connelly too. Catherine Crawford introduced me to John Sherwood's books because I'm interested in planting flowers. Jed told me you enjoy his books."

"He's right. As I age, I appreciate older heroines, so Celia Grant appeals to me. However, she isn't as old as I."

"You're not old, Mrs. Anderson; you're in the process of aging!"

When their laughter faded, Megan said, "I wonder if you remember my family, either the Malloys or the Abernathies, who lived here years ago."

"Only by hearsay. There was . . . ," Mrs. Anderson's voice faded.

Megan puzzled over her broken thought but didn't press her. Couldn't quite pull out the name she sought, maybe. Or an old scandal?

"There is someone who might help you, though. Josh Crawford. He's their contemporary, one of the few still living, I'm afraid, who is still mentally competent. He claims to know everybody who ever lived around here."

"He'll be in the phone book, I expect," Megan said. "I can call him."

"He sits under the huge elm on the square every day the weather allows. His father planted the tree the day he was born." Jed chuckled. "He'll talk your ear off, if you let him."

"Sounds like he's the person I need. I've seen him on the square, but we've only nodded to each other. I suppose he's a relation of Catherine Crawford?"

"Distantly, but I'm not sure how," Mrs. Anderson answered.

They said their goodbyes and left.

In the dim light, Jed guided Megan to the truck with his hand curling around her forearm. Trees pressed close together along the driveway. The headlights cut through shadows, which seemed almost sinister, reminding her of the Gothic novels she'd shivered through as a teenager.

When they stopped at Megan's house, she roused herself from their silence. Now what? Did she just get out? Or would that look like she was running from him? She hadn't felt this awkward since she was twelve. She took refuge in chatter.

"Your mother is nice." She hadn't pointed her finger or said never darken my door again, which was a blessing.

"I think so."

"I like her." Megan said the polite thing but realized it was true.

"I like her too. Most people love their mothers, yet I wonder how many people *like* them."

"Or even know them well enough to decide whether they're likable people," Megan murmured.

Jed clasped her hand and then pulled her into his arms, holding her a moment before lightly touching his lips to hers.

Megan pulled away. She didn't want this. No involvement was the mantra of her life. She wouldn't call herself disinterested in men, exactly. Uninterested, maybe. Was there a difference? Whatever. She took refuge in words.

"The needlework distributor comes early tomorrow. I'll have a busy day. I'm sure you will too, so I'd better say good night."

Silence greeted her words.

"You're right." Jed walked to the door with her but left with only a murmured good night.

Inside, Megan listened to the tires crunch on the gravel, the sound growing dim when they turned onto the asphalt. Memories followed her up the stairs, memories of the only kisses which meant anything: David's kisses.

She sprayed *Lancôme's Trêsor* perfume into the filling bathtub. Major mistake. Faint quivering inside reminded her that David gave her the perfume. She couldn't push his image away. His silvery eyes seemed to caress her when she pulled the plug. She settled for a quick shower instead. Too late. The light scent lingered in the air, following her into the bedroom.

There, she paced the floor, aching to hold David again. He'd acted like a jerk, but that didn't matter. Nothing mattered except her love for him. She couldn't put her arms around his memory, though, which was all she had.

She told herself to stop sifting through the ashes from an old flame, or the hurt would never go away. No one died from a broken heart—she was living proof—

but how much longer would the agony of losing him last? She couldn't chase away those memories even by reading—her usual escape from life's problems. His face came between her and the page. Her breath suddenly came in short gulps.

That wide smile wasn't David's! Her mental vision turned silver eyes to blue, silver hair to russet.

"No way," she muttered. Jed Anderson was not taking David's place. No one could ever replace him, she assured herself yet again. Scary to think she might move on.

Megan paced the floor, fighting her thoughts, until she made herself stand by the window. She stared toward the hedge, almost hoping the white thing would come again. Anything was better than the war of images in her head.

Chapter 11

The Past Reaches Out

"Good morning, sleepyhead, did I wake you?"

Megan tried to match Jed's merry voice despite her throbbing head. Her grammar went by the wayside. "Sleepyhead? *Moi*? I've already fed the chickens, slopped the hogs, and milked the goats."

He hooted. "Yeah, sure you have! Do you even know what those things mean?"

"I've heard the words or read them or something. I believe they're things farmers do every morning."

"Those are some of the chores anyway. What time does the delivery man come?"

"He promised not later than nine. Why?"

"I can lift boxes, if you need help."

Shoving his way into my business again. Megan shook off her first irritable thought. She couldn't be rude after the most pleasant afternoon she'd had since David dumped her. Besides, she could make use of him. "I certainly do. Sally's coming to help me arrange everything. You could put the boxes in their appointed place throughout the store."

"I'll be there when the delivery truck comes. There's one other thing, Megan. Do you think you'll have time to see my farm today? Mother wants to visit with you too, before you get busy with the new shop."

Megan hesitated, remembering her determination the evening before. What did he mean his mother would like to see her? "Sounds like an enjoyable afternoon if I finish the crafts."

"Great. I'll check with you later."

Jed stood on the square talking with a couple of women, when Megan reached town. His hands thrust in his back pockets, he turned from one to the other until he spotted Megan and strolled toward her, laughing across his shoulder. She wondered at the twinge which gripped her gut.

Reaching her side, Jed nodded at the sign. "Do you plan to keep the same name?"

She stepped inside. "No, the painter doesn't have the new sign ready yet. I decided on the name 'This 'n That.' What do you think?"

"Appropriate, since you'll have a wide variety of merchandise."

Turning, Megan welcomed the van driver. "Stack the boxes near the door."

She and Jed were in heated discussion when Sally arrived.

"You advise us," Megan urged. "Neither of us knows anything about crafts. We could debate the matter all day."

Sally directed Jed to place art supplies on the left of the back wall, needlework across the middle, flower arrangement items on the right.

Megan tried not to stare at the muscles that rippled across Jed's shoulders when he lifted the boxes with apparent ease.

When he finished, Megan shooed him out the door. "Thanks for doing the drudge work. We can take over from here."

"Two at your place?" Jed asked.

"Sounds great," Megan murmured, her thoughts already on the boxes behind her. "Sally, I can hardly wait to see all this stuff, even though I don't have the foggiest notion what any of it is."

Two hours later, Megan admired their achievement. "Everything looks marvelous, Sally, even professional. Still, do you think I'll sell anything?"

"Would I steer you wrong? This stuff will sell like hot cakes."

"I don't mean will people want something. I mean, can I help them find what they need?"

"You'll soon know what and where everything is. Can you handle inventory control?"

"Not a problem. My accounting program is ready. I won't need long to key in the data."

"Why not now? I can read from the delivery sheets, while you do the recording."

"Thanks. Recording will go faster if you help me." Megan led the way to her small office. "I warn you, though, I talk to the computer—not always nicely either. I mutter threatening dire consequences, if it doesn't do what I say."

"Who doesn't?"

A short while later, Sally placed the last delivery sheet in the file pocket and glanced at her watch. "I have two new, last-minute listings for winter rentals which means getting out the advertisements."

"You sound so confident about success."

"Stop your worrying," Sally scolded good-naturedly. "I'll be free to help some each day until you're more familiar with the stock."

"I'll appreciate your help and will pay whatever you say."

"Oh, no, I don't want pay at all. I want access to your customers. For years, I've toyed with the idea of teaching crafts, especially needlework. This seems an excellent opportunity. I might even pay you rent to use your back room—more central than my house."

"You can use it, no charge."

"We'll see. Okay, enough about me. What are your plans for the afternoon?"

"Jed invited me to see his farm."

"Sounds like fun. Now, I must skedaddle."

Setting out at a brisk pace toward home, Megan pondered Sally's surprised expression at the mention of Jed's farm. Was she one more in a long list he had taken to meet his mother? Or did he never take any women there?

ꙫ ꙫ ꙫ ꙫ ꙫ

"We're going to do *what*?" Megan stared at Jed. As promised, he had arrived at two. Now, half an hour later at the farm, she stood open-mouthed at his words.

Fluffy clouds floated across the sky, flirting with jet vapor streams. The afternoon was warm and breezy, ideal for a stroll in the great out-of-doors. Yet, he proposed to show the farm on a *horse*?

"Do you have something against horses?"

"They have too many feet, they're huge, and I suspect they bite." Her glare dared him to laugh.

His lips twitched. "You're telling me you don't ride."

"I've never been on a horse in my life."

"We must rectify that."

"Why?"

"Fair question. Riding lessons are in order, but for now we'll use a different conveyance around the farm."

Megan matched him step for step toward the garage, expecting to ride the Bronco since he ignored the truck. Instead, he turned toward an iron frame on wheels, no top or sides.

"Better close your mouth." Jed's eyes twinkled. "You might catch flies."

"This is better than a horse? What on earth is it?"

"An all-terrain vehicle. Goes anywhere. Lots of noise, hardly any gas."

That was supposed to reassure her? "Are you sure this . . . thing . . . is safe?"

"Safe as horses. Doesn't buck anyway. Hop on."

Megan didn't believe him, but she complied. The slight breeze carried an odor she couldn't identify.

Probably cows. Unpleasant, or perhaps that was only her heightened senses caused by fearing this mode of travel. She struggled not to wrinkle her nose.

Her hands gripped the seat until they hurt, but when this contraption didn't tip over going up a hill, Megan relaxed, shooting him a nervous smile. "Talk."

"Chicken!" he teased.

"I admit to being a wimp. I'm accustomed to paved roads, flat, mostly straight, paved roads. The road between here and Asheville is curvy in some places, and you drove me in steep mountains too, but this is wilderness."

"I wouldn't call my farm wilderness, but I understand how you can think so. You'll soon get used to uncultivated areas," he assured her with absolute certainty.

Megan didn't believe him.

For a couple of hours, they alternately rode and stopped while he pointed out interesting features. "Someday, I want to have more horses—a dozen perhaps. I'll put a horse farm over there separate from the cow pastures. Not thoroughbreds, you understand, ordinary saddle horses."

"Who would ride them?"

"Tourists. No riding horses are available anywhere near here. I might even start a riding school."

"Ah! Do you see me as your first student?"

"My guinea pig," Jed admitted. "I've never taught anyone riding before."

"Thanks a lot."

The wind changed directions. Megan took shallow breaths when they neared the pasture. She glanced at Jed from the corner of her eye guessing he didn't notice the animal smells. By the time they reached the barn, she was ready to rest her bones from the iron monster and her nostrils from the stench.

Mrs. Anderson greeted them inside the house. "I hope Jed didn't bore you to tears. When he starts on his ideas, he doesn't know when to stop."

Megan kept a poker face. She'd heard enough about cover crops and contour farming to do her forever. As for artificial insemination—heaven deliver her. She managed a light voice when she said, "He does talk when he gets started, doesn't he?"

Jed raised his hands in mock surrender. After he assured his mother that he'd been on his best behavior, he sniffed. "I'm famished. Something smells delicious. Is supper ready?"

Their conversation drifted from town affairs to local history until Megan pushed herself from the table. "Mrs. Anderson, Jed, this has been a great afternoon, but now I should go home."

They chatted, leaving the farm, but conversation dwindled as they neared Megan's house. Would Jed make a move on her? She was surprised when he walked to the porch with her, said goodbye, listened for the deadbolt to click home, and drove away. Relief flooded Megan. She didn't want kisses, not even casual ones. Not that Jed's would be casual, she was convinced, because there was nothing casual in anything he did.

ﬧ ﬧ ﬧ ﬧ ﬧ

Jed pointed the truck toward home deep in thought. Megan wasn't interested in a relationship. Why had she resisted his mild advances toward her last night? He hadn't attacked her. Quite the contrary. He'd been slow and deliberate, giving her time to reach for the door handle. Tonight, she had set a distance between them, which clearly said, "Keep your hands to yourself." She'd lied earlier. He didn't buy she was thinking about the beauty surrounding them when they visited the waterfall. What had she really been thinking? Maybe who. An old lover, perhaps? That might explain her behavior. Jed shook his head. Women! He'd never understand them.

He was a determined cuss though. He had always enjoyed challenges, so, by fair means or foul, he'd change her mind. A light-hearted relationship would loosen her stiffness, be good for her. Him too. When he finished with her, she'd be glad to head north again. The car lights cut a swath through the countryside as he drove on home, his thoughts on pouring honey.

ຎ ຎ ຎ ຎ ຎ

Standing in the square opposite her store, Megan admired the new sign. Red lettering on white background glistened in the late morning sun. Smelling the fresh paint invigorated her. Now was the time to talk with Josh Crawford. She'd been here a few months, but hadn't even told him hello, even though she saw him almost every day on the square. Megan admitted she hadn't wanted to risk yet another resident's snub. She approached the elderly man, who sat beneath a huge elm tree.

"Hello, I'm Megan Stanfield."

"Yeah, I know who you are, girl. You're your grandmother's image when she left here as a young woman. There's no mistaking you're a Malloy." His sharp eyes watched her like a cat ready to snatch a mouse.

"Is it alright if I join you for a minute?" He waved her toward the bench. "Mrs. Anderson said you might tell me something about my family, the Malloys and Abernathies. Are there any of them still around?"

"I'm afraid not. Your Malloy ancestors helped my family settle this area. I hated to see the family die out. The last man was John, who had only the two daughters, twins, Alma—your grandmother—and Eva. We don't know anything about either one after they left town right after high school."

"I never knew Grandmother had a twin." Why hadn't her grandparents told her? Talking about her would have been natural for Granddad. "My grandmother had only one child, a daughter. I'm her only child. I don't know anything about my grandfather's people. I don't remember any relatives ever visiting either of them."

"Robert Abernathy was the only one left of your paternal family when he married Alma Malloy and moved to Detroit. I don't suppose he's still living?"

"He died several years ago. His childhood stories made me move here." Memories flashed through her mind, memories of a big man who had held her hand while he shouldered his way through every crowd. Her beloved granddad, who had loved her with unreserved, unceasing candor.

"Bad ticker kept him out of the army in World War Two," Josh told her. "Is your grandmother still alive?"

"She died a few months ago. Did you know her family after she moved away?"

"I've known everyone who has lived in this town during my lifetime. Both of your great-grandparents died a few years after the girls went away. There was no one left."

"My grandmother's sister never came back?"

"No, neither ever came back. Alma was lively, kicking up larks, loved by everyone."

"What kind of larks?"

The skin around his eyes crinkled. "She was into everything from the time she could walk. She tried to climb a tree like the bigger kids, which didn't work, so she tried a sapling which came out of the ground, roots and all."

"I can see she was adventurous even in childhood. She didn't change."

Mr. Crawford recounted the school flag hanging upside down. He chuckled at the mysterious disappearance of the preacher's notes one Sunday. "Oh, she admitted her guilt right enough, nothing sneaky about Alma Malloy. She said she'd never heard a better sermon than the one he preached spontaneous-like."

"She never hesitated to give her opinion even on her death bed," Megan assured him. "I never knew anyone like her."

"She was one for the books, Alma was."

"Grandmother didn't change much. She even traveled until a year or so ago. There was always a crowd around her at home."

"Sounds like her. Now, Eva was the quiet one." He paused. "She surprised—nay, shocked—everybody when she disappeared."

Megan's breath caught. Maybe this was what Mrs. Anderson had almost told her. "Disappeared?"

"Her parents said she eloped with a soldier, spur-of-the-moment. I thought she was much too shy. They say still waters run deep, though, so I reckon it's possible. I still can't believe she'd marry a stranger, so she must have kept him a secret."

"Why would she?"

"Well, you see, Alma captivated all the young bucks, no matter who had seen them first."

"Even her own sister? Her twin?"

"Yes." Mr. Crawford stopped talking, his breathing grew shallow. Megan thought he had dozed off, so she rose, preparing to leave him to his nap.

"Jed Anderson is a good man, stable as granite. You could do far worse."

Megan felt heat rise in her face at his knowing smile. She'd left the old gentleman smiling, anyway, so maybe he would tell her more about her family.

Returning home, she glanced toward the mailbox at the end of her drive. When had she last opened it? Probably loaded with advertisements. Pulling open the door, she found only one item, a letter from the attorney who handled her grandmother's estate.

She settled beside the kitchen table and slit the envelope. Mr. Penland apologized for his delay in sending the enclosed letter entrusted to him some years before by her grandmother.

Years before? Why hadn't her grandmother told her whatever this letter contained? They were together the day before her death. Megan slit the envelope. Although she had rarely seen it, she recognized her grandmother's monogrammed notepaper.

> *My dear Megan,*
>
> *Yes, you are my dear, very dear Megan. I realize you think I don't love you. I've seen the knowledge in your face, but I do. The problem has been you remind me so very much of my sister. She's been dead for many years. I sometimes feel some guilt over her. That story belongs to the past, though, not in this note.*
>
> *Now, about the funds I'm giving you in my will. Use it wisely (I'm proud of your MBA!), but enjoy it too. You and your grandfather were very close from the day you were born. Nothing gave him more pleasure than sitting with you, talking*

about the little North Carolina town where we lived until we moved to Detroit. His memories of our Crawfordville life were happier than mine are. He loved those mountains, so I believe you would enjoy visiting there. Consider using some of the money to visit your ancestral hometown. No matter what you've believed about me in the past or the present, or even the future, please remember I love you. Grandmother.

Tears slid down Megan's face until she gave way to heart wrenching sobs. Grandmother had loved her. The bitterness of rejection seeped from her heart as it filled with the love she'd longed for. If only her grandmother had told her sooner. She wouldn't have felt so neglected if she had known, even though they seldom saw each other. She put the thought aside. Grandmother had told her at last—nothing else mattered.

When Megan glanced through the letter again, two sentences caught her eye. "She's been dead many years. I sometimes feel some guilt over her." Mr. Crawford said they left here at the same time. There must have been some connection between them later. Could this answer the terrorist question? Perhaps Grandmother's sister was the origin of the face on the flyer. Grandmother and Granddad wouldn't have talked about her if she were a terrorist.

Should she call Mike? Yes, because this would prove she was trying to help the FBI. She reached for the phone.

"Read the letter to me again."

When she finished, he said he would be right over.

Over cups of espresso, Mike questioned her, going over her grandmother's estate. No, she didn't receive anything except money and some personal items. No, she didn't know anything about diaries or journals.

"Wait a minute. I do recall Father commenting Grandmother didn't save things. He went through the attic after she died. Uncluttered to the point of disbelief, he said."

"Why did he go through the attic?"

"Mother inherited the house. Father will put it on the market after he settles the estate."

"When?"

"I don't know. Steve Penland, Grandmother's attorney, consults Father."

"The FBI might want to go through the house in case your father missed anything."

Megan nodded. "Mr. Higgins's Detroit agent talked to Mr. Penland, so he knows who to contact. There shouldn't be any problem."

Mike tipped the cup for the last swallow of coffee and stood. At the door, he said, "Thanks. The letter should help. I'll pick Mr. Crawford's brains about the sister. I understand he knows everything about everybody who ever lived here. After that, I'll pass the information to Fred Higgins."

"May I have the letter back? It's special."

"Sure. I'll make a copy and return the original to you."

Chapter 12

Sunday Visitor

The big day dawned bright and sunny. Good omen, Megan told herself as she unlocked the door of This 'n That soon after eight o'clock on Saturday. She'd been too jittery to wait longer. She was busy sorting money into the cash drawer when Sally breezed inside.

"Would you believe I almost forgot to stop by the bank yesterday?" Megan asked with an embarrassed smile. "Imagine opening a store with no money on hand."

"Nerves, nothing else. I'm glad you're taking credit cards. They're a good incentive for people to buy more than they intended."

"Will they find what they want?" Megan looked around the small store. Myriad colors in the crafts section caught her eye before she focused on collectibles. Should she have stocked sports figurines instead of the Disney *Frozen* series?

"Stop second guessing yourself." Sally read her mind. "Your stock is fine."

Megan cast a worried look out the window. "Do you really think people will come this morning? The streets are almost empty."

"They'll come! When they see those colorful posters you placed around town, they'll crowd in. You'll see."

Sally was right. Within five minutes of flipping the closed sign to open, half a dozen customers crowded into the store, each with different questions.

"Don't you have Hummels? I'd hoped I wouldn't need to go to Asheville for them anymore." The deep, plaintive voice came from a stylishly dressed woman, who either had the most beautiful complexion on the planet or the skills of a make-up artist.

"I considered stocking Hummels, but decided to special order them when I receive requests. Shall I order the current release for you?"

"No. I always see an item before purchasing." She turned on her mile-high wedgies and left the store.

Okay, if that's the way you want it. Megan turned to the next customer.

"Do you have any comic book figurines? My grandson asked me specially for . . . ," she consulted a slip of paper, ". . . Captain America. He says they're the best."

"My granddaughter says the figurines from the *Frozen* movie are the best."

Megan intervened before an argument could start. "You'll find the *Frozen* collectibles over on your left. My order for the *Marvel* series should arrive Monday or Tuesday. Be sure to come in again next week. Now, do you ladies enjoy crafts? We have a variety. I imagine you know Sally Jamison, who is helping me. Why don't you tell her hello?"

With a smile, Megan turned to a customer, who waited at the cash register, her hands filled with greeting cards. Shivers of excitement skittered down Megan's spine when she rang up her first sale and sent the customer on her way with an invitation to come again.

The Yogurt Raisin Man slipped inside the door but stopped in confusion. After a frantic glance around, he turned to leave, but Megan hurried toward him. "Good morning, sir. I've changed my business, as you can see, but I still have the snacks you enjoy. They're over here."

After she rang up the sale, she asked him to come again. He had not once looked her squarely in the face, but she didn't care. Creepy or not, he was a loyal customer.

Jed stepped inside during the first hour, gave a thumbs-up motion, and went on his way. Decidedly different from his appalling visit to Nature's Way, Megan acknowledged with silent appreciation. A customer clutching several skeins of pink yarn approached.

"Just what I need for a sweater and booties for my new grandbaby," the woman told her. "I've put it off for weeks because I dreaded going all the way to Asheville for the yarn."

"You won't have to drive there for yarn ever again," Megan assured her. "I promise you'll always find a good supply here."

Business slowed at the noon hour. Sally went to the diner for sandwiches and returned with Fran at her heels. They took turns dealing with customers, while the others ate their lunch in the office.

"I hope you will close your store for lunch, Megan," Fran commented. "I shut mine for at least an hour, sometimes two."

"I didn't want to miss any customers on the first day," Megan confessed. "If I had closed, they might not have come back. Sales have been great all morning. I don't know what I would have done without help from you and Sally."

"You would have managed," Fran answered. "Stop underestimating yourself."

Megan grinned at the friendly scolding. "I want to ask whether I've underestimated local people. I thought Hummels would be too expensive, so I didn't plan to carry them. A woman came in asking for one almost as soon as I opened the door. I told her I would special order for her, but she declined. Didn't look at anything else either."

"You've met our wealthy widow. She was Nina Bradshaw until her husband obligingly died, leaving her millions. She started calling herself 'Nee-nah' and infiltrated Atlanta society."

"Then, I suspect her shoes were not Jimmy Choo knockoffs."

"No way." Sally straightened the knitting yarn. "I imagine Saturday mornings will be your busiest time. Most of your customers this morning came from outside town. They will leave after they have lunch. Townspeople usually shop on weekdays."

"I don't expect every Saturday morning will be this busy, still I hope the novelty doesn't wear off too soon."

"We have several takers for next week's demonstrations, so you're in business for them too."

Business slacked off in mid-afternoon. Megan sent her helpers on their way and checked her stack of sales slips when the last customer left a few minutes before five. What a day, she exulted and spoke the words aloud when Jed came through the doorway.

He glanced at the shelves. "Looks like your supplies are sadly diminished. Well, not sadly by any means."

"No, not sadly, I'm thankful to say. I must fax new orders to my suppliers; otherwise, I'll run out of stock."

"How much longer will you be here?"

"An hour or so."

"Walking home after dark isn't safe. I'll stick around town." Jed closed the door behind himself, giving her no chance to speak.

Fury engulfed Megan. He had a nerve. Telling her what to do or not do. She'd known this would happen, if she let him get a foot in the door. This wasn't a big city, for goodness' sake. She was far beyond childhood too. Megan Elizabeth Stanfield had taken care of herself for years.

"I won't have it," Megan muttered. "I will not tolerate his bossiness. I'll walk when and where I please." She marched into the office and slapped down the sales slips, scattering them all over the desk. Irritated with herself now, she fired up the computer.

Finished, her deposit bag tucked under her arm, she reached for her cross-body bag. With the office light off, the store was in darkness, except for one security light. Reaching the outside door, she took an involuntary step backward.

A face pressed against the glass.

Megan put down the deposit bag and gripped her other bag by the strap, ready for battle. Only then did she open the door. "What do you think you're doing? I don't like being stared at, so be on your way!"

He almost ran, his baggy jeans flapping around his legs, his denim-clad arms pumping.

Megan turned a frowning face toward Jed, who reached her as the stranger faded into the dimness across the square. "Did you see him? I don't like the way he stares at me."

"I didn't see anybody," he told her. "Men always stare at gorgeous gals. You should expect it."

How chauvinistic and already two decades into the twenty-first century. Would men ever change? "Don't be ridiculous. His stare wasn't like that."

"Okay, okay, tell me who's been staring."

"If I knew, I wouldn't ask!"

Jed took a deep breath. "Start at the beginning. When and where did this man stare at you?"

"I see him around town a lot but caught him staring only twice. Once in the square and then in front of my store. He definitely stared at me both times. I think he peeked at me through shelves at the grocery store too. Somebody did. I saw him later, so it must have been him. I shouldn't have yelled at him tonight, though. He might have needed help."

"Yeah, or had other ideas. Let's get out of here. I picked up pizzas and salads." He grinned. "That's a clue I'm inviting myself to supper at your house, in the event you didn't catch my drift."

Megan hesitated but capitulated, too tired for an argument. "You're a gentleman and a scholar for sure."

An hour later, Megan struggled to hide her yawns when they polished off the pizza. She was not successful.

"If you keep yawning with your mouth shut, you'll get lock jaw or something. Might even blow off the top of your head. Scatter your brains all over your beautiful kitchen." He slipped an arm around her shoulder. At the door, he dropped a light kiss on the tip of her nose and left.

Megan climbed the stairs, touching her nose. A butterfly landing there would leave the same sensation before flying on its way. She wondered what Jed had in mind. She didn't really care, though, because she knew what was in her own mind. No involvement. Nothing else mattered.

ௐ ௐ ௐ ௐ ௐ

He hadn't been able to resist looking through the window, but he should not have stayed after she turned out the back light. When she confronted him like an avenging angel, the hammers started battering his head, causing more pain than if she'd hit him with her bag. Where had he seen those blazing eyes before? She was ready to attack him. Even worse, Jed Anderson had almost caught him. He couldn't risk either happening, but he also couldn't resist looking at her even though each encounter frustrated him more. He rammed his hands into his jacket pockets and headed home. Plenty of aspirin there.

ௐ ௐ ௐ ௐ ௐ

Sunday was a lazy day. Quietness enveloped Megan while she ate her lunch on the screened back porch, which had quickly become her favorite part of the house. She had never known a more peaceful place. Birds chirped high in the trees; closer a fly buzzed against the screen. A small plane flew lazily overhead. Its hum lulled her to sleep in the cushioned chaise lounge, which cuddled her body.

A distinct but not loud noise woke her. Blinking, Megan sat straight and looked around. A young woman stood on the steps, staring at her. No, not just any young woman—herself. Megan closed her eyes, shook her head, opened her eyes again. Her other self still stood beyond the screen door, flashing a smile, beckoning with one long forefinger.

Megan's heart thudded. Buzzing in her ears almost deafened her. She grasped the chair arms until her knuckles were white. No way would she leave this porch. Her legs wouldn't move even if she were willing. She made herself concentrate. Nobody can be two places at once. She was certain of one thing. Megan Elizabeth Stanfield was sitting on this side of the screen door, not standing out there.

Wait a minute, though. Maybe she could be in both places. She might be dead. This could be her spirit waiting for her body to join it. Gazing at the apparition, Megan pinched her arm. Hard. She blinked again. The image was still there, still smiling. Megan was crazy, or her brains had turned mushy. One or the other. Her behavior hadn't been rational since David dumped her. Think of her mistake rushing into the natural food business here without ascertaining need. And the terrorism threat. Either, alone, was enough to send anyone around the bend into la-la land.

Megan focused all her energy on the thing poised outside the screen door. That was not herself out there.

She refused to believe otherwise. Her own hair was shorter than *hers*, whoever she was or had been in life. Her dress was straight out of the forties. The forties? Something clicked in Megan's mind. This must be her grandmother, coming to see how her granddaughter was settling into her own former home.

Relief flooded Megan when she realized this apparition was not preparing her for an early death. Her heartbeat slowed. She wasn't sure she believed ghosts exist, still she would not, could not be afraid of this . . . whatever this is.

"Hello, Grandmother," she said. "Have you come to welcome me to your old home?"

The wraith beckoned again as she floated toward the rear of the property.

Megan spoke as if everything was real. "This will surprise you. I'm going to plant flowers after I clean out the old borders. Catherine Crawford, the librarian—you probably knew her grandparents—said I should start there. She gave me some books."

Still reluctant, Megan left the porch following the apparition, chatting all the way, hoping no one was within a hundred miles of her one-sided conversation. "Shall I show you where I plan to plant some bulbs? Daffodils for sure, maybe tulips."

Her grandmother lingered a few inches off the ground, which placed her face at Megan's eye level. She pointed toward the hedge across the back of the yard.

"Grandmother, did you plant those bushes? How industrious you were! I always knew you could do anything. Come around to the front. I'll show you where I'll start weeding this afternoon." Megan turned away, but the figure moved faster. Still hovering in front of her, the outstretched hand pointed toward the hedge. She made a lifting motion.

"What are you trying to tell me, Grandmother? I know the shrubs are ragged, but surely you don't want me to move them. That's hard work."

Megan glanced around when a vehicle crunched onto the gravel of her driveway. She turned back toward the apparition, but it was gone. The car turned around and went on its way. She listened as the sound faded. Moments passed in indecision, before Megan returned to the screened porch, half hoping, half fearing her visitor would be there.

She wasn't.

Megan sat on the steps, thoughts roaring through her mind, while she focused on the shrubs a hundred or so feet away. First, there was a white blob, followed by a white human shape, and now . . . what? Not human, despite the appearance. Had her moving into this house energized a dormant spirit? Megan hated to think she'd brought this whole nightmare on herself. She hadn't dreamed the image. Could it be magic? Hocus pocus? No. There wasn't another human nearby. Must be insanity. She'd taken the whole thing calmly too, proving insanity. Only crazy people would be calm facing ghosts. She should've been scared silly, unable to talk or even stutter. Any normal person would have collapsed in hysterics.

Megan argued pros and cons. Insane or trusting. Insane or gullible. Insane or . . . She stood, almost falling down the steps. The terrorist! Was this the image on the flyer? A being, which could appear at will? That would explain why the FBI thought copycat plastic surgery was the answer. She should call Mike and tell him . . . what? They were looking for a ghost? He would certainly laugh her out of town.

Mike told her he'd passed her grandmother's letter on to Fred Higgins, who had obtained a search warrant for her grandmother's house. Some agents had gone over it top to bottom but found nothing. Another dead end. No, Megan decided she wouldn't call Mike. She was crazy—or soon would be with all this useless thinking in circles. She'd get busy weeding the flowerbed. In only a few minutes, she piled an admirable number of weeds beside her. Megan looked around when Jed's Bronco turned into the drive. When the car door slammed, she pointed toward the weeds. "I'm making progress."

"I can see you are," Jed replied.

Megan frowned at her filthy hands.

His gaze sharpened when he bent closer to inspect the weeds she'd pulled. "You're not wearing gloves."

"They're just weeds. I didn't feel any thorny stuff."

"Not thorns. Poison ivy! Did you never hear 'leaves of three, let them be?'"

"No." She stared at him with consternation. "I'm a city woman, remember? Botany was never my strong suit."

He stared at her, disbelief on his face. "Haven't you even heard about poison ivy? You're in for an almighty rash. Sometimes chlorine bleach helps."

Megan bleached her hands, scrubbing them with rose-scented hand soap to remove the bleach smell. Didn't work. She wrinkled her nose. Great. Now she smelled like unrinsed laundry.

"I suppose I can live with the odor until it wears off. Will you have some iced tea?"

"No thanks. I came by to ask if you're ready for a riding lesson."

"I don't have proper riding clothes," Megan hedged, not liking the sound of this but with little hope she could change his mind.

"Your jeans are fine."

"Won't it make my hands worse?"

"No, I'll supply you with gloves. Now, quit stalling."

"Why didn't you call?"

"Because I knew you would think up some excuse."

Megan chewed her underlip a moment. He was right, but she relented. "I'm not sure this is a good idea. Still, okay, if you insist."

With a grin, Jed herded her out the door.

On the drive to the farm, Megan cast him a sideways glance, "Need I remind you I have definite views regarding horses?"

"Ah, yes, they have too many feet, they're huge, and they probably bite. Do I have a good memory, or what?"

"Well, just so you know. I haven't changed my mind."

Half an hour later, Megan stared at a black horse Jed led from the stable. The huge creature snorted, sidling around. "Am I supposed to get on *that*?"

"No, I wanted you to see him. Hero's Pride is my newest acquisition. Only I ride him."

"Do you have smaller horses?"

Jed handed the bridle to a farmhand and asked for Sugar Baby.

Megan laughed. "*Sugar Baby*?"

"Dad let a visiting child, a boy mind you, name her." Jed shook his head. "I refused to call her anything until I was old enough to see the humor. She's been out to pasture for several years, so she's perfect for your first ride. Flies are the only things she bites, and she only gums them. However, I can't do anything about the number of her legs. They're standard issue. She's smaller than Hero's Pride but not by much because your long legs require a large horse. Otherwise, the stirrups will scrape the ground."

"Good idea. I could use them for brakes." Megan stared at the farmhand who led two horses, a spotted gray, which ambled after a dark brown, ears pointed forward, neck held high and arched. Just looking at the brute made Megan step backward.

"This is King. He won't bother you."

"King? What kind of name is that for a horse?"

"Why not? From the minute he stood on his wobbly legs, he decided he rules the place. I haven't convinced him yet he doesn't. When that day comes, I'll demote him to Prince. Now come tell Sugar Baby hello. Here's some sugar to feed her."

"The cube is terribly small. She might eat my hand too."

She didn't trust the merriment dancing in his eyes.

"She'd spit it out because she can't chew bones."

"Funny."

"Hold the sugar in your palm."

Megan reached for the cube, never taking her gaze off Sugar Baby.

"No, don't curl your fingers. Stretch them down out of the way. That's right," he encouraged her.

Megan stood at arm's length from the gray horse, holding out her hand. The mare's lips were surprisingly soft when they closed on the lump. Having survived with her hand intact, Megan patted Sugar Baby's forehead, but kept her distance. "I didn't realize a horse's lips would be so soft."

"Muzzle."

She frowned at him. "Muzzle?"

"Horse's mouth."

"They look like lips to me."

"Muzzle," Jed repeated. "Okay, I think you're ready to mount. Come around this side."

Megan eyed the horse, which had fallen asleep, so it was okay to move. Nevertheless, she made a wide sweep around the drooping head.

"Hold the pommel—this thing—with your left hand. Now, put your left foot in my hand and swing your right leg over the saddle. Oops, not so far. Okay, slip your feet into the stirrups." He adjusted them longer and stepped back. "Now, get the feel of the saddle while I mount."

"She might run." Megan's white-knuckled hands clung to the front of the saddle.

Jed's shoulders shook. "Megan, we'll have to jump start her to get her going. Trust me on this."

Megan watched with increased apprehension when he swung himself onto the other horse, which moved closer to her.

"Now, hold the reins this way. Megan, turn loose of the saddle. You won't fall."

"I don't like heights." She released the grip of one hand and grabbed the reins.

"Both hands, Megan."

She glared at his amusement before she risked her other grip.

"Right. Okay, here we go." Jed patted Sugar Baby's neck to wake her. She followed King's slow walk, barely putting one hoof in front of the other.

Megan's jaws ached from clenching her teeth.

"Relax, Megan. You're stiff as a board."

A beautiful October day. The foliage was golden against the deep blue sky, the evergreens stood in stark contrast to the hardwoods. Megan didn't see any of it.

"Are we having fun yet?"

"You're doing fine. Just relax."

Oh, sure. Easy for him to say. He was accustomed to riding beasts. The look she gave him would wither a tree. He only grinned.

They reached a small grassy knoll overlooking the farmhouse far below. Megan lifted her gaze toward the distant mountain panorama. The only sound was a slight breeze rustling the treetops.

When Jed swung down from King, he dropped the reins on the ground. "Let's rest."

"Won't he run away?"

"No, he knows what dropped reins mean."

There went her hope. If King wouldn't leave, neither would Sugar Baby. Megan slid into Jed's arms, clutching him until her knees stopped wobbling. When they did, she dropped to the ground, stretching her full length. She didn't bother to stifle her groans. Glaring at him, she declared, "I'm dying. Without a doubt, I'm not long for this world."

He propped on one elbow beside her, his laughter echoing around them.

Even the horses thought she was funny. "Listen at them. They're laughing at me too."

"Not at you, with you."

"Do you hear me laughing?" Megan demanded and then answered herself. "No, you don't."

"I can't imagine why you didn't have riding lessons at your boarding school."

"The school was in the middle of town," she replied. "Concrete, not wide-open spaces."

Megan relaxed, only to sit upright when Jed brushed his lips across hers. She glanced at him from the corner of her eye. She'd thought she had discouraged kissing when he drove her home from the farm the other night. She must set him straight. His eyes defeated her purpose. She'd seen them icy too many times to count, but at other times, they twinkled. Now they were deep as a whirlpool. After a moment in their depth, Megan pulled her gaze away and stood.

Jed sat for an instant longer before he whistled for their mounts, which had found nearby clumps of tall grass.

Megan eyed them with disfavor. "I'd rather walk back."

"Too far. Besides, you need to ride some more."

She sat a little easier in the saddle but still gripped the reins.

"I hope you realize you're a natural on horseback, Megan." Jed helped her from the saddle when they reached the stable, holding her arms until she could straighten her legs. "I'll drive you home after we tell Mom hello."

The quick hello extended to half an hour with glasses of iced tea. When Jed helped her from the Bronco at her own front door, he advised a long, hot bath.

"Your muscles will be sore, but the solution is another ride first thing in the morning."

"I open the store at nine!"

"I'll be here at seven with both horses. We'll ride long enough to remind your muscles you're in control."

"Huh! They know better. Okay. If I must. However, I'm not sure I can trust you on this, Jed Anderson. Are you certain you aren't simply tormenting me?"

"Now would I do such a thing?"

"Yes, you would."

The crinkles at the corners of his eyes deepened. "I'll see you in the morning."

Trudging up the steps, Megan rubbed her aching derrière. Her muscles screamed. She smelled horsey, which was even worse than smelling like a jailbird. She stripped to the skin and put the reeking clothes into the washing machine, setting it for automatic soak. During a rose-scented bath, the apparition's visit popped into her mind. She hadn't thought to tell Jed. Megan wasn't sure she should. He'd think she was crazy. She shifted her aching body. He might be right.

The ringing phone forced Megan from the now tepid water. Not midnight, so not Jed. Fran maybe. Wrapped in a toweling robe, she said hello and listened in surprise. She had not expected a call from her grandmother's housekeeper.

"Megan, I need some advice. I don't know how to reach your parents, so I called you."

"I don't know how to reach them either, Mrs. Rice. I'll help if I can, though. What's the problem?"

"Many years ago, your grandmother stored a box of her belongings in my storage locker."

"I see. You didn't tell the FBI agents. Have you called Grandmother's attorney? The box is part of her estate."

"No, I haven't. Steve Penland would forget his name if his wife didn't sew a label in his jackets."

Megan chuckled. She'd already experienced Mr. Penland's forgetfulness.

"Your grandmother told me the box contained old picture albums from her young days. I thought your mother might want them."

Megan almost laughed at the idea. "She might, but I know I do. Ship the box by UPS."

"You don't think I should call the FBI? I don't know why I should, though. They weren't polite, wouldn't even tell me why they were searching the house. I called the local cops before I let them into the house." She chuckled. "Bet those agents didn't like standing outside during the drizzle until the detectives came."

Now Megan understood. Mrs. Rice always had to know everything which happened in Grandmother's house. "No, I'll contact the FBI, if necessary, after I've looked at the albums."

They chatted a couple more minutes before Megan cradled the phone. There were pictures of her grandparents in their young years, perhaps some of Grandmother's sister Eva, the possible terrorist still wreaking havoc around the world.

Chapter 13

Dancing the Night Away

When Jed rang Megan's doorbell the following morning, he wondered if she'd send him on his way with some choice words about his character. Would he go? No way. He was ready to pour honey until she agreed. Persuasion wasn't necessary. Dressed in jeans and long-sleeved shirt, she opened the door on the first ring.

"You're a beast," Megan accused him, while he led horses from the trailer attached to his truck. "I can hardly walk straight."

"Your muscles will stop protesting after a few rides. Now, into the saddle you go."

Half an hour later, Jed helped her from the saddle, holding her upper arms until she stood upright. They had spoken very little, but Jed had kept an eye on her. Her back was straight. She even held her chin high, just as she ought when in the saddle. Promising.

"Do I get invited to breakfast?" Was he pushing her too far?

"Not if you expect me to cook. My intention is a long, hot bath. You can do what you please."

"Great idea. I'll get in the tub with you."

"Oh, no, you won't."

"Aw shucks! Then, I suppose I'll cook breakfast for us. Be ready to pull yourself out by the time I get bacon fried and eggs scrambled. You do have some?"

Megan pointed toward the kitchen. "I want my bacon crisp, one egg soft boiled, and one slice of wheat toast. Buttered. There's orange marmalade too or strawberry preserves, if you'd rather have them."

"Aye, aye, Ma'am." He gave her a mock salute before turning away, hiding his grin.

With breakfast finished, Jed walked her out to her car. "Feel any better?"

"The soreness has eased some."

"For a novice, you have the best seat on a horse I've ever seen. Perfect balance. I admit surprise."

"I took ballet from age five and started ballroom dancing in my early teens. They might account for my posture."

He eyed her. Was she too big city to dance with a farmer? Another Jasmine? He wouldn't know until he asked. "You must be an expert. If I promise not to step on your toes, will you come dancing with me?"

"Yes!" Megan's answer was prompt. "Is there a place for ballroom dancing around here, or do we drive into Asheville? Or do you mean the line dancing I see on TV? Jeans and boots. I've never learned those."

"No jeans and boots. The Rambling Inn is a few miles out the highway. They hire a big band from Knoxville on weekends. Good musicians. I'll see you this week for more riding lessons, but do we have a date for this Saturday?"

"Providing I can still walk."

Jed watched Megan drive away before he guided the horses into their trailer and set out for home.

After a couple more morning lessons, Megan's independent streak asserted itself. Jed had known it would happen, just not so soon. She insisted the lessons must stop. Jed objected. She needed more lessons. Megan was adamant. She must gather her wits for the day's work but maybe later, Megan conceded. Against his inclinations, he'd agreed.

ﬡﬡﬡﬡﬡ

Megan had a hectic week at the store. She questioned everybody and compiled a list of new stock, noting what didn't sell. Between seven and nine each evening, the ladies who had volunteered to demonstrate their craft abilities welcomed all comers. Megan watched but didn't think she'd ever be adept at needlework. She might learn flower arranging, if she ever had her own plants.

Flowers came up at lunch on Thursday. Megan and Fran couldn't get their favorite back booth in the crowded diner, so they sat at a table near the middle.

"How are your flowerbeds coming along?" Fran asked

"Slowly. On Sunday, I pulled most of the weeds from the one nearest the road, but I had to stop. Poison ivy on my hands, despite the smelly bleach Jed insisted I use."

"You didn't wear gloves, but I trust you have some now?"

"Oh, yes, I went by the garden center. Bought a dozen pairs."

"That ought to do you for a while."

Megan ignored Fran's chuckle. "I'll replace the ragged shrubs out back with flowers. Do you know what grows in shade?"

"No. I admit to an abysmal ignorance of growing flowers. As you've seen, only boxwood shrubs surround my house. The man at the garden center can tell you."

"Who would I ask about digging up the shrubs?"

"I don't know, but, again, you can ask at the garden center. Or perhaps Jed would know."

"He might."

Leaving the diner, Megan bumped against a table. "Oh, please excuse my clumsiness," she told the bent head, which nodded. She turned toward her store, thinking over the incident. He hadn't even looked at her, yet she felt . . . what? Dislike? No. Antagonism.

His vibes screamed antagonism. She forgot him when she busied herself straightening yarn skeins.

On Saturday evening, Megan studied her mirror reflection. The forest green dress with rhinestone choker collar brought out the green flecks in her hazel eyes and left her shoulders bare. The full skirt ended at her knees, leaving considerable legs showing above the nude strappy sandals. Megan couldn't believe she had a date. Not just dinner, either. A real date. The first since . . . . She hurried down the stairs when the doorbell rang.

When she opened the door, Megan swallowed her surprise. Tailored suit and tie. "Don't you clean up nicely."

He winked, after a casual glance at her. "Wow! is all I can say!"

Megan grinned and locked the door after them.

"If I continue to escort a beautiful lady, I'll need a car that will do her justice," Jed commented, turning the Bronco's ignition key.

"I have no problem with this one." Dear heaven, what was she getting herself into? Their friendship was casual. One date for dancing, nothing more. Megan changed the subject to his mother.

"She sent her regards. Also ordered me to be on my best behavior. As if I were not always." Ignoring her raised eyebrows, he asked about her day.

She couldn't contain herself. "Oh, Jed, the store is a success; I know it is! I even show a profit for the week, although I placed extra orders."

"I'm glad this store is successful."

Looking around the inn, Megan ignored the covert glances in her direction but nodded at the few people she recognized. "I see Catherine Crawford is here with Mike Williams."

"Do you know him?"

She couldn't discuss the terrorism issue, although Jed knew she'd been in jail, even if he didn't know why. "Not really. I just know who he is. I believe he's an incomer like me."

"From Atlanta. He doesn't talk about it, but my friend who lives there said Mike left the city after his wife's murder."

"How terrible. Did they catch whoever killed her?"

"The last I heard, no. I'm sure they're still working on it. Cop's wife, you know."

Before she could reply, a redhaired waitress came for their orders.

Megan glanced at Jed's hair. "So much red hair—hostess and waitress—family?"

"Cousins. Gail is Marj's daughter, but don't call their hair red. I did once. Gail gave me a bloody nose. We were about six. She might be more lethal now." Jed pushed back from the table. "This music is too good to waste while we wait for our food."

She hadn't been dancing since leaving Detroit and hadn't realized how much she'd missed it. Megan marveled at how well their steps fit together when they glided into a smooth foxtrot.

Conversation dwindled when a singer approached the microphone. He did well with Frank Sinatra songs, ending with *Autumn in New York*.

"That song always makes me homesick for New York," Megan confessed.

"How long since you were there?"

"Never."

He stared at her. "Let me get this straight. You've never been there, yet *Autumn in New York* makes you homesick for New York."

She laughed aloud at his expression. "Weird, huh?"

"You think? Perhaps you should go at least once so your homesickness will be legitimate. As Fred Astaire said in one of his films, shall we dance?" A foxtrot merged into a faster two-step, slowed for a waltz, and then the band broke into a tango. Within seconds, they had the floor to themselves. Megan marveled anew at their perfect harmony. They were barely breathing hard when the music stopped. Megan smiled when they acknowledged the applause.

"I told you I'd had dance lessons, so why didn't you tell me you'd studied too?"

"At Mom's insistence—and over my vehement protests—I took lessons for five years in grade school. I think she was sorry for the dance instructor, who was struggling to make ends meet. The whole idea embarrassed me silly at the time, but I've thanked Mom many times over since."

Their conversation stopped when Mike brought Catherine to their table.

"Jed, can we change partners?"

"Sure." He rose and led Catherine onto the dance floor. Mike followed with Megan.

"I hope the band plays something sedate," Mike said. "I leave tangos to Jed. Ah, good, a waltz." He told her he'd heard nothing from the FBI. The terrorist with her face had disappeared again.

Megan lost herself in the music. They danced well together. The two men were the same height, yet their steps didn't blend, Megan realized, not the way hers did with Jed.

They were quiet on the way home, but it was a comfortable silence. When they reached her house, Jed took the key from her hand to unlock the door.

"I really enjoyed myself, Jed. Care for a nightcap?"

"Not that," he replied. He stepped inside and closed the door behind them. "This." Gathering her in his arms, he leaned against the door, studying her face in the faint moonlight, which spilled through windows.

Megan forced herself not to stiffen but to breathe easily, allowing her hands to rest on his upper arms.

"The stars don't shine any brighter than your eyes," he murmured and captured her lips in a brief kiss, which deepened with her faint response.

Jed released her lips, setting her upright away from him. Opening the door, he murmured, "I'd better leave before I overstay my welcome."

After Megan bolted the door, she stood in the darkness until the Bronco's motor faded into the distance. Would she ever kiss Jed, or any man, without remembering David?

ꙮ ꙮ ꙮ ꙮ ꙮ

After lunch on Sunday, Megan pulled on her new gardening gloves and started weeding another flowerbed. She was almost finished when nearby movement caught her eye. Glancing sideways, she stood. When she backed away, the apparition followed.

I am not crazy. I am not seeing things that are not here. I am not scared of whatever this is, either, even if the thing is a terrorist. I would rather believe it's Grandmother.

"I'm getting the beds ready for flowers. Do you think I'll ever succeed in growing anything?"

The apparition floated to the backyard, beckoning Megan. Again, she hovered near the hedge, pointing downward, then upward.

"I believe you're telling me to dig up the shrubs. I don't understand why—they're not so terribly ugly—but I will."

The figure swayed and faded away.

Megan stared at the spot, more shaken than she wanted to admit. The conversation, one-sided though it was, disturbed her. More than disturbed—irritated her that a ghost could order her around. She needed intelligent conversation with someone about this apparition. Megan considered her options.

Josh Crawford bragged about knowing everything about everybody who ever lived in *his* town, so he was her logical choice. She wondered whether he sat on his bench in the square on Sunday afternoon. One way to find out. She would need a photograph. Now was the time to open the box from Mrs. Rice, which arrived at the store earlier and occupied her car trunk.

Searching through the top album, Megan found a snapshot of the twins. They did look like her, identical facial features, but they had longer hair. One of them wore the same dress as the apparition. Her throat tightened. Coincidence? She wondered again if her moving here had energized a dormant spirit. Tucking the photograph into her pocket, she headed to town.

Megan battled the idea of dormant spirits, scoffing but believing when the apparition wouldn't go away. When she neared the square, she spotted the old man sitting under his elm tree.

"Afternoon, Megan Stanfield. What brings you into town? Not going to open your store, are you? Won't be any business, you know."

"I came to see you."

"Set yourself down. I always did like the company of pretty girls."

"I'll bet there were plenty of them too, you silver-tongued devil!" Megan joined him on the bench. "I wonder something about my family. Could you tell the twins apart?"

"Of course. Most people could, although not by their appearance. They were identical, but their actions were different."

Megan pulled the snapshot from her pocket. "Which is which?"

Squinting at the picture, he tapped one image with his finger. "This one is your grandmother, this one in the solid color dress. The one in the print dress is your Great-aunt Eva."

"You're sure?" Megan studied the picture. "I can't see any difference between them."

"You would if you'd known them. Alma was a real ham. Posed like movie stars every time anyone pointed a camera at her. Eva was the opposite. She stayed out of pictures, if she could. When she couldn't, she looked off to one side. Never failed. The only time Eva seemed at ease was when she was on a horse. Rode better than most men I've known."

"I see." However, she didn't. Definite identification didn't explain either the repeated manifestations or why it visited Megan.

"There's something bothering you, girl. Best tell me."

Megan paused, debating how to tell him without exposing herself to ridicule. "Do you believe ghosts walk among us?"

"I never saw one. I've felt the presence of people who have gone on, though. I wish I could see my Janie." He sounded so wistful Megan squeezed his hand.

"I've seen one. Twice. The same one." Megan discounted the earlier sightings because they didn't have a discernible face. They could have been tricks of light, even if she didn't believe it. "I thought my grandmother came to see me, but the apparition wears the print dress, which you say is Eva. The ghost looks exactly like the picture, the forties style dress and hairstyle."

"Oh, you can't go by the different dresses. They grew up during the Great Depression when money was tight. They wore each other's clothes. I identified her by the way she avoided the camera. Seems to me if the ghost were your grandmother, she would wear today's style."

"I hadn't thought of that. Why would Eva visit me? I can understand my grandmother might come, but why would Eva?"

"Good question. Tell me more. Maybe I can figure it out."

Megan wasn't sure she wanted to open herself to scorn or amusement, which would be even worse. However, she needed an answer for her own peace of mind, so she told the story from feeling someone's presence through both manifestations. She fell silent while the old man cogitated. She smiled at her thought. Most people would *think*. Josh Crawford cogitated.

"Their father gave me summer work throughout my teens. I helped him plant the hedge. Lilacs. He first considered extending the rose garden, which grew along the side of the yard."

"There aren't any roses there now." Megan didn't want to think about roses. Too many memories.

"No, one of the later owners pulled them up, declaring roses require too much work."

"I apologize for interrupting. Go on with your story."

"I remember the time because he was upset Alma was going to Detroit. And only a day or so later, Eva eloped. He wasn't the same man after both his daughters left home."

"The shrubs are not in good shape now. Could Eva be giving me some guidance on plants? I don't know anything about them, but how would she know?"

"Neither did she, if I remember correctly, except her African violets. Alma sneaked them into competition at the county fair one year. I don't know which girl was the most surprised when they won a blue ribbon. I always thought Alma entered the plant out of aggravation.

Maybe I wronged her. Anyhow, neither Alma nor Eva paid any attention to the yard. Well, the only thing I can say is you should take up the hedge. See if that satisfies Eva."

"The hedge is quite large."

"Ask your young man to do it for you," he said with a sly wink.

Megan felt her face heat. "I suppose you mean Jed. He isn't my young man. I'll ask him though."

"I have eyes, girl," he answered but changed the subject. "How do you like small town life after living all your life in a big city?"

"I love living here. I can't get enough of these mountains, the leaves turning into gorgeous vistas. People are friendly since they got over their initial standoffishness, which I suppose was natural."

"I noticed Jed Anderson got over his unfriendliness fast enough. Dancing last night, no less."

"News travels fast in small towns. I haven't had experience with grapevines, but I'll learn."

"Small town life will grow on you."

Megan stood. "I'd better get on back home. Thanks for talking to me."

He waved his pipe toward her. "Anytime, girl, anytime. I enjoy remembering the old days. Maybe you'll invite me out to see the picture albums one day."

"Oh, yes. Sunday afternoon? If you'll tell me what you eat, I'll take you home with me after church. You can spend the afternoon with me."

"I don't eat raw vegetables or fruit anymore, but I can manage almost anything else."

"We have a date!"

"Imagine! Me with a date at my age."

She laughed and strolled away.

They'd had a good visit, except for Josh Crawford's comment about Jed. Her young man? Preposterous!

She didn't want to ask Jed to deal with the hedge—didn't want to feel obligated to him. That's what it boiled down to, and she knew she would. Feel obligated, that is.

She switched her thoughts away from Jed to her grandmother. According to Mr. Crawford, she'd been ready for any kind of mischief throughout childhood. Could that tendency have led to terrorism in later years? The FBI agent had mentioned worldwide, and her grandmother had traveled all over the world. No, wait a minute. The terrorism started in Italy, and she didn't travel there. When Megan had asked her why, she'd said it was because the men pinched women's bottoms.

Megan laughed aloud. She hadn't thought of that in years. That must be the reason her mother didn't travel there too, because she wouldn't want to be pinched either. Thinking her grandmother might be a terrorist was almost as fanciful as thinking her backyard visitor might be.

She shivered when gusty wind swirled around her, blowing leaves across the road. The sunny sky had turned metallic gray while she talked with Mr. Crawford. In the west, heavy black clouds hid the tops of the mountain ranges.

Electricity filled the air; flickering blue light lit the sky. Megan quickened her pace as thunder rolled in the distance. Not fear—she simply didn't like loud noise. Besides, thunder always brought trouble. What would it be this time?

She soon found out.

Chapter 14

Threats

Trembling with every thunder roll, Megan jogged home under occasional flashes of lightning. With one foot on asphalt for guidance, one on the gravel shoulder for safety, she regretted she'd walked into town earlier. She shouldn't have trusted the innocent-looking clouds drifting in the western sky.

A single light barreled toward her, casting a wavering beam across the road. Megan threw herself sideways into the shallow ditch as a motorcycle sped by. Terror gripped her, until the roar faded into the distance. She lay still, watching for the light to come back, until rain started pelting her. She pulled herself upright and peered toward town. No light. Her first step landed her back in the ditch onto now soggy leaves.

She hobbled home under heavy rain.

Thunder always brought trouble.

Megan limped from her car to the diner the next morning. An ice pack on her ankle wasn't comfortable for sleeping, but the pain had eased. Aspirin had done its job too, so she could manage work if she spent most of the day on the stool behind the cash register.

"What happened?" Fran demanded, when Megan joined her for breakfast.

"I dodged a motorcycle last night and ended in a ditch. Sprained my ankle; already better this morning."

"Motorcycle? Where?"

Fran's urgency surprised Megan. "Half mile from home."

"Mike needs to know."

"The police? Why? The biker didn't hit me."

"A kid died last night when he wrecked somebody's motorcycle out in your direction. A good boy by all accounts, on the middle-school honor roll, had never caused his parents any trouble. They believe he found the bike unattended so had gone for a ride. Thirteen years old."

"Joyriding," Jed said, sliding into the booth next to Megan. "Happens too often, although rarely with lethal results."

"Did you? Go joyriding, I mean," Megan asked.

"Once. Dad tanned my hide. Only time he ever laid a hand on me. Humiliating for a fifteen-year-old. Taught me a lesson though."

"Maybe the boy's death will save some other teens."

Megan broke the silence, which followed the others' murmured agreement. Now or never, she decided. "Would you do some digging at my house sometime soon?"

"What kind of digging?" he asked.

"The hedge across the backyard."

"The whole thing? Must be a hundred feet at least!"

"I believe just one end needs moving. The right-hand end as you face the hedge."

"Maybe the owner won't want anyone changing his property."

"Don't sound so hopeful! I called him this morning. He doesn't care, provided someone else does the work. I have the impression he doesn't care what I do. He just wants the rent on time."

"Okay. How soon do you want it done? Digging will be easier if we get more rain."

"Anytime in the next week or so. I want to get the bulbs planted before the ground freezes. We're already well into October."

"Winter comes later here than up North. I plant my mother's bulbs near Thanksgiving or even later, depending on fall weather."

"Then, there's more time than I realized. Even so, I'm so slow with weeding, I'm not sure I'll get everything done."

"You'll manage," he assured her. "One way or another."

"If necessary, I'll call on you!"

ɾʋɾʋɾʋɾʋɾʋ

He hunkered down in his faded denim jacket, listening to the conversation behind him. The woman's voice wasn't familiar, too deep. Her hair was all wrong too. Well, not completely. The right color, but too short. He swallowed the last of his coffee and left the diner. His temples throbbed. He could ask somebody who she is. No, questions would reveal his curiosity, arouse suspicions. He had reached a decision. He couldn't stand the tug of war going on in his head any longer. Her fault. No woman, no headaches, his life normal again. Pondering the situation, he wandered across the square. With a sudden spurt of energy, he realized how he could learn her name and where she lived.

ɾʋɾʋɾʋɾʋɾʋ

The phone rang but stopped before Megan reached it. She shrugged and went back to her John Sherwood book. Probably wrong number anyway, because she received few calls. Half an hour later, the phone rang again. This time Megan answered on the third ring.

"Hello?"

"Leave Crawfordville before it's too late."

Megan sat in numb silence, staring at the phone, which rang twice more before midnight. Grabbing it each time, she heard only breathing. Her heart pounding, Megan lay awake for another hour, waiting for more calls. None came. She woke when the alarm went off at seven.

The day passed quietly: enough customers to keep her mind busy without too many clamoring for attention at one time. Most important, there had been only one phone call, ending when she answered. Wrong number, Megan assured herself.

She closed the store early and settled at Deborah's shampoo station, sighing with relief. She couldn't think of anything more soothing than getting her hair done.

"That sigh tells me you've had a bad day," the hairdresser sympathized.

Megan forgot she wasn't going to mention her disturbance the previous night. "I didn't sleep well. Crank caller. I had forgotten how aggravating those calls are since I left the city. I didn't expect small towns would present the same predicament."

"Obscene or just obnoxious?"

"Obnoxious. Mostly let the phone ring once or twice." Megan tried to relax while Deborah's strong fingers kneaded her scalp. The massage didn't help, but maybe talk would take her mind off the calls. "Do you take part in the Fall Festival?"

"I don't do anything except have fun."

Deborah rambled on about other fall festivals, while she wielded the blow dryer.

"Looks great," Megan congratulated her. "I'll call you again." She walked out into the early twilight from the warmth of Deborah's shop to the chill of her own worries.

Reaching home, Megan braked at her mailbox. She seldom had mail forwarded from Detroit, but she had better look anyway. She recoiled when she opened the box. What was that stinking thing? She closed the box and stared at it before climbing back into the car. What now? She should get rid of it. Obvious. How? Jed.

Farmers would know. She dug into her purse for her smart phone but put it back. Useless because she didn't remember his number. She drove on to the house for the phone directory.

"Jed? There's something furry in my mailbox. Something dead."

"Well, I've heard of dead letter offices but never dead letter mail boxes."

"Jed, stop horsing around. I'm serious. There's a stinking, dead animal in my mailbox."

"I'll be right over."

She waited on the steps until he arrived half an hour later. She didn't know which was worse, her throbbing ankle or the thoughts hammering her head. Somebody was after her—a sick somebody. The phone caller had been a man. Maybe. She was no longer sure. When Jed pulled into the driveway, she pointed at the box, keeping her distance.

Jed pulled on some gloves and recoiled when he opened the box. "Stinks, alright."

"I noticed."

Sticking his hand into the box, he pulled out the stiff carcass of a squirrel, its head crushed almost flat. Jed pulled a shovel from the truck's toolbox and proceeded to dig a hole several feet from the driveway.

"Is that the right place to bury an animal?"

"Nobody will know unless we tell them. Won't look like a grave when I finish." He finished the job, stomped the mound flat and placed a rock on it, scattering dead leaves around the area. "Looks natural. What do you think?"

Megan nodded. She felt sick, apprehensive. She should be safe in this small town. Those phone calls last night had unnerved her. Now this. Someone was stalking her. She shivered. "Who could have done this?"

Jed shrugged. "Handle dead squirrels? Probably schoolboys kicking up a lark."

"I don't think so after the phone calls last night."

"What calls?"

After Megan explained, he asked, "Is the voice familiar, one you might have heard without its registering?"

"I can't be sure. Man? Woman? I don't know. The voice sounded muffled—deep though."

"Who would want to run you out of town, for Pete's sake? Are you sure you understood him?"

She didn't hesitate. "Answering your questions in order, you are the only person who has tried to get rid of me. No, I'm not sure any longer about anything. I do know I felt threatened at the calls. This dead squirrel makes everything worse."

A stunned expression crossed Jed's face. His voice turned icy. "You can't think I would kill an innocent animal." He shot her a furious look, folded his legs into the truck, and scattered gravel as he roared away.

One thought drummed in Megan's head. Jed didn't deny he'd tried to make her leave town. Could he be her tormentor? She didn't want to believe he was so devious. Had he been friendly just to disarm her? She didn't want to believe that either.

The stench from the squirrel lingered, even seemed to penetrate her clothing. She took a quick shower. She should eat. The mere thought gagged her, but she must. Yogurt with fruit she ate at noon didn't last.

Megan swallowed the last bite of dry toast and hesitated but answered the ringing phone.

"Hello?"

"You should've left town when I told you."

Chapter 15

Nightmares

Megan studied her bleary eyes in the mirror. She couldn't let anyone see her like this. She looked like she'd been on an all-night bender when nightmares were the culprit: squirrels dancing around her while Jed urged them on.

She would take up Sally on her promise to work in the shop anytime. Thankful the real estate office had a key, Megan phoned her.

In the cold light of day, her thoughts centered on Jed. Last night, she'd almost convinced herself he wasn't harassing her. She couldn't reconcile the Jed she was coming to know with someone callous enough to kill helpless animals. Yet phone calls came too pat, exactly half an hour after he left—the time Jed needed to reach home. Who else could it be? Someone who . . . who what? Believed she was a terrorist? Even the FBI agent from Asheville was above such antics. Must be Jed.

To take her mind off him, Megan did something she'd planned as soon as she got out of jail. She fired up her laptop. Terrorism. Women. 1940s. 1950s, . . . this year. Mysterious face. She found hers. Two hours later, eyes burning from the computer glare, she shut the laptop. So much information. Her face on every site she clicked. Why had she never heard of this—these— terrorists?

Pulling on jeans and sweatshirt, Megan tugged on gloves, as she went out into cool morning air. Weeding might stop her useless thoughts.

Megan twisted around when flapping sounds drew her attention. The solemn-faced apparition floated within feet. Was it a permanent part of her life? Megan shuddered at the thought and struggled for her normal voice. In control. Ha! She should be so lucky.

"Good morning, Eva. Mr. Crawford said you are my great-aunt, not my grandmother as I thought. He told me how to tell the difference. I wonder if you remember him. He's a nice old gentleman, but I imagine he was a ripsnorter when he was younger."

Eva beckoned. She didn't go toward the backyard. Instead, she drifted along the driveway where she pointed toward the squirrel's grave.

Megan put her fingers over her lips. "How did you know?"

Eva smiled.

"Do you know who did it?"

This time, Eva floated to the backyard where she pointed at the hedge.

"Jed Anderson promised he will dig them up soon," Megan assured her. "He's waiting until rain softens the ground."

The ghost shook her head and pointed from the road to the shrubs.

Before Megan could speak again, Buddy ambled into the backyard but stopped after a few steps, hair on his neck rising. He growled and stared toward the hedge. Megan glanced from him to the apparition, which hovered there.

"Buddy, hush," Jed ordered. "Megan, I apologize for walking out on you yesterday. I should've held my temper because I could see how upset you were."

She nodded, still gazing at her unearthly visitor.

"I missed you in the diner." Jed touched her arm when she didn't turn toward him. "Sally said you weren't coming in this morning, but she didn't say why. Are you alright?"

"Do you see her?"

"Who?"

"Her." Megan nodded toward the hedge. "I see her, and so does Buddy."

Jed put the back of his hand against her forehead. "You aren't feverish."

Megan jerked away from his touch. "No, she's there. Aunt Eva is right there."

"There's nobody here except you, me, and Buddy." He cupped her elbow. "Let's go inside."

"She's gone now. I'm sorry you didn't see her too. This is the third time Aunt Eva has visited me."

Megan's clipped words fell into silence, broken only by Buddy's snuffling at the hedge. Jed turned toward the steps, tugging her arm. Why couldn't he accept what she said? Typical male, trying to soothe a hysterical female. Megan Elizabeth Stanfield was never hysterical. Furthermore, she would not let him or anyone else treat her as if she were.

Megan glared but followed him into the kitchen. Her temper simmered just below the surface. If Jed Anderson wasn't careful, he might get a taste of her anger before he left. She itched to tear a strip off his hide. She dumped the cold coffee from the carafe. Then, with great concentration, she went through the motions of making a fresh pot. Ground beans. Placed filter in basket. Poured ground coffee into filter. Poured distilled water into well. Pushed button. Only then did she speak, her voice crisp.

"Sit down, Jed. You don't need to hang over me. Aunt Eva hovers enough."

He dropped into a chair beside the table without taking his gaze from her face. Keeping his tone neutral, he said, "You haven't mentioned anyone named Eva. Why does she hover over you? Explain all this, Megan. I'm trying to understand."

"I told you about feeling someone's presence in the backyard," she reminded him. "Mr. Crawford believes she's my grandmother's twin sister. She hovers over those shrubs and insists I move them. At least that's how I interpret her movements."

The only sound for several minutes was the burble of the coffee machine and Buddy's gentle snoring. Sheer determination avoided trembling when she gave Jed a mug filled with strong black coffee. Leaning against the counter, cup cradled in her hands, Megan told him about her encounters with the apparition Mr. Crawford identified as Eva Malloy, her grandmother's twin sister.

"Aunt Eva's visit this morning was different, though. She hovered over the squirrel's grave for a second or two and then went to the backyard and pointed at the hedge. We were there when Buddy saw her. He did, you know. I've heard dogs see ghosts, even when humans can't."

Jed raised skeptical eyebrows.

"I'm not crazy," she said. "Still, this gives you reason to break my lease, right?"

Jed stood so abruptly his chair tilted. "I must get back home. The Golden Delicious apples can't stay on the trees any longer. Call me if anything else happens." He set the chair upright, and, with long strides, he left her standing in the kitchen.

"No, I don't think so," Megan muttered toward his receding back. "I won't give you any ideas to torment me more."

ꛁ ꛁ ꛁ ꛁ ꛁ

Jed jerked his Bronco into gear and scattered gravel when he turned onto the asphalt road, horrified at the idea clamoring for attention. Was Megan losing her marbles? She seemed sincere, but any sane adult knew ghosts—apparitions, whatever you called them—

don't exist. They were the stuff of fairy tales or stories to scare little kids around campfires.

She might have killed the squirrel herself. That thought jolted him as much as the pothole the tire hit. Did she invent the phone calls? She hadn't shown any signs of being irrational before. Hot tempered, yes. Stubborn, yes. Not irrational. Never that. Well, there was her belief that people around here would eat the dried-out stuff she called natural food. She got over that notion, though.

Could an evil being living in the old house have possessed her? Now who's being fanciful? If he didn't believe ghosts exist, how could he believe evil beings do?

Jed mulled over the situation, reaching a decision he considered reasonable. He'd wait to see if Megan persisted in this ridiculous ghost story. As for the phone calls, well, the least thing could scare women living alone. Megan could be imagining the whole thing. Except the squirrel, which he'd seen for himself. He could only hope nothing else turned up dead.

ꝶ ꝶ ꝶ ꝶ ꝶ

Megan's somber mood intensified the following morning. More nightmares, only this time, the apparition had John Patterson's face before turning into a squirrel with the same face. *Her* face. Both had leered at her while Jed laughed.

When she neared her mailbox on the way to work, Megan slammed on the brakes, throwing her against the tightened safety strap. Clutching her sore ribs, she forced herself from the car. After a couple of hesitant steps, she leaned toward a small cross standing next to the rock covering the squirrel's grave. Constructed of popsicle sticks, the cross had MEGAN printed in dull red on the horizontal bar. The paint had run below the letters, like dripping blood.

Dizziness washed over her. Sinking to her knees, Megan pulled up the sticks and flung them away. She swallowed the bile that was about to choke her and beat her fists against her jeans.

Jed. No one else knew about the grave, so he made the phone calls too. There couldn't be two people harassing her, could there? Megan shuddered at the possibility.

Why would he want her out of town now? Maybe her business didn't bring in much money yet, but if she made the agreed-upon lease payments, why would he care? Prompt payment hadn't stopped him before, though. So, maybe her tormentor wasn't Jed. No, she argued, it could only be him. No one else—not the FBI, not the man stalking her, not the Yogurt Raisin Man— knew the squirrel grave existed. Everything came back to the grave. And Jed. Only Jed, no matter how she tried to blame anyone else.

The thought battered Megan's brain throughout the short drive into town. How she passed the day was anybody's guess. She was quiet when she joined Fran and Sally for supper at the diner. They lingered over their fried chicken and chatted about their businesses and the festival until Mattie stared at them.

Megan glanced around the restaurant. They were the only customers still there. She reached for her purse and stood. "I believe Mattie's ready to clean up and go home."

Jed met them outside the door and followed Megan to her car at a fast clip to keep up with her. Leaning down to see her through the window, he said, "Have you seen any more ghosts?"

What was he doing still in town? Probably finding some way to harass her. Megan stared him straight in the face. No way would she let him know he had gotten to her. "Not this evening, at any rate."

He nodded. "I'll follow you home and make sure you get there okay."

"Not necessary." She bit off the words and pulled onto the road, his Bronco on her bumper, its beams shining in her rearview. Didn't he know he was blinding her? Maybe that was his intention.

When Megan arrived home, she bolted the door and hurried upstairs. She could expect a phone call in half an hour.

The phone rang right on schedule.

Megan picked up the receiver with sickening certainty of what she would hear.

"Didn't you like the grave marker?" the muffled voice inquired. "I even spelled your name right. You shouldn't have thrown away the sticks, you know. I worked hard getting the ink to run like blood. Might be your blood next time."

Megan felt heaviness in her chest when she slammed down the phone. Jed had been acting all along. Pretending friendliness, pretending he didn't want her to leave town. Directness hadn't worked, so now he was using this cruel harassment.

ﬡ ﬡ ﬡ ﬡ ﬡ

He stared out the window, his thoughts tumbling over each other. The woman was a harder nut to crack than he'd expected. He had gone to considerable trouble getting her name. Anyone else would have a name on the mailbox, but she didn't. Didn't have any mail either when he'd looked in the box. Maybe she was hiding out from somebody. Cops somewhere else. Mike Williams could have been wrong not arresting her. Turning her loose before properly investigating her. Finally, he'd picked the lock at the real estate office and searched Sally's files until he found her business lease. Megan Stanfield. Her name meant nothing to him. Why did her face cause him to have these horrible headaches? She had to go.

Chapter 16

Who Hates Me So Much?

For Megan, Saturday was a blur of people, balloons, and food. She'd never seen anything like this festival. Between stints at Sally's craft table, she had wandered around other booths. Fran joined her to help Sally pack the few items she hadn't sold. That done, Fran asked if they had plans for the next day. Sally said she needed to check rentals.

"What about you, Megan?"

"I'm bringing Mr. Crawford home for dinner after church. While he's there, we'll look at photograph albums from my grandparents' childhood here in town. The pictures aren't labeled, so I hope he can identify which ones are my relatives."

"He'll enjoy that."

"I will too and learn some town history. Did you have something in mind?"

"Nothing in particular, no."

"I don't suppose he will stay all afternoon, so shall we do something together after he leaves? Maybe we can go out for supper."

"Sounds good. We can have a nice long session of girl talk. It seems like ages since we've talked about anything except festival plans."

"I agree. I'll call you when I get back from taking Mr. Crawford home."

Exhaustion claimed Megan the moment she entered her house after the festival. If she had any phone calls, they didn't wake her, yet she attended church with an unsettled mind.

After the service, she smiled when Mr. Crawford tucked her hand into the crook of his arm and told everyone within earshot that he had a date with this beautiful lady. He got a few laughs and sly remarks, all in good fun, of course. She winked and blew a kiss to the crowd.

"I haven't been out your way in a while, so don't hurry. I want to see everything."

Megan inched the car along, listening while he talked about who had lived in each house through the years. He asked her to stop near a huge beech tree.

He gazed past her at a large white house, visible through leafless trees. "My Janie lived there. People said I was too old for her, but we were happy together until she passed away. Okay, you can drive on now."

Megan didn't rouse him from his memories until she turned into her driveway. "Here we are, Mr. Crawford."

"I wish you'd call me Uncle Josh."

"Thanks. I would like that. You remind me so much of my granddad. Has this place changed much since my grandmother lived here?"

"The trees are bigger, as you would expect." He stopped when they stepped into the kitchen. "This is different. This had been three rooms: kitchen, dining room, and your great grandmother's sewing room. Pantry through that door."

"The pantry is still there. Jed said Mrs. Caddell had the walls taken out leaving the beams for support."

"She was a newcomer in the area—brought lots of ideas with her. This was one. I wonder why nobody told me."

His peeved tone amused Megan. He prided himself on knowing everything that happened in *his* town. Megan settled him on the sofa next to a table covered with photo albums. "You look at these while I finish dinner."

"Hmmm, do I smell yeast rolls?"

"You sure do." Megan busied herself with trout filets broiled with a lemon-butter sauce, oven-roasted potatoes, steamed asparagus, and apples stewed with cinnamon.

Mr. Crawford did full justice to his meal and dozed while Megan cleared the table. Afterward, she listened while he pointed out which people were her ancestors. Even after all this time, he remembered everybody in every picture. She labeled each picture, knowing she would never remember who held what spot in her lineage.

He closed the last album with a sigh. "Brought back old memories. I had better get back home, but first, let's go out back where Eva visits you. Maybe she'll come while I'm here."

On the back porch, Megan glanced toward the hedge. "I've never tried to reach her. She always approaches me. This whole thing is her idea, though, so she might accommodate us. Aunt Eva, are you here?"

"Is she?"

His eagerness caused Megan to stare with impatience at the hedge until a shifting vapor formed into a shimmering shape and became recognizable as a woman.

"Yes, there she is. Hi, Aunt Eva, look who I brought to visit you."

Uncle Josh peered toward the shrubs. "Eva, I know you're the shyest thing in nature, but you should show yourself for old times' sake!"

"She's shaking her head *no*. Laughing at you too, Uncle Josh."

"Laughing, huh," he grumbled albeit with a grin.

"'Bye, Aunt Eva," Megan called as her ancestor faded from sight. Strolling beside Uncle Josh toward the car, Megan thanked him for coming. "You've given me a better understanding of my ancestors. Your memory is beyond belief."

Uncle Josh roused himself from a light sleep when they reached town and directed her to an old house on the outskirts. He told her he'd lived there for more than half his life. "I'd invite you in, but I'd be poor company until after I have a proper nap."

"I'll look forward to it some other time." She kissed his lined cheek.

After calling Fran, Megan sat cross-legged on the ground, weeds piled beside her, when Fran pulled into the driveway.

Fran glanced around the yard. "You're making real progress. Your diligence makes me tired, though, so stop."

Megan stood. "You're lazy. Come see the back."

Strolling around the corner of the house, Megan looked toward the hedge. Eva wasn't there.

"The garden center people will send someone with a blower one day this week. He'll turn some leaves into mulch and cart the rest away."

"You sound more like a farmer every day. Where are the shrubs Jed will dig for you?"

"Across the back yard." Megan gasped. The foggy substance was taking shape again.

"Why are you staring toward the hedge?"

"I don't suppose you can see her either."

"There's nobody here except us."

Megan ignored her. Now she must explain again—should've kept her mouth shut. She couldn't ignore the apparition, though. "Hello again, Aunt Eva. This is Fran Riddle. You probably knew her ancestors."

Fran's mouth gaped open. "When did you start talking to hedges? Does this one answer you?"

"Good-bye, Aunt Eva. Come see me again anytime." Megan's smile faded when the apparition disappeared. "I'm sure you think I'm either crazy or hallucinating."

"I don't know what I think, but will you please explain before I lose what little sense I have?"

"Come inside. We'll have coffee while I tell you a strange story."

"Make it strong. Something tells me I will need excessive caffeine."

Half an hour later, Megan sat back in her chair, exhausted. She doubted Fran would believe all this craziness any more than Jed had.

"Now I understand why you want those shrubs removed. You're doing what she wants."

"Yes."

Fran sipped coffee, eyeing Megan over the cup rim. "You've never given me any reason not to believe you. I must say, though, ghosts are a bit too much to swallow."

"You think I'm crazy too."

"Somebody else knows this?"

"Jed."

"That explains something."

"What?"

"You've changed toward him during the last few days, although he doesn't notice."

"Or pretends he doesn't."

"Okay, tell me why you think that."

After a moment of silence, Megan forced out the words. "He's still trying to make me leave town. Go back north."

Fran shook her head like dogs shedding water. "No, that can't be true. Jed has shown more interest in you than any female since he fell in love with Judy White when he was ten and she was a worldly twelve. No, I'm sure you're interpreting something wrong. Tell me why you think so."

Megan told her about phone calls, squirrel, and grave marker.

"Everything adds up, you see. The phone calls come half an hour after he leaves, which is exactly how long the drive is to the farm from here. My tormentor can't be anyone except Jed, because no one else knows about the squirrel grave. That's the bottom line, Fran."

"These actions don't add up, Megan. They're secretive, sick even. Jed would never behave this way. Besides, I've seen him looking at you when you were unaware. He's head-over-heels, although he might not realize he is."

Megan had no answer.

"What do you plan to do?"

"Ignore him. No matter how you rationalize everything, I still believe he wants me gone—anywhere except here. I won't leave. I've made this my home, not only because my ancestors lived here. I'm comfortable, have a prosperous business. I'm making friends, so here I stay."

ﬡ ﬡ ﬡ ﬡ ﬡ

"Whoever did this should be hanged by his toes and skinned alive. I volunteer for the job," Jed announced through clenched teeth.

Megan stood beside Mike Williams in the doorway of This 'n That surveying the wreckage.

The police chief had called her shortly after dawn with the news someone had forced open the back door of her shop. Her throat muscles tightened while she fought her heaving stomach. Smashed collectibles, ripped cards, torn wrapping paper, and scattered puzzles littered the floor. Yarn racks lay on their sides. Even at that distance, she could see the paper labels were off the skeins, and some skeins trailed long, loose strands.

Megan hadn't known Jed was there until he volunteered his services.

Bewildered, she asked, "What have I done to justify all these things happening? Do I deserve this much hatred?"

"*These* things?" Mike asked. "Do you mean there've been incidents you haven't reported?"

"Not vandalism, no, just crank calls, a dead squirrel in my mail box."

"This might add to your woes. Should you check the computer?"

"Oh, dear heaven, Mike. I hadn't thought about the office."

They picked their way through the mess to the small room. Tapping keys, she murmured, "Everything looks good so far."

She checked through spreadsheets, order forms, memos. "I don't see any problems."

"Do you have a safe?"

"Sure, but I don't see how anyone could open it without knowing the combination, unless professional safe-crackers live around here." Nevertheless, Megan twisted the dial and then shifted through papers and money. "There's nothing missing, so all the damage is out there."

With one last look around the store, Mike said, "Let's leave the fingerprint men to do their job. We'll go into your situation further at headquarters. There's more happening than I realized."

They huddled under umbrellas, as they sloshed across the square in rain which hadn't let up all night. An hour later, Megan shifted in the hard, plastic chair. She'd repeated every detail of her recent problems that she could remember and answered every question Mike asked. Now she felt numb all over, not just her derrière.

"Kids getting their jollies come to mind for the phone calls but not killing the squirrel. Vandalism without obvious theft doesn't fit, either."

"If you don't need anything further from me, Mike, I'd better go deal with the mess."

"There's one more thing, Megan. Has anyone suggested you leave town? To your face, I mean."

She hesitated, truth batting against her lips. There was no point in muddying the waters. "No, Mike, no one. People were standoffish at first, maybe because they didn't know me."

Mike jotted one last note. "I'll call you."

"Okay if I start cleaning up?"

"Yes, if the fingerprint men have finished. Oh, one more thing, Megan. Your face showed up on street cameras just before a building exploded somewhere in Colombia. No report yet on deaths, if any."

Megan flinched. "So, my problems are miniscule by comparison."

Rain had slackened, but they still huddled under Jed's huge umbrella as they walked back to the store.

"Just thinking about cleaning up the mess is too daunting for words. Perhaps I should just sweep out the store, call it quits."

"You'll do no such thing, Megan Stanfield, so don't even think it. Since when have you been a quitter?"

"Never, until now." What game was he playing? For weeks, Jed had made clear he wanted her gone, away from *his* town. Now, when she suggests leaving, he insists she stay.

"You're not now, either. I can't do anything on the farm in this rain, so I'll help. We'll have your store restored before day's end."

They found Fran and Sally sheltering in the doorway. The fingerprint men had locked up when they left.

When Fran held out her arms, Megan clung to her. "How soon can we start cleaning?"

"Immediately. Jed will help."

"I hate I can't stay—a new clothing shipment from New York—but Sally will."

"Sally has her own work," Megan protested. "The world doesn't stop just because somebody wrecked my business."

"No way can I show property today, so stop your fussing. We have work to do."

The number of people who braved the weather to commiserate or offer help surprised Megan. When the town hall clock struck four, her store was in pristine condition again.

"The destruction wasn't as bad as I thought." Megan surveyed shelves holding several Disney collectibles.

"The person responsible for this put down one layer of items intact and broke some on top, so the destruction looked worse than it was. I don't understand whoever did this." Jed shook his head.

Megan rubbed her temples. "Well, guys, I owe you big time for your help. I'll begin by inviting you to supper tomorrow night. I'm too bushed to do anything except collapse this evening."

"I should think so," Sally said. "Tomorrow is good for me. How about you, Jed?"

"Works for me too."

A threesome might be awkward, so Megan suggested Fran and anyone else they might want.

"Bill Sizemore, perhaps." A slight flush covered Sally's freckled face. "Fran would like it if Jack Kincaid came."

Megan knew about Fran's relationship with Jack, but who is Bill—oh, yes, the rector. "Okay, I'll call them this minute before my brain shuts down."

"You might include Catherine Crawford and Mike Williams too."

"Good thinking, Jed."

Moments later, she announced Bill will come. So will Jack when he finishes his work at the bank, but Catherine has house guests, and Mike will be on duty.

With that settled, Megan said, "My chili is the best this side of Texas, so prepare yourselves for a hot time."

"Do you use tofu or any of that stuff?"

"No, however you wouldn't know it if I did, so there, Jed Anderson!"

On this merry note, they left the store.

಄ ಄ ಄ ಄ ಄

Rolling thunder kept Megan awake. Not more trouble. Please. Hadn't she had enough? Knowing sleep was impossible, she walked the floor, occasionally peeking through the drapes. She'd done too much pacing lately.

In a flash of lightning, she saw two figures standing near the hedge. They disappeared before the next flash. Were they an illusion, or real? A product of her stressed out imagination? Maybe they were ghosts coming after her. Shivering, Megan went downstairs for tea.

Carrying the steaming cup, she wandered through the dim first floor, finally stopping at the window facing the side yard. She backed away when outside movement came closer. The cup clattered from her numb fingers, spilling tea when a gargoyle smile pressed itself against the window.

Megan moved as though in a slow-motion dream, unaware her feet touched the floor. She grasped the baseball bat—a relic from her big city days—from the hall closet. She hurried back toward the window. The face disappeared from her view.

Megan tugged the cord closing the drapes, hurrying the process with her other hand. Shivering with dread, she raced through downstairs rooms, checking door and window locks again.

Was the intruder one of the figures she thought she'd seen earlier? She was almost sure the gargoyle face was human. Could be the man in baggy jeans, who stalks her, or the Yogurt Raisin Man. He'd been near her store throughout the day every time she glanced outside. Were they in collaboration against her?

Jumbled thoughts followed Megan as she blotted the spilled tea with paper towels. She had an almost overwhelming urge to call Jed or Mike but forced herself away from the phone. The man was long gone, so what could they do?

The following evening, Megan placed an absorbent mat near the front door. Rain hadn't stopped all day, curtailing her business, but that was okay considering her depleted stock. Instead of her usual faxed orders, Megan called each vendor who commiserated and assured her she could expect next day delivery.

Her guests would arrive at any minute for chili. It would be nice if they could park their cars on the porch. The ringing doorbell chased away her ludicrous thought. Jed arrived first with Fran hard on his heels.

"Jack said everything is smooth at work, so he'll get here as soon as he shoos everyone out the door. How can I help?"

Before Megan could answer, Sally arrived with Bill, who shed his dripping raincoat with the announcement this was a great day for ducks.

Megan ushered them into the kitchen for some hot, spiced cider.

"Sally told me about the vandalism, Megan. Could Mike give any help?"

"He's looking into it, Bill, but I'm not sure he'll learn anything. Oh, well, time will tell." The phone interrupted her.

"Why didn't you answer your phone last night? You shouldn't ignore me," the voice warned. "Leave town, or I'll destroy everything next time."

Megan stood in shocked silence, the receiver dangling from her hand. She had forced herself to ignore the ringing phone last night. Too late now. He hadn't mentioned being at the window, so someone else had some fun at her expense.

"Megan, what's wrong?" Fran put an arm around her rigid shoulders.

"Was it that man again?" Jed asked. "What did he say this time?"

Her lips trembling, she repeated the caller's message.

Sally frowned. "Hey, guys, I'm in the dark here. What happened?"

"We'll explain, but first we'll call Mike."

Rescuing the receiver, Jed punched the call through to the chief. When he had explained, he admitted the caller had not threatened Megan, only her business. Jed talked, listened, talked, and then cradled the phone.

"He can't help with phone calls. Even if he tapped your line, the guy doesn't stay on the phone long enough for call tracing."

With some prompting from Jed, Megan told the whole story while they put together a heaping garden salad.

"Uncle Josh knows the person you call the Yogurt Raisin Man." Fran paused to stir the chili. "He said Patrick somebody isn't dangerous, just lonely."

Megan was not convinced.

Sally stuck her finger in the dried tomato vinaigrette. "Ummm. Good. Megan, am I right there were no phone calls, no dead squirrels, or anything else before you mentioned those shrubs?"

"I believe they started after that, yes, so there must be a connection."

"Then, the sooner I remove the shrubs, the sooner the harassment will stop." Jed glanced out the window where sheets of rain still fell. "This rain will make my job easier. These mountains are desperate for rain, though, so I hope it stays around for a few more days at least."

"Okay, let's forget it."

They couldn't. Megan's tension affected her guests, so they rehashed the cause until Jack's arrival.

"Where's the redheaded farmer?" he demanded, when he strolled into the kitchen in squishy shoes. "Hear me, Jed Anderson, this is enough rain to last you until June, so turn off the faucet!"

"Mind your manners, Jack, or I'll order more," Jed warned.

"We haven't had enough yet." Bill nodded toward Jed. "See? His head is still on fire."

Megan waved her finger in mock seriousness, glad of comic relief from her worries. "Okay, guys, calm yourselves. Jack has time for cider while I finish the garlic bread."

Fran spoke to Jack in a loud aside, "I helped her put the chili together this morning, so I can promise she used ground beef."

"You're positive she didn't use anything weird?"

"I heard that." Megan informed them with an inelegant sniff. She assumed a lighthearted air she didn't feel. "You might as well hush, because I'm ignoring both of you."

When they finished eating, the chili bowl was empty, salad gone, and garlic bread history.

"If I were not stuffed," Fran commented, "dancing would be a great way to spend the evening."

Megan swallowed a groan. She had not bargained for dancing. Nevertheless, she feigned enthusiasm. "Stuffed or not, dancing's a great idea. You guys move the furniture while I get my *Swing Years* collection. Sorry, no contemporary CDs."

Soon the strains of Glenn Miller's "In the Mood" filled the room. They changed partners occasionally and danced the evening away. At one point, Jed hummed near Megan's ear.

"I like this one—what is it?"

"Artie Shaw's version of 'I Surrender, Dear.'"

"Do you? Will you?"

Megan restrained the impulse to shout *when pigs fly*. Instead, she murmured perhaps.

"I won't let you forget," he whispered. He whirled her in a complete circle, her feet leaving the floor.

He must be sure she would succumb to his wiles. Jed Anderson had a surprise coming.

When the album ended, Megan hid her relief when she announced, "Tomorrow is another work day, so this is the last."

After they shoved the furniture back into place, Jed stayed behind when the others ran through the rain toward their cars. He returned the albums to their case, while Megan dealt with the clean dishes.

"The album covers are great photography, but why don't you get CDs? They're much smaller, won't take up so much space."

"I know, but albums remind me of my time with Granddad." Megan had never gotten over his death—perhaps never would, a fact she had learned to accept along with many others. "This might be my imagination, or wishful thinking, but I've always believed that vinyl sounds better."

"I haven't heard LPs in so many years I can't compare the two." Jed looked around. "Everything is back in place."

"You're a handy man to have around, aren't you?" Megan walked him to the door, relieved she would soon be alone.

"I aim to please, Ma'am," he drawled in his best Clint Eastwood voice. "In any way you want."

"I'll remember," she answered before she stepped away from him.

"Do. Lock up after me."

She watched him run through the heavy rain toward his truck. He must be ready to turn off the rain too by this time.

ﬡ ﬡ ﬡ ﬡ ﬡ

His baggy jeans wrapped close around his legs for warmth, the rocking chair squeak accompanied his thoughts. His wife often told him worry is like a rocking chair, no matter how much you rock, you get nowhere. Her advice didn't stop his rocking and worrying then. Wouldn't now either. She'd been gone for many years, but he hadn't stopped missing her. If she still lived, she would know who that mysterious face belonged to and why it gave him these headaches.

He'd heard other voices when he'd called Megan Stanfield earlier. He imagined her friends were advising her. Would she leave now? If she stayed, he'd think of more drastic action. He must get her alone. Get into her house somehow. He knew he wouldn't find it unlocked, still he had picked more than one lock in his time. He had tried to get inside last night but gave up rather than tangle with a baseball bat. He hadn't intimated Megan Stanfield, he admitted with grudging admiration. Something tugged at his memory causing blinding pain.

He couldn't stand much more of this. That woman with the mysterious face must go.

Chapter 17

The Shouting Match

The rain stopped sometime during the night. Megan's day at the store was busy with a steady stream of people. Most had bought something, if only a single card. All of them commiserated with her, so different from her previous store when no one entered except to stare. They must have thought this outsider had two heads or horns or something else equally weird.

Bright lights trailed her home, although from a distance. On the straight stretch beginning at the edge of town, the headlights came closer until they almost blinded her. The car passed but cut in front too close for comfort. Megan swerved onto the shoulder where the right front wheel went into the ditch. The other vehicle picked up speed and was soon gone from her sight. She eased back from the seat belt with a gasp and released her deathlike grip on the steering wheel enough to turn it.

When she tried reversing the car, the wheels only spun. After several attempts without success, she switched off lights and motor. Her seat belt had held, for which she thanked the Almighty, but sharp pain riddled her ribs. Stepping from the car, Megan fisted her hands on her hips and berated the careless Bronco driver.

Bronco?

The vehicle had looked like a Bronco. She only knew one Bronco which traveled this road.

Jed's.

Shaken, Megan hurried on home, clutching her aching side, her footsteps loud in the stillness broken only by her hard-soled shoes slapping the pavement.

Whoever ran her off the road—her mind sheared away from Jed—might come back to finish the job.

The phone rang as she entered the house. She double-locked the door and, with dread, walked into the kitchen. Gathering her nerve, Megan picked up the receiver but didn't speak. She tried. Her mouth was too dry. She heard the voice she didn't want to hear ever again.

"That was quite an accident, wasn't it? Will you never learn? I could have killed you."

Killed you. Killed you. Killed you. Megan slammed down the phone, but the phrase echoed around the room, getting louder each time until she clasped her hands over her ears, which didn't help. When the echoes faded, Megan gulped water and then dialed Fran's number.

"Did I wake you?"

"Not at all. You sound funny. Are you ill?"

Megan clutched the phone with shaking hands. "A Bronco ran me off the road. Who do I call to get my car out of the ditch?"

"Bronco? No, Megan. I know what you're thinking, but that wasn't his Bronco. A wreck could have killed you, and Jed Anderson wouldn't hurt a fly."

"I'm not a fly, am I?" She didn't mention the phone call. Wouldn't make any difference. "Just tell me who I should call in the morning."

"Hank's garage is the first place open," she replied. "Megan, will you call the police? Or are you going to assume Jed's guilt, let someone get away with attempted murder? Whoever ran you off the road won't stop his efforts to kill you. Surely, you know that! And remember, this man knows where you live! Knows you are alone."

"I know all that, but I can't deal with it at the moment. I'll see you tomorrow."

A new day didn't ease her fears. The crisp early morning breeze coming through her bedroom window didn't blow them away either. After a quick shower and her first double espresso of the day—the first of many she was sure—Megan called the garage and gave Hank directions. After she called Fran last night, she'd stared at the phone for several minutes considering whether she should call the police. She'd even lifted the receiver and put it down twice. She hadn't wanted to hear any mention of joyriding kids.

She still didn't. Thinking more clearly now, though, Megan realized there was no choice. The insurance company would require a police report. She gulped down another double espresso and steadied her breathing for the ordeal ahead. She dialed the station. and asked for Alice Morrison. When told the sergeant was off duty, she asked for the chief.

"I need to report something, Mike. I understand Alice is off duty; otherwise, I wouldn't bother you this early. I'm sure you have more important work on your desk." Megan heaved another deep breath. "Last night, someone ran my car into a ditch."

"You should have called us at the site. Don't you have a cell phone?" Impatience colored his voice. "Never mind. Where exactly?"

"On the straight stretch outside of town."

"Can you identify the other vehicle? License plate? Did it hit yours?"

"I avoided an impact. I'm not an authority on cars. A dark color. Shaped like a Bronco. I was too rattled to notice the license plate."

"Okay, I'll look into it. Kids out joyriding, I suppose, and lost control. Maybe not, though, considering your other problems."

Kids joyriding. How many more times must she hear that? "I suppose you'll tell me that the same joyriding kids vandalized my store! Also ... never mind." Gritting her teeth, she forced herself not to throw the phone on the floor and stamp on it.

Locking the door, Megan hurried toward town, not sparing a glance at the rock-covered squirrel grave. She stood by her car, when a massive, rusty wrecker creaked to a stop.

Hank looked a little rusty too, but he gave her a hearty smile. "Good morning, little lady. Ran off the road, did you?"

"Someone helped me."

"I've told them time after time they must fix that low shoulder. They don't listen," Hank complained. "There will be a tragedy here one of these days, mark my words."

Megan agreed with him and hoped she was not the victim. "The damage doesn't appear to be major, but can you call me later today at the store with an estimate?"

He glanced inside. "Air bag didn't open. Good thing because I'm not equipped to deal with those. Can I give you a lift?"

"No thanks, I'll enjoy the walk." If no cars come after me, she added silently. She needed time to think before she reached the diner because the news would already have spread. She didn't like being the main topic of conversation over sausage biscuits and coffee.

Megan handed Hank her business card and stayed until he hooked the car to the wrecker. The early sunlight flickered on the car, revealing more damage than she'd thought. The right front was a wreck. Just like her life this year. The painful thought dug into her brain and wouldn't let go. Her grandmother's death, dumped by David, animosity instead of the welcome she'd anticipated when she moved here. She thought about her problems since. Business failure, terrorism suspect, phone calls. Dead squirrel. Store vandalism. Attempt to get into her house. Now this. Megan couldn't remember having a worse year.

Perhaps the vehicle hadn't been Jed's Bronco. She wasn't even sure it was a Bronco. Might have been another SUV. The other things were innocent of physical harm. Last night's action could have sent her to the hospital. She could have gone through the windshield if she hadn't worn her seatbelt. Look on the bright side. No one would confuse her with the terrorist if glass scarred her face.

Megan tried to control her runaway thoughts. She couldn't be sure a man made the calls or drove the car. One call had come while Jed was with her. An accomplice? No, he wouldn't jeopardize his standing in the community by letting anyone know he was harassing her. Besides, Fran vouched for him. Okay, not Jed. Who else could it be? Bottom line. *No one else knew about the squirrel.*

She greeted the diner waitress with a forced smile. "Bring on the high test, Mattie. I need reviving."

"I heard you had an accident, Ms. Stanfield. Who do you think drove you off the road?" Her voice was bright with gossipy interest.

"The police think joyriding kids."

"No way." Mattie was definite in her denial. "Roger's death on the motorcycle scared them, so there won't be any joyriding any time soon."

"Who knows?" Megan nodded at other customers on her way to Fran's booth.

"You seem in fine shape this morning, Megan, despite your close call last night."

"The damage is worse than I thought, but Hank assured me he can do anything necessary. Oh, well, teenagers will be teenagers, won't they?" She almost choked on the words.

"Yes, they will," Jed agreed, sliding into the booth beside her. "They should curb their lethal tendencies all the same. Are you sure you're not hurt?"

"Only my ribs. Let's forget it. How's the harvesting coming along?"

"The silage is in the barns, and we have almost finished the apples. The Braeburns need more time."

"Farmers always have something to do, right?" Megan commented. He spent a considerable amount of time in town—when did he work? She didn't ask.

"I must leave before you guys get too deeply in conversation." Fran kept her voice low. "However, first I'm going to set a cat amongst the pigeons. Jed, can you account for your whereabouts last night? A dark Bronco forced Megan off the road."

She left, leaving a stunned silence.

Jed turned blazing blue eyes on Megan, his voice low. "You think I sent you into a ditch? Why would I risk your life?"

Stunned at Fran's betrayal even more than Jed's anger, Megan grappled for an answer. When none came, he slid from the booth and stomped out the diner door.

Battered by his words, Megan went to her shop. How long before Mike told her anything? Several days anyway. He'd say joyriding teenagers. She flirted with the idea he wanted to make crime, serious crime anyway, appear nonexistent in this small town. Not dislike of her, just automatic protection of his territory or his reputation. The more she thought about the possibility, the more she liked it, and the angrier she became.

௲௲௲௲௲

Jed ground the gears of his truck and careened down the street. When he passed the town limits, he pressed the accelerator to the floorboard and, ignoring potholes, reached home in record time. Turning into the driveway, he saw his guests loading luggage into their cars. Forced to politeness, Jed swung suitcases into the back of their SUV, chatted a few minutes, and watched them leave. He strode into the house and directly into his mother's room.

"She thinks I'm trying to kill her!"

"Who thinks what?"

He didn't answer.

She repeated her question. "Come on, Son, tell me who upset you."

Tight-lipped, he left the room. Stopping only to put on work boots, he left the house.

He barked orders at the field hands, fired up the ATV, and headed for the distant parts of the farm. Checking the creek water level, he saw instead Megan's white-faced image when she'd clung to the seat. Their friendship had progressed a long way since then, so how could she think he would kill her? First, hallucinations, now paranoia. He still muttered when he returned the ATV to the garage.

His shrill whistle brought Hero's Pride trotting toward him. The big black searched his outstretched hand for an apple and then stood while Jed saddled him. With long-handled pliers stuck in a saddlebag, Jed mounted, gripping the reins when the horse took exception.

"Cool it, boy, I'm in no mood for this foolishness. Fences need mending, so let's get started."

In late afternoon as he returned to the barn, the hollow place in his gut reminded Jed he'd missed lunch. He gave his favorite mount a rub down and headed toward the house. "Pearl, tell Mom I'll join her after I shower."

A few minutes later, he stepped into his mother's room, a smile fixed on his face.

"Who thinks you're trying to murder her?"

Jed sank into a chair beside her bed, his hands dangling between his knees. He'd long since regretted his words spoken in the heat of the moment. He should have known she wouldn't let the matter drop. He clasped her hand. "Mom, there's nothing to upset you. Have you been worrying all day?"

"Who?"

He'd learned as a child the only way her questions would stop was to answer straight out with no beating around the bush. "Megan Stanfield."

"Megan! That nice girl? What have you done to make her think you would kill her?"

"I'm automatically at fault?"

"No, Son, but she doesn't know you like I do. Megan didn't strike me as a suspicious sort of person, so she must have misunderstood something. Start at the beginning."

Jed paced the floor. "How could she think . . . okay, so I wasn't friendly when she first came. She got under my skin. I just wanted her out of my sight—but run her off the road? Risk killing her? Absurd."

"Was she hurt?"

"Bruised ribs."

"You haven't told me why she thinks it was you."

"She's convinced the vehicle was a Bronco."

"Surely you don't own the only one in the county, so there's more to her suspicion."

"I don't know what it could be."

"We'll ask her. What's her number?" She reached for the phone at her elbow. "Megan, dear, this is

Rosalie Anderson. Jed told me you'd had an accident. Are you sure you're okay?"

She listened for a moment. "Good. Will you humor an old lady? Come out here and explain all this. Yes, right now. Jed will come get you. Pearl always fixes enough supper for an army, so you can eat with us. I won't take no for an answer. You can expect Jed in half an hour or so. Come as you are."

"She protested, but she's coming. Ask Pearl to set another place."

At the garage, Jed started toward the pickup but changed his mind and settled into the Bronco.

Megan rose from the porch steps when he braked in her driveway.

"Are you afraid to ride with me?"

She met his scathing look and shook her head.

"Have you told Mike you suspect me?"

"No."

"When you do, I want to be there. I *insist* on being there."

"Okay. When I talk to him." She bit her lip. "If I talk to him."

Neither spoke another word until they reached the farm.

Inside Mrs. Anderson's room, Megan sat on the edge of a chair. "I don't really think Jed tried to kill me. I'm not even sure the vehicle was a Bronco."

"That isn't the way it looks from where I sit." The words came from deep in his throat.

"Fran spoke out of turn. I had time to think after I called her last night. You just want me away from you— not dead."

"Why do you think Jed doesn't want you here?"

"He did, from the start. Now he's started these harassing tricks."

"What harassing tricks, for Pete's sake?" Jed demanded.

Mrs. Anderson intervened. "Yes, I believe you need to start at the beginning, Megan."

"He thinks I invented the ghost when Buddy saw it too. There are those awful phone calls, *and* the dead squirrel in the mail box *and* the cross with my name on it. Dripping like blood."

Jed jumped to his feet. "I know nothing about the squirrel, except I took the body out of the mail box and buried it for you!"

"Yes, you did. You're the only one who knows about the grave, so only you could put the cross there," she shouted back.

"You're driving me insane! *What* cross?"

"Settle down, Son."

Jed forced calmness into his voice. "I'm not a mind reader, Megan. This is the first time you've told me about a cross."

"Why would I? You put it there!"

Jed spoke through clenched teeth. "I Did Not Put A Cross . . . An-y-where."

Mrs. Anderson intervened again. "Tell me about the cross, Megan."

"The cross was there the next morning, the morning after he buried the squirrel, I mean. Made of popsicle sticks, the cross stood in the ground next to the rock Jed put on the grave. My name printed in red letters was on the horizontal bar. Looked like dripping blood."

"What did you do with the cross?" Jed asked.

"Threw it away, of course. What else would I do?"

"I'll look for it tomorrow," he muttered.

She took instant exception. "Don't you believe me? You think I invented all this?"

Jed rubbed his temples, clinging to his sanity. She would drive any man around the bend. "Megan, I didn't make myself clear. The wooden sticks might have some identifying mark."

"Nobody else knew about the grave," Megan repeated. "That's bottom line, Jed. Surely, you can see that! Only you knew about the dead squirrel and the grave."

"Well, I didn't make the cross. I haven't made any awful phone calls either. Need I remind you, one came while I was with you?" He dropped back into his chair.

"If not you, who is doing these things? You're the only person who wants me out of town."

"I don't want you to leave."

"That's not the way it looks from where I sit," she said, parroting his earlier accusation.

His own words had stunned Jed. When did he stop pouring honey? When did he start meaning what he said? He didn't know. He only knew he wanted her close. She would leave, though, if he couldn't convince her he's innocent of this harassment business. But how? He didn't have a clue.

In the ensuing silence, Pearl stuck her head around the door. "If you people are done shouting at each other, you can eat before the chicken gets cold."

Over dinner, Mrs. Anderson asked again about the ghost. "What was it like, Megan? The idea of seeing ghosts intrigues me."

"Uncle Josh thinks she's my great-aunt Eva. She started as a white blob rising from the hedge." After a deep breath, Megan told the whole story.

They stopped eating while she talked.

They were silent while they finished their meal. Jed was the first to speak, his tone grudging. "I accept you saw the ghost, Megan, still that doesn't explain the rest. Ghosts don't make phone calls or grave markers. Ghosts don't trash businesses. They also don't drive Broncos or any other vehicle."

Mrs. Anderson nodded. "You're right, Jed. If we figure out why Eva wants the hedge removed, we might learn the rest. Can you find the time now, along with harvesting apples?"

"I can put off the final harvest for a few days. I'll dig up the shrubs tomorrow."

However, he didn't. When he drove Megan home, they found a stranger sitting on her steps, visible in the moonlight. Well, a stranger to Jed, although obviously not to Megan.

"David!"

Jed couldn't decide if this was friend or foe.

Chapter 18

An Unwelcome Visitor?

Foe. Jed watched, astonished, when Megan rushed into the arms of a city-dressed, silver-haired man. Her father. No, Jed decided, jealousy knotting his gut. The hug was too close, too long for any relative. He cleared his throat.

"Oh, Jed, excuse me!" Megan pulled back from the visitor and introduced them.

David slipped an arm around her shoulder. "Nice meeting you."

"Likewise. See you around, Megan." Jed turned on his heel and launched himself into the Bronco and then scattered gravel turning onto the asphalt road.

Jed fumed all the way home. She had sent him away with a good night kiss, at most, on every occasion. He'd bet the farm she wouldn't send this David Blackwell away. What was he doing here anyhow?

At the farm, he stormed into the house.

"Jed? Did you get things straightened out with Megan?"

"No. She had a visitor from Detroit waiting on her steps. Good night, Mom."

ꝶ ꝶ ꝶ ꝶ ꝶ

Megan listened to the Bronco's engine fade in the distance. The suddenness of seeing David again had sent her into his arms, but Jed's coolness had brought her to her senses. This was David, she reminded herself, the man who dumped her last spring. *Calm yourself, Megan Elizabeth Stanfield.* "Come in, David. Tell me what brings you south."

"I came to see you, Angel." His caressing tones sent quivers down Megan's body. "I expected you back home before now."

Detroit. Where, the last time she saw him, he had a petite blonde clasping his arm. Megan stiffened her spine when she remembered his cutting words. Several acquaintances had heard him and witnessed her humiliation. "Would you care for some white wine, David?"

"Don't you have anything stronger?"

"You forget, I never did." Megan motioned him toward a chair, seating herself in one across from it. "Seeing you is a surprise. How did you find me?"

Ignoring the chair, he prowled around the room, picking up and putting down miniature boxes, mostly gifts from her grandfather She gritted her teeth when he set an antique Wedgwood on the edge of a piecrust table. As casually as she could manage, she moved the box to safety and returned to her chair.

"Finding you wasn't hard. I asked your former boss where you were. She told me you had moved south. Finding this hick town was more difficult."

"Why?"

"Why? Because this place is the back of beyond! Even GPS had a hard time finding it."

"I mean why did you come?"

"I told you—to find you."

"Why?"

He took a deep breath. When words came, they sounded like something he had memorized for the occasion. "I came to find you because I've missed you. Detroit just isn't the same without you. There, does that answer your question?"

"No. I clearly remember you said you never wanted to see me again. 'We are a colossal mismatch' were your exact words."

"I only had a momentary lapse in judgment, Angel." His seductive smile firmly in place, he continued. "You shouldn't have taken the whole thing so seriously."

"Did my replacement take *the whole thing* seriously when you dumped her, which I suppose you have?"

"Forget her! She never was important." He pulled Megan from the chair into his arms. "No one is important except you, Angel."

Another shiver traveled down her spine as her traitorous body reveled in having his arms around her again. However, she retained her sense and pulled away. "David, I've had a long, tiring day."

"I have too. I'll get my luggage from the car . . . ."

"No."

He frowned. "No? Are you saying I can't stay here with you?"

"Yes, I am. You must have seen motels on your way into town. Rooms are available, I should think, because this isn't tourist season."

"You're joking."

"No. Now, be on your way before the motel office closes." Megan took him by the arm and walked him to the door, thankful that surprise curtailed his resistance. She bolted the door but didn't relax until she heard his tires screech when he turned onto the asphalt.

Megan had learned one thing—even if nothing else—since leaving Detroit. Megan Elizabeth Stanfield could survive without David Andrew Blackwell, painful though it had been for weeks.

But, oh, how right it felt to have his arms around her again!

ௐௐௐௐௐ

David barreled back through town, ignoring people jumping out of his way, screeching brakes, and blowing horns. A siren penetrated his seething mind. Just what he needed—another traffic ticket. He pulled over. Ah, a woman. Attractive too. David turned on the charm, which had never failed him. Ten minutes later, he flung the ticket for speeding and reckless driving into the glove compartment where it joined several others. The cop stayed on his bumper to the edge of town before turning onto a side street.

What did Megan see in this place? What could any halfway intelligent person see in a one-horse town? No neon lights, no bustling crowds. No music blaring from boomboxes. The stuff of life. He hadn't even seen the traffic light the cop said he ignored.

He'd thought better of Megan, the daughter and granddaughter of jet setters. She'd surprised him from the moment they met. She'd been naïve, but he'd changed everything about her. When he'd finished training her, she looked, dressed, even walked like the sophisticate he preferred. Acceptable on his arm.

Look at her now. Messy hair, no make-up, she wore jeans! His pulse quickened as he remembered the snug fit.

He roared into the motel driveway. Letting the motor idle, he pounded the steering wheel. He still wanted her. More importantly, he had to marry her. The alternative made him break out in a cold sweat.

ഇ ഇ ഇ ഇ ഇ

"I have a bone to pick with you, Frances Marie Riddle," Megan announced as she slid into their usual booth at the diner the following morning. "You should have cleared it with me before dropping your bombshell."

"Why? I figured my interference was the best way to clear the air between you and Jed."

"Clear the air? What you did was cause a shouting match between us out at the farm."

"Do tell!"

"Mrs. Anderson invited me for supper after Jed told her I accused him of attempted murder. I had already put my fears about Jed to rest, still nothing would do except tell them the entire story."

"Ghost, phone calls, squirrel, everything?"

Megan nodded.

"Did Pearl hear you?"

"Every word."

"Well, she'll keep the shouting match to herself because she won't allow anyone to know Jed could be anything other than perfect. She'll consider the ghost story fair game, though, and will tell the whole county. You can expect everybody and his brother visiting your backyard."

"That's all I need, what with David in town." He had been on her mind since she woke from a fitful sleep. Memories of good times jostled with his abandonment.

"David?"

Megan didn't hear Fran's question. "The apparition sensation might force him to keep his distance while I figure out what to do about him."

"At what point will you tell me who David is and why he must keep his distance?"

"Oh, sorry. My brain is foggy this morning. David Blackwell is a man I knew back home, one I never expected, or wanted, to see again after he decided he preferred bleached blondes. We found him sitting on the steps when we came back from the farm."

"We? Did Jed meet this guy?"

"Barely."

"The fat is really in the fire now! Jed won't relish competition. Good for him, though. How long does this David person intend to stay?"

"Who knows?"

"Hmmm. Is he staying with you?"

"No, I sent him to the motel out on the highway."

"Did he stay at a motel, or its moral equivalent, in Detroit?"

"Not always. I thought we would get married. I even wore his engagement ring, which he graciously told me I could keep when he threw me over for someone ten years younger."

"Did you? Keep it, I mean."

"No. I threw it down a street drain—in front of him."

"You didn't!"

"I have a temper," Megan admitted.

"What you have, girl, is attitude!"

"When I saw her clinging to his arm at the door of what had been our favorite restaurant, I blocked their entrance and held out the ring—two-carat diamond surrounded by smaller diamonds in a platinum setting. I asked him if he wanted it for his latest conquest. He said no, so I threw it down the drain. He was livid."

Shaking with laughter, Fran said. "You beat all I ever saw, Megan. What did I do for entertainment before I met you?"

"Cleaned the oven?" Megan quipped and slid from the booth. "Time for work."

David sauntered into the store in mid-morning.

"Welcome to This 'n That." The harsh light of day revealed he was still handsome, but his attitude was arrogance, which she had mistaken for well-deserved self-confidence.

"Nice place. Successful?"

"Definitely."

He raised his brows. "In a town this size?"

"My customers come from all over the county."

"These hicks can afford collectibles?" A sneer accompanied his words.

Megan swallowed her anger. She would *not* let him know he upset her. "While I've lived here, I haven't met any hicks or anyone arrogant enough to condemn people he hasn't met." She shrugged aside her early treatment at the hands of the locals.

David changed the subject. "What kind of entertainment is there?"

"None in the store."

She relented when she met his glare. "Much what any small town has, I suppose. Church and school activities, theater, bowling alley. Things like that."

He gazed at her in disbelief. "I noticed the little restaurant next door. Is there a nice place where we can have a decent dinner, perhaps dance?"

Willingly stand within his arms, swaying in rhythm with his body? Not happening. "We can have dinner at the Rambling Inn, not dancing. They only have a band on weekends. I don't expect you'll still be here."

"I might be, if you make staying worth my time." David stood there with one hand thrust in his trouser pocket. It didn't help that his eyes were confident, even amused.

Perhaps it did.

Her decision was sudden, yet certain. "I doubt there's any way I can make staying here worth your time, even if I wanted to. I don't."

Megan turned away from him when a customer opened the door, thankful several more followed. When David wandered outside, she watched him cross the square toward Uncle Josh. The older man would set David in a corner, figuratively speaking, if the stranger got too big for his britches, as Granddad said many times about many people.

When David came back to the store soon after the customers left, he spoke through clenched teeth. "Let's leave here for a while."

He hadn't liked whatever the redoubtable old man had said. "I can't leave my store, David. I close for lunch for an hour at one o'clock and eat at the diner next door. You can join me if you wish."

"Well, if you can't do any better." He wandered outside again.

David seemed to appear out of nowhere when she flipped the open sign to closed and locked the door behind her. Near the diner, he tucked his hand around her arm. He paused inside the door, scanned the crowd with visible distaste, and turned toward the window table. "We'll sit here."

"Okay, but first let me introduce my friends Fran Riddle and Sally Jamison. You met Jed last night."

"Do you plan to be with us long, David?" Fran studied him.

He smiled at Megan. "That depends on how long I feel welcome."

Megan ignored his hint. "You're welcome to lunch anyway. Shall we order?"

David talked throughout the meal, his subject being himself. Where he had been, what he had done, whom he had seen since she left Detroit. He dropped names right and left into the near silence, which had reigned since he entered the diner.

Megan broke into his monologue. "Time for work, David. You stay here and continue enjoying yourself."

"No, no, I'll come with you." Without examining the bill, he tossed a fifty on the table, smiling at the waitress. "That should cover it. Keep the change."

Megan couldn't believe her ears. This was a new side to the man she thought she knew well. He always figured the exact amount of the tip he left—enough to protect his image as a big spender.

"There. Now locals know how we do things in big cities. She won't forget me, will she?"

"No." Megan stepped inside her store. "Neither will anyone else. What are your plans for the afternoon?"

"Come on, Angel, relax. You don't need this place. Let's head north this minute."

"I have no intention of going back there, David. Ever. Now, excuse me, please. I have customers."

Word surely spread around town that a handsome man was visiting Megan, because more women than she'd seen before came throughout the afternoon. Most bought something; all observed him when they thought he wasn't watching. She wondered what he would say if he knew how much his presence helped her business. No way would she tell him. His arrogance already knew no bounds.

Megan had never realized his confidence was really arrogance. Now, honesty compelled her to admit she hadn't let herself realize the truth. She'd been flattered that a financial wizard—that's what people called David—would notice her, a shy person set on fooling the world into thinking she was something she wasn't. No, shy wasn't the correct word. Lacking confidence? Yes, she lacked confidence. She had less when the Detroit business she managed failed. Why had she tried the same thing here? Hadn't she learned anything? Learning had taken time, but, yes, she had. She had matured on the professional level enough to stick it out by changing her type of business and, personally, enough to recognize David Blackwell for what he really was.

Arrogant. Condescending. Shallow.

The realization made her question why she had loved him. Maybe she hadn't. Maybe she'd had a schoolgirl crush on a handsome man. She was truly over whatever it was.

When Megan closed the store at five, David pressed her to leave, but she still had paper work. She ran her totals and prepared a bank deposit, aware of his every move.

"What are you doing now?"

Patience had never been part of Megan Elizabeth Stanfield's psyche. Still wasn't, even though Granddad has emphasized the necessity. Impatience came to the fore when, first, David paced through the store and almost draped himself over her shoulder, watching her count money. She elbowed him away when he reached for a stack of twenties. "I normally do inventory control before closing and fax new supply orders. However, this one time I'll let both carry over until morning."

"Good." David slipped his arms around her. "Why don't we go to your place for a while? Later, we can have dinner in the bigger town I came through. They'd surely have nicer restaurants than here. Dancing too. I've really missed dancing with you."

"I have a better idea. Go take a cold shower. Come back in an hour. We'll have dinner closer than Asheville."

Megan stepped away from him to answer a loud pounding on the door. Hurrying from the office, Megan saw the mechanic peering through the glass.

"Hello, Hank. Another problem with my car?"

"No, I decided to bring your car, so you won't have to walk home."

"How thoughtful of you, Hank! I appreciate it." She wouldn't have to resist David, who would surely insist on driving her home.

"What was wrong with your car?" David strolled toward her.

"Fender bender, nothing serious." She introduced them.

David ignored him.

"Well, I'll be getting along," Hank said into the awkward silence.

"I'll stop by tomorrow morning to pay you, Hank. I appreciate your quick work." Megan smiled until he was outside the door, but then she scowled at David. She'd never seen him like this. He always charmed everyone he met. "Would it have hurt you to say hello, David?"

He raised his eyebrows at her. "I should be friendly with mechanics?"

She stared at him, but his face didn't change. "No, you're too aware of your importance to notice a mere repair man. Now, I must lock the door and go by the all-night deposit."

"I'll see you in an hour. With my luggage." His tone brooked no argument.

Her tone matched his. "No. Not now, not ever, David. You must understand I'm not the same woman I was in Detroit."

"Don't be so crabby." He strode out into the twilight.

Megan waited until he passed from her sight before crossing the square. She wouldn't risk another scene with him until his temper cooled. The evening was going to be trying enough without his acting like a spoiled brat.

She drove slowly, her thoughts on the past couple of years, including her relationship with David. Relief soared through her when she realized what she would have missed if she had married him. She would never have moved to Crawfordville. She had come, though. She'd found the home of her heart and friends as she'd never known in her life. This was more important than losing her first love, such as it had been.

ಋ ಋ ಋ ಋ ಋ

Fran congratulated herself when David followed Megan into the dining room at the Inn that evening. Her guess had been right. They wouldn't go to Asheville for dinner. She'd called her friends with the suggestion they gather at the Inn. She feared David would take Megan back to Detroit. Megan must see him for what he was, an arrogant man with no consideration for others. Besides, jealousy might make Jed come to his senses about his feelings for Megan. Something needed to jolt him into seeing what the rest of them had known for weeks.

Marj had pushed tables together for a crowd, so Fran, Sally Jamison, Bill Sizemore, and Jed could sit together with available extra chairs.

"Megan!" Fran hurried toward them before Marj could greet them. "There's room for you and David at our table. No, no, I won't accept no for an answer. Megan, you know we want to get acquainted with David, so come this way." She had each of them by an arm, tightening her grip when David tried to pull away.

Fran ushered them toward the table and performed the introductions without giving either of them a chance to speak. Jed was the only one who didn't greet them, just dipped his head a fraction of an inch. Fran contained her mirth with an effort. Nero Wolfe come to life.

Jack Kincaid arrived as Megan and David settled in their chairs. "Room for another?"

"The more the merrier!"

Theirs was the jolliest table in the restaurant. Perhaps, there was enough chatter that no one noticed David spoke only when he placed his order.

ω ω ω ω ω

Megan noticed.

David had been late coming for her. Still in a snit, he'd hardly spoken on the drive to the inn. She had

[194]

ignored his surliness then, but not now, on the way to her home. She released the temper she'd held through dinner.

"Couldn't you unbend enough to talk with my friends? They did their best to make you feel welcome, part of a congenial group. All you could do was sit on your self-appointed pedestal and sneer."

He didn't answer. After a couple more efforts, Megan fumed in silence.

Turning into her driveway, he slammed on the brakes. Using a voice icier than Jed's had ever been, David told her what he thought of her hick friends, the low-class restaurant, the entire area.

"You're using words suitable only in locker rooms, if there." Megan reached for the door handle.

"You hate me, don't you?"

"Hate you?" She no longer loved him, yet did she hate him? No. Her innate honesty forced her to admit she was not indifferent toward him either. "Let's just say my regard for you has changed."

"I don't believe you."

Megan pushed open the door when he reached for her. "Good-bye, David."

She slammed the door and hurried toward her house, wincing when his car tires screeched onto the asphalt road.

Whatever they'd had was over. His smile would charm her no more.

Megan probed the sore place in her heart. The ache had persisted even after she'd left Detroit. Still bruised but different now. Perhaps because she understood herself better. She had seen what she wanted to see, not what was there. David's sophistication, his easy manners, and confident walk had blinded her. What she'd seen was the stuff of every romance she'd read, every romantic film she'd seen. Brad Pitt didn't hold a candle to David Blackwell.

Megan admitted her big love was simply a man, not a knight in shining armor. At last, she could close the door on their relationship along with all its miseries.

There had been joys, she reminded herself, even if she had manufactured them. However, that door had closed too.

One last thought crowded in before she drifted into sleep. Why had he really come? She was sure love wasn't the reason.

Chapter 19

Question and Answer

"Where's the oh-so-charming dream boat with the silver hair?" Fran inquired when Megan slid into their favorite booth the following morning. "Does it come out of a bottle, by the way?"

"I have no idea. I suppose he's on his way back north. He left in such a hurry last night that he might well be there by now."

"Do you regret he left?"

Megan shook her head. "No, I'm cured. Thanks for arranging the dinner last night. You did, didn't you? I'd already realized what kind of person David is, but his rudeness toward my friends gave me the extra shove I needed to put him behind me. I can get on with my life now, whatever it might hold, wherever it might lead."

"Then my interference accomplished both my purposes. You've stopped carrying the torch, and the green-eyed monster has Jed well in its grip."

"Jed—jealous? Yeah, right."

"Yes, he is. You're the first female who hasn't fallen at his feet since grade school. He needs to know he isn't the only fish in the creek."

Over the next few days, Megan pondered Fran's words about Jed and jealousy. He didn't come to the diner for morning coffee. Avoiding her or dealing with the apple harvest? She considered the remote possibility he could be jealous. Might be nice. Might cause more problems.

Late on Saturday morning, he poked his head around the door before entering the store.

"Hi, Jed."

"Alone?" he asked. "Your friend from Detroit isn't here?"

"He decided after dinner Tuesday he needed to get back home."

Jed's shoulders relaxed. "I haven't been into town, so I didn't know. He didn't talk you into going back north."

"No. I'm still here, and here I stay. This is my home. Why would I go anywhere?" Megan's words were a softly spoke challenge, which he ignored.

"Good. Isn't it time you had another riding lesson? The weather is warm enough to enjoy being outdoors, although there's a nip in the air."

"Sounds great." Megan noted his twinkle, so she amended her answer. "Being outside sounds great, but are horses mandatory?"

His lips curved upward. "Not mandatory, but we'll let them join our fun anyway."

"Fun, ha! I've started closing the store at two on Saturdays, so I can be out there by three or so."

"I'll be on the lookout for you."

Megan arrived at the farm earlier than she'd expected. Mrs. Anderson was taking a nap, so Megan perched on the steps, waiting for Jed, who was riding fence, whatever that meant. Her vision of him straddling barbed wire didn't make sense.

Moments later, she spotted Jed at the barn and joined him. Megan stared at a prancing horse. "Do you mean for me to ride *that*? It's huge."

"Her, and yes, you've graduated to her. I've told you before you're a much better rider than you think. You can handle Lady, I promise. Come closer."

Megan stood at arm's length giving Lady some sugar cubes. The mare was not content staying so far away. She danced after Megan's retreating hand and then her footsteps.

Jed pulled the horse to a standstill. "Okay, up you go. Relax. She won't go anywhere until I tell her."

"Relax, he tells me," Megan muttered, while he adjusted the stirrups. "Easy for you to say. You've most likely been on horses since you were born."

"Not quite. Mom didn't allow Dad to put me on a horse until I was six months old."

"You're not serious! Six *months* old?"

Jed roared with laughter. "Mom strapped me in a baby carrier, which Dad held in front of him."

"I'm not sure I can believe you."

They started at a walk, increasing their speed when Megan adjusted to the different gait of the young horse. Jed kept King under firm control, and Lady stayed near him.

Jed dismounted after ambling along the trails for half an hour. Megan dismounted without help and sat cross-legged on the ground.

"Beautiful spot. So peaceful. Do I hear a waterfall?"

"Yes, below us on the left, close but too dangerous to climb down these rocks."

"Are there many waterfalls around here?"

"They're all over these mountains." He leaned over and brushed his lips across hers. Finding no response, he stared off into the distance. "The guy from Detroit is the reason you hold me at arm's length, right?"

"He hurt me. I won't risk that agony again anytime soon."

"I hope your recovery time is brief."

"Recovery is slow, but his visit showed me I'm getting there."

"Good." He pulled her to her feet. "Now, let's finish our ride."

ℵ ℵ ℵ ℵ ℵ

A couple of mornings later, Mike arrived at the diner when Megan and Jed were leaving.

"I thought I should let you know there's nothing new on your accident, although I'll keep working on it. I've ruled out the joyriders."

"I never believed joyriding kids were to blame," Megan admitted, meeting Jed's eyes.

"She thought it was me, doing all these things."

"Why?"

"When she first came, I did my best to send her away."

"I gather you've changed your mind, you dunce." Mike grinned. "I still must ask you what you were doing the evening someone sent her into the ditch."

Jed's voice was confident. "I spent the entire evening at home with our guests, the Parkers, from Weaverville. There are other Broncos around here, you know."

"Yes, I do know—nineteen inside county limits, all dark colors. Two were missing for a while that evening. I put the fear of the devil in a boy who admitted taking one. Wanted to practice driving, he said, and his dad had the family car. I've had no luck tracing the other. The owner had his ignition key, so I assume hot-wired. No kid around here has ever hotwired a car, as far as I know. I'll keep at it. Oh, by the way, Megan, your face turned up in the Middle East again. Caused havoc, of course. Thought you'd like to know."

"I don't want to know anything about that face unless it shows up here, at which time I will probably crawl under the bed and stay there until you've done your job!"

Mike left on a laugh, but Jed lingered at Megan's shop door. "I stopped by your place earlier to check the hedge. I can remove the bushes tomorrow. Can you be there?"

"You just don't want to be there by yourself. Aunt Eva might rap you across the knuckles for not believing in her."

"I'd like to see her for myself," he admitted. "So, you'll be there?"

"I wouldn't miss watching you work."

Jed missed coffee at the diner but arrived in late morning with an assortment of tools.

"Why did you bring those?" Megan pointed at the short-handled shears.

"Working around the base of the shrubs is easier if we remove the limbs first. Mom said Mrs. Caddell kept them pruned, so they're low enough to handle. Removing the limbs shouldn't take long, but the actual digging might."

"I can help with cutting off the limbs."

"Get your gloves, or you'll have blisters. Show me where Eva hovers, so I'll know where to begin. I don't fancy digging up the entire hedge."

They worked steadily, Megan trimming the front side, Jed the back, beginning with the bush where Eva hovered. They worked toward the short end of the hedge.

"I don't understand why my ancestors put the hedge here. They owned all the way back there, didn't they?" Megan flexed her cramping hands.

"This was an active farm until about ten years ago. The owner died, and farming doesn't interest his son. The hedge separated yard from fields. I'll start digging from the end while you carry the debris to the back."

When they finished pruning, she watched Jed's rhythmic work with the shovel. He didn't waste a move, as he dug around the base of the first lilac, stopping occasionally to rock the plant. Working it free at last, he knocked the dirt away from the roots and handed her the bush with a nod toward the back of the property.

He didn't waste words either.

When Jed shook the dirt from the third shrub, Megan saw Eva suspended behind the hedge. "Jed, Aunt Eva has joined us."

He glanced around. "Are you kidding?"

"Not at all. Hi, Aunt Eva. Are you making sure we do the job right?"

Jed continued shaking the plant, as he squinted toward the hedge "I wish I could see her too."

"Aunt Eva, can you allow Jed to see you?"

The apparition shook her head and pointed.

"She's pointing at the shrub in your hand. Hey, something is sticking out one side."

Jed turned the plant on its side. A long mud-smeared piece of wood protruded. Only it wasn't wood, Megan realized, when the other end broke loose from the roots.

Chapter 20

Bones

"Bones?" Mike Williams asked over the phone. "Probably a pet cemetery, Jed."

"I don't think so, Mike. We dug up three bones, which I'm confident are human. You won't believe my evidence, but I'll tell you when you get here."

"Okay. I'm on my way. Don't touch anything else until the medical examiner gets there."

"Now, what is this about human bones?" Mike asked, half an hour later after introducing Megan to the county medical examiner, who appeared to be well past retirement age.

Doc Peabody studied her face. "You look amazingly like Alma and Eva Malloy. Could be triplets."

"Uncle Josh Crawford said the same thing. Alma was my grandmother, who died in January." Megan hesitated. "I have only recently met Eva."

"She's still living, good. We've all wondered. Where is she?"

Megan pointed toward the mutilated hedge. "I believe the bones are hers. Eva is an apparition."

Mike exchanged a glance with Doc, before both looked toward Jed for corroboration.

He answered in a neutral voice. "I haven't seen anything myself. Megan says Eva has visited her on several occasions and indicated she wants this hedge removed, which we were doing when we found these bones."

Megan admired his succinctness, yet she decided more explanation was necessary. "Aunt Eva materialized when Jed pulled out the bush that she had indicated to me some weeks ago. I asked her if this was her pet cemetery. She shook her head no."

Doc directed a keen gaze at her. "Meaning?"

Megan lifted her chin. His skepticism would not intimidate Megan Elizabeth Stanfield. "Meaning the bones are hers."

Mike Williams eyed her in total disbelief.

"Jed, they don't believe me!" Megan's frustration rose. She owed Aunt Eva, whom she had come to like, despite her earlier qualms. This person, long dead, had accepted her, a stranger, albeit a relative. Megan had expected living people to welcome her, but they hadn't during those early weeks when she needed their friendship most. She would do whatever Aunt Eva wanted, no matter what anybody thought.

"Megan, you must understand this whole thing is farfetched. However, Mike, the harassing phone calls started right after Megan began talking about getting the hedge moved. All her difficulties started then."

Doc Peabody stared at her from beneath bushy eyebrows. "Young lady, I'm a man of science. I don't believe every harebrained tale somebody tells me, especially when no one else has seen evidence. Prove it!"

"I can't." Megan gritted her teeth. "Not unless Aunt Eva chooses to show herself to other people. I'm not a magician!"

Doc turned his gaze from Megan to the bones laid out in front of him. "Miss Eva was my Sunday school teacher. She made the stories come alive. Sampson holding up the building—we held up our lesson books in real he-man style. We especially enjoyed Joshua and the battle of Jericho. We marched around the table seven times and then shouted for all we were worth." Doc chuckled. "You should have seen the number of people who ran into our room to investigate. Heady stuff for a four-year-old."

"Who took over her class?"

"I don't remember. The one thing I remember was one Sunday she didn't come. Someone said she left town."

"Okay, let's look at the bones," Mike said.

Doc stooped beside the few bones Jed and Megan had dug out with their hands. He spread them roughly into human shape. "There's no doubt they're human. Female pelvic bone. So maybe, just maybe . . . ."

He stood. "I don't suppose the ghost is still with us?"

"Do you believe I can see her?" Megan needed somebody, anybody, to say she hadn't invented the whole thing.

"I've never seen one, but that doesn't mean you haven't," Doc conceded.

"Aunt Eva, are you still here?" Megan smiled when the apparition materialized beside the hedge. "She is now. Are there more bones in there? She nodded her head yes, Doc."

"Can she tell us who killed her?" Mike, who stood beside Jed, spoke for the first time in several minutes.

"She nodded yes, again. Who was it, Eva?" Megan leaned forward, staring. "She's moving her lips, but I can't be sure what she's saying."

"He's dead by now anyway."

"No, Mike, I'm sure he isn't," Jed told him. "Whoever he is, he knew what we'd find under the hedge, which is why he's been harassing Megan over the last several weeks, trying to keep his secret."

"I wish I could see her," Doc said, his voice wistful. "What's she wearing?"

Megan slipped her hand into Doc's. "A light green dress with a small white and yellow design."

"Daisies. I remember the dress well, I guess, because she wore it at church the last time I saw her. I cried because she didn't tell us she was leaving. Now I know why. She never left."

"Well, she won't be here much longer." Megan turned toward the hedge. "Aunt Eva, the minute authorities finish what they must do, I'll make sure you have a proper funeral and burial beside your parents in the family cemetery. Is that what you want?"

The apparition smiled, nodded, and faded.

"That's what she wants."

"Do you always talk to her?"

"Yes, I do." Why would he doubt it? "The least I can do is talk if she's good enough to visit me."

Mike broke the silence, which followed her words. "Doc, can you estimate how long the bones have been there?"

"No, but Eva left in the early forties. There's no reason to believe she ever came back."

"Okay, Jed, see how many other bones you can find."

Jed and Megan sifted the soil through their fingers, carefully picking up more bones. A few minutes later, they stood. Jed said, "I believe that's all."

Megan wiped her hands on her jeans. "Wait. Aunt Eva, are you still with us?"

When the figure materialized, Megan asked if they had found all the bones. Turning toward the others, she said, "Aunt Eva nodded yes."

"Okay." Mike said. "I see no reason to call this a crime scene. I can't think of any reason we will need to sift the soil further, but, Jed, put the soil back in the hole and cover it with limbs anyway. Doc, we'll need a DNA sample for the record."

"Weeks will pass before we can expect results, but I'll take samples. Megan, come by my office tomorrow for a jaw swab." Doc, sorrow marring his face, placed the bones in a bag and followed Mike to the cruiser.

Megan was silent as she watched them leave carrying her Aunt Eva. Her eyes misted. She would miss this relative. Miss watching vapor take shape. Miss the smile. The backyard would never feel the same, nor be the same, because she would have the entire hedge removed. She'd plant daisies like the ones on Eva's dress and remove anything necessary to be sure daisies received the right amount of sun.

A stray thought darted into her mind. If these bones had been under the hedge since the early forties, Aunt Eva could not have been the originator of the flyer face. If she'd been a terrorist, she would have died some other place. Megan's assumption pleased her, although she acknowledged it hindered, rather than helped, identify the mysterious face.

Megan's gaze shifted upward when Jed slid his arm around her shoulder. His smile seemed to say he understood her feelings.

"I'm sorry I doubted you. You've been right all along, while I clung to the idea ghosts don't exist."

"Admit it, Jed. You thought I was a lunatic."

The corners of his mouth tilted upward. "I'll never doubt you again. I promise!"

Jed realized how absurd he sounded and joined her laughter.

௰ ௰ ௰ ௰ ௰

Megan's discovery was the primary topic around town for several days. The old-timers recounted stories of the Malloy twins: Alma always up to something, always dragging the reluctant Eva along. Megan had more business than she could handle, so she recruited a high school girl for after-school help each day. Katie Jenkins, who worked at the inn during the summer tourist season, assured Megan she was thrilled to have a job, which she hoped would last through the holidays.

Katie's joyous voice lightened Megan's somber thoughts when people wondered aloud who had murdered poor old Eva. The conjecture she heard most often was Alma had murdered her out of jealousy, although no one gave any reason.

Uncle Josh was in his element. People crowded around him, listening eagerly to his recollections of the summer Eva disappeared.

Megan glanced out her store window, pleased he was receiving so much attention. People always waved or spoke as they passed him, but few stopped long enough to talk. The weather would soon be too cold for him to sit under his tree. What would he do then?

Glancing around her store, she considered. If she moved that counter back a foot or so and the cash register a little toward the side, there'd be room at the window for a large easy chair. He could at least see his beloved elm tree all winter.

One thing about the whole situation amused Megan no end. After school, small boys stood with their noses pressed against the windows staring at her. They had come inside only once and looked around. One little towhead said they might break something, so they scooted outside. Since coming here, she'd learned she liked little boys. They were uncomplicated and up front with people. If they wanted to know something, they asked. Leaving Katie in charge, she stepped outside.

"Hi, guys, what's new?"

"Did you really, truly see a ghost?" Eagerness battled with skepticism in the tow-headed boy's voice. "Not pretend, like people at Halloween?"

Pure ghoulishness colored the next boy's question. "Did you really find some old bones?"

"I sure did." Megan hid a smile when she heard the murmurs of *awesome, totally awesome*. "Tell you what. I'll get Pepsis from the diner, so we can sit in the square and talk. Good idea?"

They answered in unison. "Awesome!"

"Okay, you find a sunny place."

They soon sat cross-legged on the grass, listening to her with rapt attention, their drinks almost forgotten.

"You talked to her? Really talked?" inquired a freckle-faced urchin of about seven.

"Yes, several times. She didn't answer me, you understand. She nodded and smiled at me."

"Did she scare you? The first time you saw her, I mean," asked a wide-eyed lad, whose hair kept falling forward over his forehead.

"Not at all," Megan fibbed. "Ghosts aren't truly scary, you see. That's just something people say for some reason. I've never understood why, because ghosts are simply unquiet spirits, who try to tell us something."

One voice piped above the others. "She tried to tell you somebody had murdered her."

"Yes. Where somebody had buried her too."

"Awesome. Totally awesome!"

Megan agreed with them. She didn't know anyone else who had visits with dead ancestors. She marveled anew she'd ever feared the apparition.

"You're not supposed to bury people just anywhere." The biggest boy showed off his knowledge. "We have graveyards for that. My dad said so."

"He's right too. I promised Aunt Eva that I would give her a proper funeral and burial. I'm sure her spirit will be content then."

"You should ask the boys to be honorary guests at the funeral." Jed dropped to the grass beside them. "Miss Eva taught other little boys in Sunday school class, so it's appropriate for these boys to be present when we lay her to rest. How's that sound, guys?"

"Awesome. Totally awesome!"

"We'll do it," Megan said. "When the authorities finish their work, I'll be in touch with all of you."

The freckle-faced boy jabbed his elbow into the biggest boy's ribs. "Danny, ask her."

"Don't poke me, Ronnie," he muttered. "Miss Stanfield, could we see where you found the bones? Please?"

"I don't see why not. Mr. Anderson, here, found them. I'll bet he would enjoy taking you guys out there right now and showing you the exact spot where we found the bones."

"Would you, sir? Please?" They turned pleading eyes his way.

"Sure. Hop into the back of the truck with Buddy. However, hear this. If I see anybody standing, I'll turn the little imp across my knee and apply a lesson to his seat of learning. Do every one of you understand?"

With excited whoops, the boys clamored into the truck.

"You owe me for this, Megan Stanfield. One way or another, I'll collect!"

As the truck pulled away, Megan joined Uncle Josh on his bench. "I need your advice."

"Set yourself down, and tell me what I can do for you."

"I want to consult you about Aunt Eva's funeral, since you were her contemporary. What do you suggest?"

"Daisies," he answered. "She loved them. I don't know where you'll get any at this time of the year, though."

"Florists carry them," Megan assured him. "You knew her quite well to remember that after so many years."

"Like every other young buck around, I had a crush on Alma. Also like everybody else, I compared the twins, so I remember both."

"What else do you recommend for the service?"

"Will you have music? I suppose you won't want them for a funeral, but both girls loved Christmas carols, 'Star of Bethlehem' in particular. They sang it year-round when they thought no one could hear, probably because neither could carry a tune. That might be the only thing those girls had in common besides their faces."

"Neither can I." Megan admitted with a grin. "Must be a DNA thing. Well, I don't care if Christmas music is unusual for a funeral. That's what she liked; that's what she'll have. What do you think about having little boys sing 'Away in a Manger' for her?"

"Perfect," he assured her. "I wouldn't have thought of boys taking part. I wonder how many of her former students are still around. Perhaps they could tell stories they remember from her class."

"Great idea!" Megan pulled a note pad from her purse and jotted down his suggestions. "I imagine the best thing would be newspaper ads, both the *Asheville Citizen-Times* and *The Echo* here. Now, what else?"

"She enjoyed hearing church bells. Always stopped whatever she was doing and listened."

"Then, they will ring again just for her. The organ at the Baptist church plays bells, so we can close the service with 'I Heard the Bells on Christmas Day. '" This is going to be a happy funeral."

"Happy?"

"Yes, *happy*. Aunt Eva will be happy to be at rest in a proper grave at last."

"Do you plan graveside rites also?"

"Yes. I think everybody should sing 'Silent Night.' I'll ask Pastor Rogers for an uplifting prayer rather than the usual somber send-off. Okay, how does all this sound, Uncle Josh? Would Aunt Eva like our plan?"

"Yes, she would. You're a special person to go to so much trouble for old bones."

Megan stood. "Aunt Eva isn't just old bones. You see, she chose to visit *me*, a stranger, who learned of her existence so recently. She could have contacted many people over the past decades."

"I still say you're special."

She kissed his forehead. "Thanks. That means a lot coming from the town patriarch!"

Chapter 21

Unexpected Upheaval

The last two people on the planet who Megan expected to see in her store stood in the doorway. Life had just become normal after discovering Aunt Eva's bones. Now, she faced another upheaval. She closed her gaping mouth and hurried forward.

"So, this is where you are." Reid Stanfield stared around the store. "David told us you had hidden yourself away in a North Carolina hick town. We didn't believe him. I thought you were too sophisticated for something so stupid. I was wrong."

"Hello, Father, Mother." Megan hid her chagrin and gave them air kisses on the cheek. Her heart had leaped when she first saw them. They never visited her throughout all the years at boarding school, summer camps, or college. A thought shot through her mind bringing her back to the present. Aging men get more distinguished, but aging women tend to come apart at the seams. Her father followed his pattern, her mother didn't. Even in her fifties, Susan Stanfield was slender, like her daughter, besides looking almost as young. She would stay that way, Megan knew, whatever it took. "When did you get back to the States?"

"Last week, darling. We were surprised you weren't at home. Why didn't you let us know you'd moved?"

"I didn't know how to reach you," Megan reminded her mother. "I don't believe 'general delivery, Europe' would quite make the grade."

"I suppose not, darling." She glanced around. "What a *quaint* little place. Do you have much business?"

"Quite a lot. This time of day is quiet, but when school lets out, business will pick up again." Megan hesitated. She needed to know their plans so she could make her own. She decided bluntness was the answer. "Are you here for long?"

Mr. Stanfield, a tall, compactly built man in his early sixties, stared at her without blinking. "Do you have a problem with our visiting you?"

He succeeded in making her feel foolish yet again. Why did she never see this coming? Because, she answered herself, his attitude always destroyed what little confidence she had. "I asked because I want to plan some entertainment for you and introduce some of my friends."

"Don't bother." His answer was as blunt as her question had been. "We'll stay the night, if you have room for us, or we can stay in a motel. We saw one somewhere close."

Her mother intervened. "Darling, we need to leave tomorrow because I simply must shop before we board ship in Miami day after tomorrow. Ed and Jean Abbott—do you remember them?—invited us on their yacht for a long cruise around some islands."

Megan forced brightness into her smile. "I want to spend as much time as possible with you while you're here. My assistant can take charge for the rest of the afternoon. I'll ask another friend to open for me tomorrow morning. I'll call her now."

Katie hurried inside while Megan was on the phone with Sally.

"Oh." She stared at the stranger. "You look like Megan."

Megan introduced them, adding, "Katie is my right hand."

Mr. Stanfield grunted. Mrs. Stanfield murmured, "Darling, how good of you to help in our little girl's shop."

Megan gritted her teeth. At this rate, her teeth would be ground down to the gumline before they left. Would

Susan Stanfield ever admit her daughter was an adult? "You're in charge for the afternoon, Katie, while I show my parents around town. I'll be back at five. Think you can handle everything?"

"No problem."

Megan turned toward her parents. "Let's walk around town. I believe you'll enjoy seeing where our ancestors settled. I learned when I came here that Mother's family helped establish the area." She hoped all her friends were busy elsewhere. No way did she want to expose them to her father's grunts or her mother's darlings.

"The square is the heart of town." Megan managed a cheerful voice, despite their obvious lack of interest. "The Episcopal church at the upper end and the Baptist church at the lower end have stood since before the War Between the States. Several houses around town are from the same era."

"You mean the Civil War," her father corrected.

"Here they see the war differently." Megan didn't add that she'd also heard it called the War of Northern Aggression.

He grunted.

"Hey, Megan." The shout came from a car pulled alongside the square.

She bit her jaw. No way could she avoid introducing her parents to Doc Peabody.

Her father nodded without speaking. Almost as an afterthought, he stretched out his hand. "Doctor."

Her mother murmured, "Darling, how nice to meet you. Do you know our little Megan well, darling?"

"Now I know what Miss Eva would have looked like in middle age," he told Mrs. Stanfield, ignoring her question.

"Eva who, darling?"

"You haven't told them about finding Eva's bones?"

Megan had hoped to avoid talking about bones. "Not yet."

"Bones, darling?" Her mother turned toward her. "You found some bones? How *quaint!*"

Doc raised his eyebrows and muttered something unintelligible before starting his car.

"I'll tell you about them a little later," Megan assured her parents, after Doc drove away. Maybe they wouldn't meet anyone else she knew. Her hopes were in vain when Uncle Josh raised his hand, requiring another introduction.

He leaned on a cane while he surveyed her mother. "I knew your parents well. Robert was my closest friend from first grade right on through high school. I regret he never came back from Detroit. I was in love with Alma—all of us boys were."

Her mother murmured, "Darling, how interesting you knew my parents."

He ignored her comment. "The females in your family always looked alike. I would have known you anywhere. Alma and Eva were their mother's image, just as Megan is your image. I've never known any other family with identical faces through generations of women. Or men, for that matter."

On that parting shot, Josh moved slowly, yet steadily, toward his bench under the elm.

"Megan darling, I assume the Alma he mentioned is my mother, but who is Eva?"

"Grandmother didn't tell you she had a twin sister?" Grandmother had not mentioned any relatives to Megan but why not her own daughter? It seemed almost like a conspiracy of silence because Granddad hadn't mentioned her either.

"Darling, I don't recall she ever mentioned anyone in her family. You know my memory! What is this about Eva's bones?"

Megan could avoid it no longer. She motioned them to a bench and told the story from the beginning, omitting the harassment she had suffered. They wouldn't care about it. The thought shamed her. They hadn't given her much attention, true, but they'd always made sure she was in a safe place with people they trusted. Her heart eased with that realization.

"You talked to a ghost, darling? How *quaint!*"

"Has anybody seen her besides you?" Her father's raised eyebrows showed his disbelief better than words ever could.

Megan forced an amiable reply. "If so, no one has mentioned it. No one saw her at the same time I did, even though she appeared when others were there."

"Sounds peculiar. Are you on drugs of some sort?" he asked, leaning closer to stare into her eyes.

"Never!" A faint, mocking smile concealed Megan's hurt. He should know her better than that. He certainly knew how Granddad felt about drugs—he'd been quite vocal about them. She glanced at her watch. "I must close the store. Will you come with me, or would you rather wait for me here?"

Her father stood quickly. "We'll come with you. I feel like a circus sideshow while everybody gawks at us."

Megan prepared a bank deposit and locked the door. "I'll drop this off at the all-night deposit box. You can follow me home." Crossing the square, Megan introduced her parents to several people they passed, including Fran. "She's my closest friend here."

"Darling, how nice of you to be friendly with our little Megan."

Fran grinned. "Mrs. Stanfield, being friendly with your little Megan is easy."

Megan shot her friend a look which plainly said, 'I'll deal with you later,' and then she ushered her parents toward their car.

Driving along the asphalt road, Megan wondered what her parents would think about the two-story white house she already considered home. She visualized it through their sophisticated eyes, which had seen mansions throughout Europe. Megan liked the long porches that ran the width of the house on both stories, but would they? At some point, someone had added central heat and converted a small room on each floor into a bathroom, making for spaciousness instead of the usual cramped areas.

Would her mother appreciate that her ancestors had built a house solid enough to withstand storms for over a hundred years? Would her father recognize how much effort someone put into the renovations without changing the character of the house?

Megan braked at her steps and waited for them. The first time she came here, she had gazed at the house like a surprise package, spending several minutes in delicious anticipation. Was the house happy to have family back home? This place had been her hiding place only months before; now it was home. Megan waited for her parents' reactions.

Her father looked without speaking.

"Darling, how *quaint*! Wouldn't you prefer a nice, modern condo back home? Or at least in a large city somewhere?"

"No, Mother, I would not." Megan raised her chin. "I realize cities of any size are far superior to any small town in many ways. However, I've had enough city life, and I've found everything I want right here. Now, come inside."

She led them up the graceful curving staircase toward bedrooms. At the top, she pointed to her right. "The bathroom is down the hall. Come downstairs when you're ready. We'll have some wine while we discuss dinner."

Megan escaped down the stairs before they could answer. Hurrying into the living room, she checked the supply of wine and glasses. She knew they preferred something stronger as an aperitif. Nevertheless, they could settle for what she had, or have nothing. She pasted a smile on her face when she heard footsteps on the stairs.

When her father stepped into the room, he handed her a large, bulky envelope. "We found this when we reached home. When you moved down here, you neglected to tell your grandmother's attorney how to reach you."

"I never thought Mr. Penland might have further business with me since he droned on and on after Grandmother's funeral. I was ready to scream." She didn't tell him the attorney's memory was questionable. Instead, she tossed the envelope onto a table when her mother entered the room. "I'll deal with it later. Now would you like some wine?"

"No whisky, darling, or even sherry?" Mrs. Stanfield glanced around the room before settling in a Queen Anne chair, her back ramrod straight, her chin lifted. Never would she permit sagging jawlines.

"I suppose we can't expect anything stronger from you." Her father's mouth slanted into a grimace. "You must be a changeling."

"Possibly," Megan agreed without hesitation. The realization was exhilarating. Maybe she was becoming immune to their little digs, conscious or not. "Now, what do you prefer for dinner?"

"Darling, you aren't planning to *cook* for us? Isn't there a decent place around here that serves respectable meals?"

Megan gritted her teeth. Again. She must stop doing that. "Yes, Mother. The Rambling Inn is decent and serves respectable meals."

Fortunately for her temper, the phone rang in the kitchen. "Excuse me, will you?"

"Hello? Oh, good, Jed, it's you—a ray of sanity in an otherwise insane world."

"What's wrong? More phone calls?"

"No—much worse. My parents are here."

"I would love to meet them," he said after a long pause.

"No, you wouldn't, but if you think you can stand it, join us for dinner at the Inn. Please. We'll leave within an hour, if Mother can dress quickly. Can I count on you?"

"I'm yours to command. Besides, my natural desire to meet your relatives, you've roused my curiosity. I wouldn't miss meeting your parents for the world."

"Do me a favor? Don't show any surprise when you see my mother."

"Why? Does she have two heads?"

"Just don't show surprise."

Jed answered her pleading. "Okay. No surprise."

Megan took a steadying breath and returned to the living room. "That was Jed Anderson, who owns a farm near here. He's joining us for dinner."

Something Megan couldn't identify flickered in her mother's eyes.

"Darling, we look forward to meeting another of your friends."

"Now, Mother, we need to act." Megan smiled.

Susan showed a moment of bewilderment. "Oh, you mean we must change for dinner. I won't take long, darling."

Puzzled, Megan followed her. Changing to a dressy pantsuit, she returned to the living room where her father waited. "Father, is Mother ill?"

"Not at all. Why do you ask?"

"She doesn't seem quite herself."

He shrugged off her concerns. "Remember how your grandmother described her? Whimsical. She's always been changeable from one day to the next."

"I know, yet . . . ."

"I'm ready, darling. Shall we go?" Susan paused at the doorway, chiffon skirts swirling around her slender legs.

Her father drove because he contended no woman was capable. His rental was a Lincoln Town Car. Naturally. Megan had never understood how he managed to find one, almost at the snap of his fingers. She believed he would rather walk than drive a lesser automobile.

Megan waved when Jed pulled into the parking area at the Inn behind the Lincoln. Hurrying forward, he opened the doors and then stood back while Megan introduced them.

"Darling, how nice to meet another of our little girl's friends."

Megan admitted her mother was in her element meeting handsome men. Their age was irrelevant. She'd read that charm is as fleeting as beauty, which was not true with Susan Stanfield. Her charming ways were still a large part of her personality. Even at five feet eight inches tall and wearing absurdly high heels, she managed to appear dainty. No wonder men fawned over her. The thought flitted through Megan's brain as her mother linked arms with Jed.

Her father eyed him for a long moment before he stuck out his manicured hand. "Jed."

Mrs. Stanfield chattered until Gail handed menus around, bringing two minutes of silence before she started again.

While they waited for their food, Mr. Stanfield interrupted his wife's monologue in mid-flow. "Our daughter said you're a farmer. I didn't know individual farming could be successful in modern times. Only conglomerates."

"That can be true, yes, especially in mountainous regions where terrain can be difficult because of water runoff. Over time, my ancestors terraced our hillsides to control erosion. My father learned years ago that successful land business requires diversification. He added an apple orchard to his father's primary purpose of dairy farm. I will expand into a different area within ten years. I also raise the grain my cattle need with enough extra to sell at a comfortable profit. I have university degrees in agriculture and business as well as considerable veterinary knowledge."

Jed smiled above the rim of his coffee cup. "My farm has been successful for over a hundred years and is even more so today. I'm confident that won't change in my lifetime, at least."

Megan glared at her father. How dare he question her friends?

Mr. Stanfield grunted.

Mrs. Stanfield spoke in the ensuing silence. "Darling, you're the first redheaded person I ever saw with blue eyes. How did you do it?"

Megan choked on her coffee. One glance showed Jed struggled to control his rising mirth.

"My father gave me the red hair, Ma'am. My mother contributed the blue eyes."

Fortunately for Megan's self-control, several people stopped by their table. When she introduced Mike Williams, her mother gazed at him in wonder.

"A real policeman?" She flashed him a brilliant smile. "Darling, how *quaint*!"

When Mike walked away, Megan commented that some cops act superior, and she was glad Mike didn't.

"I agree, darling. Now, no dessert for me, but I'd like some decaf, no cream, no sugar."

Megan excused herself and went to the ladies' room. Several minutes later, she returned, finding her mother chattering in her usual inane manner.

Megan thanked the high heavens when they went home.

The following morning was worse. Her parents had a heated discussion because Susan couldn't find a certain scarf—the only thing I wear with this dress, darling—and then she misplaced her sunglasses, causing her to unpack her bags yet again. She found them in her purse. After they drank several cups of coffee—"Darling, we never eat breakfast. How quaint!"—Megan ushered them out the door into the mid-morning sunshine.

"I'll stop at a rise near here where you can see the entire town."

When they reached the top, Megan looked at the panorama spread before her, which always made her heart quiver with delight. This time she saw it through her parents' eyes. She couldn't imagine their quivering with delight about anything. They were much too blasé. She wondered what, if anything, would delight them to the extent this town delighted her.

Except for the congestion around the square, the residents through the years had been eager to build their homes far from each other. The broad streets on the outskirts were tree-lined, giving no hint of the subdivisions found in so many towns. The lot sizes were far from uniform. Houses were as individual as their owners could build them. Some were centuries-old rock, while others were modern ranch style with some A-frames. In the distance, the Smokies peeked through the rising mist. Far above, among drifting clouds, a plane droned on its way toward Asheville.

The tranquil vista never failed to please Megan. Not so her parents.

"Whatever possessed you to throw over a good man and come to this backwater?"

Before Megan could answer him, her mother chimed in. "Darling, that redheaded farmer can't compare with David! If you apologize, I'm sure he'll take you back. After all, his financial problems are only temporary."

Financial problems? Megan blocked out her mother's gushing. Now she understood. The financial wizard had money problems, so he came looking for her, the sole heir of both parents and their considerable fortunes. How could her father, ever vigilant with his own money, consider David as a son-in-law under these circumstances? she asked.

"His father is an old friend. I can't ignore David when he needs help."

"Is this why you came to see me? To plead David's cause?" Megan schooled her voice not to show her hurt when he shrugged. She glanced at her mother, who stared into the distance. "Give him the money he needs. Don't involve me."

He glared at her. "I can't do that. I must keep some control over his financial situation. The only way I can is if he marries you."

Megan's mouth opened but snapped shut on her retort. Megan Elizabeth Stanfield, a sacrificial lamb? *When pigs fly*! No one would ever control her through money. That would be an insult to her granddad, who encouraged her independence, and her grandmother, who never let anyone control her.

"David's financial problems do not interest me. Furthermore, I know both men better than you do. I also know I want to live in Crawfordville, not Detroit or any other big city. You must accept I'm a breed apart." Megan gazed out over the town, which she considered home. "I suppose I'm a throwback to my ancestors who moved away from the upheavals of their lives. I've found my place, which happens to be the same one they found."

"Darling, what do you see in this place?"

Megan knew they would never understand her sense of home, the continuity with her beloved granddad, so she compromised.

"What I don't see matters too, Mother. Winos and addicts passed out on park benches; prostitutes wearing spandex, strutting along crowded sidewalks in their stiletto heels, to name only a couple."

"Darling, they're everywhere."

"Not in Crawfordville. Why is it so difficult for you to understand I'm happy here?"

Her parents exchanged glances.

Her father grunted.

"Well, darling, I do think you should . . . ; however, if you're sure, we won't say another word. We love you—want only your happiness."

"I'm sure, Mother." Megan turned toward the cars. "I know you're in a hurry, so I'll tell you good-bye here. You can zip right through town on your way to the airport."

She slipped her arms around her mother, being careful not to wrinkle her clothing, and then gave them air kisses. She smiled until they disappeared in a cloud of dust, before she slumped against her car. No matter what David or her parents thought, Crawfordville was picturesque, a real community with a sense of history. Her history. Her home.

꩜ ꩜ ꩜ ꩜ ꩜

Two with that face? In despair, he leaned against the big poplar tree. Yesterday, when he saw those two women in the square, he believed he was hallucinating.

One face haunting him was bad enough; how could he deal with two? This morning, he hid behind trees across the road from Megan Stanfield's house. He'd waited, his heart pounding, until they came outside.

Yes, there were two. Two identical faces to chew at the edges of his mind. Two identical faces to give him nightmares. Two identical faces to give him unbearable headaches. He edged his way back through the woods, hopelessness sitting on his slumped shoulders.

Chapter 22

Aha! Now We Know!

Bianca settled into the comfortable seat of the Gulf Stream jet, which would take her from Asheville to Miami. She could enjoy having a private plane at her disposal. Reid Stanfield already had his nose buried in a financial journal. She'd learned one thing about him soon after they met. If it wasn't one business magazine, it was another—usually international monetary issues about which she neither knew nor cared. Reid had a one-track mind, but that was okay because business kept his attention away from her. She could relax for the first time in forty-eight hours.

The last months had been hectic, filled with jet lag and looking over her shoulder. Her escape route from Detroit, including changing her disguise three times, led to Toronto, Milan, Paris, London, where she took care of some necessary business; Zurich, New York, back to Detroit, finally North Carolina. She believed she had covered her tracks well, but she hoped never to face the necessity again.

Her only narrow escape had been in Zurich. Her time there could have been catastrophic, even more so than the fiasco in Detroit. She had not known Susan Stanfield was at the clinic where both had facial work done. It had only been three months since Susan's last appointment.

Oh yes, she knew Susan's schedule. During the past few years, she'd spent considerable time with her grandmother's American daughter, the whimsical Susan, who had never penetrated Bianca's disguise. This meeting had been fortuitous, Bianca had realized, providing the instant solution to her dilemma. Susan must disappear.

Over the past months, not even Reid Stanfield had realized Bianca wasn't his wife. She and Susan had two things in common—their almost identical appearance and a complete lack of sexual interest. Bianca endured male attention to suit her convenience. She didn't question whether there were other women in Reid's life. She didn't care. Susan probably didn't either. Now Bianca had passed the final hurdle: Susan's daughter. Megan had accepted her without question. Bianca wouldn't have cared if she had suspected. Megan was as disposable as her flighty mother had been.

No one gets the best of Bianca Rossi.

Chapter 23

The Aftermath

"Will you come and hold my hand for a while?" After wrestling with the idea throughout the bowl of noodle soup, which was all Megan could eat, she had called Jed. "Perhaps even say something nice."

His chuckle was infectious. "I'll be right over—darling."

"Jed, I'm warning you. Don't call me that. Not ever. Do you understand me?"

"Yes, precious."

"Better, but I'll settle for Megan."

"Okay, little Megan."

"Jed!"

Half an hour later Jed's Bronco braked at Megan's porch steps, missing them by less than a foot. She stepped from the shadows, greeting him with both hands extended before leading him inside. Neither spoke beyond a brief greeting.

Jed leaned back on the sofa, studying her face. He slipped his arm around her shoulder, laying his cheek against the top of her head.

"Rough day?"

Bitterness saturated her voice. "If one more person had told me how alike yet different from my mother I am, I might well have smashed collectibles against the wall."

"Does she call everybody darling, or am I special for some reason?"

"Mother throws darlings around like leaves swirling in a windstorm. She developed the habit because she simply cannot remember names. She never could. Used to embarrass me silly when she couldn't remember my friends' names. Mother did remember mine at least twice, though, so perhaps I'm the privileged one."

"You are, you know. Privileged, I mean. They may well drive you up the wall, but they love you."

"Love me. She said this morning they love me. I can't recall either of them ever saying those words to me. I would remember too because I always longed to hear them."

"Words don't come easily for some people. They do love you in their own way. Your father is certainly concerned for your welfare."

"I apologize for his pushing his nose into your business."

"There's no need for apologies. He wants the best for you."

"Their idea of best. Am I supposed to fall into their plans without a murmur?" Megan jerked away from him. "Is that what you're saying?"

"I suppose my words did sound that way. No, you shouldn't meekly accept anything from anybody. All I'm saying is keep an open mind."

"My mind is always open," Megan retorted. She should have stopped letting her parents upset her long ago. She couldn't remember any affection between her grandmother and her mother. They rarely saw each other. Like mother, like daughter, Megan feared. The lack of affection continued in the next generation. Would she ever dare have a daughter?

Megan debated with herself. Should she tell Jed the real reason her parents came? "Jed, they didn't come to see me."

"I don't understand."

"Well, they came to see me but not because they wanted to *see* me. David's having financial problems, and they came to persuade me to marry him because my father won't help him otherwise."

"Ah. I don't know how to answer that except to say it helps me understand your bitterness toward them. I can't quite see you as a sacrificial lamb."

"Nor can I."

After a moment of silence, Megan spoke again.

"I believe Mother is ill. Father said not, but she was different. Inane, yes; she's always frivolous. She just didn't *feel* like my mother. I can't explain any better, but there was a difference in her eyes too."

"Face lift?"

"No. She has those often. Judging by her lack of squint lines, her newest effort at a youthful appearance is quite recent. Her surgeon is too good to allow any strangeness in her face. I mean her eyes themselves. Her eyeballs. She looked me in the eyes only twice, which is disturbing because she prides herself on pretending to pay close attention. Her eyes were hard, no sparkle."

"Eyes do show illness sooner than other features, I agree."

"Maybe it was my imagination. I hope so." Megan wanted to believe her mother was okay, but she wasn't quite sure.

"Put possible sickness out of your mind. They'll tell you, when they want you to know anything. They probably don't want your worrying about them."

"Oh, well, I won't see them again any time soon, so let's forget them."

"Have you heard anything about Eva's bones? Are they hers?"

"Too soon for official DNA results. I'm convinced, though. Those bones are Aunt Eva, alright."

"Let's put the whole situation behind us for now." He held her close, stroking her arm.

Megan's tension eased as the silence lengthened. She didn't know when her head came to rest on his shoulder. He lifted her face for a kiss, before she pulled away.

Surprised at her rush of feeling, she told her fluttering heart to behave. Just a reaction from her parents' rejection, Megan told herself. She was a businesswoman. No involvements. She'd survived one mess and would not jump into another.

"Jed, December is almost here."

He captured her lips in a long, gentle kiss. "So?"

She pulled away, struggling to control her breathing. "Does Crawfordville do anything special for Christmas?"

Ignoring her question, he turned her face toward him. "There's a lot between us, Megan. You feel it too. Your eyes betray you."

His soft words reached her heart. She wanted to deny them. She even *tried* to deny them. She stiffened when Jed reached for her but relaxed against his shoulder when he cupped her cheek with his callused palm.

He swept his lips across hers. When she didn't resist, he deepened the kiss until she was lost in the wonder of it.

"Oh," she murmured, backing away.

"Hmmm," he agreed, pulling her close again.

"Not a good idea." She planted her hands against his chest. "I need for you to leave now, Jed."

"I could do a better job of comforting you, if I stayed longer."

Megan told him she had received enough solace for one evening.

Jed indulged in small talk but stopped when Megan urged him toward the door.

Back in the living room, Megan adjusted the screen around the fire she'd built earlier. Straightening, she saw the envelope she'd tossed onto a table the evening before. Curious though she'd been at the time, she wouldn't open the envelope while her father was there. Her business was *hers*, not his. She'd almost smiled at his reaction. He'd almost demanded to know what made the envelope so bulky.

This was the time to deal with whatever the attorney needed. If he wanted her to return the legacy, he was too late. She pulled out a single sheet of paper and a bulky envelope.

ꡒ ꡒ ꡒ ꡒ ꡒ

Dear Miss Stanfield,

You will find enclosed an envelope left in my care by your grandmother, Alma (Mrs. Robert) Abernathy, which I should have given you when we dealt with her legacy. Again, I apologize for my neglect. If either letter has caused difficulty, I will take the necessary steps to correct the situation.

Megan stared at the enclosed envelope for a full thirty seconds. The first letter Mr. Penland forwarded had contained good news: her grandmother's love. Her pounding heart told Megan this one would not. She wondered how many more letters the lawyer had forgotten, either hers or other clients' letters. Megan slit the envelope, pulled out several pages she recognized as her grandmother's stationery, and began to read.

My Dearest Megan,

So many memories. As I've grown older, the early years have become as clear as yesterday. I could wish it otherwise, because now I must reveal some of my secrets.

Your grandfather reared you well, giving you his moral standards, which is the reason I know I can trust you with this staggering situation, yet I realize I'm being unfair. You should not have the burden of carrying my sins on your shoulders. I apologize for laying this obligation on you. I can't die with this on my mind. You see, my doctor told me my time is short. Seeing Bianca traveling the same road has made me understand what my wild behavior really cost.

This puzzles you, because you don't know who Bianca is. I can't change the past, yet I also can't confess to authorities. But most important, I truly can't betray Bianca. Someone else must. I ask you to accept that responsibility.

I never expected I would put the last seventy-five plus years on paper. Over the past few years, I've had nightmares over the death and destruction I, together with my Italian family, have caused to so many people in so many places.

My Italian family. I'll begin there. I met Miguel Rossi when he was in Detroit on automobile business a couple of years after I moved here. I had started my Milan trips for work purposes, one week at a time. Over time, I became better acquainted with my supervisor and the trips lengthened. We traveled together until he realized how I felt about Miguel. That's when he stepped aside.

I quickly rose from receptionist to confidential secretary in an auto factory. I made more money than I'd ever dreamed possible. Robert's wages were even higher than mine were. For two young people from a small rural town, accustomed to living on a small allowance, so much money was heady. At first, we jointly chose not to begin our family, but later, it was my decision alone until Robert got firm about it. So, Susan was born after nearly fifteen years. I admit my romantic liaisons with other men, but I assure you—Susan is Robert's child. Even before she reached school age, I recognized Susan was lacking in the brain department. Whimsical is how I've often described her.

After Susan's birth, my marriage was over for all intents and purposes. I spent months at a time in Milan where, unknown to Robert, I gave birth to Isabella, when Susan was two years old. I accept the blame for my marriage failure. I must say, though, Robert didn't mind. I don't know or care if there were other women in his life. I can only say neither of us ever mentioned divorce.

I have always been careful about keeping my two families apart, so neither you nor Susan know you have Italian relatives. Bianca told me she has known Susan for many years, but always when in disguise.

My beloved Miguel and Isabella have met their just punishment. I will face my own when I meet the Grim Reaper within a few months. That will leave Bianca, the last of the line. Isabella gave birth only to Bianca, who also has never married. I'm aware she had two abortions. She told me she never gave birth.

Miguel and I were circumspect, if I can use that word to describe terrorists, which I now recognize we were. However, Bianca stops at nothing for the sheer pleasure of blowing up something. I can't report her without revealing my own involvement. I prefer to spend what little time I have left sitting in the sun, not behind bars.

Miguel worked with a resistance group during the war. I loved him so much I joined without caring about consequences. I only wanted to rid my beloved Italy of those horrible Fascists. After the war, we became involved in several other clandestine activities. Those were exciting years!

The years passed. I spent more time in Italy than anywhere. Robert thought I was traveling the world. I never told him differently, but being a jet setter never appealed to me. I only wanted to be with my secret family. I was a good mother to Isabella, at least I thought so. Now I know better. I was a bad mother to Susan, leaving her with Robert most of the time, so I can't blame her for doing the same with you, her own daughter.

Miguel and I talked freely in Isabella's presence concerning our work with the resistance group as well as our subsequent activities. She thought resistance was normal. We later did the same with Bianca. With her, we included Isabella's war protests and her later involvement with terrorist activities. It's natural she too, thinks terrorism is normal.

I've learned life goes on, even after the thrill is gone. A few years ago, I realized my mistake, the damage I had caused by talking in front of Bianca. I learned, then, that she had involved herself with the Italian criminal element, as her mother had done. Some months ago, an old friend in Milan reported Bianca's activities. I pleaded with her to stop whatever she was doing. I reminded her that her mother had died when a bomb went off too soon. I understood Bianca's mindset, but she couldn't understand my reaction. She pointed out she was only doing what I had done. She has continued her destructive ways until now she is out of control. In hindsight, I wonder if she would have heeded me if I had confronted her sooner, but that doesn't mitigate my guilt.

Although the destruction and death we caused horrifies me now, I still believe we acted for the right reasons. Bianca, like her mother, doesn't even pretend any sort of goodness. Rather, she reveled in telling me about setting landmines throughout the Middle East, handling ground-to-air missiles in Israel, and putting bombs in various planes. She spent time in Bosnia, Iraq, and Afghanistan blowing up whatever she could find.

As much as I miss my dear Miguel, I'm thankful he didn't live to see what his beloved granddaughter has become. She enjoys destruction, defiance of authority, even narrow escapes for themselves.

I don't know how or when Bianca's destructiveness will end—but end it must, most likely including her death. The knowledge I'm dying has made me a coward. I can't face my beloved granddaughter's just retribution. When the end comes, I pray the authorities will realize a large part of the blame for her actions rests on my shoulders and be lenient with her.

I expect a visit from Bianca in late spring or early summer. I pray I survive long enough to see her again. I also pray I don't live long enough to know what devastation she causes next.

My dear, dear Megan, I again apologize for placing you in such an untenable position. However, I reiterate you are the only person I can trust to do what is right. When you receive this letter, I will already have faced God. I admit I don't expect His forgiveness. I hope you can find in your heart, not only forgiveness for my neglect, but also

*forgiveness for this unwarranted burden.
Grandmother.*

Megan dropped the last page on the floor. She'd read it twice, not believing what she saw the first time. Italian relatives? Resistance? Mafia? It boggled the mind that her grandmother had kept her secrets. Before Granddad died, yes, secrecy would make sense, but during the years since? Megan thought back over the years remembering her grandmother's determination on letting nothing stop her. This made accepting terrorist possibilities easier.

The letter identified the woman's picture on the flyer and explained why the mysterious face had caused so much devastation for decades.

Oh, dear heaven! Megan clapped her hand across her mouth, cutting off a scream. That wasn't her mother who visited. It was Bianca! She was getting ready to leave the country with Megan's father. Was he a terrorist too?

Megan reached for the phone. "Mike? Megan Stanfield. I know it's late, but this is urgent."

"Is someone harassing you again?"

"No." She took a deep breath. "I know who the terrorist is. Mr. Higgins needs to move fast."

"Are you in danger? Is she there?"

"No, she's in Miami preparing to leave the country. She has no idea I penetrated her disguise."

"Okay. Be at my office at seven. I'll have Fred Higgins there. Did you call Frank?"

"No, only you."

"Don't call anyone. I'll call Frank."

With the assurance she would not call anyone, Megan cradled the phone. Slumped in the chair, she stared at the floor. This had been an exhausting, emotion-filled day, but she had answers to the reason for David's visit and the face on the flyer. However, the day brought another question.

Where is Mother?

Chapter 24

Where is Mother?

The knot in Megan's chest tightened. She'd known the question was coming. Here it was, shooting out of Fred Higgins's mouth like a bullet from the weapon he no doubt carried under his jacket.

After an almost sleepless night, Megan arrived at Mike's office before anyone else. The coffee she'd drunk while she waited now threatened to reverse itself and choke her. She felt cornered by the unsmiling men crowded around her. Mike Williams, Frank Anderson, Fred Higgins, John Patterson, and Nicholas Burke filled the room to a suffocating degree. Each held a copy of her grandmother's letter. Higgins tapped the original lying on the desk.

"I accept you'd never heard about Bianca Rossi. However, regardless of your grandmother's letter, your mother must speak for herself. Why didn't you tell us you knew someone else with your face?"

"Because I knew the terrorist couldn't be Mother. I didn't know there was anyone else." Megan leaned forward, willing him to understand. "Mother simply isn't capable of terrorist activities. You read what Grandmother wrote . . . ."

"If she wrote it," Patterson said with a sneer. "How convenient—this letter turning up now. You wrote this whole rigmarole yourself to send us on a wild goose chase."

"That's enough, Patterson. We don't have time for this. Go ahead, Ms. Stanfield."

Megan swallowed her anger. She had hoped John Patterson wouldn't be there. "I don't want to be unkind about my mother, but she truly is light-minded. No one with any sense would trust her with information, much less anything explosive. Everything which pops into her mind comes out her mouth."

Megan studied Mr. Higgins's face but could read nothing. At least he listened.

"Anything else?"

Megan nodded. "My parents, as I thought of them, came day before yesterday for an overnight visit. I hadn't realized they were back from Europe. Father was his usual self, but Mother wasn't. Her chatter was as inane as ever. Overall, she looked and acted like my mother, but I noticed some differences, which disturbed me when we were together."

"Explain."

"Mother has always done anything necessary for a young appearance. She believed widened eyes indicated youthful innocence, for instance. On this visit, I noticed she—this woman—kept her eyes narrowed and only twice met mine." Megan explained this woman's eyes were dull, almost dead, rather than their usual brightness. "Once when I was a child, I asked Mother if she put something in them. She said happy thoughts caused the sparkle. She was always happy. At least when she was with me."

Megan shook her head. "You might not believe eye difference is important, but, together with this, you'll realize the difference is important. Mother is fastidious to the nth degree, especially about avoiding the use of embarrassing words. She moistened her lips. "My throat's dry, could I have some water?"

After a long swig of water, Megan clutched the paper cup. "From my early childhood, Mother insisted we use the word 'act' in a natural way in a sentence to indicate my need for the ladies' room. She would answer with a sentence using the same word, and we would soon excuse ourselves. This was a secret between us. I continued when I was older simply to have close touch with her. Sometimes getting the word into a sentence that fit the conversation was difficult, especially when I was quite small. That was part of our secret game. We laughed about our secret code and promised we would never share it with anyone else."

Megan swallowed a sob. "This is hard to explain. She just wasn't her usual self, so I tested her by using the word 'act' in a sentence, not once but twice. She didn't respond. I asked my father if she was ill. He shrugged it off, reminding me Grandmother had called her whimsical."

"She's inventing the whole thing, I tell you!" Spittle sprayed from Patterson's mouth. "I've never heard anything so preposterous."

"Patterson, I said be quiet. Either keep your mouth shut or go back to Asheville." Higgins turned back to Megan. "This does sound spur-of-the moment, Ms. Stanfield."

"It isn't! I told Jed Anderson last night that I thought Mother was ill. I didn't mention our secret but did talk about her eyes. Just ask him!"

"Perhaps she decided the game was pointless because you're an adult."

"No! It's true we weren't together all the time after my early childhood, but we always used our secret code. We talked about it when we were together last January at Grandmother's funeral. Mother said she'd always wanted to have a secret with her mother, but Grandmother hadn't been interested. Mother sounded wistful when she said we would have our secret forever."

Megan blinked away tears. "Grandmother's letter convinced me that wasn't Mother who came. It was Bianca Rossi impersonating her."

The room was silent while they absorbed her words.

The sheriff spoke for the first time. "That implicates your father."

Megan nodded. Reid Stanfield was without doubt the most stubborn creature on the planet, with an answer for everything, so intelligent she had often wondered how he could tolerate his wife's near stupidity. But terrorist? Megan must accept he was until he convinced her otherwise.

"You told Mike you know where they are." Higgins said.

"They flew to Miami yesterday morning in my father's private plane. Bianca wants to shop before they board ship for a cruise tomorrow. I don't know what time."

"Can you identify the plane?"

"Twelve-passenger Gulf Stream IV." Megan focused her attention on Fred Higgins, who glanced at Mike. The knot in her chest expanded into bands circling her ribs.

"I can see what you're thinking—drugs, money laundering, whatever that entails. However, my father is a highly regarded authority on international finance, on call in many countries worldwide. There's never been even whispers about his integrity. Besides the substantial professional fees he receives, he inherited a sizeable fortune from his father, who had invested *his* father's money."

"Does he fly the plane himself?"

"Father has a license but has a combination pilot/mechanic on his payroll. He didn't say who was flying this trip. I imagine he has the pilot with him to return the plane to its hangar in Teterboro, New Jersey. Father has done that before when he didn't need the plane for an extended period. He wouldn't now because they plan an extended cruise through some islands. They didn't say which."

Fred asked about the ship.

"A private yacht owned by Ed Abbott of Manhattan. He's quite wealthy, so I imagine the ship is sizeable. I don't know anything else about him."

"Can you supply your father's photograph?"

Megan unzipped the inside pocket of her purse. The evening before, she had debated whether she should offer a picture, but, in the end, she removed this one from the double frame on her bedroom dresser. She was in enough trouble for not telling them about her mother's resemblance to the flyer photo, so she must be as helpful as possible. Megan handed Higgins the colored photograph. "This is a publicity photo made last year. I'd like it back, please."

"Okay, Ms. Stanfield. We'll take it from here. You *are* staying here?"

"Yes, I'm staying here. You'll tell me when you've arrested them?"

"I will."

"You'll find out what they've done with my mother?" Megan's voice cracked.

"I'm still not convinced this woman is not your mother. If she isn't, Interpol or the FBI will locate her. You can be sure of that."

"That woman is *not* my mother. I want to see my father too."

"I can and will arrange that." Higgins disappeared through the doorway, herding the local FBI agents before him.

"Mike, you'll be sure I get to see Father and learn about Mother?"

"Yes, if it's within my power."

"Between us, we'll manage," Frank told her. "One way or another."

His grim tone told Megan anyone who stood in his way would be lucky to come away in one piece. With a nod, she left the room, one question dominating her brain.

Where is Mother?

After leaving Mike's office, Megan hesitated on the steps. Home? No. She should eat, but hunger wasn't what drove her toward the diner. Some people still whispered and stared at her. Without doubt, this morning's long session had added heat to a boiling pot. With a smile pasted on her face, she threaded her way to the back booth where Fran eyed her with anxiety.

"I've been worried. You didn't come in or answer your phones."

Megan whispered as she slid across the bench, "I'll tell you everything when we can be private. Right now, there's no need to worry."

"Good morning, Ms. Stanfield, what can I get you?"

"Good morning, Mattie. I'll have scrambled eggs and bacon, orange juice, and coffee, please." She must get back to her normal life. Or not. These days 'normal' was sheer chaos. "Let's discuss something pleasant: the Christmas festivities around here, for instance."

Fran followed her lead. "The churches have various programs. You can be sure somebody will recruit you to take part at our church. The schools always invite the public to whatever they're doing. The town public works department hangs the decorations just before Thanksgiving."

"They had better get started because that's next week," Megan reminded her.

"Heavens, already? Anyway, they also put lights on the huge fir on the square. A tree-lighting celebration occurs on the evening after Thanksgiving. Uncle Josh, the oldest resident, throws the switch after the mayor gives a tantalizing count-down."

"Is there a parade? I've read most small towns have them."

"The committee works on that all year. Robin, as mayor, leads the parade. Santa brings up the rear. People come into town on Friday morning for shopping. They stay for the parade in the afternoon and the tree lighting just at dark. Afterward, we sing some holiday songs before going home."

"May I join you?" Jed stood by the booth, smiling at them.

Considering her morning, Megan was not surprised she hadn't until this minute thought of him. She moved toward the wall, sliding her plate along the table.

After Mattie left with the coffee carafe, he turned to Megan. "Mom is inviting unattached, no-family-nearby friends to Thanksgiving dinner. Can you come?"

"Sounds great. I'm a loner at this time of the year. Who else will be there?"

"Fran, how about you?"

"I'm another loner and gladly accept."

Jed shoved his empty cup aside. "I'll see several others this afternoon. After that, I'm leaving town for a few days."

Megan watched him stride away, and then she turned to Fran. "Time for work."

"I want to hear what happened this morning. Someone saw you enter Mike's office before seven. As a result, people have quizzed me from the minute I arrived here. You're sure you aren't worried?"

Megan swallowed a lump. "There is one worrisome thing, but I'm not in trouble."

"What—never mind. Come for lunch at my place. I'll put something together."

"Thank you. It'll be a relief to talk to somebody who isn't accusing me of every illegal thing under the sun."

Three hours of speculative glances, but few sales later, Megan hurried to Fine Feathers, where Fran wasted no time flipping the open sign to closed. She led the way upstairs where she pulled a bowl of chicken salad from the fridge. "Talk."

Megan pushed her plate away. Fran had long since finished her meal and sat in rapt attention. Megan had ignored the salad for minutes at a time while she recounted the past couple of days.

"So that's the current terrorist situation."

"You're surely in agony, wondering about your mother. We'll think positive thoughts."

"I'm afraid we're too late. Father and Bianca couldn't risk Mother coming at an inconvenient time, which must be what happened. When I get my hands on them . . . ."

Fran held her while Megan fought gulping sobs until she regained her self-control.

"Where's my mother?"

There was no answer, nor did Megan expect one. *Megan Elizabeth Stanfield get a grip.* She groped inside her purse for tissue. Facing Fran, she squared her shoulders. "No matter what comes, I can deal with it."

"I know you can."

"Have you told anybody—Jed—I was a terrorist suspect?"

"No, but he knows something is going on with you. Everybody does. Will you tell him?

"Maybe. Someday. I don't know."

"To help you make up your mind, how about some nice gooey brownies?"

"With peanut butter?"

"Is there any other kind?"

Megan laughed. "Chocolate and peanut butter— lethal combo, but oh, so yummy." She popped another brownie in her mouth. "Now, I must go."

Fran gave her a hug at the door. "Tell me the instant you hear from the Feds."

ฌ ฌ ฌ ฌ ฌ

The call, which came from Mike late in the evening, sent Megan into a spiral of despair. "Why would they leave early?"

"We won't know the answer until the authorities catch them. The FBI hasn't yet determined whether they're on the yacht. They do know the pilot returned the plane to Teterboro. He didn't see them onto the yacht, so at this point, they could be anywhere."

"What happens now?"

"Fred called Washington, who, in turn, called Interpol for assistance. Otherwise, I don't know. We just wait."

Megan cradled the phone. Wait to learn her mother's whereabouts. Wait to confront her father. Wait to stare into Bianca's dead eyes. Wait to learn if they suspected her of naming them. Wait for them to come after her.

After yet another sleepless night, Megan ran her usual five-mile loop, showered, and speed-dialed the second number on her phone: Fran.

"Oh no, Megan! They could be anywhere by now."

"I know, including this area."

"Be careful. I know. Come stay with me until they're found."

"No way. I won't risk my friends' lives. If they want me, they'll find me anywhere. They might send another terrorist. I'll stay away from my friends."

"How will you explain missing Thanksgiving dinner with the Andersons?"

"Oh, dear. I forgot about Thanksgiving. There's still a couple more days, so maybe the authorities will locate them before then. We can only hope. I won't have much of a holiday season if Father and Bianca are on the loose."

"True. Well, you must eat, so I'll see you at the diner."

"No, I'm off my feed, as Jed said the other day about one of his cows. I'll eat at home or the shop office in case what I swallow comes back."

"There is that. Okay, call me." Fran laughed. "Texting is all the rage, but I would rather hear voices than decipher abbreviated words! LOL!

Chapter 25

On the Move

Bianca stood at the railing staring into the starry sky. She would enjoy having access to Reid Stanfield's millions. When they met ten years ago, she'd looked for him in Forbes 500. What she read fueled her determined pursuit of him. Did his wealth come honestly, or did he have a side occupation? She didn't care about him; she just wanted access to his money. The jewels he'd given her through the years supported her chosen lifestyle. She'd had them replicated one by one by an expert. She dared anyone to tell the difference between the faux and the real. She still had several baubles, which would keep her going well into the future, but having his bank account readily available was better. One way or another, Bianca Rossi would make sure she could get her hands on it.

She hadn't done the shopping she'd hoped in Miami. The Abbotts had pushed them to sail early—she wondered why they were so jumpy—so here she was well out into international waters already.

Perhaps moving around was best, especially in wide-open water, where no one could sneak up on her. She hadn't stayed any one place for more than a few days since she avoided Michigan authorities on her drive into Wisconsin. From there, she crossed into Canada, after the fiasco that started her on the run this time. She would lie low for now. However, next time . . . well, the Miami airport could prove an interesting challenge.

Bianca didn't remember her mother, but she'd always been proud she was her grandmother's image. Sitting among people trying to locate her amused her no end. Her earliest infiltration had been the *Sureté* in

Paris. They never suspected one owner of that face was helping them search. The secretiveness had been almost as satisfying as watching them scurry around like a dog chasing its tail, after they had glimpsed her face. Ah, a night to remember!

The old-timers in Milan revered her because of her face and told her stories, some many times over, about their years with Alma Rossi, the name they had called her. Grandmother was dead, though. Soon her old friends would be too, so maybe now was time for a permanent disguise. She would give disguise some thought on this cruise, in case Reid ever noticed she wasn't Susan.

She'd had a brief affair with him ten years ago. Brief because he wasn't worth the effort. She had only seduced him so she could hold it over Susan's head. When she realized his wife was indifferent, Bianca ended the affair, except when she was low on funds. Since her last abortion, she'd chosen celibacy.

Reid stood a couple of feet along the rail. "My dear, I'm sorry you didn't have time to shop. I've never known Ed Abbott to be in such a hurry."

"Darling, I can shop another time." Bianca tucked her hand under Reid's elbow. "Right now, let's go to the lounge for a drink."

Chapter 26

Playing the Waiting Game

"Hello?"

"You're out of breath. Been out building your appetite?" Jed's voice came into Megan's ear.

The days leading to Thanksgiving had passed without a call from the Feds or a terrorist visit. Megan stopped looking across her shoulder. She had little business, which Fran assured her was normal, and would improve, beginning on Friday. Reduced business gave Megan too much time, brooding over her mother. Talking with Fran several times every day helped to a small extent, at least while they were talking.

Thanksgiving morning dawned clear but with a nip in the air, the kind of weather Megan liked for her five-mile run. She returned in time to grab the ringing landline. Her cell phone was on the charger. In her hurry to outrun her worries, she forgot to put it in her pocket.

"Not exactly. Since you noticed my short breath, though, I obviously should run more than I have recently. Welcome home," she added.

"Thank you. I wondered if you remembered I've been gone."

"I remembered." Megan chuckled. "No midnight calls."

"You know I haven't called so late in ages—darling."

"Jed Anderson, I told you . . . ."

"I knew that would get a rise. I hope you remember you've having dinner at the farm."

"And miss Pearl's cooking? No way."

"Great. Shall I pick you up near noon?"

"Yes, noon is good, provided you remember what to call me."

"I'll try, darling."

The phone clicked before Megan could retort, but she stood there grinning. She admitted it. She'd missed him. It would be nice if he meant the darling. The grin faded. What prompted that thought?

Shortly before noon, Megan stared inside her closet, finally deciding on a knee-length navy wool sheath, which needed something bright. Digging through her jewelry box, she found just the thing, an enamel butterfly pin painted deep gold with tiny burgundy specks. She fastened the iridescent pin high on her left shoulder.

When the doorbell rang, she hurried down the stairs.

Jed gave her a long look. "Hmmm, if I try to see the butterfly closer, will it fly?"

She turned her shoulder toward him. He leaned closer before a slow smile crossed his face, and he gathered her in his arms. Before she could react, he captured her lips.

Resting against him, Megan responded for a long moment before she pulled away. "Nice, but shouldn't we be on our way to the farm?"

"I would rather continue this." Jed captured her mouth again, this time leaving her breathless when he raised his head. "However, I suppose you're right."

Turning, he opened the door with a flourish. "Madame, your carriage waits."

Her mouth gaped. No wonder she hadn't heard the Bronco arrive. There, at the foot of the steps, stood a dark blue Mustang. "Yours?"

"Hmmm." His lips curved into a seductive smile. "I'm trying to tempt a beautiful lady into succumbing to my charms. Am I succeeding?"

She ignored his question, as she locked the door, but complimented him on his taste in cars.

"I think so. This one not only has Sirius radio, but, also, a CD player. I didn't bother getting one for the Bronco or truck, figuring CDs would skip when I drive on bumpy roads."

"I admit I would rather ride a Mustang with four wheels than one with four hooves."

"Sissy!" He helped her into the car and then hurried around to the driver's side. "I ordered it several weeks ago from an old friend, who has a dealership in Atlanta. He called Thursday to tell me the car was ready for me. I stayed there a few days catching up on his life."

"I'm sure you had fun."

Jed gave her a sideways glance. "I thought about inviting you along, but considering how fast you shove me out the door here, I decided you would say no."

Her lips tightened. "You have that right."

"Easy, now. Someday you'll realize I'm not that guy from Detroit. I hope sooner rather than later."

Nestled within the soft bucket seat, Megan was silent until he stopped the car at the farm. "I know you're not David. I just need time getting used to believing you're different."

ꙡ ꙡ ꙡ ꙡ ꙡ

Jed tossed and turned, punched his pillow, and untangled the blankets again. Thanksgiving had always been family time, the time to review the year's harvest. He hadn't been sure he wanted outsiders around the table, even ones he knew well. However, his mother had wanted the change this year for some reason. She'd made it work. By the time they reached the dining table, the others didn't seem like outsiders, especially Megan.

Megan. Jed gave in to his thoughts. He had missed her when he was in Atlanta. The women he met there had been attractive, but they were not who he wanted. Megan was beginning to care for him, or so he told himself. He wished she would trust him with the terrorism issue. Frank had told him the latest, so he knew she was no longer in danger from the Feds. Did love produce trust, or vice-versa? Regardless, he wanted both from her.

ಟಿ ಟಿ ಟಿ ಟಿ ಟಿ

On Friday afternoon, Megan closed the store to watch the Christmas parade with Katie at her side. Floats pulled by farm tractors alternated with school bands and cheerleaders. There weren't many entries but not bad for a small town, she supposed.

"What's that dance, Katie?" Some teenagers whirled by, boys wearing red and white checked shirts, girls in short skirts held aloft with crinolines. "It's different from square dancing, more upbeat."

"Mountain clogging—takes a lot of energy."

"You're so lively, why aren't you dancing with the group?"

"I wish!" Katie laughed. "I was born with two left feet, so no dancing for me."

"Have you had formal lessons? I was a real klutz until Mother enrolled me in ballet classes. They helped me, so perhaps lessons would help you too. Not ballet, perhaps, but something modern."

"No, I haven't had lessons. There's always been a different need for whatever money I've had. Look, here comes Santa!"

After they waved to the jolly old elf, Megan reopened the store, a crowd entering on their heels.

"Need some help?" Jed asked from the doorway.

"Yes!" Megan was past resenting his helping in her store. That had sneaked up on her too, but with this crowd, she appreciated all help. "You can help Katie write sales slips. See, you write the item and price, hand me the slip and money, and then wrap the item in tissue and bag it. Clear?"

"Got it."

They worked steadily until the last customer left at six-thirty, a few minutes before Uncle Josh would light the Christmas tree.

"Katie, can you come in at eight tomorrow and help me stock shelves?"

"Sure can," she answered, before joining her friends near the tree.

Megan and Jed watched from This 'n That, oohing and aahing with everyone else when the lights came on.

"There must be thousands of bulbs," Megan murmured.

"I never heard anyone say, but there are certainly plenty."

A rich baritone voice started singing "Rudolph the Red-nosed Reindeer." Soon everyone joined in. Megan dug into her memory for songs she hadn't sung since childhood. A rousing rendition of "Here Comes Santa Claus" ended the impromptu songfest.

"Jed. I'm going back inside to put together a bank deposit. Do you want to come with me?"

"You bet. I like watching people work."

Soon, with the bank bag tucked under her arm, they left the store.

"Hey, Jed, can I ask you something?" a loud masculine voice called.

"Talk to him. I'll go on to the bank."

"You're sure? Okay, I'll wait for you right here."

Megan strolled across the square, dropped her deposit bag through the slot and started back toward her store, exchanging greetings with several people on the square. A huge—gigantic—change since she opened her new store, she reflected with satisfaction. Rarely did anyone snub her. How many she knew by name surprised her.

Everybody left the square going the other way, leaving her alone. From the corner of her eye, she saw a male figure move toward her from behind a large shrub, baggy jeans flapping around his legs. Megan quickened her step, but he soon was close enough to touch her arm.

She whirled toward the man who had been stalking her. "I told you to stay away from me."

"I just wanted . . . ."

"I don't care what you want." Megan pushed his chest. "I've dealt with worse than you, so be warned. If you come near me again, I'll do you bodily harm you won't soon forget. Do you understand me?"

"I just wanted . . . ." He glanced across her shoulder and scuttled into the shadows.

Megan heard Jed calling her, but she didn't turn from watching the shadows.

"Sorry I took so long." He frowned when she didn't answer. "Megan? What's wrong?"

She pointed toward the shadows. "A man was following me, touched my arm. The one who stares at me."

Jed ran in that direction, his footsteps crunching through fallen leaves.

Megan stood her ground, peering around, alert to every sound. She spun on her heel to face oncoming footsteps, grasping her bag strap ready to swing, relaxing her vigilance only when Jed arrived.

"I lost him. We'll tell the police, and then I'll take you home."

Moments later, the desk sergeant took down the information, skepticism evident in his face. "Miss Stanfield, I'm aware you've had some problems, but can you be sure this was the same person?"

"Yes, I'm sure." Anger at his condescending manner sharpened her voice. "I chased him away when he was hanging around my store after hours. I've caught him staring at me on the square."

"Was it his voice on the phone?"

"I can't be sure because the caller always muffled his voice. This man tonight talked quite low. Who else can it be? Surely there aren't two people harassing me." Megan didn't mention her fear Bianca Rossi might send someone after her. The man in the square was local, as was the Yogurt Raisin Man, who still made her nervous.

"Okay, now this man tonight. Did you get any impression about his age? Was he agile like a teen or slower like an older person?"

"No doubt about that. He's an older man. Even hurrying away, he shuffled."

She could only give a general description because of dim light when she'd seen the man up close. Every older man she saw on the street wore baggy jeans and denim jackets. Frustration gripped her. If the cop was skeptical about her story, she felt the same about the possibility of help.

His glance on a constant move, Jed kept his arm around her shoulder while they walked toward their cars. He waited until she was inside her car with locked doors.

"Are you okay to drive?"

"I'm frustrated, not nervous. I can do this." Who was she trying to convince—herself or Jed?

"My Mustang is over there. I'll stay on your bumper all the way home."

There, he stayed close until she was inside and the lock had clicked shut.

Reaction set in when the Mustang left her driveway. Megan raised the thermostat, which didn't help her shivers, so she huddled on the sofa, a comforter wrapped around her shoulders. What should she do? Nobody believed her about this man's harassing her. Megan was in this mess alone. She wrestled with, but rejected, idea after idea. Guns scared her. She didn't own one or want one. If he got close enough to touch her again, she would also be close enough to touch him. Carrying her baseball bat everywhere was impossible.

Megan flung back the comforter and marched to the kitchen. After comparing weight and length, she chose a knife with a narrow, pointed blade. She didn't remember when or why she bought the knife but did know how she would use it, whether against local men or terrorists. The knife fit nicely in the side pocket of her cross-body bag. Megan Elizabeth Stanfield had been pushed around enough.

ꛯ ꛯ ꛯ ꛯ ꛯ

He slipped through his back door and leaned against it until his breathing returned to normal. He'd almost caught her tonight. If he'd been able to reach her, cover her mouth, before she saw him, he could have dealt with her, but he'd rushed away, avoiding Jed Anderson. He'd stood, teeth clenched, holding his breath until they'd gone.

Without turning on a light, he settled into the rocking chair which had belonged to his grandfather and then his father and, now, him. Who would get the chair after his death? His only child, a son, had died in an accident while in high school, so only nephews and nieces were left. The chair should go to a nephew, keeping the chair in the male line at least for another generation. He would write that down when he had more energy. Right now, all he wanted was for this headache to go away.

ℸℸℸℸℸ

Next morning, Fran wanted details of Megan's latest encounter, so Megan gave her bare facts before changing the subject. "I left Katie in charge, so I only have a few minutes. Where do I find dancing lessons?"

"Why? The grapevine says you're an excellent dancer."

"Not for me. Yesterday, Katie told me she can't dance, so I thought I might give her a gift certificate for lessons."

"Great idea. Wish I'd thought of it. Her family never has money for anything frivolous. A former instructor at the Fletcher School in Asheville retired here last year. I understand she gives private lessons, so you can call her."

With the woman's name in her purse, Megan hurried back to This 'n That. Mike Williams met her at the door.

"I was on my way to find you. Did you have any more trouble last night?"

Megan refrained from asking if he cared any more than his sergeant did. "No, Jed followed me home. Neither of us saw anything suspicious."

"Keep your eyes open. The other reason I came. The DNA report on the bones and your cheek swab came this morning. There's no question she's related to you, so we can assume they belong to Eva."

"I never thought otherwise. Can we have her funeral service now?"

"If a service is what you want, yes. As far as I know, you and your mother are Eva's only relatives. Will Mrs. Stanfield have any problem with holding a service?"

"*Darling, how quaint!*"

Mike roared. "Perfect, truly perfect. Go ahead with your arrangements."

Had he forgotten the woman he met wasn't her mother, or did he truly not believe it? The imitation had been spontaneous bringing spasms of pain.

Mother, where are you?

Chapter 27

Finally at Rest

"So, boys, Aunt Eva's funeral will be at two o'clock this Sunday afternoon at the Baptist church. Can you come?" Megan glanced around the boys who clustered near her outside This 'n That after school on Tuesday.

"Yes!" They grinned, high-fiving each other.

"I don't go to the Baptist church," one disappointed child told her.

"That doesn't matter," she assured him. "Aunt Eva liked all little boys, no matter what church they attended, so tell all your friends to come."

The freckled-faced lad beamed his pleasure.

"Now hear this, fellows, you must get your parents' permission. I know, let's do this. Sit with your parents until Pastor Rogers calls you forward to sing. Okay?"

With a chorus of yeses ringing in her ears, she gave hugs all around and sent them home. Glancing toward her store, she saw Jed with one foot propped against the wall, his arms crossed on his chest.

"I believe Eva isn't the only family member who likes boys," he said, when he swung into step beside her.

"I haven't been around them much, but, yes, I do like boys. They're uncomplicated. Grandmother did too." Megan hadn't thought they had one thing in common. Had she concentrated so much on hurt feelings that she'd missed anything else? Had she been so aware of surface stuff she hadn't looked beneath?

"Having youngsters sit with their parents is a good idea. In groups, these little imps tend to forget themselves."

"I hadn't thought about their behavior. I wanted to make sure we have a large crowd."

"I imagine people will push out the walls, as we say around here. Eva's funeral might be the main event of this holiday season. Her service is on everybody's lips."

He was right.

Megan dealt with questions from everyone who saw her. Can just anybody come? Yes. Would they really sing Christmas carols at a *funeral*? Yes, because those were Aunt Eva's favorite songs. Were little boys really taking part? They'll sing "Away in a Manger," so be sure your son knows it. Why not little girls too? Aunt Eva taught boys, not girls, in her Sunday school class. The questions continued until Megan was ready to hide. She told herself she didn't care what anyone thought, but couldn't they keep their negative opinions to themselves? Oh, well, their questions kept her mind off her mother for minutes at a time.

Days had passed with no word from the FBI. No one had spotted Ed Abbott's yacht. They could do nothing until they knew whether Reid and Bianca were on the yacht. Interpol had distributed the flyer, including Reid Stanfield's picture, but there had been no sightings.

Wednesday evening at prayer meeting, Pastor Rogers announced Eva's funeral service. "From what I've heard around town the past few days, we can expect quite a crowd. If you come but can't get a seat inside, you can attend the graveside service instead."

By the time Sunday afternoon rolled around, Megan questioned whether she was doing the right thing by having a public funeral. When Jed came by for her, she needed his reassurance.

"You're doing the right thing. Poor old Eva deserves the attention. She's already waited much too long. Now relax, everything will be fine."

They could see people crowding around the front door when they slipped around to the side door of the church an hour early.

"Mike has his entire force out for traffic duty here. I understand Frank has his deputies at the cemetery. Mike will escort Uncle Josh and Doc Peabody, as well as other older people who might have known Eva, to the side door, so they can sit in the front."

"I should have thought of that."

"Except for digging up Eva's bones, this is my one contribution," he reminded her. "Don't begrudge me it."

"We'll never get everybody inside." Pastor Rogers peeked out a front window. "What should we do?"

Megan thought for a moment. "I believe we should have those people with small boys come inside first. They will sit near the front. Then, we'll open the doors for the rest. Does that sound alright, Jed?"

"I think so. When the pews are full, we'll send others to the cemetery. They'll be in the front for Eva's service there."

When they opened the doors half an hour before service time, elderly people filled the two front pews on both sides of the center aisle with several seated behind them.

The other pews filled within moments, and the usher closed the door. The chattering stopped when Megan faced the congregation.

"I imagine you know my great-aunt, Eva Malloy, died under mysterious circumstances many years ago. During all this time, her body, more recently only her bones, lay under the hedge at her homeplace. We might never know details of her death, but we can know we've done the right thing by giving her a proper funeral and burial. Let's remember old times and old friends. Perhaps we'll hear Aunt Eva's words, her laughter echo across the years."

Megan sat beside Jed on the front pew, gripping his hand. "I wonder if she's here. I would like to know I've followed her wishes."

"I'm sure Eva will allow you to see her before her service is over."

After a prayer, Pastor Rogers called the small boys forward. "I was not acquainted with Eva Malloy, but church records indicate she taught the Little Boys Sunday School Class while still in her teens. For that reason, small boys of today will sing a song she taught their predecessors."

Megan blinked away tears, listening to high-pitched voices, many off key, sing about the baby lying in the manger.

Interspersed with other Christmas music, several men recounted memories of Miss Eva's leadership. The oldest people spoke in quavering voices as they recalled growing up with the Malloy twins during the Great Depression.

The church service ended with "Star of Bethlehem." The somber crowd filed out, listening as the organ chimes tolled, "I Heard the Bells on Christmas Day."

Megan and Jed followed the hearse to the Malloy family cemetery.

A hush fell on the crowd when Pastor Rogers stood beside the coffin. "Because there was no room inside the church building for everyone, I'll give anyone time to remember Eva Malloy with a few words."

Under the cover of a deep masculine voice, Megan elbowed Jed. "She's here! Aunt Eva is standing on her coffin. I'm so glad she came to her service."

He squeezed her hand. "I knew she would."

"Jed, she's coming toward us with her arms outstretched."

"She touched my face. Didn't she touch me?" he asked. "I'm sure I felt her pat my cheeks."

"Yes, Aunt Eva patted your face, Jed. She appreciates your finding her bones. Now she's hovering above the coffin again."

Pastor Rogers stepped forward when the crowd grew quiet. "After a brief prayer, we'll sing 'Silent Night' as we leave the cemetery."

After the others had moved away, Megan remained seated, unaware of anyone else while she gazed upon her ancestor one last time. When Eva reached her, Megan stood. She looked her aunt straight in the eyes.

"Are you pleased with what we did, Aunt Eva?" she whispered. "Are you at peace? Can you rest now? Can you forgive whoever left you lying under the hedge all these years?"

Soft hands patted Megan's cheeks. Eva floated back to her place above the coffin and levitated into a prone position. Megan watched her great-aunt vanish through the coffin lid.

Megan breathed a sigh of contentment, slowly becoming aware of her surroundings again. Jed stood near, studying her face.

"She's happy, Jed."

"Yes, I'm sure she is." He hesitated. "You know something? I feel blessed. I never saw Eva, but I felt her touch. I'll never doubt again."

Megan nodded. "I'm drained. Let's go home."

"Would you like to come home with me, perhaps have supper with us?"

"I don't think so. When I get hungry, I'll open a can of soup or something."

They completed the short ride in silence.

"I'd rather not leave you alone right away, Megan."

"I'm okay, truly, Jed, but you're welcome to keep me company for a while."

Megan sank onto a small sofa, lifting her feet onto the coffee table. She leaned her head back, while Jed sorted through her albums.

"Is there any Hawaiian music?"

"Hmmm, Ray Coniff, but why Hawaiian?"

"I don't know any music which will take us further from what we've experienced today, do you?"

Tension eased from Megan's shoulders as the strains of "Lovely Hula Hands" filled the room.

Jed sat beside her, clasping her hand.

Garlic scent sautéing in butter greeted Megan when she woke half an hour later. She watched Jed fold butterfly shrimp into the pan.

"How did you know shrimp scampi is my favorite seafood?"

"Hello, sleepyhead. I didn't, but scampi is easy."

"Excuse me a moment, and then I'll help."

When she returned, she had washed sleep from her eyes and tidied her hair.

He surveyed her with a twinkle. "I like the scrubbed look."

"Go on with you, flatterer. How come you can cook? I thought Pearl maintained control over the kitchen."

"I've picked up some nuggets through the years. The water is boiling for the linguini. You can mix a salad dressing."

Humming "Lovely Hula Hands," she tasted the vinaigrette, added fresh basil, and shook it again. "You even have the table set. I didn't realize I had slept long enough for you to do so much."

They talked about the funeral services while they ate. Afterwards, they loaded the dishwasher before taking their coffee to the other end of the room.

"It's getting dark out, so I'll close the drapes." Megan glanced outside but, then, looked closer. "Jed, there's someone out there."

He rushed toward her. "Where? I don't see anyone. Yes, I do, going toward the road. You stay right here."

Megan stood by the door, but the rasp of gears told them the culprit had gone. Returning to the kitchen, he punched numbers into his cell phone.

"Mike? Good, you're there. Jed, at Megan's place. There's been someone hanging around here, but he got away before I could catch him."

Jed grasped Megan around the shoulders. "No, I couldn't recognize him, didn't see the car either. Either an older model straight shift or someone has driven it carelessly because the gears made a horrible noise. I know there's nothing you can do. I only wanted you to be aware someone is still harassing her."

Putting down the phone, he cradled her in his arms. "I'm staying the night."

Megan shook her head at him. "No, you're not, Jed. Remember, I lived most of my life in a place much more dangerous than here. No one can get into this house once I lock doors and windows."

He shook her shoulders until her head rocked back and forth. "Heaven deliver me from independent females!"

"I'm not being independent." She shoved his chest. "If you stay the night here, we'll be the talk of the diner in the morning. I *will not* be the subject of gossip over sausage biscuits and coffee."

"You're a stubborn woman, Megan Stanfield, but I love you anyway."

I love you anyway. The words reverberated inside her skull until she was almost dizzy. He couldn't. *He said he did*, a niggling little voice said. He can't mean it. *He said it*. I don't want his love, just his friendship. *Will you at least try to be truthful to yourself?*

Jed tugged her along while he checked the doors and windows. He satisfied himself the house was as secure as locks could make it before he left under protest.

Exhausted, Megan shed her clothing and dragged a gown over her head. Settling between the rose-scented sheets, she slept, but not peacefully.

A faceless man chased her, his feet pounding on pavement while he taunted her with a phone held toward her. She ran from him, his maniacal laughter following her.

Megan battled into wakefulness. The laughter she could still hear was rising wind. The pounding footsteps were thunder rolls coming ever closer. Shaking off the nightmare, she brewed some chamomile tea and cradled a cup in her hands until warmth spread over her.

ℷ ℷ ℷ ℷ ℷ

He stared into the dying fire. The woman's face smiled from among the embers. The image changed from the woman with short curly hair to one with longer hair, which hung down her back. The smile stayed the same, the long hair seemed right. At least there was only one live woman haunting him now. Who is this woman with long hair? That's what bothered him. There were two women, one smile, two hair styles. Enough to drive a man insane, if he wasn't already. He wondered about the funeral, which had caused so much talk. He avoided the church service, hadn't wanted to be inside with that woman. At the cemetery, he'd watched from spruce tree shadows. He'd known both the Malloy twins, yet he could only remember them in childhood. Maybe they'd moved away while he was in the army. However, that wouldn't explain Eva's bones under the hedge.

His head throbbed with familiar pain, and he shivered the way he had last winter when he had the flu. He couldn't bear these headaches any longer. He must destroy the hold the woman had over him. There was only one way.

Chapter 28

Caught!

Bianca watched a police helicopter circle the yacht, before it settled precariously on the small deck. Had someone penetrated her disguise? Perhaps the cops want the Abbotts instead. Something had kept them nervous from the moment they boarded. There had been some air activity one day out of Miami. With little explanation, the captain changed course. He found an inlet large enough to accommodate the yacht and pulled into shadows provided by overhanging tree branches. After 48 hours with no air activity, the yacht got underway again. Bianca had thought she was safe. Now she wasn't sure.

She called on nerves of steel to see her through whatever lay ahead. She pasted on her most inane expression. Tucking her hand inside Reid's elbow, she said, "I've never seen one of those. Isn't this exciting?"

He covered her hand with his. "Be quiet, my dear."

Four men stepped onto the deck, ducking under the propellers. The chopper lifted straight up before moving away, hovering within view.

Bianca concentrated on her breathing when the men zeroed in on her and stopped within two feet of her, looking closely at her face.

"Under Interpol authority, I arrest you, Bianca Rossi, for suspected terrorist activities in the United States, Europe, the Middle East, South America, and Africa. More charges may follow. Cuff her," he told the closest agent. "No, not the plastic ties. The steel ones. Behind her back."

The agent pushed the sputtering Reid aside, while he handcuffed Bianca and laid his heavy hand on her shoulder.

"Darling, do something! I'm not Bianca. How can they mistake me for her?"

Reid stepped forward. "She's right. This is my wife, Susan Stanfield. She's nothing like Bianca Rossi."

"You admit to knowing Ms. Rossi."

"We've both known her for several years. They're close in size. However, Bianca has much darker hair, almost black, and brown eyes. You can see Susan's eyes are hazel, much lighter. Also, Bianca's face is fuller."

"We're confident of this woman's identity. Your own words indicate you are in collusion with her. Therefore, Reid Stanfield, under Interpol authority, I arrest you on suspicion of terrorism and/or being an accessory to Bianca Rossi's terrorist activities. More charges may follow. Cuff him."

The agent waved the helicopter to return. When the chopper settled on the deck, two agents pushed their captives on board and climbed in after them.

Bianca sat in tight-lipped silence, while the senior agent shouted to the two remaining agents to return the yacht to Miami.

As the helicopter lifted, one thought hammered Bianca's brain. Her plans had gone sideways. Miquel Rossi's granddaughter was in shackles. Heads would roll when the news reached her Italian connections.

Chapter 29

Confrontations

Megan gripped her hands until the knuckles turned white. More than two hours had passed since a pinstripe-suited agent had ushered her into this small room at Miami's FBI office. She'd thumbed through the few magazines stacked on a small table, as if there would be anything of interest in three-year-old business publications. Or current ones, for that matter. She had counted every spot on the ceiling twice over, getting different numbers. A fly buzzing at the window had nearly driven her berserk until she attacked it with one of the magazines.

The stormy night of horrible dreams ended only when Mike called her before daylight that morning. The fugitives were in Miami. Fred Higgins had arranged seats for her on puddle jumpers to Atlanta and then Miami. Megan was thankful he'd made the trip easy for her, even though he did so for his own convenience. He might need her to confront her father and Bianca, which was okay too, because that was her intention. With or without FBI assistance or permission, she would face her father and his terrorist lover.

The door opened to reveal another woman wearing a black pinstripe pants suit. Must be the uniform of the day.

"Please come this way, Ms. Stanfield."

"Are you taking me to my father?"

"Yes."

Moments later, Megan stood in a room only a little larger than the one she'd occupied earlier. A table surrounded by four straight chairs stood in the middle. Her father had pushed one chair away from the table and sat facing the door, his legs straight out. His face was pale, sweat beaded on his brow, his clothing was rumpled, his tie gone. She'd never seen him other than GQ perfect. He wouldn't make their cover now.

Megan wasted no sympathy on him. "Where's Mother?"

"I don't know."

She hovered over him, her fists clenched at her sides. He met her eyes for a moment, but he collapsed like her rubber ball that Jimmy Johnson punctured when she was four. She was angry then. Tears had blinded her while she pummeled him around the head. There were no tears this time. Her anger went too deep.

"Don't lie to me! You're living with a woman who looks like her, the woman who assumed Mother's identity." Megan's voice rose. She didn't care if there were people watching on the other side of the mirrored wall or listening on hidden mikes. She didn't care how many microphones or cameras there were in the room. She cared about only one thing, her mother. "How dared you bring Bianca Rossi—a terrorist, for heaven's sake!—to Crawfordville, pretending she was Mother? How dared you not tell me the truth when I asked if Mother was ill? Answer me, you sorry excuse for a human being!"

He sat in silence while her recriminations fell like stones around him.

"What did Mother ever do to deserve your treatment? True, she wasn't serious-minded. She didn't have your financial brain. Most of the time, her chatter was inane, certainly not up to your standards, so I must wonder. Did you just use her as a cover for your terrorist activities?"

At last, he spoke. "I am not—never have been—a terrorist. The very idea is against everything I believe, my every instinct."

"I'm supposed to believe you when you're living with a known terrorist?"

"Perhaps not. Nevertheless, it's true." He looked straight into her face. "Unfaithful husband and neglectful father, I must admit, but terrorist? Absolutely not. Never in this world would I deliberately place even one person's life in jeopardy and certainly not large crowds."

"If you're innocent, why did you leave Miami so fast? You said you'd be there another day because *she* wanted to shop."

"Leaving earlier was not my idea. Ed Abbott insisted for some reason. I overheard somebody here say Nancy collapsed when they turned back toward Miami, so I guess they're in trouble too. I've realized I have no real knowledge of them. Just surface stuff we know about society acquaintances."

Megan shook her head. "Reid Stanfield—icon of international finance—hobnobbing with criminals. You have your work cut out getting out of this mess, if that is even possible. Let the cards fall where they may. All I want to know is what you did with Mother."

"God is my witness. I don't know where Susan is. I am innocent of terrorism as well as whatever the Abbotts have done. I know nothing about Bianca Rossi's actions. It has become clear that I don't know anything about Bianca. The authorities won't let me talk to her. They wouldn't even answer when I asked whether she had mentioned my wife."

"You admit she's an imposter."

"I must, although she didn't answer in the helicopter when I asked her what this was all about. I repeat: I know nothing about her activities. This pains me to admit, Megan. I don't even know who she really is! Which is her disguise—the dark-haired Bianca or the Susan-lookalike?"

Megan sank into a chair opposite him. "Oh, that's right. You don't know about Grandmother's Italian family."

"What Italian family? Your grandmother joined the international jet set many years ago, but she never set foot in Italy. She told me years ago she didn't like the few Italian men she'd met and didn't want to be anywhere near them. So how can she have family there?"

"Grandmother kept her secrets well, both her Italian family and their activities over the decades. Who knows what else she took to the grave with her." Megan told him a condensed version of her grandmother's life.

His mouth gaped open. "Unreal. How do you know all this?"

"Do you remember the large envelope you brought from her attorney?" At his nod, Megan continued. "The bulkiness was a letter from her which she left in his safekeeping until after her death. She told me about her life, which included Bianca's terrorism. You can read Grandmother's letter when this is over."

"It boggles the mind how she could have gotten by with such behavior."

"Well, it boggles my mind you could fail to know Bianca wasn't Mother."

He heaved a sigh. "There's never been any reason to tell you this, but Susan and I haven't had a sexual relationship since your conception. Her pregnancy was difficult, followed by an equally painful delivery. She didn't want to go through the whole mess, her word, ever again."

Megan understood. Her mother was too fastidious for something as messy as intimacy could be. "Why didn't you divorce her?"

"She didn't want one, nor did I." He shrugged. "Susan never truly grew into adulthood. Oh, her IQ is normal. No question about that. She chose to remain younger than her years. I've never known why."

Megan had often thought her mother was childish, but she had never considered that her father might feel the same way.

"I'm curious. How did you know she wasn't your mother in Crawfordville?"

No way would she would give him details, which he could tell Bianca. "There were little things that didn't fit. I asked if she was ill, remember."

"Yes. I should have looked closer."

"How long has Bianca masqueraded as Mother? Has she used the disguise before? I'm sure not when I was around because I would have noticed."

"I don't know, but less than one year, because they were both at your grandmother's funeral last January. I thought Bianca was there to comfort your mother. Now I know better. How stupid I've been all these years."

"There's something else. This face has been known throughout the world for decades. Throughout your life, you have been an international traveler. How could you possibly have missed knowing about the terrorist with the mysterious face—the same face as your wife, your mother-in-law, and your daughter? Explain that, if you can."

He shook his head. "I don't know. Too arrogant to make the connection of *my* family with a known terrorist, I suppose."

Her always-knows-what's-best father must face his inadequacies, his humanity at last. Under other circumstances, she might have gloated. "The FBI agent said I can talk to Bianca. Maybe she'll tell me what she did to Mother."

His head jerked up. "Surely you don't think she killed Susan."

"Why not? She's killed plenty of other people."

ฌฌฌฌฌ

Although she knew Susan well, Bianca had seen Megan only the few hours in that North Carolina hick town. She'd thought, then, her cousin looked several years younger than her age, but not now. Pale, looking like she had unexploded bombs at her feet, the woman standing in the doorway appeared several years older. Bianca waited for her to speak.

"Where's my mother?" Megan's voice rose. "What did you do to her?"

Bianca caught her gaze. There was more to come, much more. Let her talk.

Megan raised her clawed hands when she lurched forward. A guard grabbed her around the waist, pulling her back despite her struggles against his taut arms. "Answer me! Where's my mother?"

Receiving no answer, Megan changed tactics. "What did you do? Sneak up behind her, like the coward you are? Stab her in the back because you don't have the nerve to face your victims? Or did you hire another terrorist to do your dirty work? Killing one woman wouldn't cause the big bang you like, right?

"How do I know? Grandmother told me. She knew you for what you truly are: an evil *thing*, not human at all, skulking around, preying on innocent people."

The reference to her beloved grandmother almost broke Bianca's resolve, but not quite. She stared at Megan, waiting for more venom, surprised when none came.

"You won't answer me. You'll let me live my life wondering about Mother, wishing I could at least visit her grave." With her shoulders slumped, Megan turned toward the door.

Bianca asked the question uppermost in her mind, when she allowed herself to wonder where she'd failed. "How did you know I was not Susan?"

Megan turned toward her, hope in her face. "There were little things, which wouldn't mean anything to anyone else."

"Why didn't you say something then? You appeared to accept me as Susan in that hick town. Maybe someday you'll tell me why in the name of sense you choose to live there, but that's for another time. Where did I go wrong?" Bianca persisted. "I know Susan well, probably better than you do."

"I thought Mother was ill and didn't want me to know. I asked Father, but he wouldn't tell me. He just brushed it off." Megan's lips trembled as tears pooled in her eyes. "Did she suffer? Will you at least tell me that much?"

For the first time she could recall, if ever, a flicker of compassion stirred Bianca. She hardly recognized it for what it was. "I'll tell you the whole thing.

"I've known about Susan for many years, because Grandmother didn't keep her American family a secret from us, even though we knew she kept us a secret from you. I always disguised myself, so Susan didn't know me. She fascinated me from the time we met at a Swiss ski lodge ten years ago. She sat alone in the lounge. I stood in the shadows absorbing her features. At that time, I didn't realize she shared Grandmother's features too. Grandmother had never told me. Even alone, Susan's face was animated. I joined her and could hardly believe her words when she introduced herself: not you, my cousin, which I had thought, but my aunt."

Megan sat on the edge of a chair, taking in every word as a dying woman struggles for air. "She always looked younger than her age."

Bianca nodded, but her thoughts were on the past. "Susan loved Switzerland, could gaze at the Alps for hours. I learned she came often to Zurich for various surgeries. I never saw Susan anywhere else until Grandmother's funeral last January. I spend a lot of time in Switzerland because I love the Alps too. I suppose we got that from Grandmother, although I don't remember she ever mentioned mountains. Anyway, I go there to relax while I plan my next adventure."

"Adventure!" Megan spluttered. "You call terrorism an adventure?"

"Do you want to hear about Susan, or not?"

Megan scooted back in her chair. "Don't stop!"

"There isn't much more. When I saw her three weeks ago, I realized she was the answer to my needs. She told me Reid was going on a three-month cruise with some friends. Susan detested boats. She didn't want to go, but Reid insisted. That was the only time I ever saw her with any expression except happiness. I told her she didn't look well and should check into her usual sanitarium while he was gone. She accepted my assurance I would tell Reid."

Megan broke the ensuing silence, her voice shaking. "Then?"

"A few hours later, I joined him at the bar." Bianca laughed. "People think Reid Stanfield is intelligent, but he has never once suspected I'm not his wife."

"Not lack of intelligence—pure arrogance. He would never notice anything different unless it had an adverse effect directly on him."

"His arrogance kept him from being a terrorist. I tried to recruit him soon after we met, but I realized there was no way he would agree. In his own way, Reid is as prudish as Susan. She was no fun either."

Megan twisted her hands. "Are you saying he didn't have anything to do with whatever you did to Mother?"

"I didn't do anything to her."

Disbelief and hope warred on Megan's face. "You didn't kill her?"

"No."

"Where is she?"

"In a clinic outside Zurich registered under her own name. She stays there when she recovers from various surgeries."

Megan covered her face as her shoulders shook with soundless sobs. Several minutes later, she lifted her tear-stained face and searched her pocket for a tissue.

Her voice husky, Megan said, "Grandmother's letter related much of your activities. She ended with the hope that, when you were on trial, the judge would recognize she was much to blame and be merciful with you. I hope the same because you spared Mother's life when you could have assumed her identity for the rest of yours."

Megan stood. "They won't let me touch you, but if I could, I would hug you. I wish we had met under different circumstances. If you had spent your childhood with my grandfather instead of yours, your life would have been considerably different."

Bianca watched her cousin leave the room. Grow up like her? Thanks, but no thanks. She preferred the life she'd lived, the excitement, the people with like minds.

How soon could she reasonably expect her friends to rescue her? Not the idiot in Detroit. After that disaster, he probably lay at the bottom of one of those lakes people think are so great. Someone from Milan would arrange her rescue. They wouldn't let anyone execute Miguel Rossi's granddaughter. Bianca smiled as the guards motioned her toward the door: one in front, one on each side, one behind. She was important, something they would soon know, not only to them. She envisioned masked faces and Uzis. Perhaps her rescue would happen when the FBI transferred her to Interpol. Her blood raced. Life had grown dull but was about to change.

No one gets the best of Bianca Rossi.

Chapter 30

This is Normal?

"Fran, ..."

"Megan! When did you get back from Miami?"

"Just now." She'd forced herself to drive home and unpack before calling. "I could use a shoulder."

"Twenty minutes."

Megan paced the porch until Fran's Mazda braked at the steps. Another two inches and she'd have to replace them, Megan told her, as they settled at the kitchen bar.

"What would we do without coffee?"

"I don't know," Fran accepted a mug with smiling faces marching around the rim. "I don't want to find out either. Now tell me all."

Interspersed with bouts of tears, Megan recounted yesterday's harrowing experience. "I couldn't believe it when Bianca told me Mother is alive."

"Thank God, she is. When you told me you'd had a call from the FBI agent who wanted you in Miami, I called our prayer circle . . . ."

"You didn't tell them!"

Fran grasped her outstretched hand. "I told them I had an urgent unspoken prayer request. I'll let them know the emergency is over. No one ever needs to know the sticky situation was yours, not mine. Everybody knows I'm forever in need of prayer about my business, so they never ask questions."

"You're a good friend. I don't know how I would get along without you."

"When will you see your mother?"

"Who knows? I wanted to fly to Zurich, but Father vetoed the idea."

"So, you saw him again?"

Megan nodded. "The authorities hadn't questioned him yet, so after I told them I just wanted to tell Father that Mother is alive, they allowed our meeting—with agents in the room, not even pretending they weren't listening."

"He doesn't want you to see her."

"Since she doesn't know about 'this incident'—his words—she'd worry if I got 'maudlin'—again his word. Mother doesn't worry about anything because it causes frown lines, but I suppose he's right that I shouldn't visit her. There's no question I would have been *maudlin*."

"If you'll forgive me for saying this, your mother sounds like she needs a lot of protection from life's problems."

"She does. I now realize Father has taken good care of her over the years. I doubt any other man would have."

Fran set the coffee cups in the sink. "Thanks for sharing with me."

"Thanks for being a person who will share my problems." At the door, Megan gave her another hug. "Back to normal life. I hope."

ꝯꝯꝯꝯꝯ

Normal? Heaven help her if this is normal, Megan thought crossing the square the next morning. The man who had been stalking her disappeared behind the library when she parked her car. At least she thought that's who he was. Could have been the Yogurt Raisin Man. They dressed much the same, the inevitable jeans and denim jackets.

Megan watched the door of her shop, one minute hoping the man in baggy jeans would come inside but in the next fearing he would. She wore her cross-body bag, the side pocket open, the knife handy, while she stocked shelves. Putting the man out of her mind, she. perched on a stool behind the cash register, and started a Christmas gift list.

Megan enjoyed buying gifts. She enjoyed wrapping gifts. She enjoyed looking at wrapped gifts. However, all this came after she had decided what to buy. She did *not* enjoy that process.

By noon, except for Katie, she'd only listed names of people she would give presents. Locking the door, she joined Fran in the diner for cheeseburgers.

"Your quick trip to Miami pushed something from my mind. I meant to tell you your aunt's funeral was unforgettable."

"The service did go well." Megan hesitated only a moment before she told Fran about Eva's appearance at the cemetery.

"Wow. I wish I could have seen her. Your face looked, oh, other worldly, I guess is the right term."

"I felt that way," Megan admitted. "I wouldn't mind having the same kind of service when my time comes."

"The funeral is over. You know your mother is alright, so why the doldrums?"

"Christmas list. I can never decide what to give anyone."

"I can relate. Every year I say I will give everybody gift certificates, but I never do."

They discussed appliqué materials for Sally. Then, Megan asked about plans for the Christmas pageant.

"I'm only singing in the choir," Fran explained. "I have no acting ability whatever. What are you doing?"

"I have no acting ability either, and dogs howl when I sing. However, I've done some dramatic readings, so I'll read the Christmas story from Luke while the children act it. Saves them from memorizing words, which I imagine is difficult at that age." She gazed at Fran with astonishment. "What's funny?"

"You should have been here last year. Mary spoke Joseph's words as well as her own. They almost came to blows. Jamie, the infant playing Jesus, shrieked in the middle, so everything stopped until his mother offered his pacifier. Can you imagine Jesus with a plug in His mouth? I can't."

Megan laughed. "Makes sense they'd use a doll this year. I've never taken part in a Christmas production. I'm looking forward to participating."

"You'll enjoy your first small-town pageant." Fran glanced at a man, who turned a chair toward their booth. "Hi, Frank, join us?"

Megan hoped the sheriff wouldn't mention her problems, even though Fran did know about them.

He waved off Mattie's offer of coffee. "Megan, I wanted to tell you that you gave your great-aunt a good send-off. I didn't know her, yet I appreciate your efforts. From all I've heard about her, she would have too."

"She did."

"You really did see her at your house, like everybody says?"

Megan nodded. "Not only at the house. Aunt Eva was at the cemetery. She showed me she was happy to be at rest."

"I've never seen a ghost or apparition. Might have scared me witless if I had," Frank admitted. "I gather only you could see her."

"I believe so. No one has mentioned seeing her."

He heaved himself from the chair, turning it back toward the table. "You're a very considerate person, a credit to our town."

Fran broke the silence, which enveloped their booth after he left. "He's right, you know. Eva wouldn't have appeared to you if you weren't special."

Megan shook her head. People would never understand what it meant to have any member of her family, even a dead one, accept her without reservation. Changing the subject, she said, "Do our usual friends exchange gifts at Christmas?"

"I believe so, although nothing expensive. Why do you ask?"

"I thought I might give a dinner party on Christmas Eve. We could exchange gifts. Or am I taking too much on myself?"

"Not at all. I think you have a great idea. Call everybody before we make other commitments."

"Alright, consider yourself invited. I'll call the others this afternoon."

An hour later, she had acceptances from Jed, Jack Kincaid, Catherine Crawford, Mike Williams, and Bill Sizemore. She left a message for Sally Jamison.

While waiting for Sally's call, Megan scanned the latest craft catalogue, until she found what she wanted for her. This was the first time she had considered giving any gift involving work by the recipient, but Sally would consider such a gift pleasure, not work. When the phone rang, she had decided on an appliqué kit for a coverlet with matching pillow shams depicting a farm scene at sunrise, complete with tiny animals and people. Intricate. Megan tensed just looking at the picture. Needlewoman she was not.

"This 'n That," she answered.

"Hi, it's Sally. Need some help?"

"Not today. I called for two reasons. First, I'm planning a party for our special friends on Christmas Eve. Everyone else accepted. Will you come?"

"Hmmm. Did you invite Bill Sizemore?"

"Yes. He accepted."

"Okay, I do too, thanks. What's your other reason for calling?"

"I need to do some shopping in Asheville. Will you mind the store for me tomorrow?"

"Sure. No way is this a busy time for realtors."

"Great." Shopping put her worries behind, if only for a little while. Surely her stalker wouldn't follow her to Asheville, so she could leave the knife at home. Megan didn't dare risk a patrolman stopping her while she carried a weapon. She'd never hear the end of an arrest from her father, who would surely hear about it somehow, some day. He'd always learned everything she would rather he didn't know. Osmosis maybe.

Late the following morning, Megan found a parking space after circling several blocks. Busy town crowded with shoppers. She must have looked through every store in downtown. Over lunch, she checked several names off her list.

A hand-painted silk tie for Jack Kincaid; for Mike Williams, a pewter Confederate chess set; and two CDs—Vince Gill and Amy Grant—for Bill Sizemore. That took care of the men, except Jed. She didn't know what to give him.

The women were easier. A leather shoulder bag for Catherine, who could never find what she needed in her overstuffed small purse. White Diamonds perfume for Fran. Megan knew she could go over her list from now till doom's day, but it wouldn't change things. She still had a blank space after Jed's name.

Setting the shopping bags on the floor, she grabbed the ringing phone as soon as she unlocked the door.

"Hello?"

"Angel, I'm really very sorry I ditched you. I want to make everything right for you."

Megan strained to understand the slurred words. Had he said *Angel*? Only one person ever called her that—she'd hoped never to hear from him again.

"David? You're drunk." He never drank before the cocktail hour, yet he was almost past coherence this early in the day. She'd never known him so far over his limit, even late at night. His near sobriety was one thing that had appealed to her. "You should be ashamed."

"Please, Angel, come home. You're my only hope."

She gritted her teeth at the reminder of his financial problems.

"David, I'm hanging up the phone now. Don't call me again. Not ever, do you understand me?" She slammed down the receiver before he could answer. She shuddered with disgust at him. At herself too, if she were honest. How could she ever have fallen for him? Was this drunkenness new, caused by his money problems, or had he hidden his alcohol problem from her? She had been so naïve that hiding problems from her was possible—even probable. Had her expected inheritance been his interest all along? That hurt too much to consider, so she pushed aside the possibility, just as she pushed aside the idea her refusal to marry him might have driven him into drunkenness. She could empathize with his financial problems, whatever they were, but that was as far as she would go.

Megan hurried to the Christmas pageant rehearsal, her thoughts on the nativity story she would read from the King James Bible, which had been her comfort since childhood. The newer versions never satisfied her, especially reading verses she'd memorized.

The choir was working on Handel's *Messiah*, which Jed had told her was the traditional adult Christmas presentation. She stood in the doorway, listening while his strong tenor voice soared above the others, and then hurried to the basement, where the chattering children waited for her.

An hour later, she hugged the last child and sent him on his way with his parents.

"Do I get a hug too?" Jed's lanky frame rose from a chair in the corner. He stretched out his arms, a smile hovering around his lips.

Megan gave him an answering smile, surprising herself by lifting her face for a kiss. Christmas season, joy to the world, and all that.

"Hmmm. I'll have some more of that."

She pulled away with the reminder they should be on their way before they got locked inside.

The janitor's footsteps clattering on the stairs reinforced her words, so after one last hug, Jed led her to the door. "I stopped by the store earlier. Sally said you were out spending all your hard-earned money."

"I did most of my shopping for my friends, so I only need some token gifts, which I can purchase here."

"Where to now?" he inquired.

"I'll check the store and make a bank deposit. Sally always sells more craft stuff than I do. Want to come?"

He clasped her hand in his as they strolled across the square, until people coming out of the movie theater surrounded them with happy chatter.

Megan smiled with delight. "I never cease to be amazed at how many people call me by name here. So few knew me in Detroit."

"You already know small town life is different."

"I like it." She cast an impish smile at him. "Not still trying to get rid of me, are you? No, don't answer. I'm only teasing."

He assumed a mock frown. "You'd better be, or I'll take matters into my own hands."

Megan laughed and then made out a bank deposit. "Perhaps I should leave Sally in charge all the time."

Standing beside her car, he brushed his lips across hers. "I'll follow you home and see you tomorrow."

Chapter 31

Confession Time

He sat at the round oak table in his kitchen, staring out the window without seeing anything. The stand of birch trees held a lot of memories. He and his wife had wandered through it, gathering the fallen bark pieces for the natural plant arrangements she'd made for the fall festival. Now, the silvery bark didn't capture his attention. He'd sat this way more often than not since Eva's burial. The funeral still bothered him. Was his reaction because any funeral reminded him death comes to all of us, or was it because that woman was there?

He transferred his gaze to the white-scrubbed table, where a revolver lay next to a ruled tablet. He must put words on the paper, words which explain everything, so people would stop blaming teenagers for what he'd done. Then, he would take care of Megan Stanfield. Himself too. She didn't deserve to live after all the bother she had caused him, and he had no reason to go on living.

He still couldn't remember why the simple sight of that woman had caused those horrible headaches, but soon his uncertainty wouldn't matter. Sometimes the thick curtain in his mind would ease open the least bit, but panic would close it again. At those times, there was only intense pain. The situation was different now, though.

Thinking about her now caused pain in his chest, not his head. He closed his eyes, slumped against the table and felt himself drift toward a tiny beam of light at the far end of a tunnel, the same one he'd ridden his bike through on a dare when he was ten, he thought dreamily as he neared the glow. He frowned when the familiar face blocked out the light. But this time she looked different. Long hair framed the face radiant with the familiar smile.

"Hello, dear. You need to forgive yourself for that long ago night. I forgave you then."

"Who are you?" His voice quavered, weakened from the fierce pain in his chest.

"Don't fight the memory any longer, old friend. You can remember now."

He clutched his chest, panic clouding his mind, and struggled for a long moment before enlightenment came. "My lost love, it's you! My lost love! Why did you leave me?"

"Think about it. Open your mind. Let the past come alive again." She began to fade.

"No, don't leave me again. I couldn't bear it!"

She answered the anguish in his voice. "You can't come yet. You still have something you must do. When you finish writing your letter, there won't be any need for your revolver. I'll wait for you, as I've done all these years."

He cried out when the vision receded. A myriad of memories engulfed him, like flames on dry wood. His chest pain sharpened. He wrote for several minutes, alternately clutching his chest and holding the paper. The pain eased when he wrote the beloved name. He slipped away on a soft breeze, which carried him down the tunnel where his lost love waited for him.

ℛℛℛℛℛ

Morning dawned clear but cold. When Megan jogged her usual route, she could see her breath going before her and felt the wind sting her cheeks. Scanning the blue sky, she wondered whether they ever have a white Christmas this far south. Did they even have snow? That was her first question to Fran, when she slid into the back booth where Fran was finishing a waffle covered with cinnamon apples.

"My lack of knowledge of this part of the country embarrasses me no end, so I have to ask about winter weather. Snow, for instance. Does it come this far south?"

"Oh, yes, we have snow this far south, but a white Christmas is rare. We get most of our snow from mid-January through early March, although we've been hit by blizzard-like storms both earlier and later many times."

"Is there enough snow to ski?"

"Outsiders are surprised when they learn western North Carolina has a good ski season, although shorter than up north. The resorts in the higher mountains use artificial stuff to supplement natural snow, but that doesn't deter skiers. Some people come through town on their way to and from the slopes, so you can expect an increase in your snacks business."

"I'll stock extra trail mix and stuff like that. Perhaps we can arrange some skiing weekends this winter. Speaking of my business, I must stock shelves before opening time."

Fran glanced at her watch. "I have an hour. I'll help."

A few people stopped Megan on her way to the door, some commenting on the funeral service. She smiled, although she recognized hidden criticism in some statements. Traditionalists didn't want funeral services interfering with their memories of Christmas carols. If they felt they could criticize her to her face, it meant they had accepted her, or so she told herself.

A loud banging on the shop door startled Megan into dropping a box of Christmas cards, scattering them across the floor. Muttering, she admitted a man holding a long florist box.

"Ms. Megan Stanfield?" he asked, glancing at each woman.

"I'm Megan Stanfield."

"Right. Just sign here."

Not noticing him leave, Megan laid the box on the cash register counter.

"Aren't you going to open it?"

Megan removed the ribbon tie and lifted the lid, revealing long stemmed red and white roses—the colors of unity—twelve of each. She knew this without counting. She also knew without reading the card who had sent them, but she opened the small envelope anyway. *"Regardless of anything else, I do love you. Please come home. David."*

Megan read the message with an expressionless face. Would she ever forget? Forget the scent of roses mixed with his masculine scent of leather and cigar smoke the first time David gave her roses? He had handed them to her personally on their one-month anniversary, just as he had on each monthly anniversary for nearly two years. Until, in fact, the last one when he told her he'd found someone else. He thought that was a classy way to end their relationship, but she had news for him.

He was wrong.

No matter how much Megan believed she was over her love for him, no matter how much responsibility she bore for her heartache, fleeting thoughts brought back all the initial pain of losing him.

She'd moped around her apartment, her emotions up and down like elevators. Then, her grandmother died, leaving her a legacy. The money gave Megan the opportunity to leave Detroit, but memories recounted by her beloved granddad—the only person who'd never failed her—told her where to go. Here to Crawfordville, surrounded by mountains as she'd never seen before, mountains that sometimes peeked through long fingers of smoky mist, giving a mysterious, gothic appearance. Shivers had run down her spine the first time she saw them, but no longer. Now she belonged in these mountains. Detroit was behind her. So was David.

She methodically tore the card into tiny pieces, watching them drift into the wastebasket. No man would ever manipulate Megan Elizabeth Stanfield with a love declaration. She ignored that slight, ever so slight, tug of sympathy too. He'd fooled her before with those words. Never again. He wanted her money, the money she would have some day; only he needed funds now.

Replacing the lid on the box, she pushed it toward Fran. "Just what your shop needs."

Fran, her eyes holding sympathy, asked, "David?"

"Yes."

"Okay, I'll take them. Thanks." Giving Megan a quick hug, Fran picked up the box and left the store.

Keeping her gaze away from the wastebasket, Megan went into the office, where she tackled the stack of sales slips accumulating about as fast as she could record them. She stopped entering the information to serve several customers throughout the morning. The stop-and-start procedure apparently didn't please the computer, because the monster began doing weird things. Work came to a screeching halt almost halfway through the stack. She tapped the enter key. Nothing happened. She tapped the page up key. Nothing. She tried typing. Nothing. The escape key didn't work. The mouse pointer was somewhere in space.

Megan glared at the monitor.

The door opened admitting Mike Williams.

"Your expression would scare a criminal," he told her when she stepped into the salesroom.

"The computer won't work. Just sits there as if it owns the place. Do you know what I think about computers? They're not machines at all. They're creatures from the far reaches of outer space, aliens. We've sat meekly by while they conquered our planet. This one has decided to drive me crazy this morning. Human beings are doomed for sure."

Mike grinned. "I decided that a long time ago, but I haven't blamed aliens. Humans do enough damage to this world."

"Give my words some thought. You'll agree with me." Megan changed the subject. "So, Mike, what brings you here this morning?"

"I have a puzzle for you. Do you know Dan Hinson?"

"Doesn't sound familiar. Why do you ask?"

"Dan was an older man who lived out in your direction."

"You use the past tense."

"His cleaning lady found him sprawled across the kitchen table when she checked on him this morning. He'd been dead for several hours."

This really topped off her morning. "I assume you're not accusing me of murdering him—you're being much too friendly—so why are you telling me?"

"There's no reason to believe anyone murdered him. The revolver lying on the table was pristine, although there's speculation about why it was there. However, the ambulance workers found this beneath his hand."

Mike handed a sheet of tablet paper toward her. "We dusted for fingerprints, so you can handle the paper."

She thrust her hands into her pockets. "Why fingerprints if you don't think somebody murdered him?"

"Automatic procedure in an unattended death."

"I don't want to read anybody's suicide letter." She kept her hands in her pockets.

"The letter is addressed to you, Megan."

"Me? Why would a stranger write to me?"

"There's one way to find out. Read it."

"I'd rather not." Megan took the letter from Mike's hand without taking her gaze from his face. "Something tells me I shouldn't, but if you insist . . . ."

A spidery scrawl ran lopsidedly across the page.

> *Dear Miss Stanfield,*
>
> *I realize you must wonder why I—a stranger—would write you a letter. I've worked up the courage to explain things. I'm behind your difficulties, phone calls, dead squirrel, vandalism in your store, even running you off the road. I only wanted to scare you into leaving town. I never meant to hurt you.*
>
> *From the first time I saw you, your face has reminded me of somebody. Every time I almost figured out who, a pain shot into my head and the memory stopped. I believed my headaches would go away if you weren't around here. I've finally remembered who you resemble. I must tell you something about the funeral service for your great-aunt. That was not Eva you buried. It was Alma . . . .*

The last word trailed off in a streak of ink.

"This doesn't make sense, Mike. Alma was my grandmother, who died last January. I know because I sat alone with her, holding her hand as she slipped away. My parents were snowbound in Zurich, so she only had me. I saw Grandmother in the coffin. Definitely her and definitely dead."

Megan's thoughts drifted back nearly a year. With her parents, she stood by her grandmother's grave, dry eyed, one distinct thought repeated itself. *Now, I'll never know why grandmother didn't love me.* Her grandmother's letter had eased her hurt, but here was another obstacle. Who *was* her grandmother?

Mike's radio interrupted their conversation. He listened and then told the faceless voice he was on his way.

"Megan, here's a copy for you. I'll keep the original in the event I need it. I don't know why I would, but I'd better stay on the safe side until Doc rules natural death. Give the content some thought. Maybe you can read something between the lines."

After Mike left, Megan held the paper at arm's length. She wouldn't be the least bit surprised if it exploded in her hand, like one of Bianca's bombs. She would think about Dan Hinson after dealing with the alien on her desk.

Lunch first. This bewildering day called for comfort food, so she reached for the phone. "Mattie, this is Megan Stanfield. Will you fix me a cheeseburger and fries? A large Pepsi too. Is fifteen or twenty minutes enough time?"

Megan waited on some customers and then went back to the office. Sitting in front of her nemesis, she said, "Now you listen to me, whatever you are. You'd better behave yourself, or I'll throw you on the landfill with the rest of the debris of my life. Do you hear me?"

"I doubt if the computer does, but I do." Jed's amused voice sounded at the door. "You were so busy fussing at the computer you didn't hear the doorbell. I could have stolen those expensive collectables. Here's your lunch."

"Hi." Megan helped herself to hot fries. "Jed, people who say 'garbage in, garbage out' are wrong. I was sitting here doing what I do every day, minding my own business, when peculiar things started appearing on the screen until it stopped working."

He planted a quick kiss on her lips. "Hmmm, salty. Let me fiddle with the computer while you finish your lunch."

"Alright. Afterwards, I have something weird to show you."

Jed tapped several keys, turned off the machine, waited, and then switched it on again. "What document were you using?"

"Accounts Receivable."

"Is this stack what you put in this morning?"

"Yes. Sally did great business yesterday, didn't she?"

"Hmmm." He compared the sales slips with the screen. "You didn't lose anything, which must be a relief."

"Yes, but what happened?"

"Who knows? I don't understand computers. I just use them. Now, what's weird?"

"A letter from someone named Dan Hinson."

Jed read it through twice, his face pale. His voice was unsteady when he handed the letter back to her. "What do you make of it?"

"Nothing. I told Mike Willians the letter had to be wrong because I saw Alma, without question my grandmother, in her coffin this past January. I don't even know this man."

"He's my maternal great-uncle. I thought he was shy, which is why I never introduced him in the diner. I thought he was a harmless old cuss. He's the last person on the planet that I would have thought might be behind your problems."

"He must have been senile."

"He didn't seem so when I talked to him Sunday. Might be mistaken identity though, meaning he might have the twins' names confused."

"Could be, I suppose."

"I need to go home. This will hit Mother hard. Uncle Dan was the only person left, whom she could reminisce with about family."

Chapter 32

Again!

We interrupt this program to bring you breaking news arriving as I speak from the Associated Press office in Miami. Terrorists have struck this city.

Megan dropped her spoon into the bowl of granola, spewing milk across the table.

Two helicopters ambushed FBI and CIA agents in three Humvees near the Miami airport. The agents were escorting a suspected terrorist to Interpol authorities. The suspect, although not yet officially identified, is possibly a female wanted by Interpol over several decades. Known as "the woman with the mysterious face," she's been in maximum security since her arrest in international waters last week.

Witnesses reported gunfire and saw a man carrying a woman leave the middle vehicle. He ran toward one helicopter, which set down long enough to pick up the two people. Seconds later, in a final horrifying act, the woman leaned out the helicopter and threw what appeared to be grenades into the midst of the Humvees. One witness reported the woman raised her arms in apparent victory. There are no survivors. Heavy smoke left by the devastation prevented anyone's noticing which way the helicopters went. We return to regular programming, but we'll interrupt with details as they arrive.

Megan sat in stunned silence. She'd thought the terrorism issue was past with Bianca behind bars. How could this have happened? How could she have arranged her escape?

She picked up the ringing phone.

"Did you hear the announcement?"

"Yes, Mike. Is there further news?"

"I haven't heard any. Frank and I are on our way. We want to ask some questions before the FBI gets here. They will surely arrive at my office ASAP."

The cops alternated their questions.

"Megan, did Bianca Rossi indicate in any way she might escape?"

"No."

"Did you get the impression she expected help?"

"No."

"Did she appear . . . ."

"She didn't show any emotion," Megan said. "She didn't move, except her eyes when she watched me. I never saw such immobility. She could've been a robot."

The questions continued until Megan thought she would scream. The cops finally left after telling her to contact them ASAP if she heard from her cousin. How could the rescue have happened? How could Bianca have contacted anyone? Heads will roll after this fiasco—FBI heads.

Megan pulled the ringing cell phone from her pocket. Before she could say anything, she heard her father's voice.

"Have you heard? Bianca has escaped."

"Yes. The cops have already been here. Where's Mother? Is she safe?"

"We're at the Zurich clinic. I can't imagine Bianca's coming here. They've tripled security, though, so she can't reach your mother."

"You'll be with her every second? You'll remember Bianca has dead eyes, and Mother's eyes sparkle?"

"Yes, yes. I won't let Susan out of my sight." Impatience tinged his voice. "You take care of yourself, or, better yet, stay with your redheaded farmer. He'll keep you safe."

The phone clicked in her ear.

Megan smiled at her father's oblique approval of Jed. She punched number 2 on her phone. "Fran, are you awake enough to listen?"

"Megan? What's wrong?"

"I hate to wake you with this news, but I'd rather you hear from me than the radio or TV. Bianca Rossi has escaped."

"Escaped! Surely, she was in maximum security. How could she manage to escape?"

"The radio announcement didn't say, but she unquestionably had help. I suppose CNN has better information by this time, so I need to turn on the TV. Mike and Frank have been here with a zillion questions already. Without doubt, FBI agents will be here soon."

"Are you going to work?"

"Yes. Working will be better than sitting here brooding. Bianca has probably left the country already. With her ability at disguise, though, who knows where she might be? Anyway, I must get on with my life, which means opening my store. I'll see you at the diner for lunch."

Megan was right about the FBI. Fred Higgins called her into Mike's office in mid-morning. Mike and Frank were there along with the local FBI agents.

She answered the same questions in various ways before Higgins would answer her question.

"How did Bianco manage to escape with so many escorts? *Three* vehicles."

"Unfortunately, what we have is surmise. Two men infiltrated the helicopter port and killed the two pilots cleared for the trip. CIA agents found their nude, dead bodies behind some shrubbery. Apparently, the same thing happened with the expected driver of the middle Humvee, because, according to witnesses, a man in that vehicle carried Bianca Rossi to the chopper."

"Why did he carry her?"

"She was in shackles. We believe he sat beside her in the vehicle."

"Do you mean he, not the pilots, killed the others in that Humvee?"

Fred nodded. "I don't see how else he could have rescued her. We found the choppers abandoned a few miles away, so they changed vehicles for the final getaway. We have no way of knowing what those vehicles were. We've closed all ports—water and air—but we aren't confident we'll catch them."

Megan rubbed her temples. "Bianca can disguise herself anyway she pleases. Otherwise, she couldn't have remained free for so long."

"Can you give us any information about her other disguises?"

"None. I've only seen her when she had my face. I love my grandmother, but I wish she had been more discriminate passing on her DNA."

Fred Higgins nodded. "I imagine there are many cops in many countries who share your wish. We depend on you to get in touch ASAP, if she contacts you."

"I will, sir, and I depend on you to keep me informed on progress." Megan reached pleading hands toward him. "Please! I need to know my mother is safe from her."

Fred nodded again. "I will do my best."

ℶℶℶℶℶ

When Megan saw Jed in the choir loft on Sunday morning, she admitted she would have been disappointed if he hadn't been there. She'd vowed not to be involved with any man ever again. Once burned, twice shy. Nevertheless, after the service, she waited for him beside her car, her turned-up collar protecting her neck from the chilly air.

When he arrived, she said, "I have an idea."

"Tell me."

"Your mistaken-identity comments the other day started me thinking. I wonder if the twins ever played tricks when they were children. I mean one pretending to be the other. I was in school with twins who did. They kept the teachers guessing."

"Uncle Josh might know."

"I know something better. I have my grandmother's diaries, but I've been too busy to read them. Perhaps we could go through them this afternoon, if you hadn't planned anything else."

"Sounds like a great way to spend Sunday afternoon, especially since the predicted rain has started. My Mustang's over there. I'll follow you."

By the time they reached her driveway, the rain had turned into sleet. They huddled on the porch, while she dug the house key from her purse.

"If the weather gets any colder, this mess will turn to snow." Dread colored Jed's words.

"A white Christmas would be fun. I'll put the kettle on for tea, while you light the fire, if I laid it the right way. Otherwise, you can build the fire too."

"I have complete confidence in your ability to build fires." He grinned when her face heated. After the fire caught, he reached for the phone. "I'll call the farm and let Mom know where I am."

"I really appreciate your thoughtfulness toward your mother."

"We're very close." Jed paused. "We've always lived in the same house, except when I was in college. I can't imagine ever living away from her."

"I can't see any reason you should. Here, have some cranberry tea, while I start lunch."

"I'll help."

"Okay, you can spread some garlic butter on bread, while I heat the seafood chowder, which might stick if I don't stir constantly."

They worked side by side, odors of food soon mingling with wood scent from the now blazing fireplace.

After they ate, Megan flipped through the album racks. "We'll read about life during the 20s and 30s, so let's have some music from that era."

"I believe I could get to like your music. Takes a while after twangy guitars, but big bands grow on a person."

Bingo, Megan exulted. His Christmas gift. CDs are plentiful.

Seated on the floor with the diaries spread around them, they leafed through the small leather-bound books until they found those covering the late twenties through the early forties.

"Jed, there's something peculiar here. This appears to be Eva's diary, not Alma's."

"Why would Alma have it?"

"I can't imagine."

They read silently, the fire crackling, soft music murmuring. The diaries revealed their household and school daily activities, but nothing about the girls' playing pranks. By the late 1930s, they had begun dating, albeit under their parents' watchful eye.

Jed rose to his feet. "I'll change the records, while you find the 1940 diary. Life should be getting interesting for those girls by then."

They didn't find anything of interest in the diaries for 1940 or 1941. Eva had entered something for each day, if only a brief mention of her boring life. However, in May 1942, there was an abrupt stop from the first through the 10th, when her life became interesting again.

"Listen, Jed. Eva mentions the man who became my grandfather."

> *Alma has decided to marry Robert Abernathy, which will set the cat amongst the pigeons since half the men around here are in love with her. I think she loves Dan Hinson but is sorry for Robert because the army rated him 4F, which means he can't go into the military. Heart trouble, Alma said. He wants to work in Detroit's automobile factories, making tanks as his contribution to the war effort. I wonder how she'll like being a nonentity in the big city after being the most sought-after girl here.*

"I can't decide if Eva was jealous or bitter, or both. After all, they were twins. From all I've ever heard, twins are especially close, shutting out anyone who tried to come between them."

"Interesting anyway. Does she give details of their leaving?"

Megan's gasp was his only answer, as she read page after page until she reached the end of that date and sat, staring into space.

"What did you find?"

"There's a lapse again until June first. Here, read it for yourself."

Chapter 33

The Past Comes Alive

June 1, 1942.
Dear Diary,
I've done it. I've shaken the dust of Crawfordville from my feet with no plans to return. Ever. After I finish writing this, I won't even think of this place again. Nobody knows how much I hated my hometown, where people always compared me, unfavorably, with my twin sister. Well, no more. No one will ever compare me with Alma again. I am her now.

I've never been able to write in my diary about my Asheville excursions because Alma snooped. She, and everybody else, would be surprised if they knew about my secret life.

The amazing thing is no one ever suspected. Well, no, it isn't amazing at all. My reputation as the timid, home-loving, dull, twin stood me well. I hid my amusement when people commented on the way Alma kept all the boys dangling after her. If only they had known! Alma was a prude, a flirt who never intended to go beyond snatched kisses in the back row at the theater.

Flirting hasn't been enough for me since I turned fourteen. That was the first time Momma took us to Asheville and left us at the theater while she shopped. I don't remember what the movie was, something for children, I dare say. I told Alma I was going to the ladies' room. I did what I said. However, on the way back, I stumbled on a step into an usher's arms. He was "an older man," twenty or so. Before I knew what was happening, he swung me around a corner and kissed me.

When I regained my senses, he whispered for me to come back again before I left. I didn't promise, just said maybe, but knew I would. I did, of course, and began my Asheville adventures.

When Alma asked why I didn't come back, I told her a guy was with her. I'd found another seat, because I didn't want to be a wet blanket. Alma believed me. She was so self-centered it would never have occurred to her that I might tell a lie. She giggled and never again mentioned my absences.

That was the first, but not the last, time I found my pleasure in the theater without seeing much of the film. The ushers changed through the next two years, but their actions didn't. They were all eager for cuddles in dark corners.

Activity at the theater ended when I got my driver's license at sixteen. I would leave home looking demure in my skirt and sweater, wearing saddle shoes with bobby socks, using the excuse Asheville's library was better than Crawfordville's. On the way, I exchanged my socks for stockings. Then, with my hair pinned up, I drove on to Asheville. I still went to theaters, but didn't stay. I left on the arm of any man I found alone. The manager and ushers turned a blind eye. They'd had their turns.

How exciting those three years were! The secrets, the daring. Remembering them makes me tingle all over.

Now for my final transformation from shy, demure Eva to fun-loving Alma.

At the supper table, Alma had told us she was going to marry Robert Abernathy and move away. Momma stared at her in surprise. Daddy reminded her she had always said she would never live anywhere except Crawfordville and that she would never leave these mountains. I asked why Detroit. She told us the army rejected Robert, something wrong with his heart. He wanted to build tanks as his contribution to the war.

We were barely seventeen. Momma tried to talk Alma out of getting married. When her arguments failed—she could be as stubborn as a mule, to use a cliché which would horrify my English teacher—they started talking wedding plans. I excused myself from the table, saying I had a headache and went to the back porch.

A man came into the yard. He couldn't see me, so I watched him stand in the shadows staring at an upstairs window, which I knew was Alma's bedroom. After half an hour, he edged his way around the house, pausing in the moonlight. Dan Hinson.

Plans for Alma's wedding progressed over the next several days. Momma wanted a big church wedding, like her own had been. However, Alma dug in her heels. Robert was impatient to leave, to do his part for the war effort, so the ceremony would take place at home.

I was envious she was leaving this backwater town, but Momma thought I was jealous, so she cornered me for a long talk. She told me I would get over my shyness someday. Then I would get interested in boys, as she called them. Containing my amusement, I said perhaps I could visit friends in Knoxville until the wedding. She agreed.

I returned home the evening before my parents expected me. I wanted to surprise everybody at breakfast. I parked short of the driveway and slipped toward the back door. I heard voices when I rounded the corner, so I stood in the shadows listening. Momma had told us that eavesdropping was a cardinal sin in family relationships. I disagree, although I never "talked back," as she put it.

Alma stood with Dan Hinson next to Momma's rose bushes. He begged her not to marry Robert because he loved her. I must hand it to Alma. She could be gentleness itself when she chose. She explained Robert needed her. He was disabled and couldn't go to Detroit alone. Dan was so distraught he grabbed her shoulders, shaking her until her head rocked back and forth.

I wondered how Miss Tease-and-Taunt would react to some rough handling. To my surprise, she resisted, punching him with both fists, but she didn't scream. I still wonder why, because she had a shrill voice that our parents could have heard. I started forward to intervene. I give myself credit on one point at least. Before I could move, I heard a distinct snap. I didn't know necks could break so easily.

Dan must have heard the snap too, because he stopped shaking her. He said her name twice. Then, he dropped her. The girl he had said he loved now lay at his feet. Dead.

The scene plays over and over in my mind. I stood, horrified, as Dan pleaded with Alma to answer, to straighten her neck, so her head wouldn't flop sideways. He straightened it himself. "She's dead, what am I going to do, God?" He walked away but turned back toward her. He stood a moment, pounding one fist into his other hand. Then, he reached his decision.

Good, upstanding Christian though he professed to be, Dan Hinson, in angry passion, had killed a woman. He not only killed her but hid his crime by burying her under some lilac bushes Daddy had planted that day at the back of the yard. Daddy had even left the spade convenient to Dan's hands. After he finished replanting the shrubs, he ran across our yard, passing close enough for me to touch him, and disappeared from my view.

I saw the possibilities immediately. I drove toward Knoxville as fast as I could maneuver those mountain curves on a two-lane blacktop road. There, I sent my parents a telegram, saying I had eloped with a soldier and would never return.

On the edge of Knoxville, I found an all-night truck stop, where I hitched a ride almost home. I left my car behind with the key in it—long gone by now, I'm sure. I wonder if anybody found the license plate and the ownership papers I buried in the dumpster.

There was a long walk from where the truck driver dropped me at the main highway into Crawfordville, but I slipped into Alma's bed before daylight, well pleased with myself.

I was present when Momma read the telegram aloud. Suppressing laughter, I showed proper surprise that dear, shy, demure Eva would do such a thing. I even volunteered to pack "Eva's" things for storage, which is how I packed my diaries and photograph albums in my travel trunks. I might change my mind about remembering my past, even though right now I don't think so. I doubt I can block my memories forever.

Dan Hinson left town the day after he buried Alma. I would love to be a fly on the wall when he comes home and hears Alma married Robert, and Eva disappeared. Regardless of Momma's admonition, I enjoy eavesdropping!

I took Alma's place in the wedding. I'll say this for our parents. They gave me a proper send-off despite their unhappiness over their other daughter.

Selfish? Yes, of course, I am. However, I will say this for myself. Not all my life in Crawfordville was a lie. I did enjoy teaching the Little Boys Sunday School Class. I like boys. I'm not sure I could tolerate giggling or whining little girls around me.

I'm ready to get on with my life as Mrs. Alma Malloy Abernathy. Although I will miss these glorious mountains, I'll take full advantage of the excitement big cities offer. I will be too busy to write in you again, dear diary, so good-bye. I hope no one finds this while I live but hope someone will find my diary after I'm dead, so people in Crawfordville will know how I outwitted them. They'll change their tune then!

Chapter 34

Who am I?

In silence, Jed placed the leather-bound volume on a table and studied Megan's averted face. Colorless. Tight. Her shoulders curved inward. She appeared to have shrunk inside herself. "Megan, what are you thinking?"

He waited a moment. "Megan, talk to me." With gentle tugging, he raised her chin until she faced him. The pain in her eyes stabbed his heart.

"Who am I?" Her voice was hardly above a whisper.

"You're Megan Elizabeth Stanfield, the same person you always were. You are also the woman I love."

She didn't react to his declaration. "The first time I talked with Uncle Josh, he said he never believed Eva eloped, but perhaps she had because still waters run deep. Those were his exact words. He was right. She didn't elope, but her still waters were fathoms deep."

"To put it mildly."

"How could she have lived that way?" Megan demanded. "She should've been mortified at her very thoughts."

"You must remember what her life was at home, in the whole town, for that matter. Always overshadowed by her twin, always coming out second best, whereas in her secret life, she was first."

"Still . . . ."

"She wasn't all bad, Megan. Remember her Sunday School class."

"Still . . . ."

"Need I remind you no one is perfect? Beginning with Adam and Eve, there's been good and bad in everybody."

"Uncle Josh also said I'm just like her. I wonder if I am."

"Why? Have you had much, uh, excitement in your life?"

Megan shot him a puzzled glance before comprehension dawned. She glared at him. "How dare you even suggest such a thing? David was the only one—only after we became engaged too. I'm not a bed hopper."

"Hey, take it easy, I was only joking. If you were like Eva in that respect, you'd have been in my bed before I knew I wanted you there, which was almost from the first moment I saw you, by the way."

Again, Megan ignored his words. "Do you realize I'm the granddaughter of a murderer?" Megan didn't wait for his answer. "Well, not exactly a murderer, but she stood there while someone killed her sister, her twin, her other half. She not only enjoyed Alma's discomfort—she turned her twin's death to her own benefit. That's unforgivable."

"I understand what you're saying, Megan. Eva would have helped her twin if the death had not been so sudden. Her diary makes that clear. Can you possibly think you inherited a defect from her? The idea is preposterous."

"I admit I'm not thinking clearly, but it seems to me Eva should have had an innate desire to protect her twin. You know, squabble among themselves but stand together against the world."

"We read about closeness between twins, about siblings in general, but how much of that is true, and how much is wishful thinking?"

"I don't know, Jed! But I just can't fathom anyone's standing by and not protecting anyone's being beaten.

"You're overlooking something else, Megan. My great-uncle was the actual murderer, even though

Alma's death was an accident. Do you think I also inherited some sort of flaw?"

He stared at her in stupefaction when she didn't answer. "You do! You believe I might harm you, kill you, even if unintentional. What have I ever done to make you think I might hurt you? You know your early fear was unfounded, so why now?"

"You shook me." Staring him straight in the face, Megan repeated, "You shook me just like he shook her."

"I don't know what you're talking about."

"Yes, you do. When we saw the man outside my house. You were angry because I wouldn't let you stay the night. You shook me. Hard."

"Oh, Megan, I do remember now. I'm sorrier than I can say. I didn't know how else to reach you. I wouldn't hurt a hair on your head." Jed shook his head when realization struck. "Those words don't mean much, do they? I suppose my great-uncle felt the same way, yet he killed the woman he loved."

Jed stared into the fire.

ͷ ͷ ͷ ͷ ͷ

Megan gazed at his bowed head and relived those few minutes after they saw the man outside her window. She *had* been angry with Jed. Angry, she acknowledged, not fearful. He *had* shaken her just as Dan had shaken Alma. He *had* shouted at her, just as Dan had shouted at Alma. However, Jed hadn't killed her.

He isn't a violent man, not really, she reminded herself. There were other times when he could have manhandled her but hadn't. After the quarrel at the farm, for instance. She hadn't worried about being alone with him even then.

Megan ticked off Jed's good points. He's thoughtful and caring with his mother. Buddy loves him. Fran thinks he's great. Even his cook-housekeeper thinks he hung the moon. Jed goes out of his way to help people. He'd certainly done everything he could for her, even manual labor. He was always courteous, patient with little boys. Another thought sneaked into her mind. *He'll be too conscious of Dan's behavior ever to hurt me.*

She studied Jed's face, which she saw in three-quarter profile. She liked the way the firelight played along the plane of his jaw. Perhaps his nose was a bit long, his chin determined. Not a Brad Pitt face. More interesting. Vulnerable, yet strong. Good combination. She nodded in satisfaction and touched his shoulder.

"I don't believe you would hurt me, Jed. I'm feeling muddled right now. Reading the diary hasn't helped."

She saw hope return to his eyes when he turned to her.

"In her letter, Grandmother said she had a different story to tell, something about her sister."

"What letter?"

Megan told him about the first letter from her grandmother, which the attorney had forwarded. "I suppose keeping her diaries was her way of telling Eva's story."

"So, between the letter and the diary you're able to understand your grandmother better."

"I always felt Grandmother didn't love me, or even like me for that matter. When I was fifteen or so, I overheard her tell my father she didn't want me around her because I was too much like what people thought she was at the same age."

"What people *thought* she was," Jed repeated.

"I suppose she said many things which pointed to who she really was, Eva not Alma, if anyone had questioned it. I didn't."

"You inherited the best of your grandmother's traits, Megan. You have her stunning beauty, according to Uncle Josh, and her love for little boys. Besides, didn't you tell me that Uncle Josh said she was a great horsewoman? You also inherited her seat on a horse. Can't you accept that and ignore her less than perfect traits?"

"I suppose."

"Do you think your grandfather ever realized her true self?"

"Heaven knows. He lived many years despite his heart problem, so it's possible. In the diary, she made him seem naïve, so the likelihood of her deception might not have occurred to him. Grandmother was right about the marriage's being over. I can't recall Granddad ever mentioning her coming home. He just accepted her when she did. That's hindsight, of course, because I didn't notice it then."

When Jed reached for her, Megan leaned away, sitting straight as a ramrod. "I've never believed in astrology, still don't. Astrology is humans interpreting God's control over the heavens, but I just remembered something astrologists say. My grandmother's birthday was May 27th."

"So?"

"Astrologists call it Gemini, the sign of twins. She was one, both literally and in her personality."

"When's your birthday?"

"March 10th."

"Then, you're not a Gemini. You inherited her good twin but not the other one, which should make you feel better."

"Perhaps." Even to her own ears, Megan didn't sound like she believed him. How could she? DNA and all that stuff might come popping out of her psyche at any moment. Then what? She didn't know.

"What will you do with the diaries?"

"Everybody around here had a high opinion of Eva. That's clear from everything I heard before and during her services. I hate to spoil their memories. Or the slur on her parents' memories either, for not knowing both their daughters better."

"I hadn't thought about the twins' parents. You have a point there. Why not let sleeping dogs lie? Tell Mike, since he read Uncle Dan's letter, to destroy the diary."

"Eva won't get her wish for everybody here to know how she fooled them. If hindsight is possible with spirits, though, I believe she would agree her wish was wrong."

"She might have changed her mind while she lived, if she remembered what she wrote in the diary all those years ago."

"Jed, why did Eva visit at the hedge when she isn't buried there?"

"Remember, Eva expressed some guilt about seeing Alma buried. Perhaps appearing to you was her way of making things right for her twin."

"Why me? I don't understand that."

"That's something we'll never know."

"There's something else, Jed. One night during an electrical storm, I glimpsed two figures at the hedge. Whimsical of me, I suppose, but I hope that was the twins' dissolving their differences."

"Makes as much sense as anything else, Megan, but you need to put the past where it belongs—in the past."

Megan's topsy-turvy life had taken yet another turn. She wondered whether she would ever again be content in her skin. Remembering everything that had happened this year, she didn't even know who she was anymore. She said so.

"I told you before. You're Megan Elizabeth Stanfield and the woman I love. I understand your uncertainty, Megan, but you shouldn't allow Alma's apparent prudishness or Eva's obvious nymphomania dictate your life. We can find the happy medium together, if you let us."

She didn't comment, so he continued. "I don't know when it happened, but I fell in love with you. Perhaps grew into love is a better way to say it. I didn't expect love, didn't even want love, to be truthful, but I'm glad now because my life is better, richer with you as part of it. I can't imagine ever again living without you close by my side."

Only the crackle of the fire sounded in the silence, as she considered his words. "How can you say that you love me? You don't know who I am. I don't even know."

"I do know who you are. I repeat: you're the woman I love. You need to accept that you are you—Megan Elizabeth Stanfield, granddaughter of a man who reared you with his principles, which are stronger than whatever your grandmother was. You are not Alma or Eva. Let them go. You should live in the present, not the past."

Despair riddled Megan's words. "I can only try."

"I'll have to be satisfied with that—for the moment anyhow. However, make it fast, will you? I'm becoming a very frustrated man."

Knowledge of her grandmother's nymphomania and identity-switch didn't bother him, but terrorism? Eva hadn't only watched her twin die. Without doubt, she'd murdered people throughout Italy. War activities, true, but her attitude of revenge showed deep-seated malevolence, no matter how she excused herself. The bottom line is genetics. Miguel Rossi could not have persuaded Eva into the resistance group, if she were not already prone to criminal behavior. Megan took a deep breath. Now or never.

"Jed, Grandmother had another secret, a terrible one."

"Oh?"

"You might have noticed I've been distracted the past few weeks." When he nodded, she blurted, "Grandmother was a terrorist."

He stared at her but didn't speak, didn't faint, or run screaming to the door, so she told him the rest. "I mentioned one letter from Grandmother, but there was another . . . ." She finished with, "I wonder how many secrets she took to her grave."

"I must confess. I already knew."

She frowned. "How?"

"Frank needed help determining whether the flyer picture was you." Jed described his conversation with the hairdresser.

Megan's temper erupted. "You told Deborah? Who else? No wonder people have pointed fingers at me. They've stared as if I had two heads. How dare you?"

"You don't understand, Megan." Jed gripped her hands. "Frank used me to rule you *out* as a terrorist before calling the FBI. I didn't give Deborah details. I only told her she was helping you. She wouldn't have told anybody, anyway. She isn't part of Crawfordville's tittle-tattle crowd. She was on the receiving end once and has avoided it since."

That mollified Megan somewhat. "Why haven't you said anything?"

"I knew you'd tell me when you were ready." He slipped his hand to the back of her neck and gently massaged. "You've had a rough time, Sweetheart. I would have helped, listened at least, if you'd trusted me."

Perhaps he would, perhaps not. She didn't know what to believe. She wanted to be alone, sort through her jumbled emotions without distraction.

Jed solved her dilemma. "I don't like leaving you alone after this upheaval, but I must deal with cattle."

Megan stared into the night after Jed left.

She'd come here to lick her wounds, hide from her past. She'd never expected to find her true self, yet that's what had happened. She hadn't even realized until now she'd been lost.

For the first time she admitted to herself that Jed might be part of her future. He was right. She couldn't look forward until she stopped looking back. She couldn't deal with the past, though, unless she looked at it once more.

Unlike her grandmother, Megan was a one-man woman. She'd never understood women who juggled several men at one time. She was satisfied with one man, David. That was over. She repeated the words, waiting for the pain. None came. For the first time since she saw him with the other woman, remembering him didn't hurt. She couldn't expect to block memories of him completely—he'd been what she needed at the time—but she could push David Andrew Blackwell to the back recesses of her mind and leave him there. The heaviness in her chest eased at last.

Exhilaration filled her. Megan took a deep breath, but the bubbles floating inside started bursting. No more David. However, she still must come to terms with her ancestor.

Was she really like Eva, as she must now think of her grandmother?

Their features were alike. There was no denying the resemblance. They both loved little boys. Was there anything else? Eva loved travel, she didn't. Eva had a bubbling personality and loved crowds. She didn't. Eva always dressed to the nines. She preferred jeans. Eva's make-up was always flawless. She rarely used anything except tinted lip balm. However, those things were all surface stuff. Megan finally faced the obvious.

Eva was a nymphomaniac. There was no nice way to describe her actions. Not an addiction to sex, no matter what psychologists say. Hers was a deliberately chosen behavior from an early age. She was proud of her terrorist activities. Megan couldn't even imagine how anyone could justify killing one person much less many.

She wasn't really like Eva in important ways, which was what counted. She was more like Alma, but not exactly like her either. Jed was right in this too. Megan Elizabeth Stanfield was herself. This thought brought relief.

Chapter 35

Different, Yet the Same

Megan and Fran spent an evening shopping at the Asheville mall, not the largest mall ever to receive Megan's business but more than adequate for her needs. The mall was crowded enough to raise her holiday enthusiasm but not so crowded as to make long lines at the cash registers unbearable.

Sitting in the food court sipping a vanilla latte, Fran went over her shopping list. "I can't figure out where the time has gone. Do you realize there's only one week until Christmas?"

Megan grinned at her expression. "That reminds me, I need decorations for the house. At Sally's behest, reinforced by Katie's enthusiasm, I decorated the store after Thanksgiving. My house is bare of anything even remotely resembling the holidays."

"Not even a tree?"

"No. A tree hasn't even entered my mind. I suppose I could get an artificial one tonight, along with the stuff to decorate it."

"Artificial? In a state known for Christmas tree farms—a state which supplies trees for the White House almost every year? You're bordering on sacrilege and had better repent, Megan Stanfield. Otherwise, I will make sure Santa fills your stocking with switches."

"Alright! I take it back. I'll get a real, honest-to-goodness tree tomorrow."

"I'll check on you," Fran warned.

Megan returned home, happy with the thought she had completed her shopping, including decorations for the tree in the event Fran followed through with her threat. Stopping at her mailbox, Megan pulled out a stack of mail, mostly Christmas cards judging by the shape. At the kitchen table, she browsed through them until she found one that was thicker than only a card. New York postmark but no return address. Inside was another smaller envelope with her name written in a bright red, flamboyant script. The contents left her breathless.

> *Dear Cousin Megan,*
>
> *Yes, you must accept you have a terrorist cousin who has no intention of changing her ways! You would join me, if you just once experienced the excitement. Think what fun we could have together. Two mysterious faces together to taunt the world! Oh, well, remembering your comment about our respective grandfathers: if you had grown up with my adventurous Italian grandfather instead of your docile American grandfather, you would grab every chance to liven up this boring world.*
>
> *When I escaped from Miami, I didn't have time to contact you, even if I'd thought about it. There was too much on my mind: the anticipation, rescue, and exhilaration of victory over people who thought they had me under control. I know everyone wonders how I managed my escape, but I won't betray my friends, who are worldwide. All anyone needs to know is this: even from hell, Miguel Rossi takes care of his granddaughter.*
>
> *Enough about my escape.*

In Grandmother's memory, I want to make amends for something I should not have done. She would never have condoned my doing anything that caused you and Susan difficulties.

Neither of you entered my mind during the Detroit fiasco. I was too intent on blowing up those tunnels. When I escaped after that fiasco, I moved around a lot, including London, which is where I learned you were in jail because of my activities. Grandmother would have been horrified at me for disturbing your life, and she would not have hesitated to let me know her displeasure. To make sure the authorities knew you were innocent, I robbed the bank in full daylight, so my face was visible. I revel in that bit of audacity!

Grandmother loved you and Susan, even though not the way she loved my mother and me. Perhaps that's my jealous prejudice.

This letter is to let you know, for her sake, both you and Susan are safe from me—also my friends. I've been the proud owner of the most famous female face in terrorism. I gave up that face reluctantly.

Yes, I've had plastic surgery as well as various other procedures. I regret I no longer have my beloved grandmother's facial features. I was always proud, not only to look like her, but also to follow in her terrorist footsteps.

The mysterious face which terrorized much of the world for so many years will

> *do so no more. Hereafter, when terrorism (I love that word!) happens anywhere on the planet—maybe even outer space!—you can be sure the face won't be yours. Remember one thing if you ever have even a tinge of concern for me.*
> *Bianca Rossi always wins!*

Megan could almost hear the arrogance in those last words. She didn't know what to feel. Relief because she and her mother were safe? Concern for Bianca's continued terrorism? I do *not* like that word! She reached for the phone.

"Mike? I received a letter from Bianca today. Do you want to see the letter tonight, or shall I bring it to your office tomorrow?"

"I assume the letter contains pertinent information, so I'll come now."

Waiting for him, Megan brewed a pot of hazelnut coffee. She had no idea whether Mike would care for flavored coffee, but she wanted the nutty flavor.

"Let's see the letter." Mike sipped his coffee after one startled whiff. After another cautious sip, he read Bianca's letter, touching only the edges even though he knew Megan had held it. Normal precaution for a lawman, she supposed.

"Interplanetary? Dear Heaven. The postmark is New York. The question is, was she there or did someone else mail the letter? Doesn't matter. She's unlikely to be there now. We wouldn't recognize her if we found her anyway. Ultimately, someone will have to catch her in the act. I'll leave that job to Interpol. For now, I'll take her letter and pass the info up the chain for what good it will do."

"Okay, but get the letter back to me, will you? I want to keep it, for reassurance of Mother's safety, if for no other reason"

Receiving his nod, Megan continued. "Before you leave, will you tell me something? You read my grandmother's letter where she asked me to deal with Bianca's behavior as well as her own. Have I done all I could? I wouldn't want Grandmother to be disappointed in me."

"Megan, hear me. There's no way you could have done more. None."

She gazed into his face for a moment and then nodded with relief. "Thank you."

Megan sat in thought after Mike left. Then she did something she'd never done or expected to do. Picking up her smart phone, she thumbed in the first number on the speed dial, the one that had been first on every cell phone she'd ever owned. This was the first time she'd used it, because he'd made clear she could use the number for emergencies only. She wasn't sure this qualified. But, heaving a deep breath, which she left out slowly, she called him anyway.

"Father, I have news of Bianca."

"Tell me."

"She sent me a letter, assuring me that Mother and I are safe from her connections, which she says are worldwide. She's had surgery which changed her appearance, so no future terrorist activity would involve what she called the most famous female face in terrorism. I don't know if we can believe her."

"Perhaps, perhaps not. I don't pretend to know anything about her true emotions."

She hesitated. "Is Mother okay?"

"Yes."

"Father, I really need to see her." Megan heard her voice break on a sob. She swallowed before she continued. "Will you bring her to see me sometime soon? Please?"

For the first time she could recall, his voice softened. "We'll be in Detroit in January to complete your grandmother's estate. I'll give you the dates. You can meet us there."

Megan knew it wouldn't do for the real Susan Stanfield to appear in Crawfordville. Even her faulty memory wouldn't cover the fact she'd never been there before. "Thank you, Father."

She clicked off the call and called Fran.

Chapter 36

Acceptance

Megan was ready for Christmas, except for the tree. She must obtain one or Fran would put her threat of switches into action, but what did she know about buying trees? Jed would know, but she felt awkward calling him. The situation solved itself the next morning when he strolled into This 'n That the moment she opened the door.

"I had to deal with a sick cow this morning, so I didn't make it into town for breakfast. I need to get back to the farm, but an elf perched on my shoulder and insisted I come into town now. So here I am, basically in all my dirt!"

Now or never. "Aha! The little elf has a direct line to my brain. I hope the cow is alright."

"Off her feed and a bit of a temperature. I isolated her before milking time and kept her milk separate. One of my fieldhands is taking a sample to Raleigh to be tested. She won't pass whatever the problem is to the rest of the herd and should be okay in a day or two. So, why the elf message?"

"Do you need to stay with the cow?"

"No, I'll check on her when I get back and watch her for a couple of hours."

Megan studied his face. He didn't appear to be overly concerned. "If you're sure, I need a favor."

"Name it."

"Fran insists I have a real Christmas tree. Will you help me choose one?"

"Sure. I'll even help you decorate it, if you speak nicely."

Megan ducked her head, folded her hands below her chin, and peeked upward through her eyelashes.

"Please, kind sir, will you help a poor, helpless female find a Christmas tree?"

"*Helpless*? Striking rattlesnakes have nothing on you!" A smile lurked around his mouth. "I'll help you anyway."

"This afternoon?"

"Is two-thirty or so okay?"

They stopped at three lots before they found a tree Jed approved. He declared the twelve-foot, perfectly shaped Fraser fir would fit in one corner of her kitchen, if they moved the furniture a little.

"The kitchen? I know it has a high ceiling, but so does the living room. Besides, who ever put Christmas trees in kitchens?"

"No one, I suppose. You're probably the only person on the planet who has a kitchen large enough. Perfect for a party too." He wrestled the tree into his pickup truck.

Aroma from simmering spiced cider filled the kitchen and mingled with the scent of fresh evergreens released by the heat. Megan felt tension ease from her shoulders. She hadn't been quite comfortable with Jed all afternoon. She wanted to tell him she had come to terms with her grandmother's decadent lifestyle. The problem was she didn't know how to bring up the subject without appearing too much like Eva. Horrible thought.

"You're right, Jed. The tree is perfect in that corner." She handed him a mug of cider. "Let's have some Christmas music while we decorate."

"Sounds good." He sipped the cider while he stood back admiring the tree. "Okay, you can help with the lights."

They worked in companionable silence for several minutes: she holding the strings of lights straight, while they inched their way around the tree, and Jed clipping the lights in place, finishing just before the doorbell rang.

"We finished the lights right on time. Go let them in."

"Them?" Megan questioned but hurried toward the front door. "Well, hello, everybody. Come in and help us decorate the tree."

Megan smiled with delight when their usual crowd trooped inside, each carrying a bag. Fran carried a couple of pizza boxes. Megan glanced at her watch when Sally greeted her with a hug. Six o'clock already? Or perhaps she closed the store early, which was okay with Megan.

"Great tree," Jack congratulated them.

"We didn't give you house-warming presents, Megan—didn't even know you then!—so we decided on tree-decorating gifts instead." Fran showed her two crystal stars.

"Your generosity overwhelms me," Megan said with a catch in her voice. "Each of you must hang your ornament in a prominent place, before we put anything else on the tree."

She admired yarn animals from Sally, a tiny book from Catherine, a silver bell from Bill. Jack and Mike gave two lengthy ropes of crystal beads. Jed was last. Standing beside the tree, he planted a light kiss on her lips, before hanging blown glass kissing angels at her eye level.

Megan smiled at him and blinked away tears, which threatened to overflow. This was already a Christmas to remember.

Fran drew attention away from Megan's emotion, when she dug into a drawer and pulled out a pizza cutter. "Okay, everybody. Let's have supper before we finish the tree, shall we?"

Megan met Fran's puzzled eyes several times throughout the evening. Had she guessed Megan's turmoil? It wouldn't be the first time. Megan held her back when the others left.

"I need to talk. Can we get together before work tomorrow?"

Fran nodded. "My turn. Breakfast at seven should give us enough time."

൰ ൰ ൰ ൰ ൰

Megan ran her five-mile loop, debating how to reveal her uncertainties. She rang Fran's doorbell promptly at seven o'clock.

"Okay, tell me what's bugging you." Fran pushed her breakfast plate aside.

Megan hardly knew where to begin. She'd gone over the whole thing time after time over the past few days, but was still unsure this morning. How much should she tell? Could she trust her friend with the whole sordid tale? Her friend. She liked the sound. It also answered her question.

"We buried the wrong woman."

Fran choked on her coffee. "We *what*?"

"Buried the wrong woman," Megan repeated. The story came pouring out, like water over the falls: nymphomania, murder, identity switch, her talk with Jed.

"Let me guess," Fran said into the silence. "You're questioning whether you're like your grandmother."

"I've tried to convince myself I'm like her only in superficial things, but deep inside, I still wonder."

"Tell your 'deep inside' to hush. You're no more a nympho than I am. If you were, you wouldn't wonder. You'd know."

"Does Jed believe me? I mean really, deep down believe me, not just a spur-of-the-moment decision he will regret. There's this whole terrorist thing too."

"You know, nothing that has happened is the real problem. I'm guessing again. You're not sure Jed believes he can trust you."

Megan bit her lip but nodded.

"You're not sure you can trust him not to lose his temper and kill you. Right again?"

Megan nodded again.

Fran pushed on. "Jed said he loves you. You say you love him. Love is the bottom line, Megan. Accept it."

"Can I? Be sure what I feel is love? Believe he loves me? I believed I experienced love with someone else, remember."

"Think back. Did you love David? Did you feel for him the way you do for Jed?"

Megan had never questioned her love for David. It was just there. Now she wasn't sure. How much of her suffering had been a broken heart? Or only a blow to her pride when he dumped her?

She had no pride where Jed was concerned. If he rejected her someday—she cringed at the thought—she wouldn't suffer only hurt pride, but deep pain. Her heart was involved now, even if it had not been with David. She was not yet sure exactly how she felt about David. His leaving had hurt, but she got over his betrayal. She wasn't sure she could get over losing Jed.

Fran broke into her thoughts. "I believe the real problem is you doubt yourself, not Jed. You're not sure you're worthy of love."

"Maybe I'm not." Megan thought about her parents, her grandmother, David, and their apparent lack of love. Granddad had loved her though. So maybe . . . .

"You know something?" Fran asked. "I could shake you till your teeth rattle. You're unlucky in your family—

also your first love affair. Don't you understand? That's their failure, not yours."

Hope filled Megan as she looked at Fran. She had been afraid to believe, afraid to trust her own heart.

"Listen, Megan." Fran clasped Megan's hands. "I know what love is. I also know what love gone wrong is. Been there and survived. I've had a loving family and friends all my life, yet part of me was missing. I didn't know what until you moved here. You filled an empty place. I could never lead you wrong, Megan. You're the sister I always wanted."

Megan curled her hands around to hold Fran's hands, her voice was not quite steady. "Me too."

Chapter 37

Peace at Last

The days leading to Christmas flew by.

Megan had difficulty controlling the children's exuberance during the last pageant rehearsal. When the parents came for the children, she invited them into the church family center, where she had earlier set out tables with platters containing Christmas cookies, decorated with green sprinkles, and pitchers of red punch. When she handed the children the small gifts, which she'd wrapped for them, she thought of the times her grandmother must have done this same thing.

The pageant was a tremendous success. Her part with the children passed without problems, much to her relief. She'd heard Handel's *Messiah* performed in large cathedrals, with better-trained choirs, but it had never moved her like this time.

The weather turned cloudier throughout the last few days before Christmas. The same question was on everyone's lips. Will we have a white Christmas? Children hoped, old-timers shook their heads.

On Christmas Eve, Megan glanced around the kitchen. She'd done everything she could for the moment. She paid close attention to her make-up, donned a bright red silk blouse with an ankle-length challis skirt of muted green, red, and gold print. Dark gold strappy sandals showed when she twirled before the mirror.

Jed arrived first. Wearing a dark blue jacket over a lighter blue turtleneck sweater, which enhanced his eyes, he hipped the door shut as he took her in his arms.

Ending their kiss, Megan leaned back against his arms. "Did I ever tell you that you're gorgeous?"

"I don't remember, but you can tell me again. Often."

"You'd be conceited in no time. Then, you wouldn't be pretty, anymore."

"Not pretty," he corrected her with a twinkle. "Gorgeous."

On a note of laughter, they walked hand in hand into the kitchen. Jed eyed the food. "The others had better get here fast, or we'll start eating without them."

The others arrived soon after, and more packages joined the ones Megan and Jed had placed under the tree. The space overflowed with gaily-wrapped gifts. Megan felt six years old again. Munching roasted nuts, she said, "I do love Christmas, the tree, the pretty packages. Maybe we should eat before I start shaking them!"

Caught up in her excitement, they filled their plates from the buffet and found seats around the table. Sprigs of live greenery surrounded chunky white candles placed at judicious distances along the red lace tablecloth.

Raising a fork toward his mouth, Jack said, "Yankee, I'm glad you don't use only candle light, because I like to see what I'm eating."

Megan observed his loaded fork with an amused smile. She'd left dim lights burning at each end of the long room, using only candles on the table. "Somehow, I always thought Yankee refers to people from the Northeast."

"No." Catherine said. "A Yankee, the way we interpret the word, is anyone not privileged to be born in the Southeast."

Her definition brought discussion of differences in word interpretation, which led to Christmas customs. Their lively discussion ended with Megan's shoving back her chair.

"The Christmas custom I'm most interested in right now is opening packages, so let's do it. Jed, will you play Santa?"

Who would have thought opening packages could be so much fun? For many years, Megan had opened each present when it arrived, thereby leaving none for Christmas morning. Now, she had seven all at once, with more for morning from her parents. She sat back, eager to see what happened next.

Jed handed one package around to each, selecting one for himself, before sitting beside Megan. "You're the hostess, so you open both the first and the last presents."

The first was from Bill.

"Ohhhh," she breathed. Vinyl was almost obsolete since the advent of CDs. She wondered where he'd found this one. "How did you know to get Hoagy Carmichael's 'The Stardust Road' for me? Mine got broken when I moved down here."

"I peeked at your album collection when we decorated your tree. He's one of the few singers from that era I know. My mother had that album years ago."

Megan paid close attention while the others opened their gifts, happy her presents pleased them as much as what they received from the others. She glanced with complacency at her own gifts: David Baldacci book from Catherine, multi-colored silk scarf from Jack, hand-crafted indoor wreath from Sally, gardening book from Mike, a bottle of White Diamonds perfume from Fran, the same gift she'd given to Fran.

She caught Fran's eye and murmured, "Two great minds working together."

Megan opened Jed's gift last—small square box, wrapped in red with a silver bow, which she carefully set aside. Opening the box, she blinked. Two golden hearts, intertwined with a small diamond where they joined, hung on a chain. "Oh, how beautiful. I want to wear it now."

She bent her head while he fastened the clasp. Megan turned so the others could admire the pendant, nestled in the cowl neck of her blouse.

With the last package opened and admired, the party ended with chatter, as they gathered the discarded paper.

Jed lingered after the last automobile sounds faded. Sitting on the sofa, he cradled Megan in his arms, his cheek resting on her head.

Could the fluttering in her chest mean her heart had sprouted wings? She might fly to the moon. She must tell him.

"Jed?"

"Hmmm."

"I've decided I don't want to be a businesswoman."

"Hmmm."

"Jed?"

"Hmmm."

"I love you."

He stilled and drew back enough to see her face. "I've wondered if I would ever hear those words from you. How soon can we get married?"

Megan cupped his face in her hands. "Must we wait?"

He answered with a kiss but drew away.

Had she been too eager? Had she disgusted him? Eva's vision jolted her. Megan felt herself shrink into a tiny knot.

Jed must have read her mind because he cupped her face in both hands. "I'm not rejecting you, Megan. Nothing is farther from my mind or wishes. However, I don't want you to think there might be a repeat experience. I'll wait until we're married, so let's set the wedding date soon."

He shrugged himself into his topcoat and opened the door.

"Look, Jed. Snow! We have a white Christmas!"

They stood in silence, watching the huge flakes swirling from the dark sky. The absolute stillness surrounded them, giving Megan a sense of peace at last.

Book Club Questions

1. Do you see attributes in Megan that mirror Bianca's?

2. The mysterious woman was known worldwide. How can you explain why Megan was not aware of the resemblance to herself, her mother, and her grandmother?

3. Also Reid, the world traveler?

4. To what do you attribute Susan's choosing to remain childlike?

5. Did Megan's move to her ancestral hometown contribute to her acceptance of her true self?

6. Did the move change her outlook on life in general?

7. Jed had one possible explanation of why Eva appeared at the hedge when she was not buried there. Do you have a different explanation?

8. Megan's grandmother declared her love for Megan after years of almost ignoring her. Did Megan accept the declaration too quickly?

9. Did Grandmother already plan to burden Megan with Bianca's behavior when she declared her love in the first letter?

10. Nature or nurture—which contributed to the malevolent spirit that Megan accused Eva of having?

Books by Peggy Lovelace Ellis

Historical Romance Series
The Uncertain Heart
The Merry Heart
The Divided Heart

Romantic Suspense
The Mysterious Face

Short Stories
Silver Shadows: Stories of Life in a Small Town

Anthologies
Challenges on the Home Front,
World War II (Second Edition)
Lest the Colors Fade
A Beautiful Life and Other Stories

Author's Note

Your opinion matters to me, so if you enjoyed *The Mysterious Face*, please spread the word by posting a review on Amazon, Good Reads, Barnes & Noble, and other sources to which you have access. Reviews are enormously helpful to the reading community, and your support really does motivate me to keep writing. Thank you!

♥ Peggy ♥